Stinger grinned. "*I'm glad you're keen* to be a Strongbranch, Thorn. I can use a clever baboon like you."

"That's . . . good," rasped Thorn. He was growing more nervous every moment. It occurred to him that Stinger might want to keep him close, just as much as he wanted to keep an eye on Stinger. . . .

"Anyway, when the right opportunity arises, I'll set you a Strongfeat." Turning, Stinger gazed into Thorn's eyes; his own glinted with a dark intelligence. "You'll prove yourself, Thorn. Don't worry about *that.*"

Thorn halted, letting Stinger walk on ahead into the night. He swallowed hard and gave his fur a shake to stop it crawling.

Why, he wondered, *did that sound less like a promise and more like a threat?*

BRAVELANDS

ALSO BY ERIN HUNTER

WARRIORS

WARRIORS
SUPER EDITIONS

Firestar's Quest
Bluestar's Prophecy
SkyClan's Destiny
Crookedstar's Promise
Yellowfang's Secret
Tallstar's Revenge
Bramblestar's Storm
Moth Flight's Vision
Hawkwing's Journey
Tigerheart's Shadow
Crowfeather's Trial

EXPLORE THE
WARRIORS
WORLD

FIELD GUIDES
Secrets of the Clans
Cats of the Clans
Code of the Clans
Battles of the Clans
Enter the Clans
The Ultimate Guide

NOVELLAS
Hollyleaf's Story
Mistystar's Omen
Cloudstar's Journey
Tigerclaw's Fury
Leafpool's Wish
Dovewing's Silence
Mapleshade's Vengeance
Goosefeather's Curse
Ravenpaw's Farewell
Spottedleaf's Heart
Pinestar's Choice
Thunderstar's Echo

NOVELLA COLLECTIONS
The Untold Stories
Tales from the Clans
Shadows of the Clans
Legends of the Clans

MANGA
The Lost Warrior
Warrior's Refuge
Warrior's Return
The Rise of Scourge
Tigerstar and Sasha #1: Into the Woods
Tigerstar and Sasha #2: Escape from the Forest
Tigerstar and Sasha #3: Return to the Clans
Ravenpaw's Path #1: Shattered Peace
Ravenpaw's Path #2: A Clan in Need
Ravenpaw's Path #3: The Heart of a Warrior
SkyClan and the Stranger #1: The Rescue
SkyClan and the Stranger #2: Beyond the Code
SkyClan and the Stranger #3: After the Flood

SEEKERS

SURVIVORS

BRAVELANDS

CODE OF HONOR

ERIN
HUNTER

HARPER
An Imprint of HarperCollinsPublishers

Special thanks to Clarissa Hutton and Gillian Philip

Bravelands: Code of Honor
Copyright © 2018 by Working Partners Limited
Series created by Working Partners Limited
Map art © 2018 by Virginia Allyn
Interior art © 2018 by Owen Richardson

www.harpercollinschildrens.com
ISBN 978-0-06-264208-0
Typography by Ellice M. Lee
18 19 20 21 22   CG/BRR   10 9 8 7 6 5 4 3 2 1
❖
First paperback edition, 2018

BRAVELANDS

CODE OF HONOR

PROLOGUE

A *thin golden glow edged the* horizon to the east, bringing the first daylight to the savannah and revealing the flat-topped acacias that dotted the grassland. *Another beautiful day*, thought Babble the oxpecker: *another delicious breakfast*. He stretched, preened under a wing, then pecked a fat tick from the hide of the rhino he rode.

This rhinoceros was a talker. He had been arguing with the other members of his crash since before dawn broke. Babble couldn't understand a word of their strange, ground-plodder language, but the conversation sounded urgent, agitated, and more than a little aggressive.

Babble raised his head and blinked. "Chatter?"

"Wait," came a muffled voice. All that was visible of Chatter was his tail; the rest of him was deep in the rhino's flickering ear. His tail wagged, and he popped out, gulping down whatever parasite he'd been digging for. "What is it?"

"I just wondered where you were," Babble replied. "Is there anything else tasty in that ear? What do you think these rhinos are talking about?"

"No idea. I don't speak Grasstongue any more than you do." Chatter fluttered down the rhino's broad neck. "I think I got the last tick, but you're bound to find something in his other ear."

Babble hopped past him, up to the rhino's head. "I wish they'd stop all the horn-tossing and head-shaking," he complained. "It's not very calming. Or easy."

"It's a nuisance, but you know what old Prattle says," Chatter told him, poking under a flap of leathery skin. *"Don't worry about today, because tomorrow there'll still be insects."*

"Well, I wish Prattle would have a word with these rhinos," sighed Babble. "They seem very wound up about something. They could learn a thing or two from us oxpeckers."

"They certainly—oh!" Chatter peered up as the call of a gray crowned crane echoed above them.

The bird soared on vast white-and-black wings, shrieking in penetrating Skytongue: "Great Flock! Great Flock!" He angled his head, staring down at the two friends. "Great Flock!"

As the oxpeckers gazed up in awe, the crane circled and flapped away in the direction of the sunrise. Distantly, they heard him calling the same words over and over, to other birds on the ground and in the trees.

"Great Flock!" chirped Babble in delight.

Chatter blinked his round yellow eyes. "I've never been

summoned to a Great Flock before. This is exciting!"

"Me neither," said Babble. "I've been hearing stories about Great Flocks since I came out of the egg, but I've never been to one."

"Let's go, then!" Chatter darted his red beak at a last insect and took off.

Babble fluttered after him. The sun was rising above the horizon now, a half circle of dazzling gold, and the sky was a cool, clear blue that was filling with birds. Crows took off cawing from their rot-flesh feasts, egrets rose in a white-winged mass, and a flock of blue starlings erupted from a thorn tree. A pair of bright green-and-yellow bee-eaters zipped past Babble, almost touching his wing.

"Hey, watch where you're going!" he chirruped, but he was too excited to be cross. The sky was growing dark with birds; many more were silhouetted against the glow of the rising sun.

"I wonder why a Great Flock's been called?" exclaimed Chatter.

A shadow raced over them from high above. A great white-backed vulture circled there; the gathered birds rose to swoop and flap around her, their cries hushed to an expectant twittering. A whole flock of vultures flew in the huge bird's wake, soaring on vast black wings.

"Isn't that Windrider?" whispered Babble. "The old vulture who speaks with Great Mother?"

"I think so." Chatter fluttered, watching her in awe.

The strange quietness was pierced by Windrider's harsh, eerie cry.

"I bring terrible news, birds of Bravelands. Great Mother is dead."

Screeches and chirrups of horror rose throughout the sky. Crows gave rasping caws of shock, and the mournful hooting of cranes mingled with a burst of disbelieving chittering from the starlings.

"No!" Chatter cried at Babble's side. "This is terrible news!"

Babble was stunned. "No wonder the rhinos were upset. They must have known already!"

Follow me. Windrider's command silenced the hubbub once more.

No bird argued; the flocks swooped and fluttered into a rough formation behind the vulture, and together the vast horde soared over the savannah, the sun gleaming and glinting on thousands of wings. The riot of colors dazzled Babble.

I wish the Great Flock could have been called for a happier reason, he thought.

Already he could see where Windrider was leading them; ahead and below, a large watering hole sparkled and glinted in the dawn. It was not the peaceful, happy place it should have been. Herds of grass-eaters milled and jostled on its banks, braying and bellowing in distress. As the birds flew lower, Babble saw a great stain on the water; something huge lay half submerged in the lake.

Great Mother.

Babble had never seen the wise old elephant before; now he wished he could never have seen her at all, if it had to be like this. She lay lifeless, torn by wounds that were dark with blood. Other elephants surrounded her, pushing desperately at her body; their enormous feet churned the bloodstained water as they struggled to get her to shore.

One of the elephants stood aside, though, staring at Great Mother. She looked young, thought Babble—smaller than the others, her legs trembling with shock. As he swooped lower he could see her huge dark eyes: filled with grief, but oddly wise for such a youngster.

The young elephant stood as if rooted to the mud, while around her grass-eaters trumpeted and bellowed, rearing up and stampeding. Zebras and wildebeests trotted to the shore, gaping at Great Mother's corpse, then surged away in a thundering, panicked mass. The squeals of smaller animals rose, then were cut off abruptly as they were trampled underfoot.

Yet the young elephant stood unmoving. She seemed transfixed by the horror of the body.

Every bird was landing now, finding perches on trees and rocks and grassy slopes. The banks of the lake became a flurry of wings as they settled, but there was no clamor of calls; only an eerie, mournful silence. Windrider and her vultures gathered on the body of Great Mother itself, wings raised as if to protect her.

"This," Windrider cried harshly into the stillness, "this is only the beginning of the turmoil that will come to Bravelands!"

She opened her beak to speak more, but a deafening crack of thunder split the sky. It crashed across the watering hole, rolling and resounding. Every creature froze in shock; Babble hunched his head into his wings, terrified.

The sky was no longer clear and dawn-blue; it had been blotted out by a dark bank of cloud. Rain exploded, hammering down on the gathered creatures of Bravelands. Babble's feathers were instantly drenched and sodden.

He stared at Chatter as rain streamed from their beaks and tails and wings. His friend looked as scared as he was.

"The Great Spirit is angry," moaned Chatter, "because Great Mother is dead!"

Babble tried to shake rain from his wings, then gave up and squatted miserably, enduring the onslaught of the torrent.

"Perhaps Prattle was wrong," he whispered. "Perhaps tomorrow won't come after all. . . ."

CHAPTER 1

This rain was the hardest he'd ever known. Thorn staggered away from the watering hole, his paws clumsy in the thick mud, his fur sodden and dripping. He could barely see for the water that streamed down his forehead into his eyes; frantically he wiped it away, over and over again. Even his nostrils were full of it.

What happened? What happened?

Great Mother died. That was what had happened. But it didn't matter how often he told himself; it still seemed unreal. *How? Why?*

It didn't matter; the Great Parent of Bravelands was dead, and she couldn't help Thorn now.

He'd gone to the watering hole to ask for her advice, her assistance, her wisdom—and because there was no other creature who could help him. Great Mother would have known

7

how to deal with Stinger Crownleaf, he was sure. The enormity of Stinger's crimes was more than any ordinary creature could comprehend. The devious baboon had murdered Bark Crownleaf, smashing her skull with a rock. He had poisoned Bark's successor, Grub, with scorpion venom—clearing the way for Stinger himself to lead Brightforest Troop.

But when Thorn had confronted him, filled with righteous rage, Stinger had only laughed. His smirk still haunted Thorn, along with his certainty that he wouldn't be brought to justice. *Do you see how far I will go to protect Brightforest Troop?*

Do you see how far I will go . . . ?

Thorn had known exactly what Stinger meant: he'd have no hesitation in killing Thorn, should he try to expose him to the troop. Thorn had had one chance to stop Stinger—one single place to look for help.

Now Great Mother was dead. And Thorn was utterly alone.

Dusk was a miserable, gray fading of the daylight; there was no sunset, no golden rays to stream through the branches of Tall Trees. Thorn crouched on the sodden earth of the Council Glade, mud soaking into his fur as if it were forming a second skin. All of Brightforest Troop was gathered before the Crown Stone; facing them were the Council members and their retinues, who flanked the broad, pale stone itself. Every baboon, from infant to aged councilor, looked drenched and dejected—except for Stinger Crownleaf. He couldn't stop the rain, and he no doubt wasn't pleased about his wet fur, but at least he had the Crown Stone to perch on.

"What do you think will happen, Thorn?" whispered Mud Lowleaf.

Thorn squeezed his shoulder. His best friend had always been small, but with his fur soaked through to his hide, he looked scrawnier than ever. "I don't know, Mud," he murmured. "Nothing like this has ever happened before."

"I welcome you all." Stinger's commanding voice drew everyone's attention. As the anxious chatter died away, he gazed around his troop with stern solemnity. "As you know, I would usually meet here only with my councilors, but the events Bravelands has witnessed today are unprecedented. Never—in all the history of these lands—has a Great Parent been murdered." Stinger raised his eyes to the sky and closed them, as if seeking aid from the Great Spirit itself. "Together we must discuss what it means for us—for *all* of Brightforest Troop."

Every baboon craned forward, eager for Stinger's advice and wisdom. There was anxiety in their eyes, but also respect, and trust. Thorn's spine felt cold. *Just a day ago, I'd have looked at him like that.*

"Mango!" called Stinger, gesturing with a long-fingered paw. "You have been scouting for news. Tell us what you have discovered."

Mango Highleaf splashed forward through the mud and cleared her throat. "My Crownleaf, no one knows for sure what happened. But many animals say that the crocodiles killed Great Mother. The brutes' tooth marks are on her body."

"That's appalling!" cried Moss Middleleaf.

"Those savages!" exclaimed Petal Goodleaf, her voice breaking with emotion.

Stinger spread his paws. "What do we expect of creatures who do not even follow the Great Parent?"

"They don't even follow the *Code*!" shouted Splinter Middleleaf angrily. "*Only kill to survive*; why, we learn it as infants on our mothers' bellies!"

Beetle Highleaf shuffled forward from the ranks of councilors. He was old and gnarled, and he had a whiff of fermented fruit about him, but all the baboons fell respectfully quiet as he spoke. "I have heard," he said in his querulous voice, "that many died in the stampede at the watering hole. Such panic was perhaps to be expected—but it will almost certainly spread, rather than lessen."

Stinger nodded thoughtfully. "The creatures of Bravelands have no guidance," he murmured.

"And no one knows who the new Great Parent is," pointed out Mango. "Great Mother did not have time to pass the Great Spirit to her successor, and that's never happened before. What shall we do?"

Moss piped up in a small, scared voice. "Maybe the Great Spirit died with her."

There was uproar. Baboons hooted in horror, others pounded the muddy ground, and babies began to wail.

"Quiet, quiet!" Stinger slapped the Crown Stone and rose

to his paws. "My troop! Other animals may panic like disturbed ants, but we are *baboons*! We will stay calm, and keep our dignity!"

The hubbub faded. Mothers hushed their babies, and Moss, looking shamefaced, muttered, "Sorry, Stinger."

Stinger turned to the baboon closest to him: Mud's mother. "What does our Starleaf say? What do the Moonstones tell her?"

Starleaf's white-streaked face was gentle and serene. Even Thorn felt calmer as she methodically laid the Moonstones before her. Each was a pebble of a different color: some were bright blue or green or orange; some were translucent, and sparkled even in the dim light; others were smooth and opaque. One was a broken shard of stone, its hollow insides revealing glittering crystals. One by one Starleaf held the stones up to examine them, her face creased in concentration.

At last she looked up, unsmiling—but then she never did smile when she was reading the Moonstones. Thorn shot an anxious glance at Mud, who nodded confidently.

"Stinger is right to call for calm," declared Starleaf. "The Great Spirit will find the new Great Parent—of that, the stones are certain."

"Well, that's good news," grunted Mango.

"But what if it's an animal that's unfavorable to us?" asked Bud Middleleaf nervously. "What if it's, say, a cheetah?"

"Or a hyena," squeaked Moss.

Starleaf gave her a kind but stern look. "The Great Spirit always chooses wisely."

"That's all very well," said Beetle, "but I must say, every animal has its prejudices, and . . ."

As the discussion turned to the merits of various potential Great Parents, Thorn stopped listening. Berry Highleaf was sitting close to her father, Stinger, and she had said nothing so far. She listened to the speakers with an expression of vague concern, but mostly she seemed sad and hurt. *And I know why*, thought Thorn, with a wrench of guilty misery.

He felt dreadful for wounding her feelings so badly the previous night. If only she knew why he had really done it. When Thorn had told her they should stop seeing each other, it wasn't because he wanted it that way. *I did it to protect you, Berry.*

But to do that, to keep her safe, Thorn had had to pretend the reason was their different ranks. He'd told her they couldn't disobey the troop's rules anymore; they must respect the laws and traditions that said Highleaves could never pair with Middleleaves.

Berry must have despised him for saying it, but he'd had no choice. Thorn was all too aware of what Stinger could do. If he found out that his daughter was involved with the one baboon who knew his secrets, or if Thorn accidentally let slip part of the truth, then Berry would be in terrible danger. Stinger might love his daughter, but he loved himself even more.

"Thorn," whispered Mud, "what's happened between you two? Berry hasn't spoken to you since you got back."

"It's nothing." Thorn shook himself, annoyed that he'd been staring so obviously at Berry.

"It's my fault, isn't it?" Mud rubbed his head and groaned. "You've fallen out because of me. You'd be a Highleaf right now if I hadn't beaten you in the Three Feats duel."

"No," Thorn said firmly. "Really, Mud, it's not that."

"Because I feel bad, and—"

"Hah. No need to feel bad!" A voice interrupted Mud, rather to Thorn's relief. He turned to see Grass Highleaf. The tall baboon was chewing on his usual grass stalk, eyeing Mud with amused disdain. His skinny friend Fly wore a cruel, chip-toothed grin. Along with Thorn, both had been part of Stinger's retinue when he was merely Stinger Highleaf, Council member.

"Yeah, don't feel bad, Mud," sneered Fly. "You didn't beat Thorn—he threw the fight to let you win."

"It was *so* obvious." Grass grinned.

"Don't talk hyena droppings," snapped Thorn, with a quick glance at Mud's shocked face. "Mud, don't listen to them. You won fair and square."

Fly giggled. "Thorn-y subject?"

Grass hooted and slapped his leg. Thorn glared at the pair of them. The fact was, they were telling the truth. He *had* thrown the fight. If Mud had lost his final Feat, he'd have been condemned to stay a Deeproot all his life—and that meant a miserable life of cleaning the camp and taking orders from the rest of the troop.

But there was no way Mud could ever know this.

"Get lost, you dung-stirrers!" he snarled at the grinning pair.

"Who's going to make us—yo— *Ow!*" Grass clutched his head and staggered back. An unripe mango had struck him right on the forehead.

Thorn gaped for a moment. Then another piece of fruit zinged through the air; suddenly the grove was full of flying missiles, striking baboons and trees indiscriminately.

Thorn leaped to his feet with the others. Their mysterious attackers were nowhere in sight, but branches swayed and creaked and rattled. Thorn drew back his muzzle and snarled.

"I smell monkeys!" shrieked Mud.

The baboons erupted in howls of anger. "Monkeys!" echoed Mango.

"There!" yelled Thorn. "In the bushes!"

Fang snarled with fury. "Those little— There's a whole gang of them!"

The monkeys bolted, hollering and screeching. Greenish-brown pelts, black faces fringed with white fur—Thorn recognized them at once.

"It's the same troop of vervets who attacked us before!" he shouted.

Stinger bounded down from the Crown Stone, enraged.

"Don't let them get away," he screeched. "Highleaves—no, everyone—*after them!*"

CHAPTER 2

Thorn sprinted after the monkeys, Mud hard at his heels. Branches sprang and showers of rainwater scattered as the whole troop pursued the intruders; every baboon had obeyed Stinger's command, except for the very elderly and the mothers with babies at their bellies. From the glade, old Beetle Highleaf screeched his encouragement: "Teach them a lesson, Bright-forest Troop!"

Stinger led the way, bounding nimbly through the foliage. As he ran he hooted orders: "Grass—circle to the left! Fang, you go right with the Middleleaves. We'll cut those monkeys off!"

Baboons obeyed him, two groups peeling away to follow Grass and Fang. Thorn didn't veer off; he kept determinedly after Stinger with the main body of the assault. Berry was at her father's side, and he didn't want to lose sight of her.

She vaulted over a half-fallen trunk and leaped for the ground. Just as she touched down she glanced over her shoulder, right at Thorn. His breath caught in his throat.

Berry didn't look hostile or resentful. All he could see in her dark gaze was relief that Thorn was still behind her, still unhurt. His heart turned over.

But there was no time to stop. The noise of the monkeys seemed more distant now; through the gray mist of rain he could see an occasional tail, or a lithe shadow leaping, but the baboons weren't gaining any ground.

Thorn raked the forest with his gaze as he ran. It might be his imagination, but there seemed to be fewer monkeys now. They were splitting up, he realized, darting off at angles, hurtling into trees and scrambling toward the canopy. High above and far ahead, he could make out branches swaying wildly, leaves thrashing. *They're scattering*, he thought. *We're losing them.*

The chase carried the baboons out of the trees and onto the broad stretch of grassland beyond. Without the shelter of the forest, the rain lashed down harder than ever; the baboons' pounding paws threw up showers of mud. The monkeys were nowhere in sight, and at last Stinger skidded to a halt in a fan of water.

"Stop!" he barked.

The rest of the troop trotted to a halt, with Grass's and Fang's groups racing to join them. Stinger reared onto his hind legs and sniffed the air, his nostrils flaring wide, snout peeling back from his fangs.

He spat in anger. "The scent's lost."

At once baboons began to sniff the ground, running back and forth. But it was no use; whatever scent the monkeys had left, it had been washed away already in the torrential downpour. All they were getting for their trouble was rain in their noses. Thorn sneezed it out.

"All right, forget it." Stinger called them back, his snout twisted with disgust. "We'll catch those monkeys another time, and show them who owns Tall Trees. Back to the glade."

The trek back was a much more morose affair. Every baboon's fur was sodden and filthy with mud, and their tired paws slipped and skidded on the treacherous ground. Thunder crashed overhead, and lightning crackled to earth; rivulets of water streamed through the grass.

"The Great Spirit's angry, I think," murmured Mud, shaking red sludge from his paws. "About what happened to Great Mother."

Thorn shivered. As he glanced at the sky, a paw touched his shoulder. He turned, surprised.

"Berry," he said hoarsely.

"Thorn." Her large brown eyes were steady and concerned. "Are you managing in this mire?"

"Excuse me, I—" babbled Mud. "I'll just—go and check with Grass that . . . um . . . something." He loped away as fast as he could in the sticky terrain.

Thorn watched him with a sinking heart. *I kind of wish he'd stayed.*

He didn't know what to say to Berry. Did he have to go through it again, his awful decision from last night? Yet hope surged inside him, too: he couldn't help wanting to hear her say, *I still want to be with you, Thorn.*

"What's wrong, Thorn?" Berry's voice was gentle as ever. "You've looked so worried all day. I noticed at the meeting you were on edge."

"I . . ." Thorn licked his jaws. "I'm just . . . shocked about Great Mother. It's a lot to take in."

"Not that." Berry shook her head. "There's something else, isn't there?"

For a horrible moment, Thorn was afraid that she could read his mind. *No. She mustn't find out about Stinger!* "Berry, Bravelands is in uproar, and nothing's certain anymore. Of course everyone's stunned. I'm just upset is all."

"I know you better than that, Thorn." Berry sighed. She stood so close, he could have reached out and embraced her. "Listen, Thorn, you *mustn't* worry. We'll be all right, don't you see? My father's in charge now. You know how wise and clever he is. He'll take care of us. He'll get Brightforest Troop through this awful time."

Thorn gaped at her. "You really think so?" he retorted. The words spilled out before he could check himself. "You don't know what—"

Berry's eyes had widened. Thorn drew a breath.

"You don't know anything about me anymore," he finished. He was shocked by how cold he sounded.

She blinked and half crouched, her gaze veering away. When she finally spoke, her voice was cool and abrupt: "Fine."

She loped away through the rain to join the others. Thorn

stared after her, his heart wrenching painfully in his chest.

I had to say it. I couldn't tell her!

Miserably he trailed at the rear, his paws heavier than ever in the mud. Ahead, Tall Trees was a dark, drooping lump, as if the whole forest was sagging under the weight of the downpour. It looked exactly how Thorn felt. Far ahead, in the undergrowth, he could hear the leaders crying out, letting the ones who had stayed behind know that the fighters had returned.

Sunk in misery, it took him long moments to realize that they were not hoots of greeting, but of surprise and anger. Some sort of commotion was breaking out ahead.

What now? Thorn sprang into a run.

When he burst into the central clearing, the rest of the fighting party was standing immobile, gaping in shock. Thorn came to a halt beside them, his eyes widening.

The clearing was wrecked, devastated. Fruits had been ripped from the trees and flung to the ground, smashed and trampled. Broken and torn branches hung half loose; twigs and leaves were strewn everywhere. Dung had been smeared on tree trunks, all across the grass, and, worst of all, on the Crown Stone.

At the far side of the glade huddled the baboons who had remained behind. They trembled with terror; mothers clutched wailing infants, and others curled on the ground, whimpering. Many were wounded, with vicious claw marks and bites still leaking blood. Beetle squatted in front of them all, cradling the limp body of another old baboon.

He raised his old eyes, bright with grief. "They killed Fig."

Stinger stalked forward, his fur bristling with rage. He rose onto his hind legs, staring around the glade. *What. Happened. Here?*"

"It was—it was all a trick." Beetle's voice was fainter and hoarser than ever. "Crownleaf, they lured the fighters away, and they . . . the monkeys came back."

A low, steady snarl was rumbling in Stinger's throat, but he stayed very still. The fighters bounded forward, exclaiming in horror and outrage, crouching over the wounded, cursing with fury at the treachery of the monkeys.

Thorn turned to Mud, who had crept to his side. "Mud, this is terrible," he whispered. "No monkey would have dared do this while Great Mother was alive."

"No," agreed Mud, trembling. "Bravelands misses the Great Spirit already."

Stinger had dropped to all fours and was stalking toward the Crown Stone. He halted right in front of it and flicked a contemptuous paw at the streaks of dung that disfigured it. Then he turned to face the troop.

"Brightforest Troop. This place is defiled." He curled his snout, baring his fangs. "We will find a new home, a better home."

There were murmurs of anxiety and a few uncertain whimpers.

"Courage!" Stinger raised his voice, and the baboons fell silent. "Brightforest Troop will never be crushed! We will rise from this stronger than ever, my friends. And *when we do*—when we do—those sniveling, treacherous monkeys will feel our wrath. They sought to destroy us, did they? My troop, we will visit destruction on *them*."

The baboons erupted, all their fear seemingly forgotten. Grinning, whooping, they sprang up and down, beating the ground with their paws. Stinger simply nodded, accepting their hollers of adulation.

Thorn could only watch, unease rippling under his pelt. *How good he is at manipulating them*, he thought. Stinger controlled the troop like a lioness steering her tiny cubs.

"My troop!" Stinger held out his forepaws and gestured for quiet. "We need to take steps to protect ourselves during this time of change, and that must begin right now. And so I propose to set up a brand-new rank for trusted, loyal baboons. That new rank will be called *Strongbranches*."

The gathered baboons murmured in awed curiosity. "How wise he is," whispered Fang, near to Thorn.

"Any baboon may apply to become a Strongbranch," Stinger went on. "From Deeproot to Highleaf, all baboons will now have a new, exciting chance to rise in the hierarchy of our troop. All that will be required is that you pass a Strongfeat: one single test that I myself will set for you. There is new opportunity for all in Brightforest Troop!"

The murmurs of excitement rose to squeals and hoots and cheers. Thorn shot a glance around the troop: yes, the baboons who were most visibly inspired were the Deeproots.

All their lives, since failing to pass the strict Three Feats challenge, they had resigned themselves to service and drudgery. *And now Stinger has given them hope of power and success. They'll do anything for him.*

Thorn chewed his lip. He had to admit it: Stinger was indeed a very clever baboon. But he, too, felt hope thrill through him.

If I become a Strongbranch, I can get close to Stinger. And then he could find evidence of his crimes and expose him to the troop. . . . "Mud," Thorn said out loud.

"What?" Mud was still gazing, enchanted, at Stinger. His dark eyes sparkled with admiration.

"Mud, listen. I'm going to apply to be a Strongbranch."

"You are?" Mud turned, startled. "Thorn, I think that's a really good idea. You're fast and strong enough—and it may help you and Berry to be together!"

Thorn did not comment on that, though his heartbeat quickened. He simply nodded, then padded alongside Mud as the troop began to make its way out of Tall Trees. Darkness had fallen completely, and crickets and tree frogs chirped around them, the sound loud enough to drown out even the splashing steps of baboons on the move. Right at the front walked Stinger, his head and tail high and proud.

Thorn broke into a lope to catch up. Stinger was talking to no one; he was a picture of courageous nobility as he led his troop to a new life.

Thorn felt as if he might be sick. He slowed a little, staying a respectful couple of paces behind his Crownleaf.

Stinger glanced back and raised his brows. "Ah, Thorn Middleleaf." His mouth twitched. "You want to join the Strongbranches, don't you?"

Taken aback, Thorn nodded; then again, more eagerly. "Yes, Stinger."

"I'm not surprised." Stinger strode on, and Thorn had to hurry to keep up.

"How—what do you mean?" asked Thorn, edgily.

"Ah, Thorn. You remind me so much of myself," Stinger murmured. The gap between them and the rest of the troop had widened, and oddly, he seemed happy to chat. "So keen, so strong and ambitious to do well. You want to be at the center of the action, just like I always did."

"I . . . I'm flattered," mumbled Thorn, uneasy at Stinger's geniality. *I threatened to expose him! Why is he being so friendly?*

"You *should* be flattered." Stinger grinned. "I'm glad you're keen to be a Strongbranch, Thorn. I can use a clever baboon like you."

"That's . . . good," rasped Thorn. He was growing more nervous every moment. It occurred to him that Stinger might want to keep him close, just as much as he wanted to keep an eye on Stinger. . . .

"Anyway, when the right opportunity arises, I'll set you a Strongfeat." Turning, Stinger gazed into Thorn's eyes; his own glinted with a dark intelligence. "You'll prove yourself, Thorn. Don't worry about *that*."

Thorn halted, letting Stinger walk on ahead into the night. He swallowed hard and gave his fur a shake to stop it crawling.

Why, he wondered, *did that sound less like a promise and more like a threat?*

CHAPTER 3

Would the Great Spirit ever put an end to this weather? Sky Strider was beginning to think not. *Perhaps this is how it will be forever, now. Perhaps the Great Spirit thinks we deserve it.*

She could no longer tell if the water that streamed constantly down her face was the Great Spirit's rain from above, or her own tears. Cold, hard drops pattered constantly on Great Mother's body, darkening her wrinkled hide to black. Sky had stayed by her for two days now. She knew that, because she had watched the sun beyond the storm clouds rise and sink, but it seemed so much longer. Surely by now it had been moons, seasons, *years.* Because how could Sky's world have changed so terribly in only two days?

She squeezed her eyes shut. When she did that, she could recall the gentle brush of Great Mother's trunk across her back. She could bring to mind that wise, gentle gaze. Without the sight of that lifeless body, she could almost feel Great Mother there beside her, full of life and strength and love.

The old matriarch of the Strider family had been Great Mother to all of Bravelands—leader, judge, and wise adviser—but she had been so much more than that to Sky. As her grandmother, she had cared for her ever since Sky's mother had been killed by lions. Great Mother had always been there, listening and consoling, taking Sky's opinions seriously, looking after her and loving her. *Just as my mother would have, if she'd lived.*

Sky's throat constricted with fear and grief. *What am I going to do without her?*

She blinked her eyes open, longing suddenly for the company of her family. The grown ones were not far away; they huddled at the edge of the watering hole, their rumps turned against the lashing rain. Now and again they would reach out to comfort one another in their shared grief.

Occasionally, though, they would turn to stare at her. Rain, the new matriarch, swung her mottled trunk and murmured to Comet. It unnerved Sky.

A small trunk touched her shoulder, and she managed to smile. "Hello, Moon," she rumbled fondly.

Her little cousin pressed his flank against hers. "Sky, what're you doing?"

She sighed. "Staying with Great Mother. I don't want to leave her alone."

Moon twined his trunk with hers. With a surge of affection, Sky realized he was trying to comfort her, the way she comforted him when he was hurt or sad.

"I wish the rain would stop," he mumbled.

Gazing up at the dark, roiling clouds, Sky let the rain lash her face and sting her eyes. "I don't think we can hope for that any time soon," she said softly.

"If the sun comes out . . ." Moon hesitated. "Will Great Mother wake up?"

"Oh, Moon." Sky stroked his trunk with hers. "I'm sorry, but she won't ever wake up. She's gone back to the stars."

Moon gave a small whimper. "Has the Great Spirit gone with her?"

A cold shudder that was nothing to do with the rain rippled through Sky. For a moment she couldn't answer. Swallowing, she said hoarsely: "I wish I knew."

Through the gray mist of rain, Sky could make out the next bay of the watering hole, where a herd of zebras paced, still restless from their panic after Great Mother's death. Their leader, a tall male with swirling stripes, stiffened abruptly and pricked his ears, snorting. At his warning, his herd raised their heads, grunting and whinnying. They were staring at something behind the elephants.

Taking a breath, Sky turned. With a heavy, thundering tread, a pod of some twenty huge, gray-skinned animals were trotting toward the watering hole. Their leader gaped his jaws wide, displaying terrifyingly huge blunt teeth.

Hippos! They were dangerous and hot-tempered; Great Mother had always warned Sky to keep her distance from them.

"Come on, Moon," she said, and shepherded him gently back to their family.

The grown ones had spotted the hippos too, and as Sky and Moon trotted into their midst, panting with fear, they formed a protective wall with their bodies.

"Stay back, young ones," said Rain.

The hippos were almost upon them, but as Sky shied in alarm, they pounded on past the elephants. Slowing, they approached Great Mother's body with grunts of sadness and formed a respectful circle. The obvious leader, a hippo with unusually large ears and a gray-pink face, lowered his broad muzzle to Great Mother's forehead. His pod watched in silence.

"So it's true," he said at last, raising his head. His small eyes glittered with fury. "The grass-eaters were right." Tipping his head back, he gave a resounding groan; his pod joined in his mourning, their bellowing voices full of rage and sorrow.

"Murdered!" The leader's roar rose above the others. "The crocodiles *dared* to murder Great Mother!"

Moon clutched Sky's tail with his trunk. "What are they going to do?"

"I don't know." Sky's heart pounded. Something awful was about to happen, she knew.

The large-eared hippo splashed into the shallows. On the muddy bank of a distant bay sprawled a bask of ten or more crocodiles. One yawned, displaying ferocious teeth, then snapped its jaws shut.

"We'll show them what happens to Codebreakers," the

hippo grunted. "I don't care if they don't follow it—they're going to pay for what they've done!"

The hippos surged into the lake, flank muscles rippling, sending up showers of water. Nostrils flaring with angry snorts, they paddled swiftly toward the crocs.

"Sky!" cried Moon. "What're they doing?"

Rain broke from the line of elephants and cantered toward the shore. "Stop!" she trumpeted after the hippos.

Her cry was lost in the rattle of rain on the lake surface, and the hippos took no notice anyway. They were almost at the far bay now, lunging out of the water in a thunder of feet toward the crocodiles. Grinning, some of the crocs darted into the water and slid beneath the surface, but one was slower than the others.

Lifting her long head, twisting to eye the threat, she was too late. The hippo leader was already on her, smashing his huge head into her shoulder. Taken by surprise, she flipped onto her scaly back, exposing her creamy underbelly. She hissed a curse in Sandtongue and writhed to escape, but the hippo lunged and snapped his vast jaws into her belly.

The crocodile flailed her thick tail, making a hideous screaming sound, but the hippo hung grimly on. He heaved backward, staggering almost onto his rump, and dragged her with him beneath the surface.

The lake erupted in a churning froth of foam. The croc's tail surfaced, slashing wildly; then, for a moment, her snapping head was visible too. But when she was hauled under once more, the foaming water turned red. As Sky watched in horror, the crocodile's twitching corpse floated to the surface, her belly shredded and bloody. Surfacing, the hippo opened his savage jaws and bellowed in victory. His pod took up the cry, their roars resounding across the lake.

At a distance the rest of the doomed croc's bask drifted, staring at the carnage with cold, stunned eyes.

Horrified, Sky shouldered through the grown ones. "It's not right!" she cried. "They're breaking the Code!" Tugging free from Moon's trunk, she bolted for the shore.

"Sky, no!" Comet shouted, but she kept running.

Fired up by their leader's successful kill, the hippos were harrying the rest of the bask. Some of the crocs met the challenge head-on, fearsome jaws gaping in defiance before they dived under; others hauled themselves from the water, racing across the sand on their stumpy legs. From the churning lake came an unearthly shriek, and another limp crocodile corpse drifted to the surface.

"Stop!" Splashing into the water, Sky raised her trunk and blared in horror, *"Stop!"*

The mud beneath her feet was soft and sucking. She wobbled desperately, lurched forward, and suddenly the lake bed was gone. Sky plunged beneath the surface, her gasp of horror stifled by a trunkful of murky lake water. Half-blind and choking, she kicked frantically.

Her feet touched the bottom. Shoving against the yielding mud, she broke into the air once more, gasping and spluttering. The hippos stared at her.

"Great Mother wouldn't want this," she cried to them,

coughing. "She—she always defended the Code." Her mouth filled with water again and she spat it out, her legs still flailing. "The Code mattered to her more than anything! Please, you must stop!"

"And let these scum get away with killing her?" grunted one of the hippos, jerking its head at the crocs. "Maybe you elephants think that's okay, but we don't."

"Please!" begged Sky, but the hippos twisted in the water, turning their backs on her. The remaining crocodiles were lurching up the muddy bank, scrambling over one another in their dash for safety; the hippos charged in pursuit, thundering up the bank and into the dense foliage beyond. With the battle moving to the land, the lake calmed and stilled quickly, its surface pitted only by the lashing rain. But where hippos and crocodiles had fought, Sky saw a dark stain rise and spread.

Feeling sick, Sky splashed back to the herd. *Is this what life will be like without Great Mother?* Her chest ached with sadness as her family trotted to meet her. She stopped. Their faces held a strange, startled curiosity.

"Was I wrong?" she asked miserably. "I know it was reckless, but I had to try to stop them!"

"No, of course it wasn't wrong." Rain exchanged a glance with the others. "That was very brave—Great Mother would have been so proud of you. But, Sky . . ." She took a deep breath. "We need to talk."

Sky felt a shiver of unease. "What about?"

"Oh, young one." Rain folded her mottled trunk around

Sky and pulled her close. "I know that your heart is still heavy with grief. All of us miss Great Mother desperately. But we must look to the future."

Moon wriggled between Sky and his mother Star. "Rain, are you our new Great Mother?"

Rain shook her head. "The Great Spirit hasn't chosen me, little one. But Bravelands does need a new Great Parent—and desperately."

Once again, all the grown ones were studying Sky, their faces thoughtful. She didn't like it.

"Your vision about the watering hole came true," Comet told her softly. "You knew something terrible was going to happen, and it did."

"You can read the bones of all creatures, not just elephants," added Star, in her singsong voice. "Only Great Mother could do that."

A jolt of shock went through Sky. "You think I'm the new Great Mother?" Aghast, she shrank backward. "I can't be. I'm *not!*"

Rain patted her gently. "It's true that we don't know for sure. And you are young, Sky; so very young. But all the signs are telling us one thing: that the Great Spirit has settled in you."

The other elephants murmured in agreement.

"It's a huge burden for you to bear," said Rain, "we know that. But we will all help you."

Sky could feel her heart thumping in her chest, and her pulse in her throat and ears. Nothing in her had changed.

Surely she would recognize anything new inside her, other than just *Sky*?

"But the Great Spirit hasn't passed to me," she whispered. "I know it hasn't. Because—Aunt Rain, Aunt Comet—" She hesitated, then blurted, "I can't *feel* it!"

Gently Rain pressed her head to Sky's. "I know it's hard. Great Mother should have had many more years, and you should have been able to grow up before your time came to succeed her. But Bravelands needs a Great Parent now. Please, Sky. We need you."

Sky stared around at her family, her throat dry. Every elephant's face was bright with hope—a hope Sky knew she couldn't fulfill.

Moon rubbed his bristly cheek against her flank, as if he was comforting her again. Her little cousin, at least, seemed to understand how she felt.

But how could she show the others how wrong they were?

CHAPTER 4

The trees gave little shelter from the downpour; drenched, they showered water onto the baboons at even a glancing touch. At the head of the troop with the other Strongbranches, Thorn splashed a hesitant paw into another muddy puddle; no, it was too deep. He retreated, testing the edges for an easier way around. They were all going to be soaked; it was just a question of *how* soaked. Some of these pools were more treacherous than they looked, and if no babies or old ones drowned on this dismal trek, thought Thorn, they'd be lucky.

Of the six Strongbranches, only four were negotiating the muddy forest; Grass and Fly Middleleaf had veered off to look for any prey that hadn't fled for shelter. Brightforest Troop would need to be well nourished for the next few days: the search for a new camp was going to be hard and long.

"Ow," complained Worm Strongbranch, who was limping slightly.

"Poor you," sympathized Frog Strongbranch. She was tall-est of them all and looked down at Worm with concern. "Does that tarantula bite still hurt?"

"It really does," grunted Worm. "I wish it had bitten my sister. She deserves it."

"Well, at least you completed your Feat," grumbled Fang Strongbranch. "When are you doing *yours*, Thorn Middle-leaf?"

Once Stinger thinks up something terrible, Thorn thought. He gritted his teeth. "Stinger said I had to pass a trial period first, didn't he?"

"Because he thinks you'll fail," scoffed Fang.

"Maybe," said Thorn. "But Stinger knows best. Until he decides differently, I'm a Strongbranch, just like you. Worm, you'd better see if there's a way through that prickly scrub."

"Go and look yourself, *Middleleaf*," sneered Worm. "Maybe we'll listen to you when you've actually done your Feat."

"Mine was the hardest," boasted Fang as he tore at some obstructing creepers. "I had to lift a boulder that was bigger than the Crown Stone."

"Liar," muttered Worm under her breath.

Frog shot her an anxious glance and spoke up loudly to drown her out. "Are you sure that's right, Fang?"

"Absolutely!" Fang glared at Frog. "And what's more, a baboon was sitting on top of it to make it even heavier."

Frog bit her lip, but silently began to help Fang with the creepers; her gentle face looked nervous. Until joining the Strongbranches she had been a Deeproot, and Thorn wondered if she was feeling as out of place as he was. He glanced over his shoulder to where Mud was helping Beetle across a treacherously slippery log. *I wish I could have Mud for company instead of this lot.*

"We need to stop for a rest," came Beetle's cracked voice, sounding out of breath. "Many of us are tired."

The baboons slumped down gratefully, shaking off rain, and mothers began to nurse and soothe their babies. Impatient and frustrated though he was, Thorn had to halt too. He was just beginning to scout for berries when Grass and Fly bounded from the undergrowth.

Despite their sodden fur, they were grinning. "Look what we've got!" announced Fly, and both of them held out paws full of fermented fruit. "Sweetpulp!"

"Ooh!" Worm brightened as she grabbed some from Grass. "Where did you find that?"

They exchanged a sly look. "Well, we didn't *find* it as such," admitted Fly with a smirk.

"Old Beetle had a stash of it in a hollow log near Tall Trees," said Grass, popping a lump into his mouth and chewing on it. "We raided his supply."

"That's not really fair . . ." began Frog.

"What, when it was just going to rot away altogether?" pointed out Grass. "He didn't have any more use for it."

"We've rescued it, that's all," said Fly. "Here, have some.

That'll calm your conscience."

"No, thank you," said Frog, turning primly away. "I don't think the Great Spirit would approve."

"Hmph." Fly shrugged. "The Great Spirit hasn't struck me with lightning yet."

"Why would it?" Worm giggled. "You're so boring, Frog."

"I think she's scared of the sweetpulp," snorted Grass. "Maybe she can't handle it."

"If she doesn't want any, it's her business," butted in Thorn angrily, and Frog shot him a grateful look. "Leave her alone."

"Fine." Grass shrugged. "If she wants to miss out, that's fine by me. Anyone else?"

Worm and Fang didn't have any of Frog's scruples; they grabbed the offerings eagerly and gulped them down. Thorn bit his lip, tempted despite himself. "What's it like?"

"You've never had it before?" Fly lifted his brow disdainfully. "Go on, you might like it."

Thorn had no wish to be in debt to them, but he couldn't repress his curiosity. He took the pawful of mushy fruit that Fly offered him and sniffed at it. It smelled strong and tangy enough to make him blink. Doubtfully he crammed it into his mouth.

It wasn't bad. Slowly he chewed, blinking. The juice that ran down his throat was sharp and made his head feel light. A rather dozy feeling of well-being crept across his brain; they were right, it did taste good. He suddenly felt a lot more relaxed about the trek ahead of them.

No! he thought in alarm. That was no way to think about

the quest for a new home; it was going to be tough and dangerous, and they'd all have to have their wits about them. Grass,
Fang, Worm, and Fly were squatting against tree trunks,
grinning and telling jokes that were little more than gibber-
ish; they weren't paying him any attention. Thorn turned
quickly and, under the guise of a cough, spat the sweetpulp
into a bush.

Wiping his mouth, he cleared his throat. Frog was the only
one who was looking, and she gave him a shy, approving smile.

"You didn't like it?" she murmured.

"I need to keep a clear head," he whispered firmly.

Frog nodded, still gazing at him with shining eyes. "I think
you're wise, Thorn."

"Thanks," he grunted. "Let's get these fools going again,
and the troop will have to follow. We can't waste time."

Frog nodded eagerly, and with quite a bit of scolding on her
part, the other four Strongbranches were chivvied into moving on through the forest. With grunts of reluctance, the rest
of Brightforest Troop followed.

"I know this place," Frog told Thorn as they tore and
smashed at a barrier of scrub. "I'm sure you do too. There's a
stream up ahead, remember?"

"I think so." Thorn was beginning to realize just how powerful the big baboon was—no wonder Stinger had picked her
to be a Strongbranch. He watched with admiration as Frog
ripped down a last tangle of small branches.

"But it shouldn't cause problems," she went on. "Everyone's
wet anyway and—oh!" Her eyes widened with shock. Thorn

followed her gaze through the gap.

Of course. They should have realized, he thought dismally.
The rain had swollen the stream massively, bursting its banks;
water had risen to cover the lower sections of the tree trunks.
The once-lazy trickle was a churning torrent of foamy brown,
with twigs and leaves and small dead creatures swirling in its
current.

"We can't cross that!" exclaimed Moss, following Frog and
Thorn out of the undergrowth.

"I'm not taking my baby in there!" declared a mother,
clutching her infant against her with a protective paw.

The baboons were all pushing through the scrub now, gathering around Frog and Thorn. As each baboon came through,
the exclamations of horror rose.

"Stop, stop!" Stinger clambered through the foliage and
scowled at them all. "I'll have none of this panic and defeat-
ism. We have an efficient team to help us now! They will get
us safely across this river." He stared expectantly at the six
Strongbranches.

Thorn and the others looked apprehensively at one another.
After a small silence Thorn said, "We should split into pairs
and look for a way across. Come on. Frog, you come with me."

The other four Strongbranches set off downstream, half-
heartedly poking at broken twigs and flotsam, while Thorn
and Frog made their way upstream. "I honestly don't see how
we're going to do this," Frog told him with a sigh.

He nodded. "It would take forever to find a way around
this water, if there is one at all. Look out!" He darted out of

the way as a rotten branch was flung ashore at their paws. As it receded a little, bobbing in a side current, he frowned. "I'd suggest using a branch like that one to get across, but did you see what happened?"

Frog nodded. "The river tossed it as if it was a twig. We'd need something a lot bigger. But what is there?"

"Something bigger." Thorn frowned. Then he brightened and pointed. "Like that!"

A sturdy mgunga tree stood right on a bend of the river, its roots now sunk deep in water. One of its branches had snapped, but not entirely; it hung drooping out over the river, reaching more than halfway to the far side.

The two baboons looked at each other, excited. "That's it!" exclaimed Frog. "It doesn't go all the way, but—"

"But there are strangler figs on the other side," said Thorn. "Look, their branches almost touch that broken one. I think even the oldest baboons could make that jump."

"And the littlest can be carried by their mothers," finished Frog. "We've done it, Thorn!"

She gave him a quick hug of celebration; Thorn was too surprised to react, and she'd released him before he could. She went bounding off back down the bank, and he loped after her.

When they reached the troop, Stinger was turning from the other Strongbranches, his face sour with disappointment. At the news from Frog and Thorn, he perked up instantly.

"Well done, my Strongbranches!" he declared, clapping his paws to draw the troop's attention. "I chose you well!

Brightforest Troop—follow Frog and Thorn. We shall once again meet a new challenge as a troop, and overcome it!"

The plan worked just as Thorn had hoped. Grass and Worm were first to cross—at Stinger's insistence—and they looked more than a little nervous as they picked their way along the flaky yellow bark, wincing when their paws touched the prickles. But they made the jump to the fig trees with ease and sat up on its branches, hooting in triumph and relief.

Satisfied, Stinger nodded. "Fly and Fang, you cross too. Thorn and Frog, stay here to guide everyone up. And then, my troop: the rest of you."

There was a new optimism among the baboons, despite the lashing rain. As Frog guided them up the mgunga tree, Thorn set to helping them cross the branch one by one. It wasn't long before most of the troop was sitting in the twisted boughs of the fig tree on the opposite bank, hooting encouragement to friends who were still to cross.

Thorn turned to find Mud at his shoulder. Mud smiled at him, nervously.

"How is it?" Mud whispered. "Being a Strongbranch, I mean?"

When he'd glanced round to make sure no one was looking, Thorn made a face. "Except for Frog, they're driving me crazy," he confided softly.

Mud grinned. "I'm quite relieved," he murmured. "I don't really like any of them. Frog's all right, but she's a bit—well, odd."

"She's very devoted to the Great Spirit," Thorn told him,

mock sternly. "Now your turn, Mud."

He watched apprehensively as his friend crept along the branch, but Mud made it to the far bank without a problem. Thorn turned to the next baboon.

"I have to carry my baby." It was a young mother, Lily, and she wore a beseeching gaze. "Thorn, will you make sure Snail gets across? She's still quite small. . . ."

Thorn glanced at Lily's older infant, who puffed out her chest and rose onto her hind legs. "I'll be fine, Mother," said Snail. "I'm actually big."

"I'll watch her," Thorn assured Lily, stifling a grin, and he helped her mother up onto the branch. With a last anxious look at Snail, Lily ventured out across the raging river, one paw shielding the baby who clung to her chest.

"Your mother and sister are fine," Thorn told Snail with a smile, as Lily made the leap to the fig tree. "Your turn now."

Snail didn't look quite as confident as she'd sounded, but she stepped bravely onto the branch, wincing as her paw touched a prickle. Remembering his promise, Thorn kept his eyes on her as she wobbled out across the churning water.

"Ow." Snail stifled a yelp as she stood on another tiny spine. She danced her paw sideways.

The bark where she set it down was flaky; it peeled under the little baboon's weight. With a yelp of surprise, Snail staggered sideways. Losing her footing, she slid helplessly and plummeted into the river below.

Lily's shriek of terror resounded over the crashing water,

and the whole troop erupted in hoots and screams. Below Thorn, Stinger charged to the bank.

"Strongbranches!" he shouted. "Get her out!"

With one glance, Thorn saw that Grass, Fly, Worm, and Fang were dithering on the far shore, their eyes dazed. *The sweetpulp.*

"They're no use," he snarled. "Frog, come on!"

He sprang down from the tree and with Frog at his heels raced downriver. A clumsy crashing of foliage told him the other Strongbranches were following, but they were far behind. He clenched his teeth in anger and picked up speed. *It's up to me and Frog.*

Out in the water, rising and falling in the surging waves, he could just make out the drenched little head of Snail. She was tossed this way and that; at one moment sucked under, the next cast up to gulp for air. He and Frog were running abreast of her now, and he looked frantically around the river in search of some scrap of hope.

"There!" he shouted. A blade of rock jutted from the water not far ahead. "If she's washed toward that, we could grab her!" Loping to the edge of the foamy water, he crouched to spring.

"No!" Frog grabbed his shoulder and pushed ahead of him. "I'm bigger, I'll do it!"

Before he could even argue, she had leaped for the rock. Frog's hind paws splashed into the river, but she hauled herself out and balanced on the rock, staring fixedly at the small bobbing head as it swirled toward her. Frog half rose, stretching out her arms; her face was taut.

Snail was facedown in the water now. As she eddied close to the rock, Frog made a grab for her, plunging her arms into the river. One paw snatched the little baboon's scruff, and Frog yanked her out, limp and dripping.

Thorn's heart raced as Frog tucked the bedraggled creature under one arm and leaped back to shore. They were bending over her when the other Strongbranches finally caught up, panting.

Snail's head lolled backward as Thorn grabbed her by the shoulders. Desperately, he shook her. Frog groaned, punching the ground in frustration. The rest of the Brightforest baboons—the ones who hadn't already crossed the river—were gathering now, and Thorn saw that Lily was there. She had recrossed the water without her baby, and she was shoving through the crowd, hooting in distress.

Oh no. Thorn shook the little baboon again, hard, and suddenly her head jerked forward. Coughing up water, she began to whimper feebly. As Lily reached her side she croaked, "Mother . . ."

Thorn staggered back in relief as Lily grabbed her daughter into her arms and rocked her. "Thank you, Thorn Strongbranch! Thank you, Frog!"

Thorn grinned and slapped Frog's back. "You did it! You got her out!"

Frog turned and gave him a hug, her eyes shining. "*We* did it, Thorn!"

Beyond Lily, who was cradling Snail and crooning softly, and beyond the other shamefaced Strongbranches, Thorn caught sight of Berry. She was staring at him and Frog, her eyes unreadable.

As his gaze caught hers, she turned away.

"We baboons are the best organizers," Stinger told the Strongbranches as he strutted across the open grasslands. "So it only makes sense that we try to bring order back to Bravelands. Since Great Mother died, things have been out of control."

"I'm just glad that we're with you, my Crownleaf," Grass told him eagerly. Ever since the debacle with Snail and the sweetpulp, the big baboon had been trying to ingratiate himself again with his leader. "There's so much disorder, anything could happen."

"I'm glad to have you here, my Strongbranches." Stinger shook his head sadly. "Even I need bodyguards."

It didn't seem that way to Thorn, but he kept his mouth shut. Every animal Stinger had spoken to had seemed wary rather than hostile. They had left the rest of Brightforest Troop sheltering in a clump of trees and now headed toward the sweeping stretch of savannah where the zebras grazed. The ground was sodden beneath their paws, and rivulets of water lay on the saturated surface, yet there was still no sign of the rain stopping. It teemed from a sky that was black with looming cloud.

Stinger had already met with a gazelle herd leader and

a coalition of cheetahs, but there were scores of other animals still to see. Thorn was weary and thirsty from the long
march around Bravelands, and he kept licking water from
his snout; Stinger would not hear of stopping to rest. As the
rain intensified, Thorn tilted back his head and let it run
into his jaws.

A cluster of bee-eater birds perched in a tree; their plum-
age, red and startling blue, looked dull and lifeless in the rain.
A lone hyena hunched under the same tree, but she didn't
even twitch as the baboons passed. Stinger, striding on with
his tail held high, seemed like the only creature in Bravelands
with any energy or purpose.

"Here we are," Stinger said cheerfully as they crested the
top of a low hill. On the plain below a herd of zebras grazed,
tails swatting, large teeth tearing at the sodden grass. Every
zebra herd Thorn had seen numbered several hundred, yet
here there were only about forty of them.

He frowned. "Where've the rest of them gone?"

"Why should we care?" Stinger loped down to the herd,
and Thorn and the other Strongbranches scrambled after
him. A stallion with curving stripes came to meet them, his
ears flicking in agitation.

Stinger nodded coolly. "Greetings to you. I am Stinger
Crownleaf of Brightforest Troop, and these are my faithful
Strongbranch escorts."

"I see." The zebra eyed Thorn and the others. Worm had
drawn herself up, her stare menacing. Grass chewed arrogantly

on a stalk of the grass he was named for. Fly's broken-toothed grin was not a pleasant one. The zebra swallowed hard, his long throat rippling.

"I am Sleekfriend," he said politely. "What brings you here, Stinger Crownleaf?"

"We live in difficult times," Stinger said, his face grave, "and I hope your herd stays strong, Sleekfriend. We came to find you first. The zebras are the heart of Bravelands."

Thorn knew these words by heart now. Stinger had already said the same thing to the gazelles and the cheetahs.

The zebra blew out a breath. His hoof pawed at the muddy ground as he dipped his head. "Hard times indeed," he agreed. "This is all that's left of my herd, in fact. Most of them stampeded after Great Mother's death, and we remain scattered." His gaze flicked to a small colt shivering at his mother's side. "If we don't regroup soon, I worry we'll be easy targets for flesh-eaters."

Stinger nodded sympathetically. "I'm hearing the same thing everywhere," he told Sleekfriend. "Discord, restlessness, herds and packs breaking apart. Nothing is as it should be." His sigh was deep and sad. "That's why it's so important to make things right in Bravelands, and quickly. We must ensure everyone's following the Code."

As if you follow it, Thorn thought darkly.

Stinger launched into the same speech he had given the other animals, stuffed with flattery and false concern. "To settle things for the good of Bravelands, I'm proposing a

Great Gathering at High Sun tomorrow. We need to find the new Great Parent—or decide how to live together until one appears."

Sleekfriend's ears were a blur of flickering anxiety. "At the watering hole?"

"Of course." Stinger gave him a sober, direct stare. "I trust the zebras will be present? We need you, Sleekfriend."

The zebra shook his thin coat, sending a shower of water flying. "Our herd . . . we feel uncomfortable at that place. Since Great Mother's death." He blinked, his long lashes glinting with raindrops. "You see, Stinger, the flesh-eaters have always left us alone at the watering hole, but without Great Mother we don't trust them. We still drink there, when we need to, but we don't linger. A Great Gathering could be . . . problematic."

Stinger slanted his gaze deliberately at the Strongbranches. In response Worm puffed herself up even more, and Grass hummed softly as he chewed; it was almost a growl. Fang plucked a beetle from the mud at his paws and bit down so hard on it his teeth clashed. Fly's chipped grin stretched wider. Frog and Thorn simply looked at the ground.

Sleekfriend shook his mane, and his hoof pawed even more anxiously at the mud. Thorn felt hot with shame, but he could say nothing.

Stinger looked thoughtful, as if he was entirely unaware of his bodyguards' hostile air. "You may be wise there, Sleekfriend. Protecting your herd is the most important thing of all." He scratched his chin. "But consider the alternative, my good friend. If the zebras aren't represented at the Gathering, how can we be sure we'll decide what's best for you? Far better if you're there to speak for yourselves. Really, it's the only way to ensure your . . . safety."

For long moments, Sleekfriend was silent. The whites of his eyes were visible as he shifted his wary stare from baboon to baboon. Then he raised his head, breathing hard.

"May animals always praise the wisdom of baboons." There was a hint of a tremor in his words. "So be it, Stinger Crownleaf. My herd and I will be there."

Stinger grinned, his fangs glinting despite the dull light. "Well said, Sleekfriend, and a wise choice, very *wise*. And now that we have the agreement of the zebras, we can invite the rest of Bravelands!"

Sleekfriend dipped his head quickly, then trotted back to his herd. Feeling more than a little sick, Thorn followed Stinger back up the slope.

"Elephants next," Stinger said cheerfully. "They won't be nearly so easy to handle."

He's too good at this, Thorn thought as he trudged behind Stinger, over the crest of the hill and slithering through a sodden stretch of brush. Even if Brightforest Troop would listen to Thorn, it would be impossible to convey just how menacingly Stinger was behaving. To rebuff him, Stinger would simply have to repeat what he'd told each herd leader. *Every word that comes out of that baboon's mouth is so polite, so reasonable—but so twisted.*

Stinger wasn't organizing this Gathering for the good of

Bravelands; that was obvious. The creatures he intimidated must know that; yet they had to comply. Stinger was leaving them no choice.

Ahead, great gray shapes loomed through the thick mist of rain: a family of elephants, shifting restively around a massive heap of torn and broken branches. As the baboons drew closer, Thorn realized with a jolt what must lie beneath them: *Great Mother's body.*

The elephants turned to confront Stinger and his escort as they approached. Thorn quailed as the huge beasts towered over them. Rain streaked down their great flanks in streams.

"What brings baboons to this place?" asked the largest elephant, flapping her ears in warning. Her swinging trunk was mottled with white patches.

"Greetings to you, Family Strider." Stinger bowed his head. "I am Stinger Crownleaf of Brightforest Troop, and these are my troop-mates." He gestured at the Strongbranches, his eyes sly as they struck their aggressive poses. "Brightforest Troop grieves for your loss, dear elephants. Great Mother was wise and generous, and we will treasure her memory."

"As will all of Bravelands," rumbled the large elephant, with a disdainful glance at the posturing Strongbranches. "I am Rain, matriarch of the Strider family."

Stinger bowed even lower. "We live in difficult times, Rain. It's our most fervent hope that your herd stays strong. I come with a proposal that, with your approval, I will carry to the other animals. The elephants, after all, are the heart of Bravelands."

Rain waved her trunk dismissively. "You seek to flatter us, Stinger Crownleaf," she said. "Just tell us why you're here."

As Stinger launched into his well-rehearsed speech, Thorn took the chance to study the elephant family. The Striders were all adults, he realized—the young one called Sky, whom he and Fearless had met when they'd come to plead a favor of Great Mother, was nowhere to be seen. Thorn hoped she was all right. It had been obvious that she and Great Mother were unusually close, even for elephants; the matriarch's death must have hit Sky hard.

Stinger concluded his speech with a flourish; to Thorn's surprise, the elephants had brightened. Rain glanced at the rest of her family, and they all nodded.

"We will come to the Great Gathering, Stinger Crownleaf," she declared.

"We're so glad to hear it." Stinger bowed his head again, but Thorn had already caught the glitter of surprise in his cunning eyes. "All the animals of Bravelands owe you a debt for your generations of wise guidance. Until tomorrow, Rain Strider, farewell!"

The elephant nodded and turned her rump.

As the baboons set out once more across the rain-drenched grassland, Thorn noticed that Stinger's jaw was clenched. In fact, his entire body was rigid with controlled rage.

He should have felt happy that things didn't seem to be going entirely Stinger's way, but Thorn found himself more uneasy than ever. Frog, at his side, seemed to think the same.

"Why is he upset?" she whispered. "The elephants agreed to come. So what's wrong?"

Thorn shrugged. "I don't know."

The two of them had fallen a little behind, and with an anxious glance at the others, Frog cleared her throat. "Thorn, I don't like this. I thought we were here to protect Stinger, but it's more like the other animals need protection from *us*."

"I know." Hope rose inside him. *Maybe Frog could be my ally! Maybe she'll help me convince the troop. . . .* "Frog, listen—"

"You two! Hurry up!" Stinger had turned and was glaring at them through the rain.

"Come on, we'd better catch up." Frog bounded on.

With a sigh of frustration, Thorn followed. *I can talk to her privately later.*

Stinger hadn't calmed down since his conversation with the elephants; if anything he looked even more annoyed. "They think they're in charge, don't they?" he snapped.

Thorn, loping at his side now, gave him an uncertain glance. "Who do?"

"The elephants, of course. Did you see the way they looked at each other?" Stinger picked up a stone and flung it at a flock of ibises; they scattered, squawking. "The Family Strider are up to something, and I don't like it."

"I'm sure they aren't," said Thorn, then added quickly, "I mean, they wouldn't dare! Elephants are always a bit . . . haughty. Aren't they? It's just . . . the way they come across. They're so big. That's all . . ." His words trailed off lamely to silence.

The Crownleaf's eyes were dark and glittering. "You know what the trouble is with elephants, my Strongbranches?"

"What, Stinger?" asked Grass eagerly.

"They think they have a Spirit-given right to be Great Parent," spat Stinger. "Well, they don't."

"No, they don't," chorused Grass and Fly.

Stinger ignored them; his eyes had narrowed. "I'd make a better Great Father than any of those colossal fools," he murmured. "Elephants can read bones. So what?" He turned his head and threw them a smirk.

"I am a baboon. And I can read *minds.*"

CHAPTER 5

The young gazelle grazed intently, tugging at the wet grass with her blunt teeth. Crouched upwind, Fearless crept forward, a few paces at a time. Her scent was diffused by the heavy rain, but when he flared his nostrils and inhaled, he could almost taste her on his tongue. The gazelle was bigger than him, but he knew he had the strength to bring her down.

He just needed to get close enough—and the need was becoming more urgent all the time. With the herds scattered and storms raging across the savannah, hunting had been meager and difficult. Fearless's belly growled with hunger, and he knew his muscles were already weakening. He and Valor could not afford to lose this gazelle. Tensing, Fearless slunk determinedly forward.

The gazelle's head jerked up. Fearless froze. She looked

around, ears twitching, but then dipped her elegant neck back to the grasses.

Now!

Fearless launched into a sprint, his legs at full stretch, his tail balanced behind him. The gazelle's eyes snapped wide; she flinched, spun, and bounded through the grass.

Fearless willed his weary legs to work faster, harrying her as she tried to evade him. The gazelle stumbled, and he sprang, slamming into her flank. She buckled and fell, her spindly legs thrashing. Fearless twisted fast, pinned her down, and clamped his jaws around her neck.

In moments, it was over. The gazelle sagged, her dead eyes glazing.

He'd made his first proper kill. Exhilaration coursed through him. Despite his weakened muscles, he felt as if he could run the length of Bravelands.

"Nicely done," remarked Valor, his older sister, as she emerged from the long grass. Her pale gold fur glowed dully in the misty rain, and she moved lithely, her elegant head high. "One day you might even hunt as well as me."

Fearless swatted her playfully. "Oh, really? Didn't you see that beautiful kill? Maybe *you* could learn something from *me*."

Valor snorted, but Fearless could see the pride in his sister's eyes. Her hunting lessons were paying off. Their mother had been the best hunter in Gallantpride, with the keenest nose and fastest sprint, and Valor was becoming just like her.

Valor stiffened. "Something's coming," she murmured.

Fearless tensed. Through the mist, a rustle of damp grass reached his twitching ears. He flared his nostrils and felt an involuntary growl rise in his throat. Together with Valor, he crouched, tail lashing, prepared to defend their kill.

Then the mist carried a scent to his nostrils: it was earthy and sharp and familiar.

Loyal!

"It's all right." Fearless relaxed. "He's my friend."

A lion's great head broke through the grass near them. A pale scar was slashed across his cheek, and his black mane was shot through with gold. "I've been looking for you, Fearless," said Loyal gruffly.

Valor eyed the newcomer suspiciously. "Did this one live with baboons too?" she asked Fearless.

Loyal growled, his crooked tail flicking. "Certainly not."

Fearless grinned at the thought. "I met him after I left the troop. You know when I rescued Ruthless from the cheetahs? Loyal helped me."

"I did. And you must be Valor," said Loyal. "I was a friend of Gallant's, long ago."

Valor's eyes sparked with joy. "You knew Father!"

Father, thought Fearless; he could never repress a stab of angry grief when his name was mentioned. Gallant had been murdered by the tyrannical Titan just over a year ago. The memory of that fight still brought a cold shudder of horror and loathing to Fearless's blood. It had been brutal, like any battle for a pride—but it had also been unjust. Unable to defeat Gallant alone, Titan had his friends intervene to attack

Gallant. Gallantpride had become Titanpride through deceit and a shattering breach of the Code—and the lives of Fearless and Valor had changed forever.

"So where do you live now, Loyal?" Valor asked, her tail lashing with excitement. "What pride do you belong to?"

Loyal tilted his head with a hint of defiance. "I hunt alone these days."

Valor stared, the fur rising along her spine. "You're prideless?"

Fearless knew what she was thinking: a prideless lion either couldn't be trusted, or wasn't strong enough to join a pride. It wasn't true of Loyal—he knew that from experience—but Valor was bound to be suspicious.

Ignoring her tone, Loyal swung his huge shaggy head toward Fearless. "Where have you been, youngster? I haven't seen you for days."

"Hunting," Fearless told him. "Valor's been teaching me."

"To hunt for Titanpride?" Loyal's face soured. "I hope you're keeping a check on that temper of yours. Titan won't forgive any defiance. I'm still amazed he lets you anywhere near his pride."

Fearless bristled. "I haven't got a temper! And I'm not a newborn cub, Loyal. I don't need looking after."

Loyal cuffed him gently. "You've got a lot of growing up to do yet," he growled. "Maybe the grass-eaters are frightened of you, but you're no match for Titan. You're not safe in Titanpride, and don't you forget it."

Fearless tossed his head. "Actually, I *am* safe. Titan made an oath not to kill me if I rescued Ruthless, and we did. Not even Titan would break an oath."

"Let's hope not." His eyes dark, Loyal gazed across the plain toward the watering hole.

Somewhere on its churned, muddy shore, Fearless knew, lay Great Mother's lifeless body. Three days ago, Titanpride's scouts had brought news of her murder; Fearless could still barely accept it was true. It was Great Mother who had negotiated Fearless's meeting with the cheetahs; Great Mother who had used her tact and reputation and wisdom to help him get Ruthless back. It was horrifying to believe that the noble old elephant was dead.

Loyal was watching him again. "I heard what happened," he said, as if he could read Fearless's thoughts. His voice was surprisingly gentle. "I'm sorry."

Fearless's head drooped. "Nothing's gone right in Bravelands since she died. Driving rain for days, and there's no sign of it relenting. The grass-eaters are scattered, and hunting is next to impossible." He jerked his head toward their kill. "It took Valor and me forever to find just one gazelle."

"I know it. Even I've had trouble hunting." Loyal shook his mane. "But Great Mother didn't control the weather, Fearless. There have always been hard times in Bravelands. Even believers in the Great Spirit suffer."

Valor flicked her ears in agreement. "This is what I've been trying to tell him," she said. "It makes no difference if there's a Great Parent or not. In the end the weather will go back to normal and hunting will be good again. You'll see, Fearless."

Fearless sighed. Their attitude wasn't surprising; it was shared by every lion. Almost every other animal in Bravelands believed in the Great Spirit and followed the Great Parent's advice, but lions had always ruled themselves. And yet . . .

He scratched at the muddy grass with his claws. "The baboons believe in the Great Spirit, and they're clever."

Loyal gave an amused growl. "Perhaps, but lions are clever too. And no one, Great Parent or not, tells us what to do."

Valor butted Fearless's shoulder. "Living with baboons has left you with some odd ideas, brother." She glanced at the looming clouds. "We should get this gazelle back to the pride."

"I'll be going then. Be careful, both of you." As Loyal padded away, he paused and glanced back. "Fearless, have you told your mother about me?"

"Not yet."

Loyal looked relieved. "Keep it that way."

"Why?" asked Valor. "She'll be pleased Father's friend is nearby, won't she?"

"Believe me, it'll be safer for her if she doesn't know." Loyal narrowed his gaze. "Will you promise?"

Fearless felt offended on his mother's behalf. "She can keep a secret," he said stiffly. "Just because she's blind now doesn't mean she's stupid."

"I know that," Loyal growled. "But promise me, Fearless. Please."

Fearless sighed. "All right. I promise."

He watched Loyal slink back into the tall grasses. Valor was already worrying at the gazelle's leg, starting to heave the corpse back toward the pride, and Fearless hurried to help her.

"What was all that secrecy about?" Valor asked him through a mouthful of leg.

"I don't know," said Fearless. He dug his fangs into the gazelle's rump.

"*And* he's prideless," Valor mumbled darkly. "What happened to him?"

Fearless raised his chin. "I haven't asked," he said. "Look, he must have his reasons. He's a good lion. I know it."

"Whatever you say, little brother." Valor shrugged. "He seems strange, that's all. And you remember what old Wisdom Gallantpride used to tell us?"

Fearless didn't reply, but Valor growled it anyway.

"Never trust a prideless lion."

The lions of Titanpride were huddled under a dripping acacia tree. Honor, Regal, and Agile, three of the former Gallantpride lionesses, had already returned from hunting; they were licking their fur clean of blood and mud. Artful, Titan's favorite mate, sprawled smirking near them, tail wrapped neatly around her plump haunches. Ruthless, her young cub, batted at her curled tail in frustration.

When's the last time Artful bothered to go hunting? Fearless wondered resentfully. He and Valor dragged their gazelle to where the other kills lay.

Titan was tearing into a zebra. His muzzle was smeared with gore, blood matting his magnificent black mane; nearby, his allies were devouring an antelope. Titan stared contemptuously at Fearless and Valor as they dropped their gazelle, then ripped another mouthful of flesh.

Once, thought Fearless, a zebra would have fed all of Gallantpride, and they would have hunted and shared it together. Now Titan demanded multiple kills, and he gorged on them with his cronies and Artful. *How does that fit with the Code?*

The junior males and the lionesses lay in a hungry circle, waiting their turn to eat. *This pride is too big*, thought Fearless; these lions would be desperate to gnaw at what remained after Titan's favorites had eaten. His chest tightened with frustrated fury. *This is not the way of true lions!*

Beyond even that circle of famished lions crouched a lone lioness: Swift. Fearless could clearly see his mother's rib bones through her thin, dull fur, and the terrible scar where one of her eyes had been. The other was cloudy and sightless.

Her nostrils flared as Fearless and Valor approached. "My cubs," she murmured. "You're back safely."

"Fearless killed a gazelle, Mother," said Valor, nuzzling Swift's cheek.

"My brave lion," Swift said. She leaned forward, searching for him, and Fearless touched her nose with his. "Your father would be so proud."

The best parts of the kills had already been reduced to bone and shreds of sinew. Fearless knew how this would go. Despite the quantities of prey, despite the fact that he and Valor hunted Swift's share as well as their own, their mother would be shoved aside until only the smallest, least desirable scraps were left. And she would be expected to be grateful.

But Fearless wasn't going to let his mother go hungry today. Keeping a wary eye on the rest of the pride, he padded back toward the gazelle. *I caught this*, he thought defiantly. *It's mine.*

He slapped a paw onto the gazelle's rump and bit down on a hind leg, then gave a violent wrench of his head. Tendons tore and joints snapped as the leg came away; grabbing it in his jaws, he trotted to a clump of acacias. Valor had watched him, eyes wide; now she butted Swift gently to her feet and guided her to the shelter of the trees. Fearless laid the leg under his mother's nose. She sniffed it and took a delicate bite.

"It's the gazelle I caught," he told her.

"Your first kill," murmured Swift, licking it. "No wonder it tastes so delicious."

Fearless swallowed hard. Once his mother had been the strongest hunter in Gallantpride. His chest ached to see her now, thin and blind and living on the charity of lions who had taken her sight and her mate. He glanced at his sister and saw the same sadness in her pale gold, elegant face.

"I'd better join the other lionesses," said Valor. She rubbed her mother's cheek and slipped away.

Swift ate a little more, then raised her head. "I've had enough, Fearless. You eat the rest."

"You've barely had anything!"

Swift licked the blood from her muzzle. "You need to eat well so you can become as strong as your father." She pushed the leg. "Go on—it's your first kill, you should enjoy it."

Fearless sighed, but as he took a bite of the rich meat he realized how hungry he was. He'd had a long day of hunting, and yesterday Titan had let him have only scraps. Giving in, he tore at the gazelle.

Her ears twitching toward him, Swift sighed contentedly. "I'm so happy to have you back. I only wish I could see what you look like now."

"Pretty much the same, I expect. Only bigger."

Swift rubbed her cheek against the back of his head. "Well, I can feel you don't have a mane yet."

"I wish I did."

Swift chuckled. "It'll come," she said. "You've got a lot of growing left to do."

Fearless sighed. Loyal had pointed out the same thing.

The sooner I'm grown, the better, he thought.

With a mane, and my full strength, I'll finally strike down Titan.

Fearless and Swift had rejoined the pride by the time Titan stood up from his meal and stretched. His powerful muscles flexed beneath his thick, healthy fur, and he shook his full black mane.

"A good meal," he grunted. "While the grass-eaters panic, the lions feast."

His tail lashed as he gazed around his pride. When his eyes locked on Fearless, they gleamed with malice.

"Ah, those foolish animals who follow the Great Parent," Titan said loudly. "Living their feeble lives in terror, and all because they don't have anyone to plod after now. Their Great Spirit didn't protect the old elephant from a few crocodiles, did it?"

Fearless's chest tightened with suppressed rage: Titan knew he had been raised by baboons, had been taught to believe in the Great Spirit. Clenching his jaws, he stayed silent, determined not to show how much Titan was riling him.

"The Great Spirit didn't even give her the sense to stay out of the water," Titan went on mockingly. "So much for the wisdom of elephants. They're no brighter than the idiotic herds who hung on her every word."

Artful and Titan's allies roared with laughter. Fearless swallowed his grunt of rage, but he kept his stare riveted on Titan's.

You can laugh now, he thought fiercely, *but you won't when I keep my oath and take back the pride. One day, Titan, I'll make you regret every vicious deed of yours.*

The lions were still huffing with laughter when one of the scouts threaded through them and padded to her leader. It was Daring, a small lioness with a scarred ear.

"I bring news, Titan," she announced. "I overheard the monkeys' chatter. There's a Great Gathering at the watering hole at High Sun today."

"Really?" Titan growled with amusement. "How exciting for the poor animals. They can bleat about how much they miss their old elephant." Resolute, Titan's closest ally, snorted so hard he choked.

"They're going to decide what to do now," said Daring. "I think they're looking for a new Great Parent."

Titan flicked his tail dismissively. "Fools," he said. "They can't wait to be told what to do." He stalked toward Fearless. "And *you*," he snarled, "you're just like them. A lion who wants to be bossed around by some grass-eater."

More laughter rumbled around the pride. Valor edged closer to Fearless, looking worried.

"Since you love the grass-eaters so much, you can spy on the meeting," said Titan. "It could be useful to know who they pick next."

Fearless bowed deferentially, hiding the hatred he knew was in his eyes. "Yes, Titan."

"Please, Titan, could I go too?" Valor asked. "They won't expect lions at the Gathering. When Fearless shows up, there might be trouble."

Titan curled his muzzle in a sneer. "You think I care what trouble this baboon-lover gets into?"

"If two of us go," Valor said quickly, "at least one of us will be able to report back to you. Even if something bad happens."

Titan shrugged. "Go if you must," he said coolly, turning away. "I can't imagine two lions I'd be happier to lose, and I daresay you'd be happy to leave. But just remember what happens if neither of you returns."

He glanced back, and his eyes burned with malevolence.

"If you're not here to hunt for your mother, she doesn't eat at all."

As Fearless and Valor trotted across the grasslands, heading for the watering hole, High Sun was almost upon them.

Fearless knew it only because the clouds were mottled with a feeble, pallid glow. The sun itself had not been visible since dawn, and still the rains fell.

"We have to be careful," said Valor. "It's like I told Titan. The animals will be suspicious if they see lions at the Gathering."

"I know," Fearless agreed. "I'll stay out of sight. But I want to speak to the baboons if I can. They'll be there for sure—Brightforest Troop is so important."

His heart lightened at the thought of seeing Mud and Thorn again. A rain-soaked, rocky kopje jutted from the grass not far ahead; in his excitement, Fearless leaped up the stones to the top.

"Important baboons," Valor huffed sarcastically, as she jumped up beside him.

"Well, they *are*. They're one of the biggest troops in Bravelands. And they've definitely got the best territory—you've never seen so many fruit trees."

Valor wrinkled her nose. "You like *fruit*?"

Fearless laughed. "Of course not!" he said as they sprang from the highest rock and set off down the far slope. "Hey, maybe the new Great Parent will appear at the Gathering! Wouldn't that be amazing?"

"Not for us," Valor growled firmly. "The Great Parents have nothing to do with lions, remember?"

"I know." Fearless gave a wistful sigh. "But it would be nice, wouldn't it? To have someone to turn to with our problems?"

Valor stopped short, lashing her tail. "Is that so?" she

snapped. "A Great Parent would solve our problems, eh? Could a Great Parent bring back Mother's sight? Or protect us from Titan?"

"No, of course not," said Fearless, offended and a little hurt. "They don't do things *for* you, they teach you how—oh, never mind. You'd get it if you'd lived with baboons."

"Like I'd ever dream of it." Valor gave a scornful snort, then shouldered him aside and jumped down from one gravelly outcrop to another. "Idiot," she grunted, but her tone was affectionate.

"Watch your paws," called Fearless cheekily. "You'll—"

—*Trip*, he had been about to mock her, but at just that moment, she did. One paw slid as it hit a puddle, and Valor stumbled. She had to take a few sideways paces to regain her balance; then she stopped and spun around, glaring indignantly at the waterlogged slope.

Her expression changed. "What . . ."

Fearless loped down to her side, and the two lions stared aghast at the devastation that lay before them. The slope was pockmarked with meerkat burrows that had not been enough to save their inhabitants.

"This wasn't the work of a flesh-eater," murmured Valor.

All across the gritty hill were strewn the lifeless, sodden corpses of meerkats: young or old, big or tiny, they had all been caught and drowned in the torrential downpour. The smell of death drifted like an invisible fog. Fearless pawed at a limp body; it was still saturated, its tiny eyes half closed and blank.

"The Great Spirit is certainly angry," he said, his voice trembling with fear. "How many more will die if this weather doesn't stop?"

Valor took a step back and shook her head sharply. "The rain fell," she said. "Like it does. Come on, Fearless; we need to get moving."

The dead meerkats had unnerved him; Fearless's spine felt cold as he followed Valor toward a steeper rise. *Valor doesn't believe, and she never will.* But he couldn't help thinking the lethal rains were too much of a coincidence after what had happened to Great Mother.

Side by side the two lions trekked to the top of the higher slope, slowing as they neared the crest. Lowering themselves onto their bellies, they crawled forward to peer down at the watering hole.

The clouded sky was shot with silver; it looked as bright as it was likely to get today. *High Sun. We made it.*

The vast stretch of the lake gleamed dully; a light mist lay over it where the constant rain struck the surface. On its churned shore, hundreds of animals formed a semicircle. Wildebeests stamped and grunted; sentry zebras and antelopes stood rigid, ears swiveling and eyes alert. A hyena, pacing through the herds, gave a sharp, laughing bark. A coalition of three cheetahs sat together, grooming one another; a leopard sprawled on a tree branch, one paw dangling, tail twitching expectantly. Fearless's gaze roamed over the huge crowd. Rhinos, monkeys, colobus, mongooses . . . all waited patiently together. Shooting a glance at his sister, Fearless saw that Valor's eyes were wide with wonder.

"How do the flesh-eaters resist all that prey?" she muttered.

"It's tradition. Oh!" Fearless brightened as he recognized some familiar baboons in the center of the crowd. "Look!" He nodded. "Brightforest Troop!"

"Your troop?" Valor wriggled forward a little, peering down with fascination.

"Yes. That's my friend Thorn, closest to the water's edge. And that small baboon next to him is Mud. His mother's the Starleaf—she reads the signs sent by the Great Spirit. And the big one?" His voice took on a note of awe. "That's Stinger. Everybody looks up to him. He's the one who rescued me from the eagle when I was little."

"What's that mound of branches?" Valor narrowed her eyes. "Oh—is that their Great Mother underneath?"

Following her gaze, Fearless swallowed. "It must be."

Rain pattered on the half-dead branches that had been draped over Great Mother's body, and their leaves rattled and rustled eerily in the faint lake breeze. Little of the great old elephant was visible, but Fearless could make out patches of her wrinkled gray hide beneath the sagging foliage. It was terrible to imagine her lying under there, her flesh already wasting away. Fearless closed his eyes briefly in silent respect. Whoever replaced her would find it tough to live up to her example.

There was motion in the crowd, a shifting of bodies, a

perceptible rising tension in the atmosphere. The muttering of gossip faded to silence as Stinger Crownleaf emerged from the horde, tail high, and stalked into the space before the assembly.

Fearless craned forward, his heart thudding. The Great Gathering had begun.

CHAPTER 6

"Thank you, my Bravelands compatriots, for your presence today." Stinger's solemn tone rang out across the rain-soaked shore. "I am Stinger Crownleaf, leader of Brightforest Troop, and it was I who requested this Gathering."

A hush lay over the assembly as he gestured respectfully at the mound of branches. "There, with us still, lie the remains of our beloved Great Mother. She was taken from us in an act of senseless violence, and all of Bravelands grieves."

A few whimpers rose, only to be swiftly silenced.

Rising to his hind legs, Stinger closed his eyes and stretched out his paws. "It is with humility that I ask you all: will you permit me the honor of leading this meeting?"

Thorn gritted his teeth. *Surely they can recognize a fake? Stinger loves being in charge.*

He turned to Mud, but his friend was watching Stinger

with bright-eyed pride. And when he glanced around the rest of Brightforest Troop, he realized they all wore the same expression. Berry, a few paces away, had her paws clasped to her chest.

Thorn's heart sank. If those who knew Stinger best couldn't see through him, what chance was there for the other animals?

"What's he saying?" a distant zebra brayed.

The creatures at the front turned, calling back, relaying Stinger's words to those who couldn't hear. A wildebeest, a giraffe, a sleek leopard, a tiny, wide-eyed meerkat: their voices rang out across the crowd, becoming a chorus of growls, grunts, and whinnies as the animals behind them took up the cry.

"Great Mother's passing . . ."

"Lead the meeting . . ."

"Stinger Crownleaf . . ."

"Stinger Crownleaf . . ."

"Stinger!"

Thorn shuddered. All of Bravelands seemed to resound with Stinger's name.

Back came the answers, as the herds called out their acceptance: a swelling roar of support that rose even above the rumble of the rain.

"The zebras agree!"

"The giraffes agree!"

"The leopards agree!"

"The antelopes agree!"

Just when Thorn thought he could bear it no more, the chorus quieted back into attentive silence. Stinger cleared his throat.

"Very well," he said, bowing his head humbly. "I will lead as best I can." He opened his jaws, his long yellow fangs gleaming. "In these days of turmoil, every animal of Bravelands is beset by worry. And so, to begin our Gathering, I invite any creature to come forward and share their concerns."

More cries rose up as his words were carried back through the crowd.

"He's doing awfully well, isn't he?" Mud said.

"Um . . . I guess." Thorn shrugged, but Mud was right—Stinger had the animals hanging on his every word. Berry smiled at her father, her brown eyes filled with pride.

A wildebeest stepped forward. "I am Grassfinder of the Traveling Herd," he said. His hooves shifted nervously, but he held his horned head high. "In the quarter-moon since Great Mother died, our lives have been thrown into chaos. The downpour will not stop, Stinger Crownleaf! Yes, we need the rains to nourish the grasslands, but this? The savannah is waterlogged! Grass is trampled into the mud, where it rots to pulp. When we can find it, we can barely eat it. Calves have drowned in the pools! We need a new Great Parent. We cannot survive without one."

A leopard slunk out of the crowd. "I am Climber," she said. "The wildebeests have no reason to call me friend, but my kind suffer too. The herds are scattered; the rain makes hunting hard and dangerous."

A cheetah hissed. "Not as hard as it is for us, cat-sister. Our speed is almost useless in this waterlogged terrain. The cheetahs starve! So do not complain to us, when you have trees to retreat to for your devious ambushes."

Climber peeled back her muzzle and snarled. "The hunting tradition of the leopards is an honorable one!"

"Please," said Stinger, raising a paw. "It is customary that we keep the peace at the watering hole."

Climber licked her jaws. "Very well. Each animal has its problems. But I think we all agree that Bravelands can't go on like this." Her powerful tail lashed. "How will we *know* the new Great Parent? No Parent has died before without finding their successor."

"Poor Great Mother never had the chance to pass on the Spirit," a dik-dik piped up, skittering on her tiny hooves. "And now it is angry. Some of my kind have drowned. These rains do not bring life, but death."

"If it carries on, we'll all starve," a gazelle chimed in.

"And our babies will drown." A vervet monkey clutched her infant tightly against her.

As the anxious voices and tragic tales multiplied, Thorn noticed movement in the crowd. Animals were shifting, backing, clearing a path for Rain the elephant as she made her ponderous way to the front. As they scrambled to make room, the animals fell breathlessly silent, eager for whatever wisdom the elephants had to offer.

Recalling Stinger's flash of terrible temper after they'd met with the elephant herd, Thorn gave him an apprehensive glance. But the Crownleaf looked perfectly composed, his face serene and solemn; only one tightly clenched paw betrayed him.

Rain's hide was soaked almost to black by the downpour, but it suited her. She looked, thought Thorn, as if the very thing she was named for gave her a deeper strength and authority. When she reached the front, she swung around to gaze at the herds, her ears spread wide and her mottled trunk curling. Thorn leaned forward.

Whatever she has to say, I don't think Stinger's going to like it.

"I am Rain Strider," the elephant declared in a ringing voice, "now matriarch of the Strider family. We elephants believe we no longer have any reason to fear. We have found the new Great Mother."

A thrill raced through the crowd. Whispers became mutters that swiftly grew to roars and bellows of joy. Even Thorn's spirits soared—with a new Great Parent, Bravelands would be safe! At last he could ask for help to deal with Stinger. Thorn felt Mud clutch his arm, and he clutched his friend back. Berry was whispering rapidly to her neighbor, Twig. Stinger, meanwhile, stood as still as the Crown Stone itself.

The excitement hushed as Rain raised her head higher. "The new Great Mother," she announced, "is Sky Strider. Sky is young, it is true, but she can read bones. Visions are granted to her, and already she seeks to defend the Code—more wisely than elephants twice her age. It's clear to us that the Great Spirit has passed to her."

The crowd erupted again. "Sky was there when Fearless

and I met Great Mother," Thorn told Mud excitedly. "I liked her!"

"Oh, that makes it even better." Mud grinned and hugged him. "This is the best news we could have hoped for!"

"Bring forward Great Mother!" bellowed a wildebeest.

"We want Great Mother!" cried a giraffe.

A chant rose up—"Great Mother! Great Mother! Great Mother!"—and beneath it swelled more voices, tinged with frantic hope. *"Save us! Save us from the rains!"*

Thorn and Mud exchanged a glance. A broad smile of happiness spread over both their faces, and Thorn cried: "Great Mother!"

"Great Mother!" echoed Mud.

The pair of them pounded the ground, growing hoarse as they yelled their acclamation with the others, over and over again: "Great Mother! *Great Mother!*"

Rain lifted her trunk and trumpeted over the clamor: "Come forward, Sky Strider!"

The animals craned their necks, desperate to see their new Great Parent. Thorn stood on his hind legs, peering across the crowd.

"Can you see her?" asked Mud. Thorn shook his head.

"Sky?" Rain trumpeted again. "Come—"

"I wish to speak!"

The bellow was deep and resounding. One by one, animals fell silent with shock as a large rhinoceros shouldered his way through a throng of antelopes and gazelles. One gazelle stumbled aside, almost falling, and its cry of "Great Moth—" was cut off in a squeak of fear.

The rhino's head was huge, heavy and square, his shoulders almost as broad as an elephant's. His tough skin hung in thick folds, and his horn—almost black at the base, and white at the tip—was magnificent.

"The elephants are wrong," he grunted into the shocked hush. "Their time is over."

Thorn shot a glance at Stinger, a tremor of unease in his gut. Stinger was frowning, scratching his chin as if in sudden doubt.

"What do you mean by this?" he asked the rhino at last.

The rhino tilted his horn at the sky. "I am Stronghide," he declared to the gathered animals, "and I bring a different story from the one the elephant tells."

Hundreds of wide eyes were riveted on him. There were no more shouts of welcome for Sky Strider; the creatures of Bravelands seemed to be holding their breaths.

Stinger turned from side to side, as if looking for counsel; then, in the anxious silence, he spread his paws. "Speak, Stronghide!"

"The night Great Mother died," rumbled Stronghide, "I dreamed of her."

There were a few skeptical mutters from the front of the crowd.

"Great Mother came to find me," Stronghide went on, his voice rising, "and she led me to this watering hole. She told me to drink, and then—she vanished." He jabbed his horn toward the pile of branches that concealed her body. "That spot? That is exactly where I was standing."

Quietening the mutters of disbelief, Stinger frowned again. Clearly and loudly, he declared: "Dreams can have many meanings, Stronghide, and often those meanings are obscured. What do you think your dream told you?"

"Isn't it obvious?" Stronghide stamped the ground with a massive foot, sending up a shower of mud. "She was passing the Great Spirit on to me. When I woke up, I could feel it inside me!"

There was a moment of silence. Then, abruptly, a one-eyed cheetah yowled with laughter.

"A rhinoceros as Great Parent? We might as well have a fish or a beetle!"

Stronghide stamped again. "It's about time!" he bellowed.

There were a few half-suppressed chuckles from the meerkats and the monkeys, and suddenly laughter erupted through the crowd like wildfire. Stinger held up his paws, shushing them all. A meerkat gave a last hiccuping giggle, and silence fell once more.

"This mockery is not appropriate," Stinger reproved them. "The Great Spirit has never chosen a rhinoceros before, it's true. But is it not *possible*? Who are we to question the Great Spirit?" Giving the shamefaced animals a stern glare, he turned to Stronghide. "Please, tell us more. Help us understand."

Stronghide flicked his tail. Two oxpeckers flew up from his flank and fluttered around his head, blinking their round yellow eyes and chirping. Flaring his top lip, the rhino replied with strange chirruping sounds and twitched his ears; the birds rose, swooping away into the dense gray rain.

"They're flying out over Bravelands to bring me news," he said proudly.

A hubbub of amazement broke out in the ranks of the animals.

"Did you see—"

"Only the Great Parent—"

"He speaks Skytongue—?"

Stronghide cleared his throat. "The time of the rhinos has come at last," he declared. "I can feel the Great Spirit within me. I am your new Great Father!"

A babble of debate erupted, the brays and bellows of the grass-eaters colliding with the growls and roars of the flesh-eaters. It seemed to Thorn that every animal was trying to make its voice heard above the others.

"A *rhino*. But there's never been a rhino Great Parent!"

"Too grumpy, aren't they?"

"Don't see why we should believe—"

"You can't deny the birds *obeyed* him!"

Stinger signaled for quiet again. "Stronghide has made a surprising claim," he said. "One that merits our careful consideration."

There were grunts and growls of agreement.

"We must think this over," Stinger went on. "What do we know?" He raised one long finger. "First, Great Mother came to Stronghide in a dream, the very night she died. Second, Stronghide talks to birds, as only a Great Parent can. We all saw him speak with the oxpeckers. And third, Stronghide can feel the Great Spirit within him."

The animals were listening now, still and attentive as the rain pelted down. Mud gripped Thorn's arm.

Stinger turned to the rhino, his gaze touched with awe. "Tell us, Stronghide. What does the Great Spirit feel like?"

Stronghide hesitated. "Like . . . I'm full of something very powerful," he said slowly. "And like I care about every animal in Bravelands."

A giraffe lowered his long neck to peer at the rhino more closely. "Interesting," he said. He glanced at his herd. "We giraffes would like to discuss this among ourselves before we come to any decision."

A bushpig snorted, the thick hair on his spine bristling. "Us too," he grunted. "We don't trust rhinos."

Stinger drew himself up, opening his jaws to speak again. And in that moment, an odd hush fell.

Thorn started. Animals were still muttering and stamping, and for a moment he had no idea what had changed. Then he realized: there was no low thunder on the lake, no steady pattering on the leaves of the trees. His fur was not being hammered by a drenching torrent.

The rain had stopped. In the blink of an egret's eye, it was gone.

The stillness felt new and strange; it was as if rain had always fallen on Bravelands, for as long as any creature could remember. The animals shifted apprehensively.

Then, across the lake, ripples surged. Every creature turned to face the water, then staggered back as they were struck by a great gust of wind. It howled across the watering hole, kicking up waves; leaves lashed wildly, and three big branches were blown off Great Mother's body to expose her gray haunch. Two of the elephants trumpeted in alarm, gaping in dismay at their dead matriarch's body.

"It's a sign," Rain cried. "A sign from the Great Spirit!"

Thorn rose up to look, and another gust of wind caught him like the blow of a giant paw. He rocked back, staggering.

"A sign!" a hyena barked, picking up the elephant's call.

"A sign, a sign!" a family of meerkats squeaked.

A terrible crack of thunder drowned out the voices. Thorn spun around; it wasn't thunder. A cordia tree had been wrenched up by its roots and flung to the ground; it rolled and crashed across the muddy bank, sending small creatures scurrying to escape.

Cries of alarm erupted. "What's happening?" Berry shouted to Twig; there was fear in her voice.

"I hear you all! A sign!" Stinger yelled against the wind. Unlike the frightened animals surrounding him, his face was lit with exhilaration. "The Gathering has heard the Great Spirit! Stronghide is the Great Father!"

For a moment, there was only the howling of the gale. And then yelps of approval and excitement broke out.

"We must make it official!" Stinger was screaming to make himself heard now. "Who accepts Stronghide the rhinoceros as our new Great Father? I believe what I have seen! The baboons follow Stronghide!"

His words were passed back through the crowd, and quickly the responses came:

"The zebras follow Stronghide!"

"The cheetahs follow Stronghide!"

"The meerkats follow Stronghide!"

"The giraffes follow Stronghide!"

On and on, each group of animals bellowed their acceptance of Stronghide as the new Great Parent. Only the elephants stood aside, wordless and disbelieving, as branch after branch rolled and tumbled from Great Mother's body, tossed by the wind. To Thorn, the Strider herd seemed torn by indecision, flapping their ears and shifting from one great foot to another, blowing and snorting in distress as more and more of their old matriarch's body was revealed.

Then, one by one, they turned their rumps. They trudged away in a line, trunk to tail, Rain at their head.

Next to Thorn, Mud's face was creased with worry. Thorn knew what his friend was thinking—the departure of the elephants didn't bode well. But none of the others seemed to care.

Stinger's snout was stretched in an ecstatic grin. He opened his arms wide, as if he wanted to embrace every animal of Bravelands. "It is decided. Stronghide is the Great Father of Bravelands! A new era has begun!"

Stronghide shambled into the watering hole, his huge feet stirring up eddies of mud. Stinger was the first to follow him, and Thorn and Mud joined the other baboons as they waded in after Stinger. Thorn's head was spinning. Could it be true?

If Stronghide truly spoke to the birds, there could be no doubt. But Thorn felt nothing like the relief that had coursed through him when he'd thought it would be Sky. *Maybe that was just because she's an elephant, and that's what we're used to.*

Wind tore and howled around the herds as they wallowed in the shallows, the water murky with disturbed mud and floating weeds. Many animals were left on the trampled shore, patiently waiting their turn. As was tradition, every creature would follow their new Great Parent into the watering hole and drink, pledging to follow his guidance.

The churned water was whipped into foamy waves by the blast of the wind; Thorn shivered as he placed his paws in the shallows. Cupping them, he scooped up water and drank; it tasted muddy, gritty, and sour, and he had to force himself not to spit it out.

Stinger was close by, his fur slick from immersion in the lake; the scar on his muzzle stood out more starkly than ever. He was studying Stronghide, his expression solemn.

The new Great Father's head was tipped back, his massive horn held high above the water. His small eyes gleamed benevolently as the animals around him paid homage.

Thorn clenched his jaws. Perhaps this was not the disaster it seemed to be.

Maybe Stronghide will help me, he thought. *Maybe today's the day Stinger's plans go wrong at last.*

CHAPTER 7

Sky ploughed across the grasslands, battling the force of the wind. From behind her, where the watering hole lay, came an outcry, but she forced herself to carry on. She couldn't do anything about it, any more than she could stop the violent gusts that tore at her ears and tail. Only one thing mattered now.

She stumbled to a halt by a bush with long curling leaves that thrashed in the wind. Kneeling, she fumbled with her trunk around its roots.

Where is it?

The sensitive tip brushed something smooth and curved; curling her trunk around it, she pulled it out. Sky gazed sadly at her recovered treasure. It was a bright, clean white shard, broken jaggedly at the end: a piece of Great Mother's tusk.

Yesterday, the elephants' sheltering baobab tree had come into full bloom. Dazed by its sudden beauty, Sky had broken off a branch heavy with creamy white blossoms, and she'd carried it to the lakeside to drape over Great Mother's body.

As she'd laid it on top of the other greenery, a few flowers had fluttered to the sandy earth. Sky had reached to rescue them, and her trunk had brushed something half buried in the mud. And there was the tip of Great Mother's tusk, cracked and broken. Sky's heart had almost shattered with renewed grief.

Now, with her trunk, Sky gently turned the tusk shard over. *Nothing. Still nothing.*

She should see *something*! She could read bones, couldn't she? Not just those of her own ancestors—every elephant could do that. But when Sky had touched the skull of the murdered baboon leader Bark Crownleaf, a vision of the killer had rushed into her head.

So why couldn't she read Great Mother's tusk?

Sky yearned to talk once more to her grandmother. Only a few days had passed since her death, and already Sky had so many things she wanted to ask the wise old matriarch—things she wished desperately that she had asked her before. *But how could I have known? How could anyone?* A chorus of raucous cheers drifted from the watering hole. Gripping the tusk fragment, Sky hurried off in the opposite direction. *I hope Rain can forgive me*, she thought. *But I have to leave.*

The wind was at her back, carrying the scents of the herds at the watering hole, but its force was capricious; it gusted and swirled, catching Sky unawares and making her stagger. When her family had last come this way, at the end of the dry season, their tread had thrown up clouds of red dust. Now the terrain was an expanse of sticky, drying mud that caked Sky's feet and made her clumsy. Grass was plastered to the ground. Creasing her eyes against the shrieking gale, Sky searched desperately for the distinctive gray slab of rock. It was the only guide that marked where she should turn off the trail.

There was no sign of it. Heart heavy, Sky trudged on. It seemed so much farther than she remembered, now that she was alone. Occasionally she paused to lay down Great Mother's tusk and nibble at muddy, flattened grass or tug a leafy branch from a shrub, but she did not dare waste time. Although windswept billows of gray cloud still scudded across the sky, a line of intense gold lay along the eastern horizon, casting shadows that lengthened with every moment.

A squishing noise behind her made her start and turn. She knew the sound; it was the one her own feet made when she splashed into thick mud. Sky peered into the dusk, breathing hard, but trees and bushes and hillocks made confused, eerie outlines against the too-brilliant sunset. It was so hard to make sense of the landscape when her family wasn't here to reassure her.

Sky's heart thudded. Clutching Great Mother's tusk she trotted on, faster this time.

Her ears twitched. There were definitely footsteps behind her. And they were speeding up as she did.

Sky bolted toward a clump of thorn trees. She slipped on a root, almost dropping the tusk, before stumbling on. The trotting footsteps were not light enough to belong to a gazelle or an antelope, and they weren't the rhythmic hoof-beats of a zebra or giraffe. It wasn't a rhino, was it? She gulped hard. Or a flesh-eater? Surely no lone flesh-eater would attack an elephant. . . .

Would they?

The dark glow of the sun was abruptly extinguished, leaving the savannah in a hazy twilight of gray and blue. Above her the dark clouds still raced in that high wind, impenetrably dense: not a single star was visible. Sky felt very alone, and horribly afraid.

The thorn trees were close, just a few trunk-lengths from the trail. Sky veered between two of them, then spun again, galloping clumsily through the trunks in the faint hope of throwing off her pursuer. She stumbled behind a dense thicket of brush and halted, trying to control her breathing.

The wind howled through the leaves. And then footsteps squelched at the edge of the copse.

Sky's insides clenched. Would the wind blow her scent away from that thing? Or would it gust in its wild way and betray her to her unseen enemy? *Will I have to fight for my life?*

A heartbroken wail rose on the wind. It drifted between the acacia trunks, lost and as lonely as she was.

"Where are you?"

Sky froze. *"Moon?"*

Shocked, she shoved back through the trees, thorns scraping at her sides. In the center of the copse, twisting and skittering on the spot in panic, was her little cousin.

"I'm here, Moon!" Sky cried. She rushed to wrap her trunk

around him. His little body was shaking. "It's okay," she soothed, "I've got you."

Moon butted his head into her neck, pressing his trembling flank hard against hers. "I couldn't find you," he whimpered.

Sky shook her ears in dismay. "Why are you here? Does your mother know you came?"

"I saw you leaving, so I snuck after you," he said in a wobbling voice. "Nobody noticed me go."

Sky cuddled him closer. "Oh, Moon. You shouldn't have done that."

"But I had to. Where are you going, Sky? *Why?*"

She ran her trunk over his bristly back. "I'm sorry, Moon. There's something I have to do. You need to go back to your mother."

"No!" Moon stared up at Sky in horror. "*Please* don't make me go back, Sky. Please!"

Sky recognized the stubborn slant of his mouth and groaned inwardly. "But everyone will be missing you. Your mother will be so worried."

"If I go back, won't *you* miss me?"

"Of course. But . . ."

"Who will you play with, if I don't come with you?" Moon pressed her. "Who are you going to tell stories to?"

Sky hesitated, her thoughts in turmoil. This was impossible. He should not have come, and yet she couldn't send Moon all the way back by himself—it was far too dangerous, and he'd probably get horribly lost. Flesh-eaters might find him in the night, and then—

And if she took him back herself, Rain might stop her from leaving again.

Besides, if they guessed she and Moon were together, her family might worry less. Oh, this was an *agonizing* decision.

Moon blinked up at her. "*Please*, Sky. Let me come with you. I promise I'll be good."

Sky blew out a resigned breath. "All right." *I don't have a choice. Oh, Star, I'm so sorry.* "But you *must* listen to me and do what I say."

"Yay!" Moon cheered. "I will, I promise! I'll be so good you won't recognize me." His ears lifted and he cantered around her, his trunk and tail swinging. Sky couldn't help smiling.

"Come on, then," she said.

The winds tossed the clouds aside, revealing a slit of the sky. In its center, a single star gleamed. Its light seemed almost dazzling against the blackness of the looming sky; the jagged crowns of the acacias were fringed in faint silver. By its glow and her own night vision, Sky shepherded Moon safely back to the trail.

Sky raised her head to gaze up at the glittering star. *Is that you, Great Mother?* she wondered. Curling her trunk tighter around the tusk fragment, she hugged it close.

"Where are we going?" Moon asked, stamping a spray of starlit water from a muddy pool. "Is it somewhere nice?"

"It's somewhere very *important*," Sky told him. "We're going to the Plain of Our Ancestors."

CHAPTER 8

Fearless crouched on the hilltop, creasing his eyes against the fierce wind. At the watering hole below, the new Great Parent wallowed up to his thighs in the murky water, his horn held high. All around him, animals drank solemnly.

"A rhino seems a strange choice," he mused to Valor. "They're not exactly popular with the other animals. I met a few once, and they chased me out of their territory."

"Well, of course they did," she said scornfully. "Why did you go into rhino territory, anyway?"

"I didn't plan it," Fearless told her ruefully. "It's a long story. But the Great Spirit knows what it's doing, I guess." He stared doubtfully at Stronghide, who was striking arrogant postures for the benefit of the admiring herds: tossing his horn, slapping the water's surface with his forefoot.

Valor got to her paws. "Come on. Time to report back to Titan."

Fearless was rising, stretching his legs, when his eye was caught by a brown blur of movement at the edge of the shore. A tall baboon was marching away from the watering hole, toward the woods below the lions' viewpoint.

"In a moment," he said. "I want to talk to Stinger first."

Valor grunted. "We're trying not to be seen, remember?"

"I'll be careful," Fearless promised her. "I just want to make sure the troop's all right."

Valor sighed. "You're a lion, Fearless. *Be* a lion. You should forget those baboons." But she sat down again, coiling her tail around her haunches. "Go on, then. Don't be long."

Fearless nuzzled her cheek, then slunk down the hill, careful not to slip on the mud-slick grass as he moved from the shelter of one tree to the next. Their foliage rattled and whipped in the wind, and when he reached a cluster of kigelia trees, he eyed their long fruit warily. His mother used to tell him not to sit under these trees, especially in high winds: *You'll be crushed either by the fruit, or by the elephants who come to eat it.*

Keeping one cautious eye on the swaying branches, he crept on. He was only a few tail-lengths away from Stinger now. The baboon sat on a boulder, staring out over the water, rubbing the scar above his nose. Beyond him, hippos wallowed in the choppy water, but he was otherwise alone.

"Stinger!" Fearless hissed.

Twisting, the baboon peered through the swaying branches.

His face lit up. "Cub of the Stars!"

He ducked under the tree limbs and wrapped his arms around Fearless's neck. Fearless's pelt prickled with happiness.

"It's good to see you, my young friend." Stinger smiled. "How's life with the lions?"

Fearless sank to his haunches and huffed. "Things could be better."

Stinger sat beside him and placed a long-fingered paw on Fearless's shoulder. "You can tell me anything, Cub of the Stars."

It was a relief to let it spill out: how cruel Titan was, and how Artful had blinded Fearless's mother. How she was hardly permitted to eat. "Titan hates me," Fearless finished. "If he hadn't sworn that oath, he'd kill me."

Stinger's amber eyes were thoughtful. "But you've not considered leaving the pride?"

Fearless shook his head. "I'll never leave Mother and Valor. And I need to stay close to Titan so I can take back the pride. For my father's honor."

Stinger smiled, his yellowed fangs gleaming. "I thought as much. You told me so when you were very tiny, when I'd just carried you down from the eagle's nest. Oh, my Cub of the Stars, you *will* take back your father's pride. But look at you: you don't have your mane yet. You are only beginning to be the lion you will eventually be. You must wait until the time is right."

Fearless wrinkled his muzzle. "But how will I know when that is?"

"Believe me," said Stinger, patting his neck. "You'll know."

Above them the kigelia branches tossed in the gale, making the long fruit swing alarmingly. "We should move from here, Fearless."

Fearless rose with him and padded at his side along the scrubby bank. Stinger picked up smooth pebbles as they walked and tossed them idly into the water. He paused, dusted his paws, and looked out at the hippos, the wind ruffling his fur.

"I've told you that Stinger isn't the name my mother gave me?"

Fearless nodded. "You took it from the scorpions, because you like eating them so much." He'd tried the crunchy little creatures himself at Stinger's recommendation, but had found them little better than rot-meat.

"That's true," Stinger said. "But it's not the only reason. I admire the scorpions, Fearless. They don't hurry. They'll eat almost anything smaller than them. Bugs, lizards, even mice. But first they'll make sure their prey is trapped, that there's no escape. Only then will they"—he slapped his paws together— "strike. Do you see what I'm telling you?"

Fearless frowned. Was he the scorpion in this story, or the lizard? "I'm not sure," he admitted.

"I'm saying that you must do the same. Titan overreaches himself, Fearless. One day, he will go too far, and he will have no escape. You'll see that your chance has come, and you'll know that you must strike. But until then, you must wait."

Fearless nodded slowly. It made sense when his friend and

mentor explained it. "Thanks, Stinger," he said. "It's hard, but I'll wait."

"It will be worth it." Stinger smiled. "Believe me, Fearless, the waiting is everything. It makes the final strike all the sweeter."

Fearless gave him a sidelong glance, a little taken aback. There was something in Stinger's voice that unsettled him, but he shook himself. "How's everything with the troop, Stinger? I wish I'd been there when they voted you Crownleaf, I'd have *loved* to see that. And how are Mud and Thorn? And Berry and old Beetle and—everybody?"

To Fearless's surprise, Stinger didn't answer immediately; he gazed out pensively over the water. A rising worry nibbled at Fearless's gut.

"I hope we're heading for happier times now," said Stinger at last. "But can I confide in you, my Cub of the Stars?"

"Of course you can!" blurted Fearless.

"The thing is . . . I'm not sure the whole troop is behind me." Stinger rested a paw against the lion's shoulder, as if he needed his physical support. "I've heard rumors that baboons are plotting against me. Baboons I've trusted their whole lives! Sometimes I even worry that they might . . . might try to get rid of me." Stinger closed his eyes. "Like poor Bark Crownleaf, and Grub who came after her."

Fearless sprang to his paws. "Who could do such a thing?" he snarled. "Do you want me to come to Tall Trees? I could guard you. They wouldn't dare try to get past me!"

Stinger shook his head. "Thank you, Fearless. That's

a brave offer. But you need to stay close to Titan, remember?" The baboon drew a weary paw down his face. "Maybe I'm imagining things. But you see, I'm not just worried for myself. After everything that's happened, the troop needs stability."

"Brightforest needs *you*, Stinger. You're the leader they've waited for, I know that. I wish my pride could have such a leader!"

Stinger patted Fearless's shoulder. "Just you wait, Cub of the Stars. They'll have that pride leader, remember? Because someday, you'll be the one leading them."

Through the swaying branches Fearless could just see a flash of pale fur moving down the hill, springing from hillock to stone. "Valor's coming to look for me. I'd better go."

"Farewell, Cub of the Stars." There was wistful sadness in Stinger's voice.

Fearless emerged from the scrub into the teeth of the ferocious wind. Blinking, he scrambled back up the hill, his paws sliding; the grass was already drying in the gale's blast, but the soil had been saturated. Pausing on an outcrop of rock, he glanced back to see Stinger still hunched beneath the trees, his face hidden in the shadows. One of his long-fingered paws was raised in farewell.

Hope scudded through Fearless like the racing clouds above him.

One day, I will face Titan, and beat him, he realized.

Stinger knows it. And when Stinger knows something, it will always come to pass.

* * *

Returning across the hilly grassland to Titanpride was a struggle. Both lions were forced to duck their heads into the wind that gusted and raged; it raked their fur, and Fearless's eyes stung from blown grit. Valor shook her head constantly, blinking and growling.

The sandy earth was spun into random, whirling dust devils around them; there was no way to be sure of the wild wind's direction. As a strong gust struck them from the west, Valor abruptly halted, sniffing the air.

"What is it?" Fearless half crouched, the wind ruffling his rump. "Let's get to shelter. This is horrible."

Valor's whiskers twitched. "Blood," she growled. Her muscles tensed. "And it's fresh."

Fearless sneezed out dust, and sniffed. There was blood, but beneath its sharp tang was a tangle of different scents— oily fur, an earthy musk, and something foul.

"Lions?" he asked his sister. "And something else, too."

Valor nodded. "Hyenas. Smell that rot-meat?" She wrinkled her muzzle. "There must have been a fight."

"But the hyenas were at the watering hole," Fearless said. "I saw them."

"Your nose doesn't lie," said Valor. "That's what Mother used to say."

They followed the trail of smells, slinking low on their haunches in the long grass. The scents of lions were muddled with the rank stench of hyena, and Fearless thought he could recognize some of them. *Is that Sly?* he wondered, sniffing. *And I'm sure that's Resolute.*

Valor jerked her head toward a nearby escarpment. A smear of dark shadow at its foot proved to be a deep hole, with rainwater pooled in its base. It stretched far into the heart of the escarpment; Fearless could make that out straightaway. He'd seen a cavern before that was just like this one.

When they reached it the hyena scent was so strong it filled his nose and throat, almost making him gag. Valor's pawsteps splashed tentatively into the water, but she slunk on into the hole, and Fearless crept after her.

Inside, it became a waterlogged tunnel, the end of which was lost in darkness.

"Must be their den," whispered Valor.

Fearless's pelt tingled. Not long ago he had ventured into that other hyena den, vengefully seeking the killers of Bark Crownleaf. It had not ended well; he had barely escaped with his life.

This is different, he told himself. *I'm not alone.*

Ears craning, he listened. All was completely silent.

It was dank, and cold, and foul with that awful scent, but at least they were out of the wind's blast. The den felt so still, it was almost peaceful. *Don't get complacent*, Fearless reminded himself.

They padded forward. The walls of the tunnel were narrow and crumbly, and Fearless's chest constricted. He hated this crushing space, not least because he knew what might await them deep inside. Shuddering, he recalled the claws and teeth of the hyenas that had ambushed him before.

Along the earthen walls, marks were visible of the paws that had dug it out—four-toed, with the raking scratch of long claws. The soil was permeated with that hyena stench of grease and foul flesh. Ahead of him Valor crept cautiously, but with each step, Fearless's unease grew. If the hyenas were here, why was it so quiet and still? If they weren't, why did it stink of fresh blood?

As they left the entrance behind, all light faded, and Valor became a blue-and-green shadow moving ahead of him. The scents thickened as the tunnel began to widen into a cavern, and with a lurch of sickening foresight, Fearless knew that now they would finally see what lay within the hyena den.

Emerging into the cavern, Valor gave a high yelp that echoed from the walls.

Hackles prickling, Fearless pushed past her. It was much like the hyena den where he'd once fought for his life. And just like that one, cracks and fissures in the roof let feeble daylight seep through, casting an eerie glow on lumpy, twisted shapes. As his eyes adjusted, his stomach turned over.

The den was full of dead hyenas. The earth walls and floor were spattered with blood. A scrawny female sprawled near his paws as if she'd been tossed there, her glazed eyes fixed on him.

The smell of lions was here too, stronger than ever. Dominating it was a sharp scent, like churned-up earth mixed with torn flesh: *Titan.*

"Maybe it was a battle." Valor stared around. "Maybe the hyenas attacked the pride?"

Fearless shook his head. Anger was building within him; his blood was hot with it. "Look at them, Valor!"

Some of the carcasses were tiny, others gaunt and thin-furred. A pup lay by the den wall, half hidden beneath an old female who must have been trying to protect it. Their throats were torn out.

"They're all too old or too young to fight," Fearless said in hoarse disgust. "They didn't come to the Gathering, and you know why? They stayed here because they were too weak to make the journey."

Tentatively Valor sniffed at the pup. "They've not even been eaten."

Fearless could barely think for his buzzing rage. "Titan's a Codebreaker!" he snarled. Turning his rump on the den and its grisly contents, he bolted back down the tunnel.

"Wait!" cried Valor, racing after him. "Fearless, stop!"

He ignored her, bounding out of the tunnel and into the chaotic fury of the wind. He blinked as dust swirled into his eyes. Valor caught up in a couple of paces, skidding to a halt before him.

"You can't confront Titan about this, Fearless. He'd love an excuse to kill you."

"I don't care!" Fearless pushed past her. All he could think about was sinking his claws into Titan's pelt.

Valor sprang in front of him once more. Her dark eyes flashed. "Well, *I* care. And so does Mother. Do you want to break her heart all over again?"

Fearless hesitated.

"*Promise* me you won't say anything."

His breath came in hard rasps. Dreams of revenge whirled in his head: *No one would stop me. No one would care. I'd be doing Bravelands a favor.*

"You don't even have your mane yet!" Valor cried in exasperation.

It was exactly what Stinger had said. As rage drained from Fearless's blood, Stinger's other words by the watering hole came back to him: *One day, he will go too far, and he will have no escape... But until then, you must wait.*

"Fine." Still shaking from the surge of fury, Fearless averted his eyes. "I promise. I'll say nothing."

Valor huffed in relief. "Finally, some sense."

But Fearless could not get rid of the stench of blood in his nostrils; not even the violence of the wind could blow it away. Somewhere inside him the fury still simmered, and when they found Titanpride sheltering in the long grass, he felt it spark back to a flame once more.

Halting, Fearless eyed the pride. Along Daring's flank ran a vicious scratch, and Resolute was licking dried blood from his paws, but those were the only signs that Titanpride had ever stirred from this spot. The lions sprawled in contentment, letting the grass billow and thrash around their heads; it was hard to believe that they'd recently massacred a helpless den of hyenas. Sly and Honor groomed each other while Regal and Artful gossiped. Ruthless was chasing a blue butterfly that lurched helplessly from leaf to leaf. The cub batted idly at the wind-tossed creature, with big paws he had yet to grow into.

"Hi, Fearless!" he called, his ears pricking forward.

Titan's ears swiveled too. Rising to his feet, he stretched, the muscles along his scarred flanks rippling. He licked his jaws, narrowed his eyes, and stalked toward them.

"Back at last," he growled. "Anything to report?"

Fearless and Valor glanced at each other.

"Well?" Titan stared down at them. Gouts of blood had dried in the black fur of his windblown mane.

"We have news from the Great Gathering," Fearless said. "Stronghide—"

"Oh, I don't care what those fools do at the watering hole." Titan flexed his claws. "I only let you go so you wouldn't whine about what I had planned for the hyenas." He grinned, muzzle curling to reveal his bloodied teeth. "Did you happen to notice their filthy den as you came back?"

Valor ducked her head. "Yes, Titan."

"Do you have any objection, Fearless?" Artful asked, amusement in her voice. She glanced pointedly toward Swift, who sat at the edge of the pride. Fearless understood the unspoken threat perfectly.

He ducked his head too. "Of course not."

Titan opened his massive jaws in a grunting roar; the pride were instantly on their feet, gathering in a circle around him.

"Our raid on the hyenas is the first of many," he announced. "The fools who believe in the Great Spirit are as panicky as ants—they'll be easy pickings. We can wipe out our enemies."

A few of the lions shifted uncomfortably. "Isn't that against the Code?" asked Daring.

Titan narrowed his eyes. "I didn't hear you objecting when we dealt with the hyenas," he snapped, and Daring shrank back. "The Code says, *Only kill to survive*," Titan went on. "Our enemies compete with us for food and territory. We can *only* survive by destroying them."

Fearless sucked in a shocked breath. Valor's jaw was trembling. On the edge of the pride, their mother turned her head away, as if she couldn't bear to hear. Some of the other lions fidgeted uneasily, but no one spoke.

"We will kill as many herd animals as we can," Titan went on. "With less prey, our enemies will starve."

Ruthless, blissfully unconcerned, was still chasing the butterfly. He pranced in front of his father, paws darting after its blue wings.

"Ruthless! Stop that!" Titan roared. Ruthless flinched and cowered. "I'm talking about the future of Titanpride. *Your* future. Act like my son and listen!"

Ruthless scampered to Artful's side and huddled against her.

"We will guarantee the safety of our pride and ensure that my son inherits a fine territory." Titan's tail lashed. "Each of you must make one kill a day. The rule of Titanpride will spread across Bravelands!"

The lions looked stunned. Regal seemed about to speak, but closed her mouth tightly.

Fearless knew what they were thinking, and he felt cold with horror. A kill a day from each lion? Not only would that be next to impossible in the current hunting conditions, but if by some wild chance they succeeded, the kills would be far more than the pride could eat. Fearless pictured all those pathetic corpses left untouched and rotting on the savannah, and his stomach lurched.

Titan was mad. What good would it do to destroy the herds? In the end that would mean death for Titanpride, too. *And here I am, forced to wait like an obedient servant, following Titan's insane orders for moons, seasons, years.*

Shutting his eyes, he tried to hold fast to Stinger's words. He needed the baboon's wisdom more than ever. But he also needed to remember the promise that had followed from Stinger's warnings.

One day my chance will come. One day I'll know the time is right.

He clenched his fangs, forcing his dark longing deep down inside him.

And then this hidden scorpion will strike.

CHAPTER 9

Thorn was dreaming of mangos and sunshine. Rich, sweet juice on his tongue, and the pleasure of nibbling the last shreds from the big stone: in his sleep, he grunted and smiled. Somewhere on the edge of his mind he knew it was a dream, but it was such a simple, carefree one, he relaxed and enjoyed it. Reaching for another mango, he sank his fangs into its skin.

It screeched in terror.

Thorn jolted awake, grabbing instinctively for a branch. The sunshine was gone; it was dead of night, and a powerful wind rocked the trees where the troop had found temporary shelter. The scream that had broken his dream had been a baboon's. Thorn was in time to see a flash of pale fur below as the falling baboon struck another branch, bounced helplessly, and plummeted to earth. Thorn cried out in horror.

Baboons were waking now, screeching in distress and

pounding the trees with their paws. In the next tree he could see the jagged scar where a branch had snapped in the wind; the branch itself was lodged halfway down, tilted between two trunks at a crazy angle.

A gust caught Thorn as he rose, almost knocking him off-balance, and he snatched for a handhold. Above him the canopy tossed, the sound of its wind-torn foliage deafening. A tremor rippled from his paws to the top of his head, and he realized his entire tree was shuddering.

A thunderous crack split the air. Thorn didn't have time to think; he raced to the end of his bough and sprang. As his paws found purchase on the next tree, he heard behind him a crash like an avalanche of boulders.

Panting, he scrabbled with his hind paws to get himself safely onto the new branch. Only then could he turn and survey the devastation.

All around the swaying trees, there was panicked hooting and screeching; some of the howls came from injured baboons below. Thorn's heart lurched. How many had fallen? *Where's Berry?*

Thorn shinned backward down the lumpy tree trunk, jumping the last short way to the ground. The glade that had been here at sunset was gone; it was a chaos of broken branches and masses of leaves, and the broad trunk of a great mahogany jutted straight across the middle. A sliver of moon flitted from the racing clouds, edging the scene in a cold pale light.

Some of the shrieks of pain were fading to whimpers that

were drowned out by the fury of the storm. "Mud!" yelled Thorn. *"Berry!"*

"I'm here." Mud was crawling from beneath a great heap of leaves, his eyes stark with terror.

"Where's Berry?"

"Here!" Berry was clambering awkwardly along a cracked branch, her paws shaking.

The wave of relief made Thorn dizzy. "Thank the Great Spirit," he croaked. "How many are hurt?"

Other baboons were jumping down from the trees now, wide-eyed and shattered; Thorn, Berry, and Mud joined them, picking their way through the devastation to search for the wounded. Some baboons were obviously dead, crushed beneath the massive trunk or sprawled at odd angles.

"Strongbranches!" Stinger's command resounded. "Get to work freeing all the trapped baboons. Find the wounded and take them to Petal and Blossom Goodleaf."

Thorn felt a tremor of uncomfortable emotion: it was disappointment. *I shouldn't wish this fate on any baboon.* But how much simpler things would have been if Stinger had been one of the baboons lying there. . . . Shaking himself, Thorn turned to work, dragging aside branches and gently carrying baboons to the care of the two anxious Goodleaves.

"We must make camp on the open plain for now." Stinger was pacing through the chaos, organizing the rescue efforts and comforting the injured. "We have no choice until this wind stops. If it can bring down that mahogany, no place in the forest is safe."

The first hint of dawn was paling the eastern horizon by the time all the wounded were retrieved and the whole troop had limped out of the forest. Settling in a shallow dip of land, they fidgeted and murmured in distress. The hollow gave little protection against the howling wind; grown baboons shivered, and babies whimpered.

"It doesn't feel right to sleep on the ground," complained Beetle. "It's not the baboon way."

"Like Stinger said, we don't have a choice for now." Thorn, padding past the old baboon, tried not to roll his eyes. "He's appointed the Strongbranches to keep watch, so try to get some sleep. It's almost dawn."

Climbing to the lip of the hollow, he tried to make himself comfortable for what was left of the night. He sensed movement beside him, but it was only Frog, joining him at his sentry post.

"Can I tell you a secret, Thorn?" she whispered.

"Of course," he said, surprised. He patted the ground beside him.

She sat down quickly. "I'm ashamed. I wasn't there tonight. When the tree fell. Because . . . I sneaked off to visit Great Mother's body."

Thorn raised his brows. "You did?"

"I don't know how to say this," she whispered, "but you're the only one I might be able to talk to. Some of the things Stinger asks us Strongbranches to do . . . I'm not comfortable with them. I have a feeling it's the same for you." Frog gave him an anxious, questioning look. "I went to the watering hole because I wanted guidance from the Great Spirit. I . . . can still sense it, around Great Mother."

Thorn lowered his voice. "Did it show you anything?"

"I'm not sure." Frog sighed. "But I think . . . the fallen tree might be a punishment. We've done wrong things, Thorn. I hate being used to scare other creatures."

Thorn nodded slowly. "You're not wrong: I don't like it either."

"I'm so relieved you weren't hurt," she blurted. Tentatively, she reached out and grasped his paw. "I couldn't bear to lose you, Thorn."

Thorn's eyes widened; all he could do was stare at her sturdy paw in his. *This is awkward.*

He was still casting for a way to let her down gently when a greasy, rotten scent drifted to his nostrils. He tensed, taking the opportunity to loosen his paw from hers. "Do you smell that, Frog?"

"Hyenas," she hissed. "We have to raise the alarm!"

Swiftly the two of them bounded to alert the other Strongbranch sentries; in a short time, the whole troop was roused and on the move.

The first sunlight was breeching the horizon anyway, sending brilliant rays beneath the rim of the storm clouds. The exhausted baboons finally halted again in a cluster of straggly trees; few of them bothered to try to go back to sleep. Thorn surveyed the troop from the edge of the trees' long shadows, hoping they wouldn't have to move again today.

A soft paw touched his arm. "Hello, Thorn," said Berry.

Thorn's heart turned over; his throat felt tight. The low sun caught the golden strands in her fur, and her eyes were as rich as damp earth. Almost without thinking he reached out a paw, but her ears flattened and she glanced away.

"Will you meet me at the Lightning Tree at High Sun?" she whispered. "It's important."

Thorn hesitated, his stomach twisting. There was nothing he wanted more, but for both their safety, he had to try to keep his distance. "I don't know—"

"I *need* to talk to you. Please."

How could he say no? Thorn nodded helplessly. "I'll see you there."

The Lightning Tree stood stark against the gray sky, its three forks seeming almost to pierce the lowering clouds. Thorn loped to its leeward side and crouched to wait, resting his forepaws on his knees. The capricious wind still snatched and tore at his fur, but he was out of the worst of it. Distantly, a small herd of zebras roamed, grazing hungrily; there seemed to be surprisingly few of them. Thorn counted them to pass the time as he wondered what Berry could possibly want.

Was she hoping for reconciliation? They'd been meeting in secret for so long; he remembered their whispered promises as they held each other. *One day we'll be the same rank. We'll be together. I'll never take another mate.* They had both said those words, over and over again. Could Berry be hoping to hold him to them?

I'd have to turn her down, thought Thorn miserably. *Again.* He picked a pebble from the grass and threw it at a pair of pied crows. They gave him an indignant caw.

More likely, he decided, Berry wanted to make clear it was over forever between them. It would be the smart thing for her to do. Thorn had been cold and distant toward her, and he'd never properly explained himself; why would she want to be with him now? A final split would be the best outcome, the smartest outcome. It would separate them forever, and Berry would be safe from Stinger; Thorn would not spend his days in fear of what might happen to her.

So why did the thought make his heart twist with pain?

A golden-brown figure emerged from the belt of trees that lay between the Lightning Tree and the troop; Berry loped toward him, sending the two crows flapping skyward. Thorn took a deep steadying breath. Berry's face was unreadable as she trotted to his side and sat down.

"Thank you for meeting me," she said.

The crows had settled once more, pecking at some insect in the grass; Berry stared at them for long silent moments. Thorn stole a glance at her, lost for words.

At last Berry turned to him. "You haven't been yourself for days."

Thorn looked back at the crows.

"I know something's wrong," Berry pleaded. "But you won't talk to me, Thorn. I could help, if you'd just *trust me*."

Thorn rubbed his eyes. For a moment he tried to imagine telling her the truth. *Here's the thing, Berry. Your father is Crownleaf because he smashed Bark's head with a stone. Oh, and because he poisoned Grub with scorpion venom. I'm telling you this because I trust you, but by the way, don't turn your back on your father. . . .*

His head sagged. He couldn't do it.

Berry was studying him intently.

"Things have been hard lately," Thorn blurted at last. He plucked feverishly at the grass. "For everyone in Bravelands. Bark dying, and then Grub . . . Great Mother, too." He glanced at Berry. "And I'm stuck as a Middleleaf forever. We can *never* be together, you know it."

Berry laid her paw on his arm. Her touch made him shiver with longing. "But you still want to be with me?"

"Yes," he whispered, unable to help himself.

"Then don't you see?" she exclaimed, her eyes bright. "Now that my father's Crownleaf, things will be different. He's always liked you, Thorn, and he's not a stickler for rules and traditions. Things could easily change! If I talk to him—"

"No!" Thorn jumped up, dislodging her paw abruptly. "Don't ask him. You mustn't!"

Berry flinched. "But why not? I've been thinking and thinking about how we can be together, and it's obvious now. Father was voted Crownleaf precisely *because* he's willing to adapt. Because he listens to new ideas!"

Thorn gaped, his mind empty of excuses. "I just . . . it's such a bad time for the troop," he babbled. "I don't think we should bother Stinger. Not now, not with everything he's got to worry about. He wouldn't change the rules anyway."

Berry frowned. "Why do you say that?"

Thorn floundered for a reason but came up with nothing. "I just don't think he'd want to," he said lamely.

Berry jumped up, her eyes flashing. "Why don't you like Father anymore? Oh, don't lie, Thorn! You two used to be close, and now you're avoiding him—just like you're avoiding me."

"I'm not —"

"Don't you realize how lucky we are to have Father?" Her fists were clenched with fury. "He came to Brightforest Troop as a stranger, carrying me on his back. He had to make his own way and prove himself, and now he's Crownleaf! All he's ever done is try to help our troop." She was shaking now. "I wish *you* were more like Father!"

Thorn's eyes burned; his chest felt so tight he could hardly breathe. He spun away, staring at the crows.

"Wouldn't it be easier if you told me the truth?" she growled behind him.

His gut lurched and he turned. "What truth?"

"You've found someone else, and you're too cowardly to say it." Berry's tone was so contemptuous, it was like the stab of a fang in his gut.

"I haven't—"

"Oh, come on. I've seen you and Frog cozying up together." Berry's snout curled. "It doesn't say much for you that you're denying it."

Thorn was so stunned he couldn't reply.

"You've made it clear how you really feel." Berry took a deep breath. "I'm going back to the troop. Don't bother to come with me."

She stalked off across the grassland, ignoring the angry

protests of the crows. As she disappeared into the belt of trees, Thorn sank to the ground, his head in his forepaws. How could Berry have misread his feelings—or his lack of them— for Frog?

"It's for the best," he muttered to himself. "It doesn't matter. What counts is that I'm keeping her safe."

Along with the pain, a roiling anger was building inside him. This was all down to Stinger: all of it. *I need to do something!*

He didn't know what, that was the trouble. No other baboon even shared his suspicions, let alone took his side. *Except maybe Frog . . .*

Berry might be scrambling up the wrong fig tree about Thorn's feelings for the sturdy, solemn baboon, but it was true that he liked and respected Frog. She was the only Strongbranch who felt the same way about the orders Stinger was giving them. *She told me as much this morning.* He could go to Frog with his knowledge, confirm her suspicions, ask her to help him beat Stinger . . .

And then what? prodded a voice inside him.

Frog might be a big, strong baboon, but that hadn't saved either Bark or Grub. If Thorn made her his ally, he could be sentencing her to death by scorpion poison, or a rock to the skull, or worse. Could he live with himself?

Thorn raked at his neck fur in frustration. There had to be another way, someone who could help—someone Stinger couldn't threaten. He just couldn't imagine who that might be.

Staying away from the troop any longer would look suspicious. With a sigh, Thorn rose and plodded back across the grassland, ignoring the crows' cackling Skytongue. Ahead of him, in the tree line, a flock of blue starlings erupted from the canopy, chattering in alarm, but he was too preoccupied to worry. He loped into the trees and almost immediately heard a raucous screech. A pair of lilac-breasted rollers burst up through the canopy, swooping and diving toward the grassland. They'd left the shelter of the trees even though it exposed them to the violent wind. Thorn frowned, snapping out of his reverie. Something was disturbing the birds.

A screech heralded a crashing of foliage. Leaves and branches swayed and shuddered. Then, on the stiff breeze, the odor of fruit pulp and nuts reached Thorn's nostrils. . . .

Monkeys!

He broke into a run. One baboon, alone, stood no chance against a troop of vervets. High in the trees behind him he could hear their echoing calls: "This way! This way!"

Thorn wove and dodged between trunks, but whichever way he turned he could still hear the monkeys behind him. When he paused, panting, to glance over his shoulder, he caught sight of a score of green-brown bodies racing through the branches. Their white-fringed faces brimmed with malevolent excitement.

They're coming closer. They'll see me!

All he could do was hide and hope. Ahead was a clump of crotons, their sunset-colored leaves brushing the ground. Thorn leaped and dived into their midst—and collided with something large and furry.

"Oof!" he gasped. *A monkey!* His stomach flipped and he tensed for a fight.

"Thorn?" The voice was querulous with surprise.

He blinked, squinting into the dappled shadow. After a moment he made out a familiar face, scowling through parted leaves.

"Nut?" Thorn squinted at his old enemy. "Is that you?"

Nut wriggled through the leaves. He looked filthy. Thorn remembered him as a large-framed, muscular bully, but he looked shrunken and thin. Nut's once-fine fur was matted, he smelled as if he'd rolled around in a pile of dung, and his sunken eyes held the hunted look of a grass-eater. Life since his exile from the troop had not been kind.

Nut bounded forward and shoved Thorn's chest, sending him sprawling.

"This is my bush. Get lost."

Thorn's old dislike flared into loathing. Hadn't his day been bad enough already? Nut had always been a bully—he'd almost gotten Mud killed during the Three Feats.

And yet, staring into his hollow, haunted face, Thorn couldn't repress a surge of pity. Nut had deserved a lot, but he hadn't deserved to be run out of the troop. Thorn of all baboons knew he wasn't guilty of the crime he'd been accused of. He certainly couldn't leave him to be torn apart by monkeys.

"Shut up and listen," he snapped. "There are monkeys coming and we've got to hide."

Nut sneered. "I'm not helping you. I never want to see you again. You or that weedy Mud."

Thorn growled and pointed at the trees. "Listen to that racket. Do you think you can fight all those monkeys alone? We'll be safer together."

Still glaring, Nut hesitated. An earsplitting screech made him start and glance up at the treetops. He curled his snout in angry defeat. "Fine. This way."

Thorn scrambled after him up the cracked bark of a big kigelia tree. In a fork between two branches at the top, a smear of black shadow revealed a hollow; Nut twisted and lowered himself in. The space looked tight, and Thorn balked for a moment at the idea of squeezing in there with the malodorous Nut.

Nut rolled his eyes at him. "Well, get in!"

With a sigh of resignation, Thorn wriggled in beside him.

"Keep your elbows to yourself," Nut grumbled.

"Keep that stink to yourself," Thorn retorted, trying not to breathe too deeply. There were disadvantages, he thought, to being out of the wind.

Craning his neck, Thorn glimpsed a few monkeys as they bounded screeching through the canopy. He squirmed tentatively up and peered around.

A branch to his right dipped wildly and bounced as two monkeys leaped onto it.

"Do you smell that?" one monkey said, sniffing the air.

Thorn held his breath. Beside him, he felt Nut twitch.

"Baboon?" the other monkey asked. "It's probably blown

in on that wind. You couldn't escape baboon-stink if you flew up to the Great Spirit in the sky. They smell worse than rot-meat."

The monkeys laughed like hyenas; as they loped on, Thorn ducked down. Huddled in the hollow, he and Nut kept still until the chattering and screeching faded.

"Well, they're right about one thing," Thorn remarked, rubbing his nose. "You could do with a groom."

Nut squirmed past him, pulled himself out of the hollow, and scrambled down the tree. "What're you doing here any-way?" he snapped as Thorn followed. "Having a break from bowing down to Stinger?"

Thorn jumped to the ground and dusted his paws. "I never bowed to Stinger."

"Whatever you say," Nut sneered. "Go on—run back to your precious Crownleaf."

He turned his rump on Thorn, stiffening his matted shoul-ders as he stalked away with what passed for dignity. Once again Thorn felt a pang of involuntary pity. Then something else stirred inside him: the beginning of an idea . . .

"Nut, wait!"

"What?" Nut snapped over his shoulder. "I did you a favor: I helped you hide. Don't push your luck by asking for another one."

"I hate Stinger too."

Nut stopped, his ears twitching. Slowly, he turned.

"I hate Stinger," Thorn repeated, slowly and clearly. "And, Nut—I know you didn't kill Grub. Stinger did."

Nut's jaw fell open.

"He killed Bark, too," Thorn went on, now that he had Nut's full attention. "He wanted very badly to be Crownleaf. And now he is."

"*What?*" Nut snarled. "Stinger exiled me for *something he did?*"

"Yes," said Thorn.

Nut made a strange squeaking noise. Snatching up a pawful of gravelly dirt, he flung it at the trees; some of it rattled on the leaves and bark, and the rest gusted back into his own eyes. A tormented growl emerged from his throat as he rubbed at them. At last he slumped onto his haunches. "He's crazy, isn't he?"

Thorn squatted beside him. "I think he's worse than that. I think he's cleverer than all of us. He got just what he wanted. And what's more, the troop loves him."

Nut's muzzle twisted. "They deserve him."

"You don't think that," said Thorn. "Not really." He felt a sudden wild urge to hoot with laughter. After everything, the only creature he could talk to was Nut. "Besides, we can save the troop from Stinger *and* from themselves. We can drive Stinger out."

Nut snorted. "*We?* I don't want anything to do with *you!*" He flapped a paw at Thorn. "I hate you, remember?"

"Fine." Thorn shrugged. "I'm not asking you to like me. But I'm the only baboon in Bravelands who knows you're innocent."

Nut fell silent. His eyes narrowed.

"You want to come back to Brightforest, don't you?" Thorn

pressed. "That'll only happen when Stinger's gone."

"It's not possible," Nut muttered. "He's too clever, as you point out. Too *powerful*."

"For us, maybe. But there's someone we can ask for help. Someone who's much stronger than any baboon."

Nut frowned. "Who—" Realization dawned on his mean features, and he raked his paws across his patchy-furred skull. "You don't mean—"

Thorn nodded firmly. "Yep."

Nut groaned and sank his head into his paws. "You're going to ask Big Talk."

CHAPTER 10

"Would you hurry up?" snapped Thorn. "I've been away from the troop since dawn. Stinger will be getting suspicious."

He stalked through the trees ahead of Nut, his hide prickling with irritation. He might have cajoled Nut into coming with him, but the bigger baboon had made it painfully clear he wasn't happy about it.

"This is ridiculous," Nut griped, as they crouched at the edge of the open plain, flinching at the blast of the gale. "You're going to get us both killed."

"I don't see you coming up with a better idea." Thorn bounded out into the long grasses, the wind tearing and tugging at his fur. Grass blades whipped, lashing his face, and he sneezed and spat. He glanced back to check that Nut was following. He was, but the scruffy baboon's broad forehead was crinkled into a scowl.

"Why Big Talk?" grumbled Nut. "He won't help us."

"Fearless is my friend, remember?"

Nut snorted. "He's *Stinger's* friend. Trust me, he won't be on your side."

A sliver of doubt stirred within Thorn. He remembered all too clearly Fearless's rapt adoration while Stinger taught him the ways of the baboons. *But I used to feel the same way*, he reminded himself. *Stinger fooled all of us.*

He shook his fur. *I must have faith in Fearless.* "He'll be on our side—when we tell him the truth."

"Sure. That's if we can even find him," Nut pointed out. "You can spend all day poking around in the grass if you like— I'm going for a nap. Don't get blown all the way back to Tall Trees." With a disdainful flick of his tail, Nut stalked over to the lee of a baobab tree.

The shelter of its vast trunk did look tempting, Thorn had to admit. But he shot a glare at Nut as he slouched down against it. *Just a bit of help would be nice. . . .*

He opened his jaws to tell Nut exactly what he thought of his attitude, but at that moment he felt a tremor in the earth beneath his paws.

Thorn bounded to the baobab tree and seized Nut's arm. "Something's coming!"

"Get off!" Nut slapped at his paw. "I've only just sat down."

Thorn shook him. "We need to *go!*"

Dragging the reluctant Nut to his feet, Thorn raced back into the long grass and ducked out of sight. Nut slumped down beside him, looking truculent, but half rose to peer out over the tossing sea of grass.

Over the crest of a slope thundered a galloping zebra. His eyes rolled in terror, showing the whites, and his breath came in guttural rasps. Streaks of sweat ran down his chest and flanks.

Moments after him, the flesh-eaters appeared. *Lions*, thought Thorn; *he's doomed.* The big cats' golden bodies were strong and lithe, and they barely looked out of breath. Three sleek lionesses were closing in from the side as a powerful-looking male with a scarred nose drove the zebra forward. To the right, two cubs bounded, cutting off the escape route: one was half grown, the other much younger.

As the cubs veered closer, Thorn gasped. The half-grown cub was Fearless.

"Big Talk," whispered Nut. "That's handy. Get his attention."

Thorn, though, felt his belly quail. He had never seen Fearless hunt a full-grown, hoofed grass-eater, so he'd never seen that expression on his face: fangs bared, ears cocked, glittering eyes fixed on the prey and nothing else. The young lion looked intent, and bloodthirsty, and entirely deadly.

The zebra veered and jinked, trying to shake off its pursuers; with a lurch of his heart, Thorn recognized the pattern of his curving stripes. "That's Sleekfriend," he hissed to Nut. "I visited him with Stinger, right before the Great Gathering."

Sleekfriend dodged again and bolted past the baboons, his eyes glazed with terror. His pounding hooves struck up plumes of red dust that swirled in the wind, but his legs trembled visibly; he was already exhausted. Thorn could hardly bear to watch.

Please let him get away!

But the lions were closing their ambush. They swerved, keeping pace with Sleekfriend, and the lionesses angled toward him as the cubs held the flank. There was a jolt of hesitation in Sleekfriend's hoof-beats as he tried to double back, only to find his way blocked by a muscular lioness.

His moment of indecision was enough. A tawny lioness sprang. She landed on Sleekfriend's haunches, digging her claws deep. Sleekfriend staggered and swayed. He tried to buck her off, kicking out with his hind hooves, but his forelegs gave way and he fell to his knees. The other lions piled onto him, crushing Sleekfriend to the ground. Fearless was at the forefront of the ambush; Thorn saw him lunge with open jaws for the zebra's straining throat.

Thorn looked away. He heard a single desperate whinny that was strangled to silence. After that, there were only the triumphant grunts of the lions.

Thorn gulped. The struggling heap of bodies out on the plain subsided into stillness; Sleekfriend's thrashing leg trembled, stiffened, and sank to the ground. It was over.

Beside Thorn, Nut was shaking, his breath coming in quick, nervous pants.

"Ruthless!" Fearless's familiar roar resounded across the plain. "Ruthless, come here!"

Thorn peered back at the killing site. The lions had risen to their paws, leaving Sleekfriend on the ground, and they paced and circled a little distance away. Ruthless—Thorn recognized him now, the tiny cub he'd once helped Fearless save from cheetahs—must have fallen behind during the hunt; now he was pounding eagerly toward the rest of the pride, his tail high.

"What are they doing?" Nut whispered indignantly. "That zebra's not even dead!"

With a jolt of horror, Thorn saw that Nut was right. Sleekfriend's bloodstained ribs pulsed with shallow breaths. That leg was still twitching. His eyes were glazed, but there was life in them.

Thorn felt sick. Lions hunted and killed; of course he knew that. But they followed the same Code as all the animals of Bravelands: *Only kill to survive.* Why would they bring down Sleekfriend and not hurry to eat? Weren't they ravenous after their hunt?

The worst of it was that Fearless looked perfectly calm, his tail flicking as he called to Ruthless again. The Fearless Thorn had known would never have left Sleekfriend to suffer. Had life with the lions changed him so much?

The biggest lion, a male with three long scars across his muzzle, was sniffing the air. He took a few paces toward the long grass where Thorn and Nut crouched, and his shoulders tensed.

"Baboons!" he roared. "Come on, we each need a kill today. Get them!"

Of the six lions, Fearless was first to react. With a grunting roar he sprinted toward them. Thorn froze, as rooted to the ground as a baobab. Was his friend *hunting him*?

Nut grabbed Thorn's arm and yanked. "Move, you idiot!"

Thorn stumbled, his paw scraping against a rock; finally the reality hit him. With a gasp, he broke into a run, racing at Nut's side toward the woodland. One glance over his shoulder told him Fearless was in hot pursuit.

Thorn's breath burned his lungs, and his muscles felt uncoordinated and clumsy. This was like being caught in a nightmare. Deep in his heart he could barely believe his old friend was hunting him down. Yet with every pounding pace he knew what was coming: Fearless's sharp claws in his back, Fearless's weight forcing him to the earth, Fearless's fangs piercing his throat . . .

"Make for the trees," rasped Nut. "Thank the Great Spirit he's a useless climber."

For the first time Thorn knew what it was like to be truly hunted by a flesh-eater. Flashes of Sleekfriend's expression came to mind: the rolling eyes, the flared red nostrils, the soundless scream of terror. Thorn knew he must look exactly like that; it was almost as if he was detached from his body, watching it all from above. *Fearless is going to kill me. My friend, my troop-mate, Fearless . . .*

Closer to the trees there was blown debris everywhere: snapped branches, tangled twigs, dislodged fruit. Something sharp pierced Thorn's paw, but even as blood seeped between his fingers he kept running. The cool green of the forest was ahead, so very close. With a final desperate spring, they were beneath the trees.

"Climb!" Nut screeched.

Thorn reached for a branch, but in a sudden gust of wind it sprang out of reach. With a whimper of despair he tried again, and snatched a handhold. The foliage lashed at his face; the wind was so unpredictable there was no way to dodge it. His snout was bleeding too now; he could feel a trickle of warm blood beneath his nostrils, but he didn't care. Leaping for a branch that bounced and tossed in the gale, he grabbed it and swung, holding on for dear life. His paws trembled so badly, he could barely cling on.

Branch by swaying branch, the two baboons dragged themselves into the treetops.

"Farther in!" Nut yelled.

Burrs and broken twigs whipped their faces as they risked crazy leaps from tree to tree. In theory, retreating deeper into the forest should have sheltered them a little from the storm, but they were so high in the canopy now that it made little difference. Another branch jerked suddenly away in a powerful gust, and Thorn was left hanging on to a cluster of twigs. Nut grabbed his arm and dragged him to safety, and they bounded on.

At last, near the top of a sycamore fig, Thorn dared to stop. Nut did too, slumping against the trunk, his broad shoulders heaving. Parting the foliage with trembling paws, Thorn peered at the ground far below. Something moved down there, but as his breath caught, he realized it was only a warthog, grubbing in the brush. Of Fearless there was no sign.

"I think . . . we're safe." He flopped along the branch, chest heaving.

Nut glared, his breath still rasping. "I . . . told you it was . . . a stupid idea. I *said* we couldn't trust Big Talk."

"You did." Thorn's whole body sagged with misery and exhaustion. "You were right."

His stomach churned. Fearless had been his *friend*. They'd grown up together. That cruel killer was nothing like the Fearless he knew. Thorn didn't understand how he could have changed so much, and so suddenly, but he couldn't deny what had just happened. Nut lurched up, propping himself against the trunk with one paw. "So much for fighting Stinger," he panted, starting to climb down the tree. "This has been a huge waste of time."

"Wait!" cried Thorn.

He lowered himself carefully down after Nut. Not until he was close to the foot of the tree did he risk the final jump to the mossy forest floor; he felt a lot more fragile and killable than he had only this morning.

"I need your help, Nut. Please. You're the only one who knows the truth."

Nut shrugged and shambled off through the trees, scratching at his dirty fur. "Forget it," he growled. "And if you have another bright idea, don't come bothering me with it."

"Fine," Thorn muttered, coming to a frustrated halt. "I won't."

He watched Nut disappear into the green shadows of the

woodland, then heaved a sigh and turned back toward the savannah. He didn't need Nut's help, he tried to tell himself; after all, that baboon had never been anything but trouble.

He just wished he didn't feel so *alone.*

No Nut, he thought, swatting at a termite nest. *No Fearless. No plan.*

No hope?

Maybe not. But he had to try.

The trek back to Brightforest Troop felt far, far longer than he'd remembered. As he finally padded, exhausted, over the rim of their hollow, he paused, one paw half raised.

Low hoots and wails were audible, though muffled, as if desperate baboons were trying to keep silent when they wanted to screech in rage or pain. Thorn's throat constricted. *What's happened?*

He sprang forward, energized by fear, into the troop's midst.

Lily Middleleaf, her baby in her arms, turned her agonized face to him. Starleaf squatted by a jutting slab of rock, gripping a Moonstone in each paw and muttering. The Goodleaf baboons, Blossom and Petal, were hunched over a pathetic heap of fur that lay huddled on the short grass.

"You're back!" cried Mud. He ran to Thorn, grabbing his shoulder. "You're back, thank the Great Spirit."

Thorn stared from Mud's tormented face to that motionless figure on the grass. He took another pace, though his paws seemed suddenly too heavy to lift. The figure was a baboon;

she was spattered with gouts of blood, and he couldn't make out if she was breathing.

Even in the clouded afternoon light, her matted fur was shot through with sparks of gold.

"Thorn." Mud tugged at him urgently. "Berry's been hurt!"

CHAPTER 11

Fearless creased his eyes against the blustering wind. *It's a good thing I was here*, he thought. *They'd have gotten themselves killed.*

Thorn and Nut were moving much faster now, thank the Great Spirit, and in moments they were lost in the foliage above him. Fearless wondered what Thorn was doing with Nut in the first place. He knew Thorn couldn't stand him—Nut had thought it hilarious to twist Mud's tail and steal his fruit, but his vicious sense of humor had taken a much darker turn during the Second Feat. He had almost gotten Mud killed when he riled up the crocodiles.

Fearless shrugged. Perhaps Stinger had sent Thorn and Nut off together to complete some kind of task and teach Nut a bit of team spirit? Yes, he decided, that was it: Stinger was admirably wily and wise.

At least he'd managed to drive them away before any of the

other lions could catch up. Fearless took a deep breath. He let his tail droop, hung his head, and forced disappointment into his face as he shambled back to the lions.

"Useless." Resolute glared at Fearless down his scarred nose. "Can't even catch baboons."

"Sorry." Fearless mustered a huge sigh.

Honor pawed uneasily at the ground. "We should finish off that zebra," she told Resolute. "Let me kill it and be done."

Fearless glanced to where the zebra lay shuddering on the ground. Valor had taught him to kill quickly and cleanly, and the sight of the suffering creature appalled him. He'd longed to suffocate the life out of the poor thing even as he gripped its throat, but fear of Titan's retribution had held him back. Fearless couldn't let him hurt Sleekfriend any more.

"Don't touch that zebra, Honor. Fearless was following orders, for once." Resolute swung his maned head toward Ruthless. The little cub crouched by Regal's side, batting at a red beetle that tottered along a grass stalk. "Ruthless will make this kill."

Ruthless looked up, his eyes wide. "Me?"

"He's too young," Honor protested.

"Nonsense." Resolute tilted his head, his voice teasing. "Ruthless is a very special cub. He deserves a chance to prove it."

Ruthless stared at the zebra, his jaw slack. "I can't choke that. It's enormous!"

"You can do it, Ruthless," Regal said, licking the top of his head. "Use your teeth. If you put one paw on the neck and

push the head down, you'll see the line where the blood flows.
Bite that line and he'll be dead in a heartbeat."

Ruthless's eyes widened. "Will there be a lot of blood?" he
asked faintly.

Daring flicked her ears. "Don't listen to her, Ruthless,"
she said. "It's better to straddle the zebra so he can't kick you.
You'll have to lean over his neck, but just make sure to really
tear with your teeth. It might take a little longer, but you'll get
the job done."

Ruthless swallowed and looked fearfully at the zebra.

"Come on, Ruthless," Resolute coaxed him. "Show us why
your father chose your name." His tone was light, but Fearless
saw an excited gleam in Resolute's eye, as if he were stalking
prey.

He wants to humiliate the cub.

All the lions were watching Ruthless now. He hunched his
little shoulders and stared at the ground. Honor looked worried, but the other lions were egging Ruthless on.

"You can do it!" Daring urged.

"Hurry up, Ruthless," said Resolute. There was a tinge of
impatience in his voice now. "The zebra's all laid out ready for
you. We've done the hardest part. You just have to make the
kill."

"Your first kill is something to be proud of," Regal chimed
in. "You'll never forget this day."

"What will your father say," Resolute wondered, "if he
hears you refused?"

Ruthless trembled. He crouched lower, as if he wanted to disappear into the grass.

Fearless sucked in a breath. Before anyone could react, he sprinted toward the zebra. "Fearless!" Resolute roared behind him.

He didn't look back. Reaching the zebra, he remembered Valor's advice: *Bite deep and bite hard, right where the neck meets the head.* His fangs closed on the zebra's throat, warm blood filled his mouth, and the zebra jerked once, convulsively. Then it went limp, dead at last.

As he backed away, licking blood from his jaws, a hard blow caught him in the ribs, bowling him over in the grass.

"You *never* steal another lion's prey!" Resolute roared. "Are you a fool or a traitor?"

Regal bounded up and clouted his head. "You have no right to steal Ruthless's kill! He is Titan's heir!"

Fearless staggered to his paws. He reeled from the blows, but hot indignation coursed through him. "He's too little," he spat. "Anyone can see that."

Regal snarled and drew back a paw to strike again, but Resolute shoved her aside with a muscular shoulder. "We'll let Titan deal with him," he said. "Let's get back to the pride."

With a disgusted shake of his mane, Resolute strode back toward Titanpride territory, Regal right behind him. Ruthless followed, his head and tail sagging. Without even glancing at Fearless, Honor and Daring grabbed the zebra's legs and dragged it after them. Fearless trailed last, his body sore and his gut tense. His anger was fading as an uneasy regret crept in. *I shouldn't have done that. How's Titan going to react?*

He scowled at Regal's haunches. He'd known her all his life; she had been a lioness of Gallantpride and a friend of Valor. Yet now her loyalties seemed to lie with Titan and his cronies. Fearless's skin crawled beneath his pelt. Was she that scared of Titan? Or was it simpler than that, and Titan's viciousness was infecting the whole pride one by one?

"Thank you for helping me," squeaked a soft voice. It was Ruthless, who had dropped back to walk close to Fearless. His pale brown eyes were full of trust, his belly still round with cub fat. "I'm sorry you got in trouble."

"It's okay," said Fearless. "I'll be fine, I promise."

Ruthless's tail drooped. "I should have been able to kill that zebra."

Fearless gave his shoulder a nudge. "It'll get easier."

Ruthless perked up. "Will you teach me to hunt? You're really good at it."

Fearless grinned. "I'm still learning, just like you. My sister, Valor, though—*she's* a great hunter. I could ask her to help you."

"Would you?" Ruthless's whiskers quivered. "*Thank* you, Fearless."

Side by side, Titan and Artful were waiting for them. Fearless saw that Valor was already back from her own hunt, sitting beside Swift; Valor snuggled against their mother, her head on her shoulder. In the center of the camp, prey was haphazardly strewn in a pile, and Daring and Honor hauled the zebra toward it.

Titan turned toward them. "You've made your quota of kills today?"

Both lionesses ducked their heads as they dropped the zebra. "Yes, Titan."

"They did well, Titan," Resolute told him. "Honor took down a gazelle by herself, and Daring killed a bushbuck. They're on the prey pile already."

Titan nodded, rising and dismissing the lionesses with a jerk of his head. He sniffed at Resolute and Regal, letting them pass without comment, then bent low over Ruthless. The little cub cringed guiltily.

"Why don't you smell of prey?" Titan growled. He put a heavy paw on Ruthless's back.

"He's so young . . ." Artful murmured.

"My son is no ordinary cub," Titan snarled. "He will be the finest of hunters, and I want to know why he hasn't made a kill today."

Silence fell. Ruthless opened his small jaws, the pink of his tongue lolling. "I—"

"It was my fault," Fearless cut in. "I stole Ruthless's kill before he could make it."

Ruthless shot Fearless a grateful look and Artful's shoulders relaxed. But Valor sprang to her paws and Swift's ears pricked, her whiskers trembling. Fearless felt the fur along his spine rise.

Titan paced toward Fearless, his powerful muscles bunching and stretching beneath his pelt. "How dare you," he growled. "How *dare* you steal from my cub!"

Fearless could feel the stares of the whole pride, some vengeful, others anxious. His pelt prickled.

"I didn't—I didn't realize it was so important," he said. "I thought . . . I wanted to help Ruthless. . . ."

Titan loomed over Fearless. His black mane whipped in the wind, his nostrils flared red, and his breath smelled of blood. Instinct urged Fearless to back away, to run as far from Titan as he could, but he dug his claws into the earth and held his ground.

"That," snarled Titan, "is no excuse. My orders were clear."

"I'm sorry." Fearless swallowed. "How can I put it right?"

"You can't," snarled Titan. "An insult to my son is an insult to me. I won't forget it." He glanced over at Swift, and his muzzle curled into a grin. "You, Fearless, must go and make another kill. And as punishment, neither you nor your mother will be permitted to eat."

"But Titan," blurted Honor, "there's barely any prey! And we already killed what we could find."

"It's an outrageous demand!" Valor lurched forward, eyes flashing, but Swift staggered hurriedly to her feet and nudged her flank.

"We understand, Titan," Swift said meekly, blinking her milky eye in his direction. "Don't we, Fearless? Valor?"

Valor clenched her teeth. "Yes, Mother."

Fearless could barely speak. At last he managed to mutter, "Yes."

His stomach shriveled like a frog left out in the sun. In his ostentatious pity for Ruthless and a dying zebra, he'd forgotten to have any for his mother. He'd known what his disobedience would mean for Swift, but that had flown out of his head in the heat of the moment. He did not want to imagine what Loyal would say if he heard.

The rest of the pride eyed him as he slunk away, their expressions ranging from disdain to sympathy. If there was a single lion who wanted to challenge Titan's judgment, they clearly didn't dare. Fearless padded on, his heart heavy as he crossed the border of Titanpride territory. Hunt again? He could barely lift his head; his weariness cut right down to the bone.

I hate Titan. Leaning forward into the wind, he protracted his claws, raking up chunks of earth as he walked. *I hate him so much.*

At least he had to battle the wind; it kept his mind off his longing to fight Titan. Everything that brutal lion did was rooted in needless cruelty: terrorizing his pride, forcing them to kill far more than they could eat, alternately indulging and terrifying poor Ruthless. Even more than he hated Titan, Fearless hated that he couldn't do anything to stop him. For now, Stinger was right: all he could do was wait.

Fearless blinked, realizing his paws had led him to Loyal's den. Wind howled around the bleak kopje, blustering grit and sand into his eyes and whistling eerily through the gaps in the rocks. Above him he could make out the dark slash of the den entrance, half hidden by a jutting stone.

The tightness in his gut loosened, just a little. Fearless scrambled and leaped up the shelves of rock, finally bounding onto the flat patch of sandy earth where the weather-bleached bones of long-dead grass-eaters lay scattered.

"Loyal?" Fearless called.

There was a stir of sound inside the den; a shadow moved at its mouth. "Fearless?"

Loyal's voice was fuzzy with sleep. His familiar head emerged, squinting into the wind. Catching sight of Fearless, he leaped down. "What's wrong?"

"Titan. Of course."

Loyal growled. "What's he done now?"

Fearless slumped onto his haunches. His misery could no longer be suppressed; his words tumbled over each other as he told Loyal everything.

"And I can't go back until I've caught more prey," he finished miserably. "And even if I do, Mother won't eat today."

Loyal's amber eyes darkened to glittering bronze. "You shouldn't go back at all. It's too dangerous."

"But Mother and Valor—"

"I know, I know." Loyal tapped his crooked tail against the ground. "You won't leave them. But what good are you to them if you get yourself killed? You could stay safely here instead. What do you say?"

It was very tempting. For a fleeting moment Fearless let himself imagine it: living with Loyal in his den, bringing back kills he could eat himself. Sunning himself on the kopje when the storms finally passed . . .

Closing his eyes, he sighed. "I can't leave them with Titan;

who knows what he'd do? And if I brought them here, he'd come after us." His voice lowered to a growl. "Besides, Loyal, I need to avenge my father." He flexed his claws. "For that, I have to be there, watching Titan. Stinger said I'd know when the time was right to kill him."

"Stinger said *what*?" Loyal's shoulders tensed, and he bared his fangs. "That kind of recklessness will get *you* killed."

"I'm being careful," Fearless assured him.

"By insulting Titan's son and stealing his kill?" Loyal shook his mane violently. "What a crazy risk, Fearless."

"I had to do what I did! And Ruthless was glad. He—"

Loyal cut him off with a snarl of frustration and launched into frantic back-and-forth pacing. "What does a *baboon* know about how a pride works? What does Stinger know about Titan? He's got no business telling you what to do." He swung to face Fearless, the wind blowing his mane back; Fearless felt the full impact of his enraged expression. "Leave Titanpride. Now, Fearless! Before you do something *really* stupid."

"But I won't do anything stupid!" Fearless protested. "And Titan can't hurt me that badly. He made an *oath* not to kill me."

Loyal stared at him for an agonizingly long moment.

"Oaths can be broken," he said quietly.

Fearless snorted. "Not even Titan would break an oath," he said. "He's a cruel, Codeless brute, but he's still a *lion*."

Loyal turned away. The gale-tossed clouds over the kopje were darkening to purple, roiling and churning. Flocks of birds darted beneath them, heading for shelter.

"More rain's coming," Loyal growled at last. "Come on, youngster. If you insist on going back, you'd better have some prey to take with you. We're going hunting."

CHAPTER 12

The sunset was almost violent in its intensity, as if it were compensating for the dismal grayness of the day. Its dying rays stained the cloudbank with purple and orange and a blazing yellow. The gales still raged, pinning back Sky's ears.

Great Mother's tusk fragment felt heavy in her trunk; the trek had been so long and tiring, yet Sky knew they had not made enough progress. Every step had been a struggle against the blast and tug of the wind, and she and Moon were still nowhere near the path that would lead them where they needed to go.

Moon stumbled, steadying himself against her with his trunk. "Sorry, Sky," he yawned.

"Time to sleep, I think."

"I'm not tired, I can keep . . ." Moon said, but his words were swallowed by another yawn.

"This wind's too much." Sky caressed his ear fondly. "Come on. I think I can hear a stream over there—let's have a drink. I need to rest, even if you're tough enough to walk all night."

Moon drew himself up with pride, then stiffened. His ears flapped forward. "What's that?"

Sky had heard it too, a distant trumpeting call carried on the wind. She went still, listening. It rose and fell with the breeze, making it hard to tell its direction.

"Is that a rhino?" breathed Moon. "Rhinos are dangerous, Mother told me."

Sky shook her head. "Don't worry, Moon, it's not a rhino. It's another elephant—a lone male, I think." As Moon brightened, she added, "But they can be dangerous, too! We'll keep out of his way, all right?"

"All right, Sky. If you say so." Moon nodded obediently. "I *told* you I'd be good."

Stifling a chuckle, Sky led the little elephant down a worn patch of ground. The stream was loud now, even above the roar of the gale, and as they neared it the ground underfoot became softer, dotted with tussocks of lush grass. It was much more pleasant for Sky's aching feet than the hard, endless track. In dense mgunga trees, hundreds of egrets were settling to roost; beneath them Sky saw the water at last. It was high and fast, swollen by rains and whipped into crests by the wind.

Here in the grassy hollow, sheltered from the driving wind on the savannah, scents seemed to linger. Sky raised her trunk, uneasy; there was a meaty, musky tang in the air that she recognized with a shiver. *Lions.* Perhaps they weren't close, she thought hopefully; perhaps their scent simply lingered in the damp foliage and the relative stillness.

Moon was already dabbling and splashing his toes in the swift current. Sky sucked up a trunkful of water and squirted it gratefully into her mouth. It tasted fresh and clear, and so very welcome.

Moon splashed his foot harder, sending up a small shower, and giggled. "It's cold!"

"It certainly is. Feel this!" Sky pointed her trunk and blew a spray of water over his head.

Moon squealed and trumpeted in delight, all his tiredness temporarily forgotten. Pleased to distract him, Sky played water games with her little cousin until he grew bored; then they both set to ripping up the sweet grass and pulling down slender thorny branches.

At last a twig fell from Moon's mouth even as he chewed. His eyelids were sagging, and he gave a great yawn. Sky folded her trunk over his neck.

"Time to sleep," she murmured.

Tucking Moon under her trunk, and Great Mother's tusk fragment safely beneath her leg, Sky lay down. Moon cuddled closer, his head warm against her flank.

"Do you think my mother misses me?" came his small voice.

"I'm sure she does," Sky told him softly. "I miss her, too. And Rain and Comet and Cloud and Twilight. But you know what?"

"What?" whispered Moon.

"We'll be back with them very soon. I bet Star will wrap

you up in her trunk and keep you next to her for days and days." Sky stroked the bristly hair on Moon's back. "You'll get so mad when she doesn't let you run off to play."

"I won't be mad," Moon mumbled. "I'll stay right beside her. Forever and ever and *ages.*"

He snuggled tighter against her, his heart beating through her hide. Her own eyes were growing irresistibly heavy. Somewhere overhead a bird flew, calling out a long, throbbing song.

"What was that?" Moon looked up with a start.

"Just a nightjar," Sky reassured him. "They fly in the dark. Haven't you heard one before?"

"I don't think so," Moon said doubtfully. "I'm always asleep then. With Mother."

"They're nothing to worry about, I promise."

"Are nightjars *big*?"

"No, they're little brown birds," Sky told him. "If one landed on your back, you'd barely feel it. Great Mother could talk to them, like she could talk to all the birds. They used to fly down to perch on her ear and tell her what they'd seen in the night."

"Oh." Moon shifted his head from side to side, his cheek digging into Sky's stomach.

After a moment, he sat up again. "What's that?"

"Where?"

"Over *there*," Moon whispered, pointing with his trunk. "I think it's a hippo."

Sky peered at a rounded shape that loomed above the water,

moonlight gleaming on its smooth gray surface. Was it moving . . . ?

Then she made out one jagged edge and a pitted hollow. "It's just a boulder."

"I don't like it."

Something shrieked overhead, far louder than the nightjar, and this time they both jumped.

"What was *that*?" Moon whimpered.

"Just another bird," Sky said, but she wasn't sure. Something about the sound made her skin crawl. She peered up at the sky, but there was nothing but darkness and the racing clouds.

Moon buried his head against her side. "I don't *like* it," he repeated. "I want my mother. I want to go home!"

Something—a hyena?—howled far away, and Sky flinched. "We'll go home soon, I promise," she said. "Shall I tell you a story? Maybe that will help you sleep."

She felt Moon's eager nod.

"Okay. Let's try a story my mother used to tell me, back when I was even littler than you."

"I'm not that little," Moon said, sounding less frightened and more indignant.

"No, of course you're not. This is how the story goes: One day, back when the first elephants were walking across Bravelands, back when the grasses were growing for the first time, there was a little elephant named Cloud. Cloud was so brave that she—"

"He," Moon mumbled against her hide. "I want Cloud to be a he."

"Okay. Cloud was so brave that he wasn't ever afraid, not even of lions or crocodiles. And he was so smart that he could understand what the birds were saying, just like our Great Mother could. And he was so strong that if a tree fell across his family's path, he would just pick it up and toss it out of the way. And his mother and his aunts and his cousins and his grandmother were so proud of him, and they all loved him very, very much."

"And he loved them." Moon sounded calmer now, and his ears craned to listen.

"Of course he did. One night, Cloud's whole family fell asleep after a long, long trek, but he was still awake, watching the sky. And a star fell down. Did you ever see a star fall?"

Moon nodded against Sky's belly. "One time," he said. "Mother saw it, too."

"Yes, but when you saw it, it fell far, far away, right?" Sky caressed his twitching ear with the tip of her trunk. "The star Cloud saw was big and bright. It fell with a great *boom*, so he knew it had landed somewhere near him. Maybe just over the next hill . . ."

"Did Cloud go find it?" Moon asked.

"Well, he whispered in his mother's ear that he would be right back and not to worry about him. And he started walking across the grass toward the star."

Moon raised his head, looking out into the darkness. "Sky," he whispered, his voice sharp. "Sky, there's a rhino over there."

"It's only a rock," Sky told him with a smile. "Just like the hippo was."

"Sky!" Moon sounded terrified. He pointed with his trunk.

There was just enough moonlight to see a shape, far back beside the path. The something was big and still, and there was a curve to it that *did* look like the high hunch of a rhino's back.

Had the shape been there the last time she looked? Sky couldn't remember.

She didn't think so.

Was it a rock? She'd surely have heard it rolling down onto the track, even on this soft ground; and besides, it was so *big*. Sky opened her mouth to whisper something reassuring to Moon—

—And the shape turned its head in the moonlight.

Yes, that was *definitely* a head. Sky could see the tufted ears and unmistakable long horn of a rhino. Her blood chilled.

"I'll go look," she murmured, steadying her voice. "You stay here, Moon. If I trumpet, run away. Run *as fast as you can*."

"No, stay." Moon wrapped his trunk around Sky's leg, but she shook him gently away.

"It's going to be okay," she told him, trying to sound as firm and calm as Great Mother always had. "I'll be as quiet and as quick as a leopard." It was impossible to walk silently; reeds and grasses whispered and rustled beneath her feet. With every step Sky winced, fear rippling through her blood. When she reached the barren ground closer to the path, her tread crunched on gritty earth and rattled loose pebbles. She halted, her heart pounding.

The rhino didn't move. It lay on its belly, chin against the ground, top lip quivering with its snores.

At least it wasn't the biggest rhino she had ever seen; it was close to her own size, not yet fully grown. Sky glanced around, but there were no more rhinos in sight.

She crept back to Moon. "The rhino's asleep," she whispered. "It doesn't even know we're here."

Moon blew a shaky, relieved sigh. "Maybe we should go, before it wakes up."

"No, but let's leave before dawn. We won't bother the rhino, and the rhino won't bother us."

Sky settled down again, the small elephant tucked against her side. "It's late," she whispered. "Look there, where the clouds have parted. You can see the moon up in the sky, little Moon."

"Little Sky," Moon murmured.

"The big moon looking down on the little Moon," Sky said, making her voice soft and dreamy. "Think of all the things the big moon can see, all over Bravelands."

Moon's breathing deepened and slowed, and Sky's own eyes grew heavy. The moon drifted back behind the scudding clouds, creating a smear of bright silver. If only the river of stars wasn't hidden; Sky liked to gaze up at it when she couldn't sleep. She'd watch its glittering swirl, follow its arcing path from horizon to horizon. The silver clouds weren't the same, she thought as they blurred and spun in her vision.

They didn't soothe her as the stars always did. . . .

* * *

Sky woke abruptly to the sound of splashing in the stream. Weak daylight shone through the churning cloud, and Moon was playing happily in the wave-tossed water.

"You're awake, Sky!" he squealed. "That rhino's gone!"

Sky looked back along the bank. It was empty. *Thank the Great Spirit.*

Feeling with the tip of her trunk, she found Great Mother's tusk fragment still tucked in the grass beneath her. Relieved, she plucked a mouthful of grass and popped it into her mouth.

Cold water spurted over her face, and she gasped.

"Got you back for yesterday!" Moon shrieked, capering away.

Sky shook the water from her ears, grinning. Filling up her own trunk, she gave chase. Moon cantered away, his trunk swinging, and Sky pretended to miss, splattering water over the grass.

"I win!" cried Moon.

"You win," agreed Sky, grabbing him and curling her trunk around his.

When they'd eaten enough grass and green twigs and leaves, Sky gathered up the tusk fragment and they set off back up to the track. If anything, the wind seemed stronger than ever; out on the open savannah Sky had to lean into it, battling its force, and protecting Moon as best she could with her rump. Dust swirled into her eyes; it did not help that the track was rising now. She heard that bull elephant's blare again, but distantly. And the faint odor of lions still drifted occasionally to her trunk, but in this wind they could be miles away.

It was hard to judge the passing of time when the sun was obscured by that layer of scudding gray cloud. All the two elephants could do was plod on, one heavy footstep after another; the verdant green bank and the sweet taste of water began to feel like a distant memory. *Poor Moon*, Sky thought. *This must be so hard for him.*

Her throat was too dry to ask him how tired he was; she simply halted to let him rest. As he sagged against her rump, Sky stared back along the track, trying to judge how far they had come.

A stocky form shimmered in the distance, trotting briskly toward them.

Sky felt a shock, as if a hoof had struck her gut. "What?"

Moon turned wearily to follow her gaze, and his eyes widened. "The rhino," he gasped. "Why is it following us?"

"I don't know." Sky felt her fear rising. Moon looked on the verge of panic: *Calm down*, she told herself sternly, and she tickled his ear. "Don't worry. It's just going the same way as us."

They hurried on, trying to make faster headway against the wind. The well-worn migration track was long and straight, and the marker stone was easy enough to spot; when they turned off, the new track tapered into a blue distance and vanished into hazy hills. When Sky glanced back, she saw that the rhino, too, had turned at the marker stone.

Why would it do that? What does it want?

The track rose steeply and narrowed. Walls of rock pressed in, finally forcing them to walk in single file. At least that protected Moon a little from the blowing grit and the dislodged shingle that whirled past. The howl of wind and the clatter of falling stones echoed unnervingly from the sheer rock walls, yet there were sharp sounds behind them that were even louder. Sky heard rocks rattle, and they sounded too big to be blown even by this storm; there was a rhythmic crunching that was definitely footsteps.

Anxiety gnawed at Sky, and she picked up speed.

Mist gathered as they climbed, a gray dampness that clung to the folds of their skin. At last, after many false summits, the rocky path reached what Sky knew was the true crest. She halted.

Beyond this point, Sky remembered, the path dipped, and the walls of stone would broaden suddenly, opening out into wide, flat grassland strewn with scattered bones: the Plain of Our Ancestors. Was it possible the rhino was going there too? The ground was sacred to elephants; what business of the rhino's were the bones of dead elephants? Yet as far as Sky knew, the track led nowhere else.

Squaring her shoulders, she nudged Moon, urging him to squeeze ahead of her.

"Moon, keep going," she said. "I'll wait here for a minute, but you follow the path and keep going to the valley. You remember it? You'll be safe there."

Moon nodded. He glanced back past her, and she knew he'd heard the rhino too.

"Be careful, Sky," he whispered, then trudged on upward.

Sky waited as the bleak wind moaned and howled. Her

heart felt like an oxpecker bird fluttering in her chest. Below her, the path angled behind a blade of rock, and she couldn't see beyond it. But she heard a grunt and the tread of heavy feet.

The rhinoceros emerged, ploughing upward. It was a female, breathing noisily, her eyes fixed on the ground as she hauled her hefty body up the steep track. Sky had been right—the rhino was no bigger and probably no older than Sky was. But she still looked dangerous, with her massive body and sharp horn. *Give me courage, Great Mother.*

Now or never, Sky realized, stepping forward to confront the rhino. Angrily she raised her trunk and spread her ears.

"Why are you following us?"

The rhino halted, her black eyes glittering. She raised her head, and her long horn gleamed in the pale light.

CHAPTER 13

The rock of the escarpment was already weather-smoothed, but it seemed to Thorn as if these gales might wear it away altogether. The wind howled across the slope, flattening the few tufts of vegetation on its barren face; it made an eerie wailing sound in the tunnels where the troop sheltered. The small cavern near the entrance was as far as they'd ventured for now, and capricious flurries of breeze gusted in to rumple their fur.

Brightforest Troop had found the abandoned den by chance, and despite the constant, unsettling howling of the gale, Thorn knew they were lucky. The floor of the cave was damp with pools that lingered from the rainstorms, but at least they were out of the worst of the blast. The Strongbranches and some of the fitter baboons had gathered branches and wedged them as tightly as they could across the tunnel's opening; the foliage rattled and shook, but the screen was holding. The tunnel itself receded farther into the hillside, but no one wanted to probe deeper to see what was down there. A faint odor of rot-meat, which no baboon chose to mention, seeped from the depths.

They had enough problems of their own.

Berry was in a hollow off the small cavern. She lay motionless on a bed of soft leaves, her face slack in feverish sleep. The Goodleaves bustled around her, bringing cool water and poultices, but Thorn could only crouch, staring at her beautiful face, willing her to wake up.

Beneath her closed lids, her eyes twitched rapidly. *She must be dreaming*, thought Thorn. *I hope they're not bad dreams. I hope she isn't living through the attack again.*

"This is my fault," he whispered to her. "Berry, I'm so sorry."

She'd been attacked right after their argument at the Lightning Tree, by the same monkeys he and Nut had eluded. A foraging party of Middleleaves had heard her cries and driven the monkeys off, but by the time they found Berry she was battered and semiconscious from bites and scratches. But worst of all . . .

Thorn looked down at the stump of Berry's severed tail, the bloody mess hidden by the Goodleaves' dressings.

If only we hadn't argued. If only I hadn't let her walk away alone. The thought raced around his mind, over and over again.

"I . . . I haven't seen it," Berry mumbled.

"What, Berry? What do you need?" begged Thorn, leaning closer.

But Berry went still again. Blossom Goodleaf touched her cheek. "She's very warm," she said, her brow furrowing. "Petal, come help me."

The other Goodleaf hurried to her side with a handful of fresh leaves, and together they carefully unwrapped Berry's tail stump. "More honey, Petal," said Blossom. "We have to stop the wound from going bad."

Berry struggled feebly as the Goodleaves uncovered her wound, as raw and bloody as a half-eaten carcass. Thorn winced.

"She's so weak," Petal murmured, carefully rewrapping the stump as Berry whimpered and twitched. Thorn wished he could hold her paw and comfort her—but he couldn't, not in front of the Goodleaves.

"When will she be healed?" he croaked.

Petal and Blossom exchanged sorrowful looks. Blossom shook her head.

Terror clawed at Thorn's throat. *They're wrong*, he thought. *She will get better. She has to!*

The Goodleaves wrapped the last jackalberry leaves around Berry's tail stump, then Blossom hurried away to tend to baboons who had been injured by the falling tree. "You can't stay long," Petal warned Thorn before following Blossom. "Berry needs rest more than anything."

As soon as they were alone and unobserved, Thorn reached out to stroke Berry's cheek. She lay very still now, but her usually sweet mouth was twisted into a grimace. "Berry," he whispered. "Berry, can you hear me at all?"

He craned over her, his breath in his throat, but she didn't even twitch.

"I'm so sorry," he whispered at last, clasping her paw. "*So* sorry. I wish I'd come with you. I could have helped you fight off the monkeys, or hidden with you." He shut his eyes tightly. "You were right, Berry. There is something wrong, and I wish I'd told you the truth. . . ." He squeezed her fingers. "It's your father, Berry. He's done terrible things."

Berry didn't react. She couldn't hear him, Thorn knew. She lay right before him, yet she was so far away.

"I'll tell you everything when you're better. I promise." With one last caress of her face, Thorn padded reluctantly back into the main cave.

Mud was crouched in the shadows against the wall, talking in a low voice to the other baboons, but when he spotted Thorn his eyes widened. He hurried to meet him. "How's Berry? Is she going to be all right?"

"I don't know." Thorn realized his voice was trembling.

"Oh, Thorn." Mud touched his shoulder. "Are *you* okay?"

"I'm fine, I . . ." Thorn hesitated. While Berry lay drifting in and out of consciousness, did it really matter how he felt?

He was spared having to finish his answer; a bark of summons came from the Strongbranches, who were emerging from the deeper tunnels. "Thorn," called Worm. "Help us bring the food out."

The healthy members of the troop turned as one to the Strongbranches, but eager glances faded quickly to grimaces of distaste. Thorn suppressed a shudder as he helped Frog carry a greasy, blackened thigh to the center of the cave.

"We investigated the rest of the tunnels," Frog said with a shrug. "They're full of dead hyenas."

"It's food, isn't it?" snapped Grass. "Stop making those faces, all of you."

It was true that in the high winds, and with many flesh-eaters prowling, hunting outside was hard. This pungent rot-meat would have to satisfy the troop, thought Thorn as he helped distribute the dismembered corpses. Still, as Starleaf took a rotten foreleg from his paws with a smile of gratitude, he felt a pang of shame. The Strongbranches, their duty done, were gathering around a small pile of berries, insects, and dead rodents; they'd managed to forage a few tasty things near the den entrance, but they were keeping them strictly to themselves. As Starleaf called Mud over to share her chunk of carrion, Frog hailed Thorn from the Strongbranch corner.

"Thorn, come and eat with us."

Reluctantly, Thorn sat down with his fellow Strongbranches. He couldn't deny that his lizard tasted better than dead hyena, but guilt gnawed at him.

"Stinger!" Grass brightened as the Crownleaf padded over. "Here, we've saved you a scorpion."

"And we found some grewia bushes," added Fly eagerly. "These are delicious, Stinger."

Stinger eyed the orange fruits and popped one into his mouth. "Save some of these for Berry," he ordered. "And the tamarinds. She likes those."

Yes, Berry did love tamarinds. She'd suck the tangy flesh off the seeds, her eyes bright with delight. Thorn stared at the remains of his lizard, his appetite gone.

"Come on, Thorn." Stinger slapped his back. "Eat up. You're a protector of the troop now—it's your duty to keep up your strength."

"Hey, you," Worm barked at a passing Deeproot. The little baboon started, and turned with wary eyes. "Bring me some leaves. I need to rest this foot. It got bitten by that tarantula I killed, remember?"

The Deeproot darted to his store, rushing back with an armful of date palm leaves.

Worm growled, "No, softer ones! I want solanum. Why haven't you got any of that? Yes, yes, leave those for now, but get me some solanum before the day's out."

What a bully, Thorn thought. *They all are, apart from Frog.*

Out of the corner of his eye he saw Fang lob a bone at Mud. It was small, but it smacked him right between the shoulder blades.

Mud spun around, glaring at the Strongbranches, and Fang pointed at Thorn.

"It was him!" he hooted.

Mud's eyes flicked to Thorn, full of disbelief and hurt. Thorn, startled, opened his jaws to protest, but his friend had already turned away, his shoulders hunched.

"Right," said Stinger, gulping down a fat caterpillar. "Stop messing around. We need to talk about those monkeys and what we're going to do about them."

"We're going to chase them down and massacre them," growled Worm.

"Yes. Teach them a lesson about tangling with baboons." Fly's snout twisted.

"Wait," put in Thorn. "Is that wise? We can't rush into anything."

"They bit Berry's tail off," snapped Worm. With a sly glance at Stinger, she added, "Doesn't that bother you, Thorn?"

"I'm furious about what they did to Berry!" he retorted angrily. "And the others! But we've seen how dangerous the monkeys are."

"And there are an awful lot of them," said Frog. "I agree with Thorn."

"And so, as it happens, do I." Stinger stared through narrowed eyes at Worm, who flinched in surprise.

"I don't understand. . . ." Fly licked his jaws. "Stinger, don't you want to get revenge?"

"I *want* to," said Stinger. "I want to punish the monkeys just as much as you brave baboons, and I'm grateful that you want to avenge my daughter." He picked at his teeth. "But Bravelands has a Great Father for a reason."

Fly, Grass, Worm, and Fang gaped at him.

"But, Stinger—" yelped Fang.

"We can't let them get away with this," growled Worm.

"What would that rhino know about this?" whined Fly.

Stinger turned to him with a glare that froze him to silence, and Fly bit nervously on his lip. Frog looked shocked to the bone.

"Sorry," muttered Fly.

"Quiet, all of you." Stinger held up a paw. "And *never* let me hear you question the Great Parent again. We are better than the monkeys. Do not *ever* forget that." He shot another withering glance at Fly. "We will go to our Great Father, and we shall ask him for justice."

"Stinger Crownleaf! A word, if I may!"

As old Beetle Highleaf hobbled forward, the Strongbranches turned to stare. The grizzled baboon was huffing and puffing as he stopped in front of Stinger, his jaw working in agitation.

"Speak, dear Beetle." Stinger extended an encouraging paw.

"I am here to represent the Council, Stinger," said Beetle. "I must make that clear first, because there has been a meeting in your absence. While you were, er . . . busy."

"A meeting?" asked Stinger silkily. "In my absence?"

"Yes, indeed. Well, you know, the Council rules do allow for such a thing." Beetle scratched nervously at his neck fur. "There was some, ah—concern. About the way the troop is being run."

"Go on, my wise friend." Stinger dipped his head.

Beetle seemed more sure of himself now. He nodded back politely at Stinger. "Some baboons are not happy, Stinger. You see, there's a feeling that the Strongbranches are perhaps— well, throwing their weight around a little."

"My Strongbranches?" Stinger looked wounded. "But their purpose is to protect the troop, not to harm it."

"Just so, just so. But there's been a tendency to, shall we say—to tell the other ranks what to do. To take the best food for themselves. It doesn't seem entirely proper."

Stinger nodded thoughtfully. "I appreciate your coming to me, Beetle. My Strongbranches do need to keep their strength up, of course, but I have made it very clear to them that they are here to serve the troop, not to command it."

Grass opened his mouth as if to contradict him, and Thorn distinctly saw Stinger elbow him in the chest.

"Good, good." Beetle looked relieved. "Perhaps a little reminder would be appropriate, Stinger? Just to make sure the ways of the troop are respected?" He glanced nervously at Worm and Fly. "After all, it's a very new idea. There were no Strongbranches in my day."

"Quite." Stinger gave him a broad smile, his fangs exposed. "I am glad you brought this up, and I'll deal with it straightaway. Grass, Fly: go with Beetle, please. Take him outside the den where you can discuss this properly, will you?"

Grass grinned, and Fly jumped to his feet. Beetle's eyes shot from one to the other. "Well, indeed, I—"

"Come along, old baboon," said Grass, taking his arm. Fly seized the other, and they began to march him away.

Uh-oh. Thorn leaped to his paws, ready to follow as Grass and Fly escorted Beetle swiftly from the cave. But he felt claws grip his shoulder and dig in.

"Now, Thorn, what did I tell you?" Stinger smiled into his eyes as he pushed him firmly back down. "You need to eat so you can be a good Strongbranch. Carry on with your meal, please."

Thorn swallowed. Stinger's eyes were locked on his, and he was still wearing that brilliant, intimidating grin.

Defeated, Thorn went limp. He picked up a fig and tried to chew on it, though it tasted like dust. Frog caught his gaze; she looked deeply disturbed.

As he forced the fig into his mouth, piece by tasteless piece, Thorn strained his ears, but no sound reached him from beyond the tunnel. Whatever was happening outside, it was drowned out by the wailing howls of the wind.

Great Father stood on the wind-scoured bank of the watering hole, his thick gray legs stained up to the knees with mud. His tail flicked impatiently as three golden-brown gazelles pleaded with him.

"Titanpride has been slaughtering our kind, and the grass-eaters all across Bravelands," said the tallest gazelle, tossing his slender horns in agitation. "They're not killing to survive— they aren't even eating those they kill!"

"We've lost so many of our herd," added a sorrowful female. "And the worst of it is, they've just left them for the vultures."

"It's against the Code," said the first gazelle. "Great Father, we need you to intervene." Waiting with Stinger and the Strongbranches for their own audience with the Great Father, Thorn listened apprehensively. What the gazelles were saying sounded exactly like what had happened to Sleekfriend. Titan was developing an unnerving hunting pattern.

"What should we do, Great Father?" The third gazelle spoke up, her huge dark eyes pleading. "Our herd won't survive if this goes on."

Stronghide grunted. He raised his horn, his small dark eyes searching the sky. "Let me think," he said ponderously. For a moment he stirred the drying mud with a huge foot. Then he flicked his tail across his rump, and his two oxpeckers rose into the air, twittering.

Flaring his top lip, Stronghide made a few peculiar chirping noises back at them. "Yes, my friends," he rumbled. One of the oxpeckers darted down to pull a tick from the Great Father's ear, swallowed it, and trilled noisily.

"My bird advisers say you're telling the truth," declared Stronghide with a decisive nod. "Titanpride is killing too many of the grass-eaters."

The gazelles brightened, exchanging eager glances.

"So, Great Father, what should we do?" asked their leader.

Stronghide raised his horn again and stamped one foot on the mud. "Fight."

The gazelles stared at him for a wordless moment. Their leader swallowed hard.

"I'm sorry, Great Father," the small female said at last, very politely. "We don't quite understand."

Neither did Thorn. He gaped at Great Father, longing to shout out a protest. *How can gazelles fight lions?*

It wasn't just him and the gazelles: even the other Strongbranches seemed perplexed. Fly and Grass stared at each other in puzzlement, while Frog shifted uneasily on her paws. Only

Stinger's face remained perfectly composed.

"We . . ." The tall gazelle flicked his ears and stamped a hind hoof. "We can't fight lions, Great Father."

"You've got horns, haven't you?" Stronghide tilted his head, frowning. "You've got hooves, yes? You outnumber the lions by about a hundred to one, don't you?"

"But—"

"My advice is final," Stronghide grunted. "Go and fight."

The gazelles hesitated, sharing fearful glances. At last they turned and trudged away, their horns bowed into the gale. They looked defeated and despairing—and little wonder, thought Thorn. If they followed Great Father's advice, they'd be slaughtered.

Great Father looked rather pleased with himself. He turned to the other members of his crash, who milled on either side of him, seeming slightly bored.

"This Great Father business is hard work," grunted Stronghide. "But very rewarding, very satisfying indeed. Now who's next? Ah, yes," he intoned grandly. "Baboons of Brightforest Troop, bring me your problem, and I shall solve it!"

Stinger loped forward, the wind rippling his fur. "Great Father, the baboons of Brightforest Troop come to you for guidance," he said, bowing his head respectfully.

"And guidance you shall have," declared Stronghide, glancing around for his crash's approval; they nodded their horns in encouragement.

Stinger cleared his throat politely. "A monkey troop raided our territory," he told the rhino. A shadow passed over his face. "And a day ago, they attacked my own daughter, Berry. There was no provocation, no reason for them to do this." His voice faltered and cracked. "She may die."

Thorn flinched, picturing Berry, limp on her bed of leaves. Stronghide was pawing at the mud again, leaving deep scrapes. The oxpeckers had settled on his rump, and they twittered constantly to each other, but he didn't appear to be listening to them this time.

"Be like the rhinos," he grunted at last. "Fight the monkeys."

The Strongbranches stared at him. Grass's big shoulders shook, as if he were trying not to explode in derisive laughter. Through stifled gasps, he mumbled, "This has got to be a joke."

"He's telling everyone the same thing," hissed Fly. "He'll make the meerkats take on the hippos next."

Stinger shot them a withering look, and they fell silent. "Thank you, Great Father," Stinger said, bowing low. "Your wisdom signals the Great Spirit within you, and we will abide by it."

He strutted away from the watering hole, Thorn and the others trailing behind. Grass and Worm were giggling together, whispering sarcastic remarks about the rhino. Fly and Fang simply looked confused. For once, Thorn was on their side.

He and Frog padded in silence, side by side, until they were almost back at the escarpment. Still unnerved by the Great Father's nonsensical advice, Thorn finally glanced at Frog.

She looked shaken to her core.

"Are you all right?" he murmured.

"Thorn." She turned her agonized face to him. "Stinger's wrong. How can that have signaled the Great Spirit inside Stronghide? It wasn't wisdom at all!"

"He's new to the job," said Thorn doubtfully.

"The Great Spirit inspires every Great Parent," she told him, raising her eyes respectfully skyward. "What comes from the Spirit is *always* wise. I'm worried." She sounded choked with emotion. "Thorn, I don't think that rhino is the true Great Father."

Thorn swallowed and glanced at their Crownleaf, stalking ahead of them. Only Stinger, as usual, seemed to take the rhino's behavior in stride. *Nothing rattles him*, Thorn thought with frustration. *He always has an angle. He always has a plan.*

At the crest of a low rise, Stinger halted and turned to his Strongbranches. He did not look at all displeased with the advice Stronghide had given him.

"Fly, go back to the den," Stinger ordered him, "and tell every baboon who can fight to meet us on the far side of the stream." Fly loped off, and Stinger smiled at the others, pointing a paw toward the plain. "Everyone else, come with me. We'll head straight for the acacia woodland. That's where the little brutes are, most of the time."

"We're going after the monkeys?" asked Fang eagerly.

"That is what the Great Father has counseled. Be warned: the trees there are not dense. It won't be possible to sneak through them without being seen." Stinger dusted his paws in satisfaction. "So we will conceal ourselves by the stream that runs along the southern edge and wait for Fly's reinforcements."

To Thorn it sounded as though Stinger's plans were remarkably detailed already. He didn't dare even look at Frog, but he was aware of her tension as she walked ahead of him. Fang, Worm, and Grass were garrulous as they approached the woodland and eventually had to be hushed by an irritated Stinger, but Frog and Thorn were quiet, each wrapped in their own worries.

The sound of a running stream roused Thorn from his reverie. Here, just a little way from the thick belt of trees, the earth seemed much drier and sandier than at Tall Trees. There were the acacias, their crowns blending into one another to create a flat canopy, but he could barely see any fruit trees dotted among them. He wasn't surprised the monkeys had tried to steal the baboons' territory.

Stinger had halted by the stream; he signaled to them all to crouch low. If anything, the wind was even stronger; dry sand and red dust whipped around them. Thorn could feel it working into his fur, right down to his skin; there was grit between his fingers and toes. And his eyes stung badly; he rubbed them with a frustrated paw, which only made it worse.

There was the sound of pattering pawsteps behind them, and Fly appeared, leading every Highleaf and Middleleaf well enough to fight. It was unusual for Lowleaves and Deeproots to join a battle, but Fly had brought a few of them, too; it made sense, Thorn conceded. Brightforest Troop's fighting strength was short right now, after the disaster of the falling tree. And besides, he couldn't help his heart lifting when he spotted Mud. He raised a paw in grateful greeting and his small friend nodded, his large eyes scared but serious.

They all want to fight for Berry, Thorn thought, his chest tight.

With a bark of summons, Stinger drew himself up and strode forward. His fighters fell in behind him; Thorn was sure his was not the only heart that was beating hard and fast as they crossed the line into the trees.

Almost at once, shrieks and cackles of alarm filled the air. The monkeys had been nowhere in sight; now they swung and bounded from tree to tree, rattling the foliage, screaming out warnings.

"Baboons!"

"Filthy baboons!"

"Spite, we're under attack!"

Long acacia seed pods and broken twigs pelted down onto the baboons. A pod clipped Thorn's shoulder, and he stifled an angry yelp of pain as he marched staunchly on with the others.

"Stupid, smelly baboons!" a monkey shrieked from a branch, baring her small fangs. "Get out!"

"We'll peel your hides off!" screamed another, leaping to scratch at a Deeproot before scuttling back up a tree.

The acacias thinned even more toward the center of the woodland; the baboons emerged into a broad clearing to find the monkeys' leader waiting for them. Thorn's hackles sprang

up at the sight of him; the big brute was instantly recogniz-
able, his white-fringed black face contorted with malice and
resentment.

Stinger halted and rose onto his hind legs. His calm voice
resounded with determination.

"I am Stinger Crownleaf," he said, "and I come here for
vengeance."

The leader rose up too; he was huge for a vervet, bigger
even than some of the baboons.

"I am Spite Cleanfur," he snarled, "and you are a fool to
enter my territory."

"Then I am a fool who will shortly have his revenge,"
Stinger said evenly. His eyes were as cool as a night wind.
"You, Spite Cleanfur, almost killed my daughter. Now you
and your troop will pay."

Spite peeled back his muzzle from his fangs, threw back his
head—and laughed. The monkeys in the trees instantly joined
in, and the air was filled with raucous, ear-shattering hilarity.

Thorn's paws clenched, but Stinger ignored the laughter.
"The Great Spirit is on our side," he said. "Great Father told
us to fight you. Get ready to lose."

Spite smirked. "You've made a big mistake, Crownleaf.
You're in *our* territory, remember, and we've never lost a battle
here."

Stinger waved a paw dismissively. "Oh, I'm not looking for
a battle."

Thorn started in surprise. The other baboons murmured

in confusion. Why were they here, then?

Spite frowned. "You don't want to fight?"

"I didn't say that." Stinger rubbed his scar. "But a blood-bath is pointless. No matter who wins, both our troops would be weakened. In these troubled times, that would be foolish."

Spite's face furrowed. He curled his long tail around a branch and nodded. "So what do you propose?"

"A duel." Stinger spread his paws. "One baboon, one monkey, one fight. It'll be clear who's won and who's lost. The losing troop stays away from the winner."

Spite smirked, baring his short fangs. "An interesting idea. But I need to discuss it with my band."

Uncoiling his tail, he leaped onto the neighboring tree and clambered up into its crown. From the host of monkeys who circled the glade, individuals began to peel off and follow Spite, leaping into his tree and scrambling up after him. *That's his equivalent of our Council*, Thorn supposed. Half hidden by the foliage, the monkeys were chattering rapidly. From the high-pitched jabbering, all Thorn heard was "risky" and "worth it" and "fools."

At last Spite emerged from his council, his face hard and satisfied, and swung down to the ground. He punched his fists into the sandy earth and fixed his cold stare on Stinger.

"We agree to your terms."

Stinger nodded. "Sensible," he drawled. "Pick your best and strongest monkey. You'll need him."

"He is already chosen," said Spite with a slow grin. "Step forward, Sneer Grayfur."

The monkey who dropped to the ground was even bigger than his leader. He was, thought Thorn with a dry gulp, the biggest vervet he'd ever seen. The monkey's ridged brow was broad, and his muscular shoulders even thicker; his eyes glittered darkly. His fur was marked with the scars of dozens of fights. Sneer flexed his powerful arms, and his muzzle split in a grin.

In silence, the baboons stared at him. At last, Frog turned to Stinger, her eyes fierce.

"I'll fight him," she muttered. "I'm the biggest Strongbranch. I can take this brute."

"Go, Frog!" whispered Fly, looking more than a little relieved. "Beat him to pulp!"

"Wait." Stinger was still scratching at his scar, and his eyes were locked thoughtfully on Sneer Grayfur.

Taken aback, Thorn and the other Strongbranches glanced at him. For another agonizing moment, the Crownleaf remained lost in contemplation. Then he turned to them.

"This fight belongs to Thorn Middleleaf," he told them brusquely. "It can be his Strongfeat."

Thorn thought he'd misheard. He blinked at Stinger.

Then Frog blurted, "But Stinger, you can't mean it!"

"*Him?*" exclaimed Worm in disbelief.

The whole troop was staring at Thorn now, and he tried not to shake. Now that it had sunk in, he knew exactly what was going through Stinger's mind. This could not end badly for the Crownleaf. In the unlikely event that Thorn won the fight, Berry would be avenged. If he didn't—Thorn shot a glance at Sneer Grayfur and swallowed hard—then Stinger was free of him. He'd never have to worry again about Thorn exposing his crimes.

"Stinger, please," Frog was begging the Crownleaf. "Let me do this. I know I can win."

"No, Frog." Stinger patted her shoulder, at the same time pushing her firmly backward. "Thorn is many things, but he is not a coward. Are you, Thorn Middleleaf?"

His amber eyes glinted gold, and the tiniest smile quirked at the corner of his mouth. Thorn knew there was no way out. Turning toward the monkeys, he paced forward with as much bravado as he could summon.

Sneer Grayfur bared his fangs and reared up onto his hind legs, towering above him. Thorn gritted his jaws and bunched his shoulder muscles.

How can I possibly beat that?

CHAPTER 14

In the dappled shadow, Thorn and Sneer Grayfur prowled around each other. The dueling ground was silent but for the moan and rush of the wind in the acacias; the baboons had withdrawn into a tense semicircle at the edge of the clearing, while the monkeys craned from the branches, eyes glinting with bloodthirsty excitement. His stare never leaving Sneer, Thorn tensed his muscles, waiting for an opportunity to spring.

Sneer looked lithe for a monkey of his size and power. His rangy body moved fluidly, and he still wore that confident smirk. *Maybe too confident?* Gulping in a breath, Thorn twisted suddenly and flew at him, but Sneer ducked and darted out of reach.

In the treetops, Sneer's troop-mates shook the branches and jeered. "Too slow, baboon!"

At that, the whole clearing erupted with rival hoots and screeches. Brightforest Troop pounded their fists on the ground, drawing their lips back and chattering to drown the monkeys out. "Get him, Thorn!" he heard Notch whoop.

Thorn lunged again, but this time Sneer feinted and came in low, smashing into Thorn's belly. The breath knocked out of him, Thorn was flung back, and Sneer leaped to straddle him, his claws raking. Thorn felt them dig deep into his flank, and shock was replaced by searing pain. He howled, kicking out and squirming, and somehow wriggled away from the huge monkey. Panting, he twisted sharply, scrabbling backward. Sneer was still advancing, his fangs bared.

The big monkey drove him back into the circle of baboons, who drew away hurriedly. Thorn had a momentary glimpse of Mud's terrified face before he focused all his attention on Sneer once again.

"Thorn, fight!" came his friend's desperate voice.

I'm trying, Mud. Clenching his jaws, he rolled out of reach of Sneer's lunge and jumped to his feet. Sneer's fangs closed on his tail, and as Thorn whipped it away, he saw blood spatter the dust.

"Watch that tail," Spite Cleanfur taunted from the trees. "Don't be like your pretty friend. Tails are tasty and fresh!"

Infuriated, Thorn flexed his claws. As Sneer stalked closer, he ducked and flung himself forward, slamming into the big monkey's chest. Taken by surprise, Sneer fell backward and Thorn pressed his attack, clawing and biting. Sneer twisted beneath him, wiry and strong; Thorn knew he couldn't keep him pinned for much longer. He could feel Sneer's claws tearing at his shoulders even as the brute squirmed, and those vicious jaws caught the sensitive edge of his snout, shooting a bolt of pain across his face. Thorn got in two more scratches and a bite on Sneer's neck; then, with a massive heave, Sneer threw him off.

Sneer Grayfur got to his feet, touching his neck with a paw. It came away bloody. The big monkey curled his muzzle in a grin of malice.

Great, thought Thorn, his breath rasping painfully. *All I've done is make him mad.*

Thorn was bleeding too. He didn't dare look down at his smarting limbs and tail. It was obvious now; Stinger's double strategy was going to go the worst way for Thorn. Windblown dust whirled, stinging his eyes, and he blinked hard. *I'm sorry, Berry. So sorry.*

"Finish him!" Fly howled, and for a moment Thorn felt so dazed he didn't know which of them he was talking about. "Finish him, Thorn!" Sneer was advancing again, his four legs stiff with menace.

"Thorn!" Mud's screech was hoarse with terror.

Above and around the clearing, the wind had risen even more, making the acacia crowns whip violently. It seemed appropriate weather to die in. More blood dripped from Thorn's shoulders, but as soon as it hit the ocher earth, the gusting wind obliterated it with dust.

The wind . . .

Thorn's head jerked up to see Sneer advancing for his

final lethal assault. He dodged and darted sideways, bolting
upwind.

"He's on the run!" screeched the monkeys. "Sneer! Sneer!
Kill him!"

Sneer gave a growl of mockery and twisted to follow. Thorn
waited, his heart pounding. The huge monkey was only a tail-
length away when Thorn dug his claws into the gritty earth
and tore up a great billow of dust. The wind caught it and
hurled it into Sneer's face.

Sneer Grayfur gave a howl of pain and reared up, clutching
at his eyes. Thorn couldn't afford to hesitate. He barreled into
the monkey's exposed belly, knocking him to the ground, and
there was a hideous cracking sound.

Sneer's skull had hit a stone. A low moan of pain gurgled
from his throat as he clawed at his eyes; blood had begun to
trickle from a spot behind his ear. Desperate, Thorn shoved
him to the side and wrenched the blood-spattered stone from
the earth. Without pausing to think, he smashed it hard down
onto the monkey's head.

His heartbeat throbbed so loudly in his ears, it was as if the
whole world had gone silent. Thorn panted hard, poised above
Sneer's limp corpse, terrified he would suddenly leap up and
fasten those bloodstained fangs in his throat.

But Sneer Grayfur didn't move. Sand and grit blustered
across his body. *Only kill to survive,* Thorn told himself through
the ringing in his ears. And if not for that rock, he'd be dead
in the monkey's place. *Thank you, Great Spirit.*

"Well." Stinger's voice broke the silence, and Thorn couldn't help hearing a note of resignation in it. "That settles that."

Spite Cleanfur was staring at his dead champion, his lips peeled back from his fangs in disbelief. He raised his glittering eyes to the baboons.

"Thornwood Troop," he screamed. *"Attack!"*

"Now, wait a minute—" Even Stinger sounded surprised.

Monkeys poured from the trees like ants swarming from their nest. There were scores of them, far more than had shown themselves before, covering the tree trunks so thickly they looked like rippling moss. Thorn scrambled toward his troop, but the monkeys were already upon him. Small, strong bodies pushed him down into the dirt, tearing at his skin. Something heavy slammed into him, and there was a moment of piercing pain. A monkey had landed on his back, Thorn realized; it dug its teeth into his neck. Flailing, he shook it off.

"Thorn!" From under the mass of monkeys, he heard Mud's scream. The baboons were rushing into battle, fangs flashing. Thorn was released as the monkeys spun to meet them, and he staggered to his feet.

Notch swung a sturdy branch, striking monkeys left and right, and Fly bit and tore with his chipped teeth. Frog was fighting her way through a mass of greenish fur, sending monkeys flying. But the baboons were heavily outnumbered. A big monkey had its long arms twisted around Mud's neck. Another monkey leaped, and Mud crumpled, disappearing beneath scratching, biting furies.

"Get off him!" With one blow, Thorn sent a sharp-faced monkey tumbling head over tail off his friend. Knocking another to the ground, he dragged the wounded, shaking Mud to his feet.

"Fall back!" Stinger's command rang out across the chaotic battle. "Brightforest Troop, *fall back!*"

Thorn slashed at a monkey blocking his path. Dragging Mud along with him, he scrambled through the acacias after the rest of the fleeing troop. Monkeys hung from the branches above the retreating baboons, hooting and jeering, flinging nuts and twigs.

"Run away, long-snouts!"

"Cowards!"

Limping across the grassland, hauling their wounded, Brightforest Troop straggled back toward their temporary den. Even though it stank of death and hyenas, even though it was dank and sodden, Thorn had never been so glad to see its yawning entrance. One by one, the baboons crept into its shelter. Thorn sagged with relief as he shepherded Mud inside.

Gently, Mud pushed him away. "I'm all right," he said. "You're more hurt than I am. It's just a few scratches. You'd better go join Stinger."

Thorn gave a shaky nod. Only now was he beginning to feel the true pain of his wounds. With a last reassuring hug from Mud, he limped across to the other Strongbranches.

"Ah! Our champion!" Stinger clapped his paws together as Thorn approached, and the other Strongbranches turned to stare. Frog's eyes shone.

"Congratulations, Thorn Strongbranch!" Stinger went on. "Your victory is one thing we can celebrate today. We are all proud of you! I knew you had the brains to beat that thug of a monkey."

Thorn was too exhausted to do anything but nod. He wasn't sure *Thorn Strongbranch* was a name to be proud of.

"You are truly one of us now. You'll do anything to defend our troop, won't you?" Stinger slapped an arm across his back and squeezed his shoulders.

Thorn flinched with pain and shuddered. "Yes, Stinger," he managed to mumble.

"Fly did a great job," said Worm. "Those teeth may not be the prettiest, but by the Great Spirit, they're effective."

Fly puffed up with pride and exposed his chipped fangs. "Stinger, did you see how Worm pummeled that monkey's face into the dirt?"

"We're the Strongbranches, and we whip monkey-tail!" bellowed Fang, slapping the ground.

"We did all right," murmured Frog, "though there were too many of them. We can't be complacent."

"Well," said Worm with a shrug, "you did fine, Frog, but some of the others from the troop were just make-weight. Mud Lowleaf was useless."

"Waste of space," sneered Grass. "I don't know why he came."

"Thorn had to save him," said Fly, shooting an ingratiating glance in his direction.

Thorn glared at him. "That's just not true," he lied. "Mud got in some good hits. Why don't you worry about your own performance, Grass?"

Grass glared back, but the conversation was interrupted by other baboons who crept forward to reassure the Strong-branches about their own achievements. Notch was tugging on Grass's fur, telling him about his prowess with the branch; Moss was reenacting her battle with three monkeys.

Frog edged to Thorn's side. "Grass is just jealous," she whispered. "You were wonderful, Thorn! I was so afraid you'd lose. I mean . . . I was scared for the troop, of course. But mostly for you."

"I was scared for a while myself," Thorn told her, trying to keep his voice lighthearted.

She touched his scratched and bleeding arms and gazed down into his eyes. "I hope they don't hurt too much," she murmured.

"Frog . . ." Very gently, Thorn drew his arm away. "Listen, I . . . I'm sorry." He bit his lip. "I like you, I really do. A lot. But I'm in love with someone else."

The change in her eyes struck his heart; she looked desolate. "Oh. Thorn, I'm sorry. I didn't mean to . . ." She swallowed hard and backed away. "I understand."

He'd hurt her again. Thorn's stomach twisted with remorse. *It's all I seem to do to my friends these days.*

Gathering herself, she gave him a smile, one that was a little forced. "Can we still talk, though? There's something I need to tell you."

"Of course," he said. "What's happened, Frog?"

She was solemn again, her brow furrowed. "I've been back

there," she whispered. "To Great Mother's body. And I found something strange."

He watched her intently. "What?"

"I can't explain. Will you come with me and see?" Her eyes slanted away. "I promise I won't make it awkward."

"Frog, of course I'll come," he assured her. About to squeeze her arm, he restrained himself. "But we'd better be careful. I don't think we want anyone else to see us."

"No." She nodded in agreement. "But this can't wait, Thorn. We need to go soon."

CHAPTER 15

Sky's legs trembled, but she held her head high as she faced the rhino down. She was all too aware of the narrowness of the rocky pass. If the rhino chose to charge, Sky had nowhere to run. At least Moon was already heading for the Plain of Our Ancestors; she would block the rhino long enough for him to get there, and perhaps find a hiding place among the protecting bones of his forebears.

She won't get near him unless it's over my body.

The wind howled through the ravine, dislodging scree and grit that swirled in flurries into Sky's ears and the folds of her hide. She ignored its sting, fixing her stare on the deep-set black eyes of the rhino. She looked young, thought Sky, and not nearly as dangerous as Stronghide. But she was still a rhino, and rhinos were not to be underestimated.

"You've been following us all day." Sky spread her ears wide in fierce challenge. "What do you *want?*"

To her surprise, the rhino lowered her eyes and shifted from hoof to thick hoof. Now that her posture was meek, she seemed small standing among the vast walls of rock.

Sky lowered her trunk. This wasn't what she'd expected at all. It felt like facing an equal, not an enemy.

"I just . . ." the rhinoceros mumbled, and hesitated. "I wanted to ask you something."

"Ask us . . . ?" Sky's ears flapped in confusion. "We thought you were . . . going to attack."

The rhino flinched. "No! I wouldn't do that."

"Oh," said Sky lamely. The angry determination was draining from her muscles.

"I didn't mean to worry you," said the rhino, her top lip working anxiously. "I was following you because I guessed where you were going." She swallowed and looked up. "I know this place is sacred to the elephants. I know how special it is to you, but please—may I go there?"

Sky let her ears relax. She had never seen or heard of another animal venturing onto the Plain, but neither had she heard of a rule against it. She paused, playing for time. "Why?"

The young rhino glanced away. For long moments, she stared at the rock walls, her throat jerking. At last she said hoarsely, "I did something bad. Don't ask me what, please. I can't tell you what, but I'm so sorry about it." She swallowed hard. "I hoped that maybe . . . maybe, if I visit the bones of the Great Parents, I can start to make up for it."

Sky's heart warmed with instinctive sympathy. "That's a

good idea," she said gently. "Whatever's happened, whatever's gone wrong, being on the Plain always helps."

The rhino visibly sagged with relief. "Thank you, uh . . . ?"

"I'm Sky," Sky told her. "Sky of the Strider family."

"Thank you, Sky Strider. My name's Silverhorn."

"I'm glad to meet you, Silverhorn." Sky realized with surprise that it was true. "Come on, follow me. It isn't far."

Her heart much lighter, Sky led the rhino up the last stretch of the pass and over the crest. The walls of the valley opened out before them, and she heard Silverhorn take a sharp breath of wonder.

Side by side, the new companions walked forward onto the broad sweep of the grassy plain. Almost at once, the wind dropped. Clouds still raced overhead, but here on the Plain the lush grass rustled in a warm and gentle breeze, and delicate flowers bloomed undisturbed. Instead of the howl of the gales, there was only birdsong and the hum of bees.

Sky took a deep breath of the scented air. It was so peaceful here, despite—or maybe because of—the sun-bleached bones scattered through the grass.

Silverhorn tilted her horn, gazing in awe. "It's so beautiful," she murmured, her voice trembling with reverence. "The bones . . . there are so many. Are those the Great Parents?"

"Not just the Great Parents," Sky said softly. "When an elephant knows they're going to die, they make the journey to the Plain. If they can't come, their family carries their bones. We come here to remember all the elephants who have gone."

"Oh," whispered Silverhorn. Her eyes lingered on a skeleton

nearby, its tusks jutting skyward. "Rhinos don't have this tradition. It must be . . . nice."

"It is." Sky's gaze roamed the valley. "And it's safe here. Ah, Moon, there you are!"

In the shadows at the edge of the meadow, her little cousin waited, sucking nervously on the tip of his trunk. His gaze was riveted on the rhino. Sky beckoned, and at last he crept toward them. Sky reached out her trunk to draw him closer.

"It's okay, Moon," she said, stroking his ears. "This is Silverhorn. She didn't mean to scare us. She just wants to visit the Great Parents." She turned to the rhino. "This is my cousin, Moon."

"I'm very pleased to meet you, Moon." Silverhorn bowed her horn.

Moon started, his eyes widening, but recovered his nerve. He dipped his head awkwardly, then wandered a little way away, peeking up through his eyelashes at Silverhorn.

"He'll get used to you," Sky whispered.

"I hope so," said Silverhorn wistfully. "I'm sorry I scared him."

Still holding carefully to Great Mother's tusk shard, Sky gestured with her trunk to the calodendrum in the center of the plateau. Its wide canopy was in bloom, its long green leaves almost hidden by clusters of pink. "Do you see those blossoms, Silverhorn? That's the Mother Tree. The bones of all the Great Parents lie beneath it. When my family travels here again, we'll bring Great Mother's bones, too, so that they can rest with the others." *Great Mother's bones . . .* Sky caught her breath at the thought and blinked hard. "Why don't you visit them now?"

Silverhorn nodded. She stared at the tree for a moment, then shambled toward it, her horn dipped in respect. Moon was still watching her; he had retreated once more to the shelter of the rock walls.

Carefully Sky placed Great Mother's tusk fragment on the grass. "I'll be right back, I promise," she whispered. "I know you'll understand. I want to see my mother."

The skeleton she longed to see again was at the very edge of the plateau. Grass studded with delicate violets had grown over the bones, but not high enough to conceal the great skull and spine. Sky parted the grass gently with her trunk, exposing her mother's bleached white ribs.

"I'm back," she said softly. "I'm sure you didn't expect me so soon."

Her own bones ached with sorrow. It had been a long time since her mother had been killed by lions—Sky had been very small then—but she still missed her fiercely. She imagined she always would.

"Mother," she whispered, "I need your help. The family thinks I'm Great Mother, but I know I'm not. I don't know what to do."

Despite her longing, Sky hesitated. The last time she had touched her mother's bones, expecting a beautiful memory, she had instead been shown a terrible vision: a burning red landscape, a watering hole turned to blood, Bravelands lurid and distorted. Striding through the ominous flaming colors had come a huge lion and, riding on its back, a sinister, evil-faced baboon. The vision had shaken her to her core.

Much later, she had learned that the twisted baboon was the murderer of Bark Crownleaf. But even now, with the vision of the bloodstained watering hole fulfilled in the worst way possible, Sky had no idea what the rest of that vision meant, or why she had been the one to see it. If she touched her mother's bones now, would she see something just as terrible? Or even worse?

There was only one way to find out. Sky took a deep, shaking breath, and laid her trunk against her mother's skull.

Grasslands stretched around her, flat and empty in every direction. No animals, no birds, just a gentle breeze stirring the sun-touched grass so that it rippled, golden and green, as far as Sky could see.

And in the center of it, straight ahead, stood a tree.

It was an acacia, but its canopy rose higher than any Sky had ever seen. She walked closer, her feet silent on the grass.

The tree's trunk rose high into the air, and, above her head, branches twisted and spread out, dark against the blue, blue sky.

Something in the silhouette of the branches seemed strange and wrong. High above her, she could make out a huge shadow. Sky creased her eyes, straining to understand.

And then she recognized it: the stocky form of a rhinoceros. It balanced there impossibly, each foot on a branch.

With a rumbling, awful shudder, the tree began to shake. Its thick branches bounced and creaked, shifting wildly below the rhino's feet. "Watch out!" Sky tried to call, but no sound came.

The rhinoceros lifted its heavy head toward the sun, oblivious to the danger. Below its feet, the branches snapped and cracked, yet the rhino stayed there still, its horn high, gazing at the white dazzle of the sun—

The vision faded. Swaying, Sky pulled away from her mother's skull.

It hadn't been as bone-chillingly terrifying as the last one, but this vision was just as confusing. Was the rhino Silverhorn? Was she in danger? *Mother, I don't understand!*

In a daze of bewilderment, Sky plodded back to collect Great Mother's tusk fragment, then carried it toward the calodendrum. Moon, emerging from his shelter by the rock face, trotted in her wake.

When Silverhorn caught sight of the two elephants, she backed respectfully away from the bones beneath the tree. Sky studied her bulky shape from the corner of her eye. The rhino in her vision had been bigger than Silverhorn, surely? But it was so hard to tell. Beating down her perplexity, Sky tried to focus on finding a place for Great Mother's tusk fragment.

"Sky, what are you doing?" Moon prodded her curiously with his trunk.

"This is why I brought Great Mother's tusk," she told him. "This is where it belongs."

There was a patch of green, soft grass between the bones of two other Great Parents; Sky parted the blades with the tip of her trunk and laid the tusk fragment there. It gleamed in the sunshine, and it seemed to Sky that it was whiter than any of the other bones around it. *Like the sun surrounded by stars.*

Whenever Sky had tried reading that shard of tusk, she'd seen nothing. Would it help that it was here now, where it belonged, among the Great Parents who had gone before her grandmother? Drawing a deep breath, Sky laid the tip of her trunk on its smooth surface.

Please, Great Mother. Tell me who the new Great Parent is. Tell me what I should do.

Nothing. The tusk might as well have been a rock or a stick.

"Did Great Mother tell you where the Great Spirit is?" asked Moon eagerly.

Silent, Sky shook her head.

Moon's voice wobbled. "But we came all this way!"

"We'll try something else," she assured him.

Maybe one of the other Great Parents could help? Sky let her gaze roam over the grass beneath the pink blossoms. Something drifted into her memory: her very first visit to the Plain of Our Ancestors, when she had been even younger than Moon. Great Mother had brought her here, and she had shown Sky something very special. . . .

There. The ancient bones were just fragments now, and Sky parted the tangled grass with a gentle touch. Over the years the tree's roots had grown and spread, coiling around the bones; one had thrust through an eye socket of the skull. The Mother Tree had made this skeleton part of the Plain itself.

"The bones of the first Great Mother," she told Moon softly.

He craned forward, then shut one eye. "They're broken."

"They're very old," Sky said. "They've been here a long, long time."

Reverently, she stroked the worn bones. *Can you hear me,*

ancient Great Mother? Sky closed her eyes tightly, hoping against hope.

And the First Great Mother heard her.

Darkness. Storm clouds and densely growing trees, their heavy boughs thrashing.

A howling wind blew back Sky's ears and drove into her face and chest, almost shoving her to her knees. Yet there was something very important up ahead, Sky knew, something she had to see. She creased her eyes against the storm and leaned into its force, battling forward.

Something was approaching, something vast and powerful that broke through the trees as if they were twigs. The ground trembled, branches cracked and snapped, and leaves tumbled down. It was a dark shape, huge and familiar and comforting, and its gaze was locked on something distant.

Joy surged through Sky. "Great Mother!"

The heavy, well-remembered head began to turn.

And then the great elephant vanished.

"Great Mother!" Sky wailed. She was abandoned, she was lost. . . .

A white light bloomed among the trees and Sky gasped. The glow of it shimmered, more beautiful than anything Sky had ever seen, and for the first time in a long while, she felt filled with peace. . . .

Until the light began to shrink.

"No," Sky whimpered. "Don't go!"

She stumbled forward. The light was changing, forming an outline of spread feathers. A bird, Sky realized: a bird with impossibly wide, shining wings—

She staggered, her knees weak with shock. She was back on the Plain, with a bright sun overhead and a gentle breeze shimmering through the grass.

"Sky?" Silverhorn trotted close, alarmed.

"What did you see?" Moon asked, grabbing her trunk with his. "What happened, Sky?"

Sky blinked, trying to collect her thoughts. "I don't know— I saw Great Mother, and a bird . . . I don't *know*," she exclaimed in desperation. "Maybe the Great Spirit is in the air some- where? Looking for the right Great Parent?"

Before either Moon or Silverhorn could reply, a harsh call split the sky, echoing from the rock walls. A shadow swept across the grass with the breeze.

"A bird!" Moon cried. "Like you saw, Sky! It's a good sign, isn't it?"

Sky stared up, her heart swelling with hope. But as the bird spiraled down out of the sun's dazzle, Sky's throat grew tight with fear. It was a vulture—an eater of the dead.

The vulture screeched in Skytongue as she circled, sending a shiver along Sky's spine. The bird was not beautiful. Her wings were vast and black, her face wrinkled and wattled, and her long neck was almost bald. The three companions flinched as she angled her broad wings and swooped down beneath the calodendrum.

She took a lurching hop through the grass, and her talons raked the ground. With a cry of triumph, she seized the shard of Great Mother's tusk.

"No!" Sky cried, lunging forward. "No! Please don't take it!"

Ignoring her, the vulture flapped up into the sky. Out of Sky's frantic reach, she swept over their heads, then soared above the narrow pass of the Plain's entrance. As Sky sobbed with frustration, the bird gave another harsh scream, then circled once again.

"She's stolen her!" trumpeted Moon, galloping back and forth, his trunk swinging with fury. "She's stolen Great Mother!"

"But why?" Silverhorn's black eyes were angry. "Sky, why would a bird do that?"

Sky was immobile, staring up at the vulture. Her heart turned over. *Why would a bird do that?*

And she realized she already knew.

"We have to follow her!"

CHAPTER 16

"Slash at his eyes," Titan said, pacing around a pair of tussling young lions. "Now kick him with your hind paws."

The stillness of the savannah gave an ominous atmosphere to the fight training. The wind had dropped so abruptly, it felt almost eerie. The violent gales had been replaced, in what seemed like the blink of a lion's eye, by a motionless, shimmering heat that left the young lions drained and lethargic. Even at a distance, Fearless could tell they were struggling to find their fighting vigor.

One of the lions had a pale pelt that was almost white; perhaps he wasn't suffering quite as badly as the darker-furred lions, because he found the energy to twist and slam his powerful hind legs into his opponent. The rival, whose fur was dark amber-gold, yelped and sprawled. Yielding, he flopped, panting in the dusty heat.

"Good, Forceful!" Titan growled. The pale lion tossed his patchy mane triumphantly, while his opponent slunk away. "Let's see you take on Proud."

A big young lion with a short brown mane leaped toward Forceful. Roaring, they reared up on their hind legs and crashed together.

Fearless sat with the lionesses, between Swift and Valor, his claws working in and out as he imagined joining in the fighting practice. Of course, these lions were older than him; not quite grown yet, but old enough to have left the prides of their births. He envied them the tufty manes they'd started to grow.

"I don't understand what those youngsters are doing here," Daring muttered. "Proud left the pride when Gallant was our leader. Why has Titan asked him back? And that one with the amber fur—Clever—he left ages ago too. Remember old Constant? She was their mother."

"I remember Constant," Valor murmured. "She must have hoped her sons would start prides of their own."

"That's harder than it used to be," pointed out Sly. "Forceful and the others from Dauntlesspride have been roaming Bravelands for the last few moons, and they've still not managed to establish prides. Maybe they think Titanpride will give them a better life."

Swift raised her dusty head from her paws; it seemed a massive effort for her in the broiling heat. She stared sightlessly toward the sounds of fighting. "There shouldn't be too many grown males in a pride," she said, sounding oddly wistful. "It always leads to trouble."

"That's up to Titan," Regal snapped. "If he invited them here, he must have good reason."

"That's what I'm afraid of," Swift murmured.

Forceful and Proud were struggling in close combat, their muscles straining as they bit and snarled. Fearless watched uneasily.

All the new young males looked powerful. Taking on Titan was one thing, but no matter how strong he became, Fearless couldn't fight Titan's allies too. After all, Titan wasn't exactly averse to bringing in his cronies to help him fight—he'd done just that in his duel for Gallantpride.

Ruthless, who had been stalking crickets in the long grass, flopped at Fearless's side with a grunt. Fearless butted the little cub's head. "Hot, isn't it?"

The cub opened his jaws, panting rapidly. "I almost preferred the wind."

"How are your hunting skills coming on? Catch anything?"

"A lizard," Ruthless said. "For a bit, anyway. Then it hid under a rock." He grimaced. "I don't like these new lions. Father watches them fight all the time instead of playing with me. I wish they'd go away."

"Me too," Fearless murmured.

Proud looked exhausted, swaying as if he was wilting in the heat. Forceful sprang, toppling him off-balance and sending him crashing to the ground. He whacked the side of Proud's head and straddled him. Proud stayed down, flanks heaving, tongue lolling.

"Forceful is the winner!" Titan roared. "You were named well, young one." As he grunted a summons to the new lions, Fearless counted them through the quivering heat haze: eight young males, all of them large and powerfully built.

"Titanpride is the finest in Bravelands," Titan declared. "We want only the best and strongest males as we expand our territory. While Forceful has shown himself the strongest, all of you have fought well and proved yourselves worthy."

Rising to their paws, the rest of the pride grunted their approval. Even Daring and Valor, who had been complaining about the new lions, got to their feet. *They're too afraid not to*, Fearless realized.

As if hearing his thoughts, Valor turned to glare at him, narrowing her eyes and lashing her tail. Belatedly, Fearless got the message, and he grudgingly stood up too.

Titan was still pacing haughtily before the youngsters. "There is one more demand I make." His black mane rippled over his powerful shoulders. "You must swear an oath of loyalty."

The new lions exchanged apprehensive glances as Resolute rounded them up into a line. Some of them shifted nervously; Forceful stood stiffly, his head high. There was an arrogant curl to the pale lion's muzzle that reminded Fearless of Titan himself.

Titan prowled closer, looking the young lions up and down. "By the laws of our ancestors," he roared, "I, Titan, welcome you to Titanpride. My pride will protect you and feed you, give you a home and a family. This I swear."

Resolute stared expectantly at the young males. "Respond," he grunted. "By the laws of our ancestors . . ."

"By the laws of our ancestors," they chorused in unison.

"We pledge our loyalty . . ." he went on.

They followed his prompts obediently. "We pledge our loyalty to Titanpride. We will raise no paw against Titan. We swear to protect him and his pride in all ways."

Titan had moved to face Forceful. With a quick swipe of his paw, he scratched a long bloody line across the pale lion's throat.

"My oath is given." He moved down the line, scratching the neck of each lion.

"Now you lot," growled Resolute as Titan stalked back to his dominant position.

One by one, prompted by Resolute, the young males stepped forward. Some of them trembled, but every one of them raised a paw and drew a swift claw scratch across Titan's throat.

"My oath is given," growled Forceful.

"My oath is given." That was Proud.

"My oath is given. . . ."

The heat was so oppressive, Fearless felt almost groggy; perhaps, too, it was the memory of his own oath, the one he'd had to give Titan when he was forced by circumstance to join Titanpride. He remembered all too well the longing that had surged through him: the longing to dig his claw harder and deeper, to end Titan's life then and there. It had been impossible, barely even thinkable. But he'd thought it, and he thought it again now as he watched Titan bind yet more powerful young lions to his will.

The new lions slunk back into their obedient rank; Titan surveyed his recruits, nodding with satisfaction.

"The blood oath of a lion is the most precious thing he has to give." A thin trickle of blood ran through the mane at Titan's throat and down to his chest. "Breaking an oath is shameful. Every lion in every pride turns his back on an oath-breaker. This is the way of our ancestors."

"I knew a lion once, called Bold," growled Resolute, pacing along the line of youngsters. His muzzle curled. "*Coward* would have been a more fitting name. He swore an oath to protect his leader, then refused to battle another pride because he was afraid. No lion could atone for such shame; he was driven out of the pride. He became Bold Prideless, skulking the land alone. In the end he grew so thin and weak, the hyenas finished him off." He shrugged his broad shoulders. "That's how oath-breakers die."

As one, the pride grunted in approval. "Well said, Resolute," rumbled Titan.

Despite the horror of the story, Fearless felt a little lighter on his paws. Loyal's fears must be groundless. If this was an indication of Titan's respect for oaths, he would undoubtedly keep his own vow not to kill Fearless.

Titan stretched out his forepaws, clawing the earth, his muscles flexing. The blood had stopped trickling from his oath wound, but there was still a dark clotting trail across his chest. "Today, you will honor the oath you have made to Titanpride," he told the young lions. "You have work to do. Come with me."

What kind of work? As the young males followed Titan and Resolute to the very edge of the long grass, Fearless narrowed his eyes. What was Titan talking about?

The pride dispersed, finding whatever shade they could from the dazzling glare of the sun. Swift fell asleep beneath a fever tree, her thin flanks rising and falling. Valor and the other lionesses sprawled in the dappled shadow of an acacia cluster, grooming one another. Fearless studied Titan's group at the edge of the long grass, his foreboding growing ever worse. The young lions' ears quivered as they hung on their leader's words.

Something batted at Fearless's tail, making him jump and glance around; it was little Ruthless. "I'm so *bored*," he whined. "No one will play with me."

Fearless shot another look at Titan and the young males. He got to his paws. "Lucky I know some fun games, then."

Ruthless's tail shot up. "You'll play with me? Thank you, Fearless!"

Fearless grinned. "Have you ever played Snake-in-the-Grass?"

Ruthless shook his head.

"Valor and I played it all the time when we were little," Fearless said. "One cub hides in the long grasses, keeping low, the way we do when we're sneaking up on prey. The other cub looks for them. If they find the cub who's hiding, they win, but if the hider manages to sneak up on them without being seen, *they* win."

Ruthless's tail twitched with excitement. "I'll hide first!"

"Okay," Fearless said, shutting his eyes. "I'll count a hundred heartbeats. Then I'll come find you."

"No you won't!" came Ruthless's cheerful voice, and then there was the rustle of his paws moving away through the grass.

The cub's pawsteps were clumsy and obvious, but Fearless wasn't paying attention anyway. When he opened his eyes, Ruthless was out of sight. Fearless caught his scent at once— nectar-like, from all the insects he caught—and realized he'd headed toward a clump of scrubby trees, well away from Titan and the young lions. Ignoring the cub's trail, Fearless wandered closer to Titan's group.

"Where has that tricky cub gone?" he said loudly, sniffing the air.

Behind him, he heard the long grasses quiver. *Good. He's following me.*

Fearless padded on. "I can't find the scent," he pretended to grumble. Glancing back, he saw ripples in the grass—Ruthless must be shaking with excitement. The cub was going to have to practice a lot more. . . .

Fearless turned his rump and wandered idly on.

There was a quick patter of paws and Ruthless leaped on him. "I got you! I got you!" he yowled.

Fearless threw himself down with a grunt. "Oh no! Where'd

you come from?" He tussled with the cub, rolling him over in the grass while Ruthless yelped in delight. A couple of the young males glanced up at the commotion, then, ignoring the cubs, looked self-importantly back at Titan.

"My turn now," said Fearless. Hardly able to keep still, Ruthless shut his eyes.

Fearless idled toward the lions' gathering, trying to look aimless. When he was sure no one was watching, he crouched low in the grass and slunk forward on his belly.

"Two young ones is what Daring told me," came Titan's low growl. "Traveling alone. The rhinos and elephants think they rule Bravelands, but this will teach them a lesson."

There was a rumble of agreement from the other males. Fearless stopped crawling, hardly daring to breathe. He couldn't see anything but grass and had ended up closer to the group than he'd intended. He was suddenly terrified of sneezing.

"But how could we kill an elephant?" a young male asked. "Or a rhino?"

Fearless recognized Resolute's snarl. "I thought they called you Clever? Titan said we're hunting young ones, not fully grown fighters."

"Killing zebras and gazelles is one thing," said Titan. "Any cheetah or leopard could do it. Taking down the young of the giant grass-eaters will show all Bravelands the power of Titanpride."

Fearless clenched his jaws and curled his tail tight against his rump to stop it from thrashing. Lions might not follow the Great Spirit, the way the baboons had taught Fearless, but they did live by the Code. Titan was already a Codebreaker; now he was planning to tear the Code apart like a piece of meat.

By killing young ones . . .

Sky, thought Fearless in sudden horror. The wise young elephant had been kind and friendly, and she had helped him when he'd met with Great Mother. Now, if Titan had his way, she'd be dead.

He wriggled backward through the high grasses, putting distance between himself and Titan's lions. He had gotten a little distance away when paws landed on his back. Fearless froze, his heart leaping into his throat.

"Found you!" Ruthless yowled triumphantly.

Panting with relief, Fearless rolled the little cub over in the grass. "Good job," he said. Glancing back at Titan and the others, he caught Resolute's eye. The big lion stared at him for a long moment, and Fearless's skin prickled. Had he realized Fearless was listening?

But Ruthless squirmed out from under Fearless's paws and hopped onto his back again, squealing with excitement. Resolute rolled his eyes and turned back to the others.

Ignoring Ruthless's pleas for more games, Fearless made his way back to the rest of the pride. He thought of the rhinos and elephants who were right now grazing in peace at the watering hole, oblivious to Titan's plans.

I have to warn them.

* * *

"Are you sure about this?" Valor halted, panting in the heat.

"Of course I am," growled Fearless.

Valor glanced nervously at the lionesses padding ahead. She and Fearless had dropped to the back of the hunting party so they could talk without being overheard, but Regal or Daring might turn at any moment.

"You'd better go, then." Valor gave a sigh of resignation. "If anyone asks, I'll say you've taken off after a new scent. Try to bring some prey when you come back."

Fearless rubbed his cheek against his sister's. "Thanks for helping."

"Good luck," Valor whispered, glancing toward the other lionesses again. "And for our mother's sake, *be careful.*"

Staying low, Fearless ran at a long, loping pace away from the hunting party. When he emerged from the long grass, the land dipped and stretched out before him, its yellow grass spreading nearly to the horizon. The acacias were few and far between; there was a large copse of them in the distance that Fearless wished was closer. He was going to need shelter, not just from the blazing sun but from his own pride.

Now that he was out of their sight, he picked up speed and bolted, panting, the hot air drying his tongue. His head swam with the glare, but urgency pulsed through him like a second heartbeat, and he didn't dare slow down.

It felt like an endless, grim run, the land shimmering around him until he was no longer sure it was staying where it ought to be. Dizzily, he wondered if Bravelands itself was against him. Perhaps he would run across this broiling expanse forever and never reach the watering hole.

He was on the point of collapsing into a panting, sprawling mess when he spotted, not far ahead, the hill from which he and Valor had watched the Great Gathering. Fearless sagged with relief as he bounded over the kopje and plodded up the slope; he was no longer capable of running. Reaching the crest, he crouched and peered down.

The new Great Father stood at the edge of the watering hole, his legs in the muddy shallows, surrounded by wilde-beests. As Fearless watched, Stronghide lowered his heavy head, tossing his horn and pawing at the water. A great crowd of gazelles, zebras, and buffalo clustered nearby; waiting their turn, Fearless reckoned, to bring their troubles to the Great Father.

Fearless didn't have time to wait with them. Now that he had caught his breath and the end was in sight, he sprinted at full tilt down the hill, the incline giving his paws extra speed. He bowled toward the grass-eaters, almost cannoning into a herd of antelopes, who whickered in alarm and drew swiftly back. As whinnies and squeals rose around him, he shoved and wriggled through a forest of long, hooved legs and finally burst into the open, right in front of Stronghide.

The Great Father scowled at him.

"What do you think you're doing, cub?" He lowered his horn. "Wait your turn."

"This is important," Fearless gasped. He swallowed hard,

bringing his breathing back to normal. Remembering his baboon-taught manners, he dipped his head. "Great Father, you have to do something. Titanpride plans to kill the young rhinos and elephants."

The closest animals blinked at Fearless, startled, and a murmur of shock and disgust rippled through the crowd. Two zebras pawed the ground in agitation, and a buffalo bellowed in anger. Yet Stronghide's small eyes remained blank.

"See what I mean, Great Father?" grunted a wildebeest. "Titanpride is breaking the Code every day. They've been killing far more of us than ever before, and they don't bother to eat half their prey. Please—tell us what to do!"

Stronghide lowered his head, looking truculent, and swished his stiff tail back and forth. "I've already *told* you what to do. Fight!"

The wildebeest looked stricken. In the hordes of grass-eaters near Stronghide, frightened exclamations of disbelief grew in volume.

Fearless huffed. "Fight? Great Father, do you know who Titan is?"

The rhino turned toward him, swinging his horn. "Do I *what?*"

Fearless hastily took a step back. "I didn't mean to be disrespectful."

Great Father glared at him. "How do you know Titanpride's plans, anyway?"

"Well . . ." Fearless shot a nervous glance to both sides. "I'm in Titanpride."

A nervous whinny went up from a zebra. Hooves stamped and rumbled as the grass-eaters shifted in a mass away from him.

"I mean I'm in the pride," Fearless added hastily, "but I'm not a *Titanpride* lion. Not really. I hate Titan. I don't agree with what he's doing. Any of it."

The wildebeest leaned closer, its breath musky with the scent of chewed grass. "What do you mean, you're not really a *Titanpride lion*? You're not a flesh-eater? You haven't been killing our kind?"

That was a tough one to answer honestly. Fearless took a couple of awkward steps back. "No. Look, I'm a lion. Obviously. What I mean is—"

"I knew I recognized him," a zebra neighed roughly. "This cub was with the pride that hunted our leader Sleekfriend. Hunted him for fun, as far as we can tell. They didn't even eat him, just left his entire carcass for the rot-eaters."

"You don't understand," insisted Fearless, his words tripping over one another as he struggled to justify himself. "I tried to help him. I killed him!"

The zebras reared back, neighing in horror. "Codebreaker!"

"Codebreaker!" The other grass-eaters took up the cry, but they weren't shying back now. They were pressing closer, the herds tightening around him.

"That's not what—" Fearless's protests were cut off as a hard hoof punched into his flank, sending him tumbling. The wildebeest lowered his wide curved horns, pawing at the ground.

Fearless scrambled to his paws and backed away. "I'm telling the truth," he shouted to Great Father. "Just protect the young ones! Tell the elephants and the other rhinos. *Please!*"

The grass-eaters were trotting toward him in a great hostile mass; there was no more time. Fearless bolted, darting through the striking hooves, swerving, ducking from horns. At any moment he expected the rake of a vicious horn or the hard blow of a hoof against his ribs, but he kept running and dodging, making for the hill. Were grass-eaters good climbers? He hoped not; he hoped his paws would provide surer grip than their clawless hooves.

Reaching the foot of the slope, he bounded halfway up, then glanced back, trembling and panting in the oppressive heat. The grass-eaters had fallen back and were gathered once more around their Great Father.

Fearless padded to the top of the hill, his muscles aching, and flopped onto the grass. His heart was pounding hard and he licked at his sore ribs. *That was some kick.* What had happened to the peaceable traditions of the watering hole? Fearless wasn't sure how it had happened, but he'd messed everything up.

I don't even know if Stronghide believed me, he thought miserably.

There was nothing for it: he'd have to warn the elephants.

He peered down the hill again. The grass-eaters were arguing with Stronghide once more, their voices raised high in protest. *No wonder, if he's telling them to fight Titanpride.*

Much farther along the shore, so far away that it looked like a bird's nest, was the heap of branches that concealed Great Mother's body. Near her stood the great elephants, some of them tearing down branches for food, others talking intently.

Fearless circled along the top of the hill, staying high on the slope until he was sure he had left the grass-eaters at his rear. The sun was fierce and his neck and spine burned, but he didn't dare head down into the shade of the trees until he was sure he wouldn't meet any angry wildebeests. At last he bounded down a long spur of gravelly rock toward the elephants.

One by one they raised their vast heads to stare at him, their ears tilted forward. Fearless's hide prickled. They were just so *big*, and some of them had tusks that were longer than he was. His heart sank as he realized Sky wasn't among them—he was pretty sure *she* would have been friendly.

The huge creatures didn't take their eyes off him, but they watched him calmly, as still and steady as the great trees of the forest.

"I remember you," said one of them. She had kind eyes fringed with long lashes.

Another, older than the others, with heavy wrinkles criss-crossing her face, pointed her white-patched trunk at him. "You came with your baboon friend to meet with Great Mother. Fearless Titanpride, isn't it?"

"That's right." Fearless winced a little at the pride name.

"I am Rain Strider," the old elephant told him. "I'm the leader of our family now that Great Mother is gone. What brings you here?"

Fearless took a couple of tentative forward paces. "I've come to warn you, Rain Strider. Titan is planning to attack young elephants and rhinos."

The elephants shifted in alarm, their trunks swaying. "Why?" asked Rain, in a voice that made his stomach quiver.

"Sometimes lions have killed our weakest, and our youngest," said the long-lashed elephant, her voice much grimmer now. "But why would Titan *plan* such a thing?"

"If he kills the young of the great grass-eaters," Fearless went on steadily, "he thinks every animal will respect him."

"Have you spoken of this to Great Father?" Rain gave him an unsettling stare.

"I tried to talk to him," said Fearless, swallowing, "but I don't know if he believed me."

The elephants huddled together, talking in frightened whispers, their tails stiff. Rain stayed quiet, deep in thought, her face a combination of anger and deep anxiety.

"Titan has not yet begun on this plan?" she asked at last.

Fearless shook his head. "He was talking about it for the first time today. I overheard."

"Thank the Great Spirit," one of the elephants breathed.

Rain eyed Fearless down her trunk. "It's unusual for a lion to warn us of such things," she rumbled, with an edge of menace. "Is this a trick?"

"No!" exclaimed Fearless, his ears pinning back. "I just . . . I don't like what Titan's doing."

"Few animals do. But I didn't know that included any of his pride." Rain flicked her tail.

Nervously, Fearless glanced around the elephant family. "Is Sky here? I know her. I hoped she would be, because . . . because I think she'd listen to me," he finished lamely.

Rain tilted her head, and the other elephants stared. "You know Sky?"

"I've met her," he said. "When I asked Great Mother for help. I had a problem and they both helped me fix it."

The elephants withdrew, talking once more in their deep, rumbling voices. Fearless wished he could hear their words; he hoped they didn't include *Squish that lion.*

The long-lashed elephant gazed at him. "Rain, if he knows Sky . . . maybe the cub can help us?"

"Maybe he can, Star." The old elephant studied Fearless, her eyes so penetrating he felt a shiver run along his hide. "Fearless, we shall confide in you and hope that your motives are true. The two youngest members of our family are missing."

Fearless's mouth went dry. "You mean Sky?"

"And my son," said the elephant called Star, her voice cracking. "My little Moon."

Two young ones: that's what Daring said. Traveling alone . . . Fearless's heart skipped, and he felt a hollow of dread in his gut.

So Titan already knew. He would be hunting the youngsters: *these* youngsters. Now Fearless had to hunt them too—and be sure to get there first.

"Do you have any idea where they went?" he asked with sudden urgency.

"We know they're together," Rain told him. "Their footprints showed us that. We've waited here because we were sure they'd come back, and we don't want to be gone when they do."

"What if Moon came and I wasn't here?" Star swayed and swung her trunk, looking tormented. "But Rain, now it's different—"

"Titan may be hunting them," Rain said grimly. "We won't catch up in time if that's true."

"We're too slow," Star moaned, as the other elephants gathered around to comfort her, pressing their bodies close.

"I'm not slow," Fearless growled. "Will you show me where they went?"

Rain gazed at her herd. "My sisters. We don't have a choice."

Another of the females gave him a look of misgiving. "I agree. We have to trust the cub."

Exchanging reluctant nods, the elephants turned to lead him along the shore of the watering hole. They shambled past yet more animals who had come to consult Great Father: an anxious-looking gerenuk who tossed his elegant horns, three giraffes who browsed idly on the tallest trees, and a sounder of warthogs who trotted away at the sight of Fearless, their tails stiff and high.

The elephants led Fearless into a lush patch of greenery, then pushed through thorny bushes and up to the edge of the scrubby grasslands, where everything became drier and browner, shimmering in the heat to a flat horizon.

"Their tracks led here," Rain said, pointing with her trunk. On the dusty ground, Fearless could see prints left by two sets of elephant feet, one smaller than the other. He followed them for a few paces, but they disappeared when they reached more well-trodden ground, obliterated by the prints of a multitude of feet, paws, and hooves.

"Their prints are lost here, where the ground becomes rocky," Moon's mother said. Her eyes were wet. "But their scent lingers. Can you smell it?"

Fearless huffed at the tracks, his nostrils flaring. The hot dry ground held little scent but that of insects and dust; this was going to be harder than he thought.

Then he caught it: the dry, warm smell of elephant, mixed with grass and baobab flowers—*Sky*—and with it, something soft and milky. *That must be Moon.*

"I can scent them," he said excitedly. "I'll find them for you—and bring them back."

Moon's mother lowered her head to him, her eyes dark and pleading. "Will you?"

"I promise," he said. "For Sky."

Relief rippled through the elephants in a murmur. Rain stepped before Fearless and placed the tip of her mottled trunk on his muzzle. It felt dry and warm, and slightly ticklish, but he bowed his head and remained still.

"Thank you, young Fearless," she said. "All our hopes rest with you. May the Great Spirit guide you in your search."

Fearless nodded. Whiskers twitching, he picked up the trail once more and set off at a bounding run.

CHAPTER 17

If the constant wind had been unbearable, this turn of the weather was worse. At least the hyena den had provided shelter from the blast, but there was no escaping the suffocating heat. There was shade from the blaze of the sun, but the stench of hyena rot-meat was overpowering. Eating it had become a trial of endurance.

Thorn pressed a chunk of the foul carrion into Beetle's paws; the old baboon lifted it to his mouth and chewed, looking pathetically grateful. Beetle was missing a tooth and one of his eyes was swollen shut, and even through the reek of rotting hyena Thorn recognized the pungent smell of sweetpulp on his breath and skin. *He's using it to numb the pain,* Thorn realized, feeling sick.

What did Grass and Fly do to him? He didn't like to think about it.

"Try to finish that," he murmured to Beetle. "You need your strength."

Beetle gave a dejected nod, and Thorn rose and padded outside into the shimmering heat. He had to find more food, even if it meant traveling a little farther; Beetle and the others couldn't live off rotting corpses forever. And the others included Berry, he thought as his heart turned over. How was she expected to recover on a diet like that? Even though Stinger demanded the best of the foraged haul for her, supplies were getting desperately low.

Nothing seemed to be going right for Brightforest Troop at the moment. If they had a leader they could trust, a leader who truly wanted the best for every baboon, it would all be so different. The weight of Thorn's secret knowledge was almost intolerable. *If only I could confide in Mud.*

But there was nothing to be done, not right now. He could no more put Mud in danger than he could risk Berry's safety.

The berries and nuts from the nearest bushes had all been stripped, the roots dug up. His head reeling from the intensity of the sun, Thorn made for the ditch that lay between the den and a copse of scraggy trees. There was at least one fig tree among them, he knew: maybe the other Strongbranches hadn't cleared it yet.

The ditch was no more than a blurred line in the wobbling heat, the copse barely visible beyond it; sighing, Thorn trudged across the arid grassland, hoping the long walk would be worth it.

Distant screeches made him look up; there were black dots

in the sky that became clearer as he drew closer. Vultures were circling over the little gully. Maybe there was a fresher corpse he could raid, he thought gloomily. But the vultures weren't settling, which was odd.

The odor of hyena drifted into his nostrils, fresh and strong. If the survivors had found a new den near here, he'd have to be careful. It certainly looked like it, Thorn thought as he flinched from a fresh pile of droppings.

He frowned. The vultures seemed agitated. They were almost right above him now, soaring and wheeling. What was wrong with them?

Whatever it was, it lay at the bottom of that ditch. Thorn scrambled down into it, his nerves alert for trouble.

He stiffened, bristling. There *was* a body, sprawled in the muddy trickle that was all that was left of the rapidly drying stream. His heart clenching with dread, Thorn loped toward it.

He couldn't stifle his yelp of horror. "Frog!"

The big, gentle baboon lay facedown, lifeless. Turning her over with trembling paws, Thorn stared at her clouded eyes. A surge of grief rocked his body.

"Frog," he whimpered hoarsely. "Oh, Frog, what happened to you?"

There was not a mark on her brown-furred body, yet she was already rigid. Thorn touched her with trembling paws, his heart aching. No bites, no slashes; had she fallen?

Poor, strong, softhearted Frog, with her quiet devotion to the Great Spirit; Thorn knew already how much he was going to miss her. He glanced up at the vultures. *Why haven't you touched her?*

His mind was in turmoil. Vultures had been Great Mother's messengers; they'd brought her evidence of bad deaths. They wouldn't eat a corpse that had been killed in breach of the Code. Was that why they'd left Frog alone?

Frog had talked about Great Mother, he remembered. She'd gone back twice to the body beneath the branches. Was it possible someone had overheard her telling Thorn about that? Or had seen her going to and from the troop—perhaps Stinger himself? Crouching over the body, Thorn flared his nostrils tentatively.

No hint of scorpion venom—at least, not that he could detect. It was hard to say for sure, though, with the smells of dry earth and the failing stream, and the faint but growing odor of death.

Thorn rose to his paws. Clambering up the gully's far side, he gathered windblown twigs and branches and carried them down to Frog's body. When she was covered, he sat and watched over her. The elephants had done this for Great Mother; it was the least he could do for his own friend.

Not quite all, though. Frog had wanted to take him to Great Mother's body; she'd wanted to show him what she'd found there.

He owed it to her to fulfill that wish.

Thorn's pelt prickled as if a hundred eyes watched him in the night. Hippos bobbed in the shallows, sleeping. A herd of kudus dozed close to Great Mother's body, their elegant brown hides turned to white-striped gray in the darkness; a few kept watch with glowing eyes, their spiraling horns raised high. Thorn flinched as a night bird screamed.

Milling around Great Mother's body, their huge shapes silvered by starlight, were the elephants. They were so close, Thorn's nostrils were filled with their earthy musk, and he could hear every blow and sigh. Night had fallen completely, and the prickly bush where he crouched was dense, but still he felt as if every animal could see him; worse, open grassland stretched between him and Great Mother's body. Every creature in Bravelands would see him and know what he planned, and every creature would turn from him in disgust.

He backed farther beneath the bush. A few half-dried berries were clustered among its leaves; Thorn chewed some, wrinkling his muzzle at the bitterness. There was movement in the night; a cheetah slunk to the water's edge to lap at it, her coat spotted gray, her eyes fiery orbs. Ponderously, the elephants moved toward a copse of trees, guiding each other with their trunks—so lovingly that Thorn felt a pang of loneliness.

He'd already lost Fearless. A ravine seemed to be splitting open between him and Mud, becoming ever wider with the secrets Thorn kept from him. And as for Berry . . . Thorn clung to the hope that she'd recover, but would she ever want to speak to him again?

He mustn't think too hard.

The clear silver moon was rising higher: it was almost full, the shape of an elephant's ear. The elephants themselves were

lost in the shadows of the bush. With infinite caution, Thorn
crept out, thorns snagging on his pelt. Crouching low, he scur-
ried across the grassland.

The mound of greenery that covered Great Mother's body
rose far above Thorn's head. On top rested a branch of white
flowers—they were dead, but their dried petals looked like
scattered stars. *Forgive me, Great Spirit.*

Finding handholds on the branches, he climbed lightly to
the top of the mound. Great Mother had been dead for several
days, and by now Thorn would have expected decay, especially
in this oppressive heat. By now she should be rot-meat, her
body parts scattered by scavengers. Instead he could smell
nothing but leaves and flowers, and when he pulled aside a
branch, he drew back in surprise—Great Mother's skin was
deeply creased, but her body remained firm. There was no
swelling or hollowing, and she was unmarked by any scaven-
ger. The old elephant seemed untouched by death.

The Great Spirit must be protecting her body, he thought in wonder, *because it once made its home there.*

The idea made him a little less afraid, and a little less
ashamed. Somewhere on this body lay whatever Frog had
wanted him to find, and Thorn had a sense that the Great
Spirit wanted him to find it too. Quietly, he lifted more
branches.

On Great Mother's trunk and forelegs there were vicious
bites, still clotted with dried blood. Peering at the rows of
tooth marks, Thorn hesitantly explored them with his finger-
tips. Deep and tapering, they were definitely crocodile bites.

Horribly, he could picture the scene: powerful jaws tearing at Great Mother's legs until her knees buckled, long teeth fastening into her trunk, scaly bodies thrashing as they dragged her head beneath the surface . . .

But why had they attacked her? The crocodiles didn't follow the Great Spirit, he knew, and they didn't even know the Code—they might have thought her an ordinary elephant, alone in the water. An elephant in their territory, maybe? And, furious at the invasion, they killed her?

Thorn tried to imagine it again—Great Mother wading deep into water that was filled with crocodiles. That was the part that didn't make sense. Even the stupidest monkey knew how dangerous crocs were, and Great Mother had been the wisest animal in all of Bravelands.

So something made her go into the water.

Or someone . . .

His only hope of discovering the truth was Great Mother's body itself. Thorn studied it as well as he could in the moonlight, raising branches and exploring her belly, her side, her legs. *Oh, Frog, I wish you were with me. What did you find?*

Deep gouges slashed the old elephant's flanks and hind legs. Thorn ran his paws over them. They were different from the wounds made by the crocodiles—broad and ragged, and far from being neat rows, they were scattered unevenly. His heart raced. He was right—another animal had forced Great Mother into the water. *But who?*

Thorn felt the gouges. Not bite marks, and too deep and broad to be claw marks. Horns? Tusks? They were high on her body, near the top of her thighs—the animal who'd made them had been large, but still smaller than Great Mother.

As he paused, thinking hard, there was a shuffling, scratching sound at the edge of the watering hole. Thorn froze, his heart turning over. Had he been seen? Slowly, he turned.

From the bank, an ibis watched him, its long, curved black beak as delicate as a butterfly's proboscis. It ruffled its white wings and cackled at him in Skytongue.

"Hush!" Thorn hissed. "Please be quiet!"

The ibis called again. It picked its way across the bank on its long legs, then bent its beak to probe at the ground. Looking up at Thorn, it gave another cackling cry.

Thorn waved his paws. "Go away! Shouldn't you be roosting?"

The ibis cocked its head, spread its wings, then folded them and pecked at the ground once again. Between every stab of its beak, it cackled what sounded like a summons. Stifling a groan of anxiety, Thorn backed down off Great Mother's body, trying not to disturb more branches.

"What's the fuss about?" he hissed.

The ibis did not fly away. It simply stared at him, with eyes that were blacker than the night. With a sigh, Thorn crouched and patted the ground in front of it.

He frowned. The mud here was dry and already cracking in the heat, but he was sure this patch had a loamier texture, as if it had been recently disturbed. Finding the edge of the looser earth, Thorn began to dig at it. The ibis watched, silent at last.

Deep in the crumbly mud, Thorn's fingers touched something hard and ridged. His heart thundering, he clasped it with both paws. *Frog. Whatever this is, you buried it.*

He tugged it out and brushed away clumps of dried mud. The thing was heavy, a solid cone that tapered to a sharp point. The broader end felt rough and jagged against his palms, as if it had broken off something larger. Thorn turned it in his paws. There was a dark stain on the point. Thorn lifted it to his nose and sniffed. *Blood.*

Thorn's heart began to race once more. He spun around to the ibis—but the bank was deserted. The bird had gone.

A thrill rippled along his spine. Great Mother had been close to the birds—she'd spoken their language of Skytongue, like all Great Parents. Did the ibis know more about her death?

The thing in his paws was like a broad broken tooth, from some large creature; Thorn had seen something like it before, he was sure. Clutching it with difficulty in one paw, Thorn loped back to Great Mother's body and scaled the branches once again. With a deep breath he pressed the tooth into one of the deep gouges in Great Mother's flank.

It matched exactly.

Frustrated, Thorn stared at the tooth, picking mud off it with a claw. What kind of animal had teeth that were so brown and ridged? In some ways it wasn't like a tooth at all.

He scoured the bank for the ibis again. Out on the lake there was a flash of white, the gleam of a long beak, the shadow of black tail feathers against the water. Relieved,

Thorn bounded toward it, leaping from stone to stone and splashing up to his knees.

"Come back!" he called as loudly as he dared. "I need you!"

The black-and-white shape rippled and fractured. Suddenly it wasn't an ibis at all; it was nothing but moonlight breaking on the dark water.

A shiver crept through Thorn. Staring at the lake, he backed swiftly toward the bank. Nothing moved out there now but the eerie reflected moonlight.

His paw closed tightly around the tooth, and he bolted for his temporary home.

It seemed almost like a different moon that cast its light on the baked earth in front of the hyena den. Here, its silver shimmer felt reassuringly familiar, even welcoming. Thorn felt a tremor of relief as he caught sight of the tunnel entrance.

A slender figure sat just outside, crouched over something on the ground. Recognizing Starleaf, Thorn hurried to join her.

"It's stuffy in the den, isn't it?" he said.

She glanced at him. "It's not much cooler out here, but I needed some space and peace." She gestured at the Moonstones laid out on the sandy earth. "I'd hoped they would tell me when this awful heat will lift, but I see nothing. First the rain, then that windstorm, and now this. I've never known Bravelands so troubled."

That sent a frisson of unease through Thorn. Starleaf was

old enough to have seen a lot of trouble. He licked his jaws, uncertain what to say. *I'd like to give her some comfort, but I can't.* He could hardly tell the wise old baboon that things were even worse than she thought.

"Starleaf, can I ask you a question? I don't want to disturb your reading, but . . ."

She smiled at him. "Of course you can, Thorn. I'm glad of a distraction."

He nodded and held out his find. "Can you tell me what kind of tooth this is?"

Starleaf took it from him and balanced it on one palm, lifting it to the moonlight. Her eyes narrowed, and she scratched the white streak on her face.

"This is no tooth," she said. "It's the tip of a rhinoceros horn."

That's it. That's where I've seen it before. Thorn's mouth went dry. Of course it wasn't a gigantic tooth. It had been snapped short; that was what had confused him. It was darker and a little less ridged, but it had the same look and texture as the tip of Stronghide's horn.

Stronghide. Thorn's head swam. Stronghide and his crash must have killed Great Mother so that he could become Great Father. The rhinos had always been jealous of the elephants; that night they had decided their time had come. It made a sudden, horrible kind of sense. *Mud was right*, he thought. *Our Great Parent really is a fraud.*

Starleaf handed back the horn. "Where did you find it? It

must have hit something hard to break like this."

Thorn winced, imagining the horn smashing into Great Mother's thick leg bone. "I . . . I don't know," he mumbled. "Just lying around." Taking his rapid leave, he hurried into the den.

Stinger sat on a pile of leaves just inside the first tunnel, sinking his teeth into a fig. He chewed on a mouthful, wrinkled his muzzle, then tossed the rest to the ground. It rolled to a stop against a cluster of more half-eaten figs.

"Sweet," he said, chewing. "But it doesn't have the tang of scorpion."

Thorn halted, swallowing hard.

"Thorn *Strongbranch*," Stinger greeted him emphatically. "What can I do for you?"

Thorn licked his jaws. "Frog's missing."

"Is she?" Stinger picked up another fig from the stack beside him. "Let's try this one, it might have a little more edge."

"I can't find her," said Thorn, his gaze fixed on his leader, "anywhere."

Stinger gave an irritated shrug. "She'll have wandered off on some solitary hunt. Frog's a strong one, but not too bright."

The rage that rose inside Thorn almost choked him. His paws shaking, he thrust the broken rhino horn beneath Stinger's nose.

Stinger stopped chewing. His eyes flickered over the horn.

"The rhinos did it," croaked Thorn. "They drove Great Mother into the water, knowing the crocodiles would kill her."

Stinger went entirely still. He lifted his eyes, watching Thorn for long, silent heartbeats.

Then he slapped the ground and hooted with laughter.

"Well, well," he cackled. "Maybe Stronghide isn't as stupid as he seems. You know, I have a reluctant admiration for him. He got what he wanted, didn't he? He's Great Father now—may the Great Spirit help us all." He snatched the horn and turned it in his hands. "Clever work, Thorn. Go on, off you go."

Thorn stared at him. "But what about Stronghide?"

Stinger picked fig pulp from his long teeth. "What about him?"

"Aren't we going to tell Bravelands what he did?"

Stinger licked a finger, his eyes bright. "Why should we?"

Thorn stiffened in disbelief. "Because he *murdered Great Mother.*"

"Looks that way." Stinger shrugged and went back to picking his fangs.

Thorn wanted to shriek, or better still to claw at him. "This crazy weather, the conflicts with the herds, the way we're hiding in a stinking hyena den—it's because we've got Stronghide pretending to be Great Father. The Great Spirit is angry!"

"Oh, I agree with you," said Stinger cheerfully.

Thorn clenched his fists. "So what are you going to *do about it?*"

"Nothing."

Thorn's jaw felt slack, and he couldn't say a word. Thoughts went racing through his mind like skittering spiders, too fast and confused to catch. *He's surprised. And he's not surprised. He's seen that horn before, or he knew about it.*

But he's shocked that I have it. He didn't expect that. Not yet.

Oh, Frog, I don't know what to do.

"Thorn, Thorn, Thorn." Stinger spat out a fig seed. "I'll do nothing, and nor will you. This is one of those times when we'll have to let others fight our battles for us."

Thorn felt a growl rising in his throat. "I . . . What does that even mean? We have to tell—"

"*Careful.*" Stinger's tone was suddenly, terribly different. He stepped down from his leaf pile and drew himself up. Thorn had almost let himself forget just how big Stinger was: intimidatingly so. He was staring down at Thorn now, his amber eyes very cold.

"Remember who you're talking to. I'm your Crownleaf and commander, Thorn Strongbranch. And I forbid you to say a word about this to anyone." Stinger's upper lip peeled back, revealing his long yellow fangs. It was nothing like a smile. "*Do you understand?*"

A bolt of sheer, chilling fear went through Thorn's rib cage. How many times had he told himself, *Stinger might kill you . . . ?*

For the very first time, he knew in every bone and sinew of his body that it was true. It was true, and very real, and if he didn't leave right now, it was imminent.

The words barely rasped through his constricted throat. "I understand."

Slowly he backed away from Stinger, until he was outside

the tunnel and beyond the glow of the big baboon's deadly eyes. Then he ran, desperately, for the safety of his troop-mates.

Another secret, he thought. *I'll have to live with it. But for how long?*

CHAPTER 18

The sun had risen to its highest point, shortening the shadows almost to nothing, and its heat thrummed on Sky's back with what felt like malice. She and her two companions trudged through a long, narrow valley that was lush with soft grass and thick flowering bushes, but already Sky saw signs that the heat was taking its toll: flowers drooped and shed their petals, and the tips of the grass were drying to yellow. So often she had gazed toward the hills and seen them shrouded in mist, but now the sky was a hot intense blue from horizon to horizon. Not a shred of cloud interrupted its dazzling arc.

At the farthest end of the valley a mountain rose, hazy with distance. Sky gazed longingly toward it. A flock of starlings flew from one wind-twisted tree to another, their blue and red feathers flashing, and the rasping honk of hornbills echoed through the valley, but Sky was focused on just one bird: the great black vulture that held Great Mother's tusk fragment in her talons. The bird hunched at the top of a crooked tree, a little way ahead. She was always a little way ahead. Every time Sky, Moon, and Silverhorn drew close to her, she would spread her wings and flap a little farther, waiting in the next convenient tree.

It was so dispiriting. *Oh, Great Spirit, please let that glitter in the grass be a stream. . . .* The Great Spirit must have heard her. Exhausted, Sky came to a halt before the shallow gully. There was bedraggled grass high on its banks, but below that an expanse of drying mud; the stream itself had clearly shrunk and was little more than a murky trickle. All the same, Sky was glad of it, and she gave a murmur of thanks to the Great Spirit. She sucked up water as well as she could and poured it gratefully into her mouth.

As Silverhorn trotted down to join her, Sky reached out her trunk for Moon, and he too stumbled down the bank and leaned against her.

"You must be thirsty, little cousin." She used some of the precious water to spray his shoulders. "Come on, take a drink. Then roll."

"It's so hot," he whimpered. "I'm so tired."

"It'll be better when the sun goes down." She glanced up at its glaring white light, willing it to sink toward the west.

"How far is that big bird going to take us?" asked Moon after a while, licking his lips. He already seemed sprightlier; Sky had begun to worry he would drink the stream dry.

"I think she's leading us toward the mountain," Sky said,

kneeling and rolling to cake her hide in soothing mud.

"I've never been on a mountain!" said Moon. "Have you, Sky? What's a mountain like?"

Silverhorn lifted her dripping muzzle from the stream and grunted. At first, the rhino hadn't believed that the vulture was leading them anywhere, but it had gotten harder to doubt it: yesterday, the bird had led them on, step by weary step, until it was too dark to travel. Sky had been afraid to stop and sleep in case the vulture vanished, but this morning, there she'd been again: a black shape wheeling in the morning sky.

"I've never been on a mountain either," Sky told Moon, checking that his skin was thoroughly muddy. "We can find out what it's like together."

In her tree, the vulture turned her bald head to stare at Sky. Spreading her black wings, she rose once again into the air.

Moon broke into an impatient scamper. "I want to get to the mountain! It's all blue! Do you think it has trees?"

"I don't know, Moon," Sky said. "And calm down! You'll tire yourself out."

The vulture landed on the branch of a black ironwood, farther up the valley. Sky and her companions left the stream behind and followed.

"Maybe the *trees* are blue! Maybe it's really cold, and there are animals with lots and lots of fur," Moon suggested. "I bet they look like monkeys, and they climb on the mountain rocks, but they're so furry they're squishy and round."

"Like those puffball mushrooms in the forest," said Sky. "Only not poisonous, I hope."

Moon giggled and whacked her side with his trunk. "You wouldn't eat a monkey!"

Sky laughed, too. "Maybe if I got hungry enough! Or a sweet little elephant!" She shook her trunk at him and he scampered away.

"I think there'll be lots of water on the mountain," Silverhorn chimed in longingly. "It looks so blue and cool."

"Ooh, yes," Moon said. "So much water we can't drink it all. And we'll have to wade through it, and silver fish will swim around our legs."

"Oh, Moon, don't," pleaded Sky. "You're making me thirsty again."

"The mountain looks so high, though." Silverhorn's gray ears twitched. "We'll have to walk up a long way. My legs aren't great at that."

"You can do it," Sky told her. "Elephants aren't natural climbers, either, but we'll manage if we just keep trudging along. One foot in front of the other, that's all."

Moon's eyes widened. "Maybe we'll see where the stars fall to the earth," he exclaimed, "like Cloud did in the story? Stars would land in a high place, and that mountain's *really* high."

A hoarse cry interrupted them. The vulture had flown from her perch again and was rising higher than ever.

"Is she moving already?" Silverhorn sighed. "We're not even close to her yet. How does she expect us to keep up?"

Sky furrowed her brow and stared. The vulture's long bald neck was stretched out, and her head twitched as if she was scanning the earth below. Her guttural screech sounded again, loud and urgent, and although Sky didn't speak Sky-tongue, there was no mistaking her meaning: it was a warning cry. She glanced at Silverhorn, whose small eyes had grown wide.

Sky hesitated, glancing up and down the path. "I don't see anything."

While Moon hopped and flapped his ears, she turned and climbed a few paces up the valley's steep side. Stopping with her feet wedged against rocks, she peered around, her heart thumping. She had not liked the tone of the vulture's cry.

Silverhorn was clambering up the opposite slope. "Nothing to see from here," she cried.

"Nothing here either," called Sky. She trod carefully back down to the track, and Silverhorn joined her.

The vulture swooped low, the draught of her wings raising the sparse hairs on Sky's back. Her shriek hurt Sky's ears, and it sounded more frantic than ever.

"What *is* it?" Sky asked helplessly. "I don't understand!"

Moon had stopped capering. His trunk trembled. "Sky, I'm scared."

Silverhorn was scenting the air, her top lip flaring. She gave an abrupt grunt of dismay.

"Lions!" she cried. "Run!"

"Moon!" Sky threw her trunk over his shoulders and pushed him ahead of her.

The three of them thundered up the valley toward the mountain, their panicked footfalls making the ground tremble. Just above their heads the vulture soared, her hoarse screeches urging them on.

The rank, blood-tinged scent of lion flooded Sky's trunk. She didn't want to glance to the side, but she had to. And there they were, plunging out of a line of scrub and sprinting toward them—nine powerful male lions, their jaws parted to reveal savage teeth. Ahead of them charged a huge, muscular leader, his mane jet-black.

Silverhorn was keeping up beside her, the rhino's sturdy legs working faster than Sky would have believed possible, but she could see that Moon's pace was slackening. He glanced back and squealed with fear.

"Moon, keep going!" Sky trumpeted. "Don't look, just run!"

"Sky, I can't," Moon sobbed, stumbling.

Sky was aware of blurred, tawny shapes running to her right and left; the lions were gaining, pinning them in an ambush. The dried-blood smell of them was dizzying, and Sky could almost feel their hot panting breath on her rump. "Keep going, Moon! *Run!*"

We need help. She barely dared slacken her pace, but the lions were alongside them now. And she knew instinctively that she and Silverhorn would not be enough to fight them off. *That bull elephant we heard, is he still close?* Slowing as much as she dared, catching a great gulp of breath, she let out an instinctive rumbling call, deep and tremulous.

At the edge of her vision something huge and golden sprang past her. Shying in terror, Sky saw the great black-maned lion, his long legs extended, slamming into Moon's rump. He clung on with his claws, almost as if he were hugging the little elephant. Moon squealed in pain and shock, staggering; then he stumbled to his knees.

"*No!*" Sky skidded on the gritty earth. The lion was hanging onto Moon's flank now, biting and shaking his great maned head. Moon squealed and thrashed, his eyes huge in his panic.

"Get off him!" Sky trumpeted, and charged.

Before she could reach the lion, a heavy weight thudded onto her own rump. Swaying, she fell to her knees. She couldn't breathe—why couldn't she breathe?

She was smothered in hot stinking fur. Another lion slammed into her shoulder, and she felt sharp teeth sink into her neck. The stench of lion choked her. *Get off me!* she tried to scream, but something was constricting her throat. With a massive effort she struggled back onto her feet; a lion dangled from her throat, its fangs and claws snagged deep in her skin. It hurt so much she could barely think. Thrusting herself desperately onto her hind feet, she slammed her forefeet into the ground and felt the lion fall away. It rolled beneath her and sprang back to its paws.

The lions encircled her now, and they were stalking forward. A pale-furred male jerked his head at his cronies. "You three, get the rhino."

She heard Silverhorn bellow and turned to catch a glimpse of her charging. The rhino slammed her horned head into an amber-gold lion, sending him tumbling to the ground. As another leaped, she swung her horn at him, forcing him to retreat with a yelp. The vulture swooped, screeching, and raked her talons along another tawny flank.

Sky's attacker lunged again, clawing at her face. She swung her head violently, catching his belly with one of her short tusks, and he dropped with a grunt of pain. Hot blood was running down her face and trunk, but she didn't care. All that mattered was—

"Moon!" She thundered toward him.

She slid to a shocked halt. The black-maned lion, still crouched over the little elephant, looked up and met Sky's eyes. Slowly, he licked Moon's blood from his jaws.

Rage coursed through her and she charged, head lowered. The lion reared back, raising his paws to strike at her. As her forehead slammed into his tawny shoulders, she felt his protracted claws rip the top of her ear, and new pain blossomed. She flung him away from Moon, and he landed with a grunt in the dust.

Moon's eyes were closed to slits. Terrified, Sky ran her trunk over his bloodied body. "It's me," she said, her voice choked with tears. "It's Sky. Can you hear me?"

Moon's eyelashes flickered.

The black-maned lion was already getting to his paws. Sky spun to face him. She reared up on her hind legs, slamming them into the ground before the big lion. "You won't touch him again!"

The lion curled his muzzle in a smirk. "To me, Titanpride."

At once, the other lions abandoned their fights with Silverhorn and the vulture. They ranged themselves beside their leader, jaws snarling in menace. Silverhorn lurched to Sky's side and stood shoulder to shoulder with her, blocking the lions from Moon.

"Now you've tasted the might of our pride," growled the black-maned lion. He was far larger than the others; Sky could see now that they were mostly young, with tufty, half-grown manes. "Let your elders know this is Titanpride territory. Soon all of Bravelands will be ours."

Silverhorn quivered with rage. "Lions don't own—"

"Elephants and rhinoceroses aren't safe here anymore," Titan interrupted. His eyes were lit with a fierce glow, and his tail lashed. "Your size has made you arrogant, and your arrogance has made you soft and weak. I, Titan, rule Bravelands now."

A faint whimper rose behind Sky. She longed to go to Moon, but she had to keep the lions at bay. . . .

"A true leader wouldn't attack a baby," she said, her voice trembling. "Look at you, you're not starving. You're no ruler. You're a Codebreaker!"

Titan threw back his head and roared, his long teeth stained red. "Insolence!" He lowered his shoulders to spring.

A bellowing trumpet echoed from the hillside. For a moment it was impossible to tell its direction, but Sky at last swiveled her head toward the source. It came from farther down the valley, beyond a bend in the path. Titan went still, his ears flickering.

The second blaring call was much closer. A distant roll of strange thunder became footfalls that hammered on dry earth; then, around the bend in the track, charged the biggest bull elephant Sky had ever seen.

She gave a sobbing gasp of relief. *Thank the Great Spirit!*

The bull was tall and broad, with dark gray skin and long, cream tusks. With a last angry bellow, he charged the lions.

"Battle formation!" Titan roared.

The lions scattered, spreading out for their ambush strategy. The bull merely dipped his head as he ran, catching the pale-furred lion on his tusks. His colossal head jerked up, flinging the lion against the rocks of the hillside. The bull swung to Sky and Silverhorn, his ears spread wide in aggression.

"Get out of here!" he bellowed.

The lions, dodging his heavy feet and the thrust of his tusks, snarled defiantly. But they were smart enough to know they were beaten; as he charged, they twisted in their tracks and bolted back down the valley.

Only Titan held his place for a heartbeat longer. "Warn your elders," he snarled at Sky and Silverhorn. "Titanpride hasn't finished with you."

The bull curled back his trunk, his tusks shining; it was enough. Titan turned and bounded after his fleeing pride. The pale lion, dazed, staggered from the rocks and limped after them.

Sky lurched forward to kneel at Moon's side. All around his head and haunches, the pale earth was stained red with blood.

Frantic, Sky ran her trunk tip over his injuries. Deep gouges were clawed across his rump, and bright red blood welled far too quickly from his neck. Sky pressed her trunk across the savage bite, trying desperately to staunch the bleeding.

"Oh, Moon," she murmured, over and over again. "Moon, it's all right. They've gone now, you're safe."

The little elephant's flank rose and fell rapidly, but his gasping breaths were shallow and weak. Silverhorn stared down, her face crumpled.

"Can I help?" asked a deep and gentle voice.

Sky glanced up through a blur of tears. The bull elephant's deep-set eyes were a startling green, and they were filled with compassion. He was younger than Sky had assumed, and far less scary than she'd feared. Though his tusks were far longer than hers, they hadn't yet reached their full length. It probably hadn't been many years since he had left his own mother's herd.

The thought of a mother herd made Sky almost choke on her grief. *Oh, Star, what have I done . . .*

"Maybe I could carry the little one to his mother?" offered the bull, and Sky felt the hesitant touch of his trunk on her shoulders.

Sky shook her head helplessly. "She's too far away. I brought him too far!"

Oh, why hadn't she turned back when Moon came after her? If she'd insisted on taking him home, he'd be safe now. *Safe, instead of . . .*

"We don't even know you!" she blurted, trying to blot out her thoughts.

"My name is Rock," the bull said gently. "I heard your

distress call. Here, let me help."

He pressed his trunk down next to Sky's, trying to stop Moon's blood. Was it Sky's imagination? *The flow is lessening....*

"I came as fast as I could," murmured Rock, staring down with pity at Moon, "but I wish it had been faster."

"You saved us," rasped Silverhorn. "Thank you."

Sky's throat was too tight to speak. Yes, the flow of blood was slackening, but the hope that had flickered was dying inside her. Less blood welled from Moon's throat, but only because most of it was already pooled beneath the little elephant's head and neck.

Rock came in time to save two of us, she thought, and hot tears stung her eyes.

Gulping, she stroked Moon's plump baby cheek with her trunk. "Moon," she whispered hoarsely. "You remember the story I was telling you?"

He whimpered a little, his eyes glazed and far away. *I don't even know if he can hear me.*

It didn't matter; there was nothing else she could do for him now.

"Little Moon," she went on, her singsong voice catching in her swollen throat. "Do you remember how Cloud was looking for the fallen star? He searched everywhere." Sky nestled closer, wrapping her trunk around Moon's body and holding him tightly. "Cloud walked and walked, tired and thirsty. He traveled far, through the woods and across the savannah, and up a steep, steep hill, and finally he reached the top. And way down in the valley below, he saw a bright light shining. It was the brightest, whitest light he'd ever seen, and it was beautiful. He didn't feel tired anymore and he wasn't thirsty. He didn't stop to eat grass or to drink water or to play. All he wanted was to find his star. He was the bravest little elephant there has ever been."

Moon seemed quieter now, his tension drained. She could hear his weak breathing, one slow gasp after another. She thought that perhaps his ear twitched.

"He was so strong, so determined, and all his family knew it, and they were so, so proud." Sky did not know how long her breaking voice would hold out. "At last he reached the star, and its light was dazzling. Cloud knew he'd reached where he was going, and all his journey had been worth it, every bit. And Cloud stretched out his trunk to touch the light—"

With a last, rattling breath, Moon went still. His flanks sank, and did not rise again.

"And he touched the star and he was *happy*."

The last word was a wail of unbearable grief. Hot tears, released at last, began to flow down the creases of her face.

Was it really Moon's small heart that had stopped? Because Sky was sure the lions had torn out her own.

CHAPTER 19

The heat barely relented with the setting of the sun. Thorn felt it pressing down on him like a smothering paw as he gathered with the other Strongbranches in the dusk outside the hyena den. His fur felt clammy with it, and he wished just a breath of breeze would return from the earlier gales. The ominous mood made it even worse.

Stinger sat on a low shelf of stone, the Strongbranches—Thorn included—ranged on either side of him. Facing them stood old Beetle, his chin defiantly tilted.

"I must say," Stinger drawled, "I'm disappointed that you haven't seen sense, old baboon. You go on challenging my rule, even when you know how wrong you are."

Beetle's voice was the same old quavering wobble Thorn had always known, but it held a new element of stony strength. "I shall go on asking difficult questions, Stinger Crownleaf, and if you call that *challenging*, then so be it. I certainly will go on *challenging* you."

"I was made Crownleaf by popular acclamation," said Stinger in his silky voice. "Who are you to question the will of the troop?"

Beetle set his jaw. He was clearly scared, and Thorn could only admire his courage. "The will of the troop was never that your Strongbranches would have a free paw to bully and intimidate."

"Do I condone bullying?" Stinger's eyes widened with horror. "I have no knowledge of such behavior. If I did, you can be sure I would discipline my faithful Strongbranches. But all I see, Beetle, is loyal fighters who care for the troop, who love Brightforest, who will do anything to defend it."

"They will do anything." Beetle snorted. "Indeed they will. That's why you value them more than the Council. Your devoted thugs can beat me all they like, Stinger, but they won't stop me asking questions."

Stinger's hackles bristled. "And there we have it. You refuse to see my status as the will of Brightforest Troop; therefore you no longer belong with us. As of this moment, traitor Beetle, you are exiled."

"Stinger, no!" Thorn hadn't meant to open his mouth, but this was too much. "Beetle's old and frail. Please, Stinger, show mercy. He won't survive on his own!"

Stinger swiveled his head to fix his amber stare on Thorn. It was chilling, and Thorn found his admiration for Beetle growing even stronger.

"That's Beetle's problem. He should have thought of that before he chose to be an enemy of the troop. If he wanted to be one of us, he should not have undermined his Crownleaf. Do I make myself clear?" Stinger's gaze lingered for a long, unnerving moment on Thorn, then turned back to Beetle. "Go. Get out of my sight, old baboon."

"I will." Beetle did not lower his eyes. "I will go, knowing that my fate will one day be yours, when the troop discovers the truth about you."

His heart clenching with dismay, Thorn watched the old baboon limp away with as much dignity as he could muster. His progress was slow, and the Strongbranches hooted and chattered in mockery, but Beetle didn't flinch. He hobbled farther and farther into the dusk, until he was nothing but a shadow against the graying grassland; then he vanished altogether.

Thorn knew he would never see him again.

"Well, well." Stinger dusted his paws. "Now that that unpleasantness is dealt with, we can rejoin the troop for the Moon Reading."

Grass moved his stalk around his mouth with his tongue. "Where are we going to have it, Stinger? The clearing in Tall Trees was perfect. That patch of sky—the moon rose straight into it."

"There's nowhere like that here," agreed Fly, picking his chipped teeth. "Can't see the moon from a hyena den."

"Does it matter?" said Stinger irritably. "It's a load of monkey-brained claptrap, anyway. I'm only indulging Starleaf to keep the troop happy."

"Oh." Fly's eyes widened in surprise.

Grass's jaws went still on his chewed stalk. Then he nodded enthusiastically. "You're right, Stinger. It's nonsense."

"Why are we doing it, then?" asked Fang.

"I told you." Stinger glared at him. "Don't you *know* that traditions keep the troop happy?"

"Yes! Yes, of course. You're wise, Stinger." Fang nodded too, so eagerly that it seemed like a competition between him and Grass.

"Besides," said Stinger more smoothly, "occasions like these are handy for spotting troublemakers like old Beetle there. All of you, keep your eyes peeled and your ears sharp for gossip. Now that Frog's gone we'll all have to work harder, but I know I can count on you."

Thorn stared from one to the other, shocked. The Moon Readings weren't just some hoary old tradition; they were the heart of troop life. Starleaf had always used her skills to advise the Crownleaf, to warn of impending trouble. Did Stinger really not believe in them? Worst of all, his fellow Strongbranches were fully invested in mocking Starleaf's work now, giggling and hooting with derision. He dreaded to think what Frog would have made of it.

He didn't even like to think about Stinger's other orders. Watch the troop for troublemakers?

What is Brightforest Troop becoming?

Stinger had decided that the shallow dip in the plain, where they'd sheltered on their trek, was an ideal spot for the Moon

Reading. It was nothing like the Moon Clearing at Tall Trees, Thorn thought as he glanced around, but at least it was roughly circular. The moon would not rise majestically above the canopy into a clear ring of sky, but Starleaf was clever. She'd know when it reached its zenith. She had arranged her Moonstones in a semicircle in front of her and now waited in patient silence.

Mud nudged Thorn's elbow as he walked past to take his place. "Thorn, I just want to keep you up to date," he whispered. "Berry's still sick. There's been no improvement. The Goodleaves say the wound went bad."

Thorn's heart wrenched; it was what he'd feared. "But she's no worse?"

"No worse, but—"

"Thanks for telling me," Thorn said quickly, catching Worm's eye. She was staring at him suspiciously and muttering something to Fang. "You'd better go to your place."

Mud stared at him for a moment, shocked, but he shook his head and walked on. Thorn felt the familiar sting of guilt: *I hope Mud doesn't think I don't care.* They couldn't stand there talking, even about something so important; the Strongbranches would report Mud to Stinger faster than a striking cobra. Regretfully, Thorn watched his friend settle into the circle. Mud was avoiding his eyes now.

Along with the other Strongbranches, Thorn had been detailed to stand at the edge of the troop, watching from just outside their circle. The others were moving into place, hunching at points around the hollow, their glittering eyes fixed not on Starleaf but on their fellow troop members.

Looking for troublemakers. Thorn shivered.

To give Stinger his terrible due, it seemed to be working. Every baboon was on their best behavior; there was no talking, no gossip, no nudging and whispering. They all sat quite still, their eyes fixed obediently on Stinger; he stood next to Starleaf, ready to introduce the solemn proceedings. Only occasionally did a baboon glance nervously at the watching Strongbranches.

Starleaf stood with her Moonstones in the center of the shallow dip, glancing around. She scratched the white streak on her head. "Stinger," she said softly, "we can't start yet. Beetle hasn't arrived."

"Beetle will not be joining us," said Stinger. "He has been exiled as a traitor."

There were muffled gasps around the circle. Thorn watched his fellow troop members keenly, his heart thumping. Would they really stand for this? Beetle had sometimes been a figure of fun to the younger baboons, but deep down, they had all respected him. This might be the moment they began to question Stinger's decisions.

His heart sank as he realized no one was going to speak up. The murmurs faded under the steady glare of the Strongbranches; a few baboons actually nodded in agreement.

"He *was* a bit of a loudmouth," whispered a baboon near Thorn.

"You can't blame Stinger," replied her neighbor softly. "Brightforest Troop needs unity."

"He knows what he's doing." The first baboon nodded and they fell silent again, watching Stinger and Starleaf.

They're not just scared of the Strongbranches, realized Thorn with a stab of despair. *They're starting to justify their own cowardice.*

Starleaf seemed dumbstruck for a moment at Beetle's fate, but she shook herself, glanced at the dark sky, and inclined her head to Stinger. "The moon is about to reach its place, Crownleaf."

Stinger took a seat on a boulder near the front, which Thorn and the Strongbranches had earlier rolled into place to act as a Crown Stone; they at once moved down through the crowd to squat around him. Fly shoved Notch Middleleaf aside so he could take her place; Notch opened her mouth to object, but closed it when she saw several Strongbranches watching her. She shifted a few tail-lengths away, her fur ruffled.

As Thorn padded across the circle, Mud at last met his eye, gesturing to the spot he'd saved beside him. Guilt tugged at Thorn—he and Mud always sat together, and even after Thorn's brush-off, Mud was reminding him of that. But Thorn gave a quick shake of his head and walked past Mud to take his place at Stinger's feet.

Mud turned away, his shoulders drooping.

Thorn glanced at Fang. The muscular baboon wasn't even looking at Starleaf, but was scanning the other members of the troop, his brow aggressively furrowed and his large paws clenched. *Who would dare question Stinger with that brute watching?*

Starleaf's face was tilted toward the sky, her gaze intense

and unblinking. The moonlight made her eyes glitter. "It's a Blood Moon tonight," she said at last. "A time of turmoil and danger."

Looking up, Thorn gasped with the others. The moon was indeed stained with dull red.

Starleaf picked up one of the Moonstones—a purple one, almost black in the moonlight—and held it to the sky, peering through the crystal. Slowly, she worked her way around the semicircle of Moonstones, changing their angles, moving them closer or farther from her eye. The troop sat in breathless, attentive silence.

Almost. Fang gave a muffled snort, and Thorn knew what was going through his head: *Old fraud.*

But that wasn't true, Thorn was sure of it. Hadn't Starleaf always guided the troop wisely? She'd told them where to gather the freshest fruit, what parts of the forest to avoid in the rainy season. Long ago, before Thorn was born, she'd guided them to Tall Trees. Thorn glanced at Stinger, whose face was perfectly still and unreadable. Starleaf's Moon Readings always benefited the troop. Why would he want them to doubt her?

Starleaf placed the last Moonstone—a white crystal—back in the circle. Her face was drawn with fear, her lips trembling.

Stinger leaned forward with mild curiosity. "What's wrong, Starleaf? What did you see in your . . . stones?"

Starleaf passed a paw over her face. "Death and despair."

The shallow dip rang with gasps and frightened exclamations. Females clutched their babies tighter. Mud was staring at his mother, wide-eyed.

"*Death and despair?*" Bug Middleleaf shrieked. "What's going to happen?"

"Should we leave? What should we do?" hooted Lizard Deeproot.

Stinger Crownleaf remained perfectly composed. Lazily, he lowered himself from his boulder and made his way to the center of the circle.

Sitting down, he raised a paw. "Let's not panic," he said. "After all, the signs are unclear. Look—the moon is turning white again."

"I don't think you should interrupt Mother," Mud called out bravely, making Thorn wince with apprehension. "We need to hear what she has to tell us."

The Strongbranches gave Mud lethal glares, but Stinger nodded good-naturedly. "Of course," he said. "I want to hear what Starleaf has to say, too. But if she's not completely sure, she should look for other signs."

"I am sure," Starleaf said, softly but clearly. "The moon turned bloody tonight, and even now ragged clouds obscure it, blown first one way, then another. For days, it stormed and lashed with rain; now do you feel this unbearable heat? Drinking water vanishes; even the trees are dying. Bravelands was battered by high winds, but even those were not constant; they veered from south to north, and all points between. And this morning, I found rotting moss upon the trees. The signs are clear: Brightforest Troop has lost its way. And there will be much trouble before we regain the right path."

Thorn turned to Stinger. *It's true, every word*, he thought darkly. *And all because of you.*

For a fleeting instant, Stinger's muzzle twisted with irritation, before he donned a bland look of concern. It was enough. Thorn knew, with a sickening certainty, that Starleaf's Moon Reading had bitten him to the bone.

The baboons were growing increasingly distressed, and even the threatening stares of the Strongbranches could not stop the whispers and stifled cries of anxiety.

"What does it mean?" Lily Middleleaf clutched her baby and held little Snail close. "Are our young ones safe?"

"It's Stronghide," said Twig, his paws clenched. "The Great Spirit is punishing us for accepting him."

Several of the baboons shouted their agreement, but Jackfruit Lowleaf pounded the ground with his fist, baring his fangs at Stinger. "The troop's gone wrong since you drove my son away!"

Thorn had almost forgotten that Nut was Jackfruit's son—after all, Nut had always done his best to distance himself from his Lowleaf parents.

"Your wretched Nut murdered Grub Crownleaf," growled Fang with menace. "We should have executed him. Maybe *that's* where the troop went wrong."

Jackfruit howled with anger, and his mate, Pod Lowleaf, took a bounding pace forward. "There's no proof!" she snarled. "So our son handed Grub his dinner. So what? Anyone could have poisoned it!"

Stinger himself paced forward, then rose up onto his hind

paws to tower over Jackfruit and Pod. His voice was a penetrating growl. "How . . . dare . . . you."

The two Lowleaves seemed to know at once that they'd gone too far. Exchanging a frightened glance, they crouched, hunching their shoulders submissively. An ominous silence fell.

"I cared for Nut like he was my own son," Stinger hissed, "just as I care for all our young. Am I not father to every youngster here? Perhaps a better one than some of the baboons who birthed them?"

Jackfruit and Pod gave frightened nods. Thorn couldn't bear to imagine what it cost them.

"I tried to guide Nut as he became a Highleaf," Stinger went on, turning his face nobly toward the sky, "but his ambition became too much." He leaned once more toward Jackfruit and Pod. "If a fruit is rotten, is it the fault of the baboon who finds it? Or the tree from which it grew?"

Jackfruit sucked his teeth, his eyes darting from side to side. Pod simply stared at the ground.

Stinger spun contemptuously away from them. "Starleaf, have you anything more to tell us?"

"I've told you what I've seen." Starleaf gave him a beseeching gaze. "We must try to save ourselves."

"We all appreciate Starleaf's wisdom," he told the troop smoothly. "And she's right. We *were* in danger of losing our way, after Bark and Grub were killed. That's the bloodstained chaos she saw in the moon. But now? Now we're back on the right path, and I, Stinger, guide our steps."

Most of the troop relaxed at this, though there were a few remaining murmurs of alarm. Starleaf and Mud looked rigid with shock.

"But we must fear for the rest of Bravelands," Stinger went on. "There is a blight of cruel leaders: Spite Cleanfur, for instance, and the brute Titan. I fear that Starleaf is right, and there will be much unrest before Bravelands is secure and peaceful once more. We must be vigilant. We must be *united*. We must watch at every moment for danger, both within and without."

"But Crownleaf," Starleaf protested, "the moon itself has spoken—"

"The moon has passed its peak now," said Stinger. He gestured toward the night sky; the moon had indeed edged away from its zenith. "We thank you for your guidance, Starleaf. At the next full moon, we will seek it again."

One by one, small groups of baboons left the hollow. No more mutters rose, and no questions were yelped; their fear had vanished like a puddle dried up by the sun. Only Starleaf and Mud, gathering up the Moonstones, still looked anxious and subdued. Mud glanced at Thorn and opened his jaws as if to speak, but a single glance at the Strongbranches silenced him.

I believed your mother, Mud, thought Thorn. *I wish I could tell you that.*

In a matter of moments, only the Strongbranches were left in the shallow dip on the plain. Stinger rubbed his scar. "So," he said, "what did you make of that?"

"Monkey-brained claptrap," sniggered Fly.

Grass shoved him. "Jackfruit and Pod are the troublemakers." He grinned, as if he'd cracked a difficult nut.

Stinger waved a paw. "Jackfruit and Pod? They're sour because their precious son's a killer. No one takes them seriously. No, we saw a much bigger troublemaker tonight than those two."

Thorn stiffened. *No*, he thought. *No, no, no!*

"Who?" asked Worm.

Stinger's lips twisted into a smile. "Clever Thorn knows who I'm talking about. Don't you?"

Thorn grew hot under his pelt. He shook his head.

"He's being modest," crooned Stinger. "It's Starleaf, of course." His expression darkened, and his fur bristled. "I won't have her telling them such rubbish, tradition or not. She's frightening the troop, causing dangerous alarm."

Fly slapped the ground. "Should we deal with her now? A few scratches will shut her up."

"No," said Thorn quickly. He felt sick at the thought. "We can't do that."

Stinger picked at his lip thoughtfully. "Thorn's right," he said. "It'll take more than that to handle such a turbulent baboon who endangers our peace and unity."

"Perhaps," ventured Grass uncertainly, his eyes creased as he focused on his leader, "she should be gone altogether?"

Stinger gave a long, sad sigh. "I think, I fear . . . yes. Yes, Grass. That would be best for the troop."

Thorn felt as if a stone had struck his chest. He turned

in agitation to his fellow Strongbranches. Surely even they wouldn't stand for this?

But Grass looked as if he'd been handed a prize mango; he was grinning from ear to ear. The other Strongbranches nodded vigorously, clearly eager to make up for their slow thought processes.

"I agree." Fang thumped his chest.

"Nothing better for Brightforest Troop," hooted Worm. "We *all* want what's best!"

"*Better for Brightforest?*" Thorn exploded. "You can't mean that. Grass, Fang! You know what Starleaf's done for us over the years. For every baboon in the troop!"

Stinger showed no sign of losing his temper; thoughtfully he stroked the scar on his snout. "Ah, Thorn," he murmured. "How true that is. And we have been taught since we were young to accept the word of the Starleaf, because every Starleaf is special, and wise. But this one . . ." His voice lowered almost to a breath. "Is she? Is she really?"

Fly got in the first reply. "No! No, she isn't!"

"No!" chorused the others.

"Starleaf has tricked you into thinking her fantasies are the true path," Stinger said sadly. "And now she is leading Brightforest Troop into danger. I don't want to hurt her. I don't want *anything* but peace in Tall Trees. But which is better—for one baboon to suffer? Or the whole troop to be destroyed?"

"You can't do this!" The panicked words burst out of Thorn. He turned on the Strongbranches. "You know this is wrong!"

"Surely you're not siding with an enemy of the troop, Thorn." Stinger looked hurt.

The other Strongbranches glowered. Thorn knew that with one word from Stinger, they'd turn on him too. They'd rip him to hyena-food, right here and now. And then who would be left to save the troop?

He swallowed hard, clenching his fists. "Of course not."

"Good." Stinger nodded with satisfaction. "Do it when no one's around. I know I can trust you all." His gaze lingered directly on Thorn. "So don't let me down. Don't let the troop down."

"Yes, Stinger," chorused the Strongbranches. "Long live Brightforest! Long live Stinger Crownleaf!"

CHAPTER 20

Thorn hadn't given much thought to the sleeping arrangements in the hyena den, but now even that racked him with guilt. Only tonight had he really registered how much better the Strongbranches' area was; it was dry and free of puddles, it was distant from the stink of dead hyena, and the sandy floor was thickly covered in the softest leaves. There was even a crack in the wall that let in a faint dank breeze from the lower tunnels; in the rest of the den, the stifling heat left baboons limp with exhaustion.

The realization took away his appetite—or whatever appetite he had left, after he contemplated what Stinger planned for Starleaf. His Strongbranch colleagues seemed to have no qualms at all. They hooted and giggled in high excitement, stuffing their faces with the pick of the foraged food. Grass was sharing it: figs and spiky melons, roots and marula nuts, fat cockroaches, small birds and mammals. Thorn knew the rest of the troop wasn't eating nearly so well. When Grass shoved a chunk of dik-dik flesh into his paw, he shoved it away.

"Now, now, Thorn," mocked Fang, "you've got to eat to keep your strength up. Stinger said so."

"And you don't want us to tell Stinger you're being rebellious, do you?" Fly sniggered.

Worm elbowed him sharply, and Thorn growled and crammed the meat into his mouth.

The foulness struck his tongue immediately, making him gag. He spat out the meat, coughing violently, unable to rid his mouth and nostrils of the stench. *Dung.* There was dung hidden in the meat.

The other Strongbranches were almost helpless with laughter; Fly was actually rolling on the floor. "Good trick!" he yelped.

Thorn stretched his jaws wide in a grin and managed to choke out a laugh. "Very funny."

"Hoo hoo hoo." Grass was wiping away tears of mirth. "Eat up, Thorn!"

He wanted to fling himself at the sneering baboon and rip at his snout with his claws, but that would be fatal. It was probably what they wanted. Keeping the stiff grin on his face, Thorn picked out his own fig from the pile and ate it.

They hate me. Well, the feeling's mutual. If he could thwart their plans for Starleaf, that would be revenge enough.

They'd stuffed their bellies so full, it didn't take long for them to fall asleep, one by one. It probably wasn't what Stinger had ordered, but that certainly didn't bother Thorn tonight. Leaving them snoring, he crept as quietly as he could from their sleeping quarters.

Placing his paws with infinite care, he moved down the main passageway, peering into the side tunnels. They were all far more crowded than the Strongbranch den. Baboons dozed and snuffled in a tangle of legs and arms. *This isn't how baboons should sleep*, he thought. *We should be nesting in trees, curled in our own spaces. Everything's wrong right now.*

Peering into the dimness of a small cavern, he recognized several Highleaves; it seemed a likely place to find Starleaf. Cautiously Thorn stepped over the slumbering bodies at the mouth of the cave, then picked his way through a tangle of sleeping baboons. No one stirred.

His paw nudged a loose pebble that rolled on sloping rock and bumped into Moss's nose. As he held his breath, rigid, she snorted, huffed, and rolled over.

He padded on, every pawstep an agony of tension. From somewhere to his right, there was a whistling sound; he gulped, but it was only Twig, snoring, her head propped at an awkward angle against another Highleaf's belly.

The scents in the cave were a mishmash of familiar baboons. Pausing in a tiny gap between sleeping bodies, Thorn flared his nostrils, searching for Starleaf. *Maybe she isn't in this cave at all?*

Then he caught it; a faint, clean, warm scent to his left. He edged toward her, painfully slowly, only just avoiding stepping on Branch's tail.

When he reached Starleaf, he had to pause to recover his

composure. Then he crouched over her. She was curled on a scratchy bed of mahogany leaves, her face relaxed in sleep. She looked so much like Mud, Thorn's heart twisted. *I miss him. . . .*

Right next to her, Splinter was sprawled, one paw twitching in a dream. Splinter was one of the baboons who'd cheered Stinger the loudest tonight; if Thorn was to have any chance of success, Splinter absolutely must not wake.

He had to make sure Starleaf stayed quiet too. *I'm really sorry,* Thorn thought. Taking a silent breath, he clamped his paw over Starleaf's mouth.

She woke with a jerk, her cry muffled against his fingers, her eyes bulging. She twisted beneath him, claws flailing.

"Don't be scared," Thorn whispered, as loudly as he dared. "It's me, Thorn. I've come to help. You're in danger."

Recognizing him at last, Starleaf stopped struggling, and Thorn drew his hand off her mouth. "What's going on?" she asked softly.

Splinter muttered and shifted, his hand slapping at his bed of leaves. Thorn glanced at him nervously. "Follow me," he whispered. "Whatever you do, don't wake anyone."

He turned and crept back through the cavern, seeking the path he'd found before. Starleaf picked her way behind him; she was so silent, he had to check to make sure she was still following. But at the mouth of the cavern, she stopped.

"Come on," Thorn whispered. "We don't have much time."

Starleaf shook her head, gazing intently into his eyes. "Not until I know what's going on."

Something rustled in the darkness nearby. Thorn's heart

was pounding, and he felt light-headed. "Please, Starleaf, before we get caught."

"Caught? By who?"

Thorn took a shuddering breath, half afraid to speak the name. "Stinger."

Starleaf stared at him. A light of disbelief glowed in her eyes.

"Stinger thinks your reading was about him," Thorn whispered hurriedly. "And he's right. He's the one the Blood Moon warned you about. He's . . . done terrible things. I can't explain now, but you *must come*. Stinger wants you dead so you can't warn the troop."

Starleaf's eyes widened in horror. She flinched back. "I have to fetch Mud!"

A grunt came from the cavern, and Thorn stiffened.

"You'll have to leave him," he whispered. "I'm sorry. I'll take care of Mud, I promise."

Starleaf backed another pace. "I'm not going without my son," she hissed.

Now there was a loud rattle of leaves and a murmuring yawn.

"Someone's awake," growled Thorn. "No more time!"

Seizing Starleaf's resisting paw, Thorn dragged her through the mouth of the den.

"I have to go back." Starleaf's cry was heavy with sorrow. "I have to see Mud. He'll be so worried."

"You can't," Thorn said grimly, clambering over a fallen

trunk. He was still gripping Starleaf's paw, and heaved her over it too. "It's too risky."

They were deep into the belt of trees beyond the grassland, and the branches overhead were so broad and dense they blocked the moonlight, making the woods almost as dark as the hyena den. Thorn's fur was clammy with the heat, and his breath came in short, sharp pants; he could make out only the vaguest shapes in the undergrowth, and as they stumbled along, twigs snapped and small animals skittered out of their path. Thorn hoped that they weren't being followed; they would be very easy to track.

But whenever he paused to listen, he heard only the stir of leaves in the hot night breeze, and the soothing rhythms of cicadas and frogs. At last he released Starleaf's paw, and she kept close behind him as they moved through the darkness.

"You'll tell him why I've gone?" she asked, her voice trembling.

Thorn hesitated. He wanted to, so much—but if Mud knew the truth about Stinger, he'd be in immediate danger. It was exactly what Thorn had been trying to avoid.

"I *will* tell him," he told Starleaf. "But not until it's safe."

She gave a long, shaky sigh.

"I'm so sorry," Thorn added helplessly. "But keeping this secret is the only way I can protect him."

"I understand," Starleaf said. Her voice sounded a little firmer, as if she were gathering her strength. "Where should I go, though?"

"I'm taking you somewhere safe."

Thorn pressed on, shoving the undergrowth aside, until he recognized a familiar clump of crotons. The canopy was thinner here, the moonlight stronger, and close by he could make out a huge kigelia tree.

"Nut!" Thorn called up.

A rustling came from the hollow at the top of its trunk. Nut's head popped out, his mangy fur more rumpled than ever.

"Oh, great, it's you." Nut's broad forehead creased into a scowl. "Got another brilliant plan?"

Starleaf was staring at Thorn in horror. "Nut?" she exclaimed. "I can't hide with that murderer!"

"Hey!" shot back Nut from above. "Who says you're staying here? Is this your latest plan, Thorn? It's worse than going to see Big Talk."

"Nut didn't kill Grub." Thorn gripped Starleaf's paws and gazed into her eyes. "Stinger did. He framed Nut for his own crime. He killed Bark too."

"What?" Her voice was hoarse.

"It's true. There's no time to explain. I confronted him, and he admitted it all."

Starleaf licked her jaws, stunned.

"Now do you see how much danger you're in?" Thorn said gently. "You need to stay here with Nut. He's not that bad." His muzzle twisted. "Well, he's not a killer, anyway."

Nut climbed down the tree, jumping to the ground. "Starleaf!" He gaped at her. "I . . . I didn't recognize you in the dark," he said, scratching his neck. "What happened?"

"Stinger's planning to kill her," said Thorn brusquely.

Nut's eyes widened. "Really? He'd even kill *Starleaf*?" He turned to her, his face suddenly very serious. "Then you're welcome to stay here. Anything I've got, it's yours."

"I would be honored," Starleaf said graciously. "Thank you, Nut."

The sky was lightening to a soft purple, and it wouldn't be long until the sun rose. Thorn knew he had to get back before he was missed. "You'll be safer together. And I'll keep figuring out how to fix this. It won't be forever."

"Probably will be, by the time you think of something," muttered Nut.

Starleaf took Thorn's paw and squeezed it gently. "Be careful, Thorn. And please, please, look after Mud."

"I will. I promise." He clasped her paw in both of his. Then he lurched forward to give her an impulsive hug.

With a last anxious glance, Thorn bounded back the way he'd come. *Now comes the hard part*, he thought as he hurried through the cloying dawn heat toward the hyena den.

He had to convince Stinger—and, far worse, Mud—that he knew nothing about Starleaf's disappearance.

"Thorn! Thorn!" Bird Lowleaf shouted as soon as Thorn approached the den. She bounded toward him. "Have you seen Starleaf? She's missing!" Panting in the heat, she drew to a halt in front of him. "First Frog, now Starleaf. What's *happening*?"

The hyena den was in an uproar. Knots of baboons

clustered at the tunnel entrances or in the caves, huddled in frantic conversation. Moss and Splinter loped from one bush to another, poking them with sticks as if they expected to find Starleaf concealed there.

"Mud hoped she was with you," said Bird.

Thorn shook his head. Bird pointed to a cluster of stunted trees at the foot of the escarpment. Mud was huddled beneath them, clutching his mother's Moonstones to his chest.

Thorn bounded toward him. Mud's small face was crumpled, his shoulders shaking, and his expression as he turned to Thorn was grief-stricken. The reality of what he'd done struck Thorn like a kick from a kudu's hoof; the subterfuge might be necessary, but what effect was it having on his friend?

"I'm sure she's all right," he said, wrapping his arm around Mud's shoulder.

Mud looked up, his red-rimmed eyes filling with hope. "Thorn! Do you know where Mother is?"

Thorn's mouth soured. He shook his head, and Mud's eyes dimmed. "It doesn't mean anything bad's happened," he said. "Maybe she went to look for food, or to think about her Moon Readings—it could be anything."

Mud twisted his paws together. "No, something's wrong. She hardly ever leaves the troop, and never without telling anyone. And look at this."

He held up the silver Moonstone: a crack ran right through its heart. Thorn shivered.

"It's a bad sign," Mud said miserably. "I know it is."

Thorn looked from the stone to Mud's desolate face. Could

he just hint that Starleaf was safe? "Listen, I—"

"Mud," said a smooth voice.

Thorn turned, his heart flipping.

"We're all so worried." Stinger's face was creased with concern. "Get some rest, Mud. I'll make sure you hear as soon as we know anything."

Mud nodded. Bleakly he gathered up his mother's Moonstones. "Thank you, Crownleaf," he said. As he trudged toward the hyena den, his shoulders sagged, and Thorn's heart wrenched with guilt.

A heavy paw gripped Thorn's shoulder, its claws digging into his pelt. Stinger leaned into him, so close that Thorn could smell the tang of scorpions on his breath.

"Starleaf had better be past finding," Stinger murmured. "I hope you've made sure of that."

Thorn tried to pull away, but Stinger's paw tightened, making him wince.

"I've questioned the other Strongbranches, and none of them know where she is." His scorpion-breath was hot and clammy on Thorn's ear. "Did you kill her yourself? Alone?"

For a moment, Thorn's heart faltered. "Yes," he choked out. "I killed her."

"Good, good." Stinger gave Thorn a bone-rattling shake. "It would be awful if she was still alive," he crooned in a singsong voice. "Because then I'd have to kill *you*. And I'd . . . take my time."

He released Thorn, patting his face. Thorn stiffened, trying not to flinch.

"Now go join the other Strongbranches," Stinger said. "You've got work to do."

The others slouched in the shade of the den entrance, panting irritably in the increasing heat. Fly tugged idly on Fang's tail, and Fang twisted and snapped his fangs. Catching sight of Thorn, Grass scowled.

"About time. Where have you been?"

"I took care of Starleaf," Thorn mumbled. The words tasted like rot-meat.

The others gaped. "You did?" Grass whispered.

Fly shoved him hard. "What? That job belonged to all of us!"

Worm jostled Thorn's other side, pulling his shoulder fur viciously. "Selfish!" she hissed.

"The next troublemaker is *ours*," said Fly.

"Whatever." Grass shrugged and spat. "Come on. We've got work to do."

Thorn had no choice but to follow, though he was dazed from lack of sleep and already woozy from the relentless sun. Grass set a fast pace, and as they loped across the grassland, Thorn straggled wearily at the back. The mere sight of his fellow Strongbranches revolted him. They had *wanted* to kill Starleaf. What had Stinger turned them into?

"Bug Middleleaf tried to take the best figs this morning, but I stopped her," Worm bragged. "'You can't push me around anymore,' I told her, 'I'm a *Strongbranch*. If you think you can still treat me like some Deeproot, you'd better think again.'"

"Uppity Middleleaves," sneered Fly, licking his chipped teeth. "They haven't got any power now and they hate it."

"Right." Fang nodded. "You've got to show them their place. They thought they were better than us and now they know they're not. Ha!" The very thought seemed to put him in a good mood. "So come on, Thorn, we forgive you. Tell us how you finished off Starleaf."

"None of your business," Thorn said wearily.

"You're as boring as Frog," growled Grass. "Come on, we want details."

"Yeah," agreed Worm. "You can't take the job for yourself and refuse to tell the story."

They went on pestering him, but Thorn ignored them, letting their badgering fade until it was as indistinct as the drone of mosquitoes. He was surrounded by baboons of his own troop, yet he'd never felt more alone.

The others halted, and Thorn only just stopped himself crashing into Worm. Looking up, he saw that they stood among widely spaced acacia trees.

"We're in Spite's territory?" he asked.

"You noticed." Fly sniggered. "Moron."

"Shut up, Fly," Grass said. "If you'd been listening when I explained our orders, *Thorn Strongbranch*, Stinger wants us to take care of the monkeys. They're off raiding another troop's territory today, the little bandits, so the camp's empty."

"Take care of them?" Thorn repeated apprehensively.

Fly grinned, baring his chipped fangs. "We're going to snap the upper branches. Not quite all the way, though. They'll look fine and safe, until a monkey climbs up, and then . . ." He slammed his palm against the ground.

"Oh." Thorn swallowed. He looked up at the highest branches, far above his head, and pictured helpless shapes plummeting to their deaths.

"Good idea of Stinger's, eh?" Grass said cheerfully.

"Only he could have thought of it," Thorn muttered.

Sauntering farther into Spite's territory, Grass patted the trunk of the nearest tree. "Thorn, you start with this one."

With a deep breath, Thorn dragged himself up the trunk and swung into the highest branches. He was shaking so much when he reached the top, he had to grip with all four paws to steady himself. From far below, his four colleagues stared up at him.

"Go on!" hooted Worm. "Get on with it!"

If he didn't, Thorn knew, they would rush to tell Stinger. And then Stinger would have the perfect excuse to get rid of Thorn, and with him the truth about his crimes.

His guts twisting, Thorn reached for the nearest branch and cracked it between his paws.

CHAPTER 21

Fearless's head ached from the heat, and his gullet burned with thirst. His paws were sore from running, his stomach empty—and worse than any of it was the heavy stone of shame in his chest. He'd failed the elephants.

He'd managed to follow Sky and Moon's scents for a long time. Sometimes the two had been together, and sometimes apart. Other animals had crossed their trail, confusing it: he'd caught the sour tang of rhinoceros and the sharp odor of monkeys. By the time he'd tracked them to flatter, drier lands, the trail had grown faint; then it was gone altogether, dissipated by the winds. He'd lost them, after promising their family he would reach them in time. He couldn't bear to face Rain Strider again, or worse, Moon's sad-eyed mother.

I just hope Titan lost their trail too.

He plodded along in a daze of guilt. It was so all-consuming, he had almost stepped on the gazelle before he saw it.

Fearless sucked in a breath, withdrawing his paw. He was hungry, but this gazelle was not much more than its skin. Fur was stretched over bones; its empty-eyed head craned toward the grassland beyond. Fearless followed its eyeless stare.

His gut quivered with shock. Before him on the plain lay the rest of the herd—twenty or more of them—and every single gazelle, young or old, was in the same state as the first. They sprawled where they'd stumbled and fallen on the desiccated grass. Every tawny body was a dried-up bag of hide and bone, and the gathering vultures tugged listlessly at shreds of skin.

A few had been dismembered by rot-eaters, but there was no pooled blood and he could see no bite marks on throats or haunches. Fearless knew little about the lives of grass-eaters, but even he could tell it was thirst that had killed these creatures. He did not like to imagine their stumbling, hopeless trek in search of water.

Shuddering, he picked his way through the shriveled corpses, not tempted to take so much as a bite. No doubt Titanpride had no such problems; one thing there was plenty of was live prey and thirst-quenching blood.

The fate of the gazelles distracted him from his worry about the elephants; by the time he was in sight of Titanpride, he almost hoped he'd find Titan and the young males lounging with the others, eating all the prey and bullying the lionesses.

But Titan wasn't there. None of the full-grown males were. The lionesses dozed under broad-topped acacias, almost piled on top of one another in the shade; obviously they reckoned the warmth of huddled bodies was preferable to the full blaze of the sun. Ruthless was curled against Artful's side, his tail tucked across his nose. Fearless's chest clenched tight. Where were the adult males?

And where were Swift and Valor? He stopped, his fur prickling. His mother and sister were nowhere to be seen.

Artful rose and stalked toward him, her haunches heavy from eating so well. Ruthless glanced up at his mother, his small face tight with worry, then dropped his head onto his paws again, pretending to sleep.

"Where are Mother and Valor?" Fearless demanded.

Artful clouted him on the ear. He stumbled, the side of his head stinging, but he locked eyes with her defiantly. "Where are my mother and—"

"Silence!" she growled. "Where have you been?"

"Hunting," he lied.

Artful's paw slammed into his head again. Fearless shook himself, his ear buzzing like a hive of angry bees.

"You're always disappearing," she snarled. "Don't think I haven't noticed. Don't think *Titan* hasn't noticed."

Still Fearless held Artful's gaze, holding his aching head high. "I'm not doing anything wrong."

Artful's tail lashed back and forth. "Stay with the pride," she growled. "Titan might have decided not to kill you, but we haven't forgotten you're Gallant's brat. From now on you're not leaving my sight—so if you stir up trouble, I'll know. Understand?"

She glared for a moment longer, then turned and flopped next to Ruthless again. Ruthless kept his head down and his eyes closed, but Fearless was sure from the twitch of the cub's ears that he'd heard everything.

Despite his defiance, Fearless felt unnerved. It was foolish to cross Titan, he thought as he paced away. *I have to be more careful.*

He slumped down beneath an acacia next to Honor. He'd grown fond of the lioness since she'd stood up for Ruthless, when Resolute had tried to force the cub to finish off the zebra.

Honor flicked her tail. "Don't annoy her, you idiot," she muttered. "The best thing you can do is keep your head down, like the rest of us."

"Do you know where my mother and Valor are?" he asked quietly.

Honor shook her head. "No," she said, "but they left together. Probably hunting."

"They'll have to go a fair distance, then. There's a herd of dead gazelles not far away, and there's no flesh on them. The grass-eaters are dying, Honor."

"I know." She nuzzled him. "It's bad. But Valor will look after your mother, don't worry."

Fearless sprawled in the grassy dirt beneath the tree's shade; even that felt uncomfortably warm against his belly. His clammy fur prickled with the heat, and he panted hard. A tchagra bird gave a piercing call in the branches, and he blinked up to see the little bird searching for insects, a blur of gray and red-brown. His eyelids felt heavy; Honor's had closed already, and her sides gently rose and fell. He mustn't do the same. Turning his gaze to a horizon that wobbled in the glare, Fearless watched for his mother and sister—and for Titan.

But in the heat, it was so hard to stay alert. When he became aware of blurred shapes moving, he jerked up his head, realizing he'd almost fallen asleep. *Mother?*

No. With a lurch of dread, he saw that the lions were Titan, Resolute, and the young males. Forceful, the pale-furred lion, trailed behind the others, limping badly. *They're not dragging prey,* he thought, his hopes lifting.

"Father!" Ruthless jumped up as the males drew closer. The rest of the pride stirred too and rose to greet them; Fearless followed Honor as she dutifully padded to join the other lionesses.

Ruthless scampered up to Titan, then jolted to a halt, his small muzzle wrinkling. "You smell bad," he said.

Titan cuffed Ruthless affectionately, rolling him in the grass. Fearless could only stare, his stomach twisting: the lions were spattered with rank, clotting blood. They had certainly killed *something*.

Ruthless yelped with excitement as Titan nuzzled his belly and licked his nose. When Ruthless scrambled back to his feet, his small chest and muzzle were stained red, and Titan nodded in satisfaction.

"There," he growled. "Now you look like a proper hunter."

Artful smirked, while Ruthless peered uncertainly down at his bloodied chest.

Titan paced back and forth, his powerful muscles flexing. "We have won a great victory today," Titan roared. "We tracked and killed a young elephant. It was a hard fight"—he glanced at the injured Forceful—"but Titanpride was triumphant. Now the elephants and rhinos know what we're capable of."

Resolute and the young lions roared in triumph, their heads thrown back. As the lionesses grunted and huffed their congratulations, Fearless clenched his teeth, digging his claws into the baked earth. Was it Sky or Moon who had died? *For nothing more than a display of Titan's arrogance . . .*

Titan nuzzled Ruthless, streaking more blood across the cub's face. "I do this for you, my son," he said. "One day, you will rule all Bravelands."

Rearing up on his hind legs, Ruthless pressed his paws against Titan's chest and touched his nose with his own. "Yes, Father," he said, but his expression was puzzled. He kept glancing from his mother to his father.

Titan's tail lashed the air. "Now that all of Bravelands has learned to fear Titanpride, we must keep up the pressure. Today I will lead you in the next great step." He gazed around, meeting every eye. "It's time to take Dauntlesspride."

The pride roared in approval. Even Honor joined in, though Fearless couldn't tell if she was sincere. But no matter how he tried, he couldn't join the chorus of grunting roars. Into his head flashed an image: Titan and his allies stalking over the hill onto Gallantpride territory, and his father leaping forward to face Titan's challenge like the honorable lion he was. Fearless could almost hear the terrible grunting roar as the lions had collided in midair, could feel the ground shaking as they slammed down, locked in combat. And once again, he saw the awful, treacherous moment when Titan's allies had sprung into the battle against all the laws of lions and killed his father.

His breathing was suddenly rapid and harsh. *I'm going to have to watch the same thing happen again.*

"Titanpride, follow me!" Titan roared. As he strode across the grasslands, heading out of his territory, the other lions fell into position: Resolute beside him, the young lions forming up behind. The lionesses followed, Ruthless weaving his way between their legs; Fearless could do nothing but trudge after them, his paws heavy as his heart.

"This will make us the most powerful pride in Bravelands," Regal murmured just ahead of him.

"Dauntless is old, and he's getting weak." Agile hunched her shoulders. "It's about time someone took over his pride."

Fearless gulped back a snarl of anger. Regal and Agile had been Gallantpride lions—had they already forgotten what Titan had done to his father? And Forceful had been *raised* in Dauntlesspride! Yet Fearless could see the pale-furred lion limping up ahead, talking cheerfully to Fierce, showing not a single qualm of regret.

Of course lions took over prides—Gallant had won his from another pride leader, and Fearless wanted to claim his own someday—but Titan wasn't like other lions. *Titan Codebreaker.* Suddenly Fearless was glad that his mother and sister weren't here. At least they had been spared reliving their worst memory.

Titanpride moved quickly and fluidly through the yellowed grass. As they passed a grove of trees, a monkey shrieked, foliage rattled, and Fearless caught a glimpse of small greenish shapes racing away through the branches. *Every animal in Bravelands is afraid of Titanpride*, he thought darkly. *And that's just what Titan wants.*

Ruthless dropped back to walk next to Fearless, his eyes shining with pride. "I never saw a real fight before," he told Fearless. "I think my father can beat any lion, don't you?"

A sharp pain went through Fearless; he remembered saying the same about his own father, just before his death. But the awful thing was that Ruthless was right. Titan would win any fight at any cost; Gallant had lost because he fought with dignity and honor. *I wish Ruthless didn't have to find out what Titan is.*

"He probably can," Fearless said at last. *And if he can't, he'll cheat.*

The trek to Dauntlesspride territory was a long one under the unforgiving glare of the sun. Fearless's paws, already tender after a night spent searching for the young elephants, throbbed and ached. As the lions paced on, the land turned from flat grassy plains to low dry hills, where the grass grew in clumps and groves of scrubby trees dotted the landscape.

"Look," Honor said, craning her neck. "They've seen us coming."

Fearless peered ahead. The rival pride was gathering on a hilltop, their bodies long golden lines of tension; he could hear their apprehensive growls. Dauntlesspride was a lot smaller than Titanpride: the old lion who was their leader, eight or nine lionesses, and few half-grown cubs about Fearless's age. Ranged on the crest of the hill, they stared warily down as Titanpride advanced.

Dauntless himself was tall and rangy, his fur tipped with silver, his face craggy with a long life's experience. A lioness with dark brown eyes—his mate, Fearless guessed—pressed protectively against the old lion. At Dauntless's other flank stood a half-grown lion about Fearless's age. Brown-eyed and long legged, he was clearly their cub. His fur was dark gold, his features sharp and anxious, and he stood with every muscle taut, working his claws against the ground.

Dauntless grunted and padded forward to meet Titan. His gait was stiff, as if his joints ached, but his gaze was steady. "Titan of Titanpride," he said. "What brings you to Dauntlesspride territory?"

Titan roared, his powerful chest swelling. "By the laws of our ancestors, I, Titan, come to claim this pride of Dauntless."

Dauntless's cub clenched his jaws, but neither he nor any other Dauntlesspride lion moved. *They knew this was coming*, Fearless thought.

Dauntless gazed at Titan, his eyes cold and hard. "All lions know that Titan is a breaker of the Code."

A low growl rose from the Titanpride lions. Titan himself snarled, his muzzle peeling back to expose his deadly fangs.

"Lies!" he roared. "Everything I've done has been for the survival of Titanpride."

Dauntless shook his silvered mane. "You don't fight to survive," he said contemptuously. "You fight to make sure others don't. But I will fight you, according to the ancient laws of our ancestors." He swept a long, scornful look across the lions gathered behind Titan. "We all know how you defeated Gallant. If your pride attacks, Dauntlesspride will retaliate."

"Agreed," said Titan smoothly.

Dauntless turned to the lions around him. "Stand aside, Dauntlesspride," he said. Obediently, they moved back, their tails low. The dark-eyed lioness touched her nose to Dauntless's, and he murmured something before she padded away.

Only Dauntless's cub hadn't retreated. "I want to help, Father," he said. "I can protect the pride, too."

The old lion rested his muzzle on the cub's golden head. "Not today, Keen. Not yet. This is a battle I must fight alone."

The cub swallowed hard. He nodded, pressed his forehead to his father's, and retreated to his mother's side.

Dauntless turned to Titan once more. He curled his muzzle and gave the roar of response.

"By the laws of our ancestors, I, Dauntless, fight to keep this pride."

Titan didn't hesitate. With a snarl, he leaped for Dauntless's throat, and the old lion reared up to meet him. They grappled and rolled on the ground, growling, then broke apart and scrambled to their feet.

As the two lions circled each other warily, Fearless saw that the older lion was already limping, although his gaze was steady and not yet clouded by pain. As both prides roared encouragement, Ruthless hopped from paw to paw, his eyes wide.

Dauntless swiped at Titan, but his movements were slow. The huge black-maned lion dodged the blow. With a snarl, he pounced, slamming into Dauntless's side and forcing him to the ground. The older lion struggled, but Titan pinned him down with one paw on his shoulder and one on his flank. He opened his jaws wide and plunged them into the older lion's throat. Dauntless's legs kicked once, and then were still.

It had been so quick.

Titan lifted his bloodstained muzzle. "By the laws of our ancestors," he roared, "I, Titan, claim this pride."

"No!" yowled Keen. *"No!"* He bolted to his father's body, his tail thrashing with distress. For a long, aching moment he pressed his face against his father's; then he straddled his body as best he could, facing Titan. The cub trembled, but his shoulders were hunched in threat, and his brown eyes flashed.

"Step away, little cub," Titan growled.

"I am Keen Dauntlesspride," the cub snarled. "And I won't yield my father's pride to Codeless lions!"

His mother sprang to his side, her head high. "I stand with my son," she said. "We are not Codebreakers. And we do not wish to be ruled by one."

A golden lioness joined her, then several more. Together, they lined up alongside Keen. Fearless shivered. A guilty memory rippled through him: when his own father had been killed, Fearless had run for his life. He couldn't help but be impressed by the young lion's staunch bravery.

But he knew it was hopeless.

Titan's tail lashed. "You do have a choice, young Keen. Certainly you can refuse to join Titanpride." His fangs bared. "You may choose the alternative. *Death*."

His lunge was sudden and violent, and Titanpride charged forward with him. Fearless shoved Ruthless away with his shoulder.

"Get clear of the fight!" He paused, just long enough to see the startled Ruthless scamper away, then hurtled into the battle. He wouldn't harm these lions, whatever Titan's orders, but he had to look convincing or he'd die himself. Snarling, he swiped at Dauntless's mate, his claws deliberately tearing empty air.

Thundering on, he passed Agile grappling and rolling on the ground with another lioness, then Regal snarling at one of the males, her muzzle and paws streaked with blood. The Dauntlesspride lions' faces were tight with grief and terror, their eyes glassy. It was horribly reminiscent of the day Titan killed Gallant.

Fearless dodged and darted between them, roaring and lunging without letting his claws and teeth meet flesh. There was no need to, he realized with a lurching sickness in his gut; Dauntlesspride was losing the battle, swiftly and badly. Not only were they outnumbered, but not all the Dauntlesspride lions had joined the fight. Some stood aside, heads and tails drooping. Fearless felt a deep pang of pity. They didn't want to obey Titan, he knew, but the laws of their ancestors said they must follow the victor. It was a hard tradition to defy.

A dark golden shape leaped into Fearless's path, and he jerked to a stop, paws skidding. *Keen!* He was smaller than Fearless, but he crouched low, shoulders hunched in fury, and bared his fangs.

"I'd rather die than join you!" He sprang.

Fearless rose up onto his hind legs just as Keen crashed into him. Twisting, he shoved the smaller cub away with his forepaws. Keen rolled, staggered upright, and crouched again.

"Stop," Fearless growled desperately. "I don't want to fight you!"

"I won't follow Titan!" Keen yowled. Wildly, he slashed at Fearless.

Fearless reared back, then threw his whole weight at him. Together they rolled and bounced across the earth, Fearless ducking his head to dodge Keen's snapping jaws. As his burst of furious energy drained, Fearless twisted and pinned him down.

He panted as Keen glared up. The cub's brown eyes were full of fear and anger, and Fearless recognized grief there too. "Go ahead," Keen grunted, breathless. "Kill me if you want to. I'll never follow Titan."

"Weren't you listening?" growled Fearless. *"I don't want to fight."* He shifted first one paw, then the other, from Keen's ribs. "I'm Fearless Gallantpride. Titan killed my father too. He's as much my enemy as he is yours."

Keen staggered to his feet, breath rasping, never taking his eyes off Fearless. "You mean it?"

Fearless nodded. "Don't stay here, they'll kill you. Run,

Keen Dauntlesspride—and take as many of the others as you can."

Keen studied Fearless, a glint of doubt in his eyes. Abruptly he blurted, "Come with me, Fearless. You don't have to stay with Titan."

"I do for now," Fearless said with disgust. "Until I can fight him—and kill him."

For a moment longer, Keen stared at him. "If I can help you do it, I will." Turning, he huffed over his shoulder, "Thank you, Fearless Gallantpride. Good luck!"

The cub darted low into the fight, dodging the slash of paws as he grunted to the Dauntlesspride lions. A few younger ones broke from their battles and fled after him, dashing into the cover of the scrubby trees nearby. Honor and Sly ran in pursuit, but drew up when Keen and his group reached the woods.

I hope they'll be all right, Fearless thought, watching Keen's golden outline disappear into the shadows.

He was still staring after them when a heavy blow caught the back of his head. His legs buckled as he slammed onto the ground. Wheezing for breath, he struggled and flipped himself over.

A furious Titan straddled him, black mane soaked in blood, slaver dripping onto Fearless's face.

"Traitor," he snarled, his breath hot on Fearless's muzzle. "You helped our enemy escape. Now you die."

CHAPTER 22

"*I didn't!*" Fearless yowled. *He tried* to scramble away, but Titan's heavy paw slammed down onto his throat. He flailed uselessly with his paws, his breath jerking.

"Liar," Titan snarled. "I saw you. You weren't fighting Dauntless's cub, you were talking to him. And then you let him go."

Titan was horribly close. All Fearless could see was his huge head. Hot air puffed from Titan's nostrils, and flecks of drool spattered from his long yellow teeth. "No, I didn't," Fearless rasped, forcing out the words. "He escaped!"

"You've betrayed me," Titan growled softly. His breath smelled of blood. "*You're* the oath-breaker, Fearless. *You're* the traitor. My oath means nothing now."

Fearless stilled, his heart pounding. Surely this wasn't where everything ended? *I can't die now*, he thought, dazed and horrified. *I haven't beaten Titan yet.* He was aware of silence all around them, in a baking heat that was almost as heavy as Titan's paw. The battle must be over.

"I'll be glad to be rid of you," Titan growled. "I only wish I'd done it when I killed your father."

Terror shot through Fearless. He struggled again, but Titan's weight was a boulder bearing down on him, and drawing every breath was its own battle. Titan's jaws opened, his fangs shining. Before long the vultures would be gathering above his body. *I'm sorry, Mother,* Fearless thought. *I'm sorry, Valor. Loyal, I've let you down.*

"*No!*" A piercing yowl cut through the silence. "Father, no!"

Startled, Titan paused. Fearless felt his grip lessen, just enough that he could twist his neck to see Ruthless. The little cub's eyes were wide with fear.

"Father, I *saw* them," he panted. "Fearless was fighting that cub. He knocked him over and he took a really big swipe at him."

Titan's eyes narrowed.

"He *got* him, too," blurted Ruthless. "That cub won't be around much longer. The hyenas will catch him and eat him if he's bleeding like that."

"Are you sure of this, Ruthless?" Titan asked, "It's very important that you're absolutely certain."

Ruthless nodded. "I'm sure, Father. Fearless fought really well."

"Artful!" Titan roared. The plump lioness shambled over. "You heard what Ruthless said? What do you think?"

Artful paused, looking down at Fearless with cool golden eyes. "Ruthless wouldn't lie," she said. "Not to you. Certainly not for the benefit of Gallantbrat."

Titan pressed down again, forcing a strangled yelp from Fearless's raw throat. "I should kill you," he growled, his dark eyes glittering. "But Ruthless's word has saved you today. Understand? You owe my son your life."

He lifted his paw. Fearless lurched to his feet, taking great gulps of the clammy air. He staggered across the hilltop, willing his head to stop reeling. The battle was indeed over. Several Dauntlesspride lions sprawled, dead. The rest huddled together, edgy gazes locked on Titan.

"This land is Titanpride territory now," Titan declared. "Follow me."

He didn't even have to glance over his shoulder; every lion followed his command without question, the new Titanpride lions falling in behind the existing ones. Fearless limped along at the back, beaten and aching.

"Fearless? Are you okay?" Ruthless had dropped back to pad beside him.

"Because of you I am." His voice sounded rough, and it hurt to speak. "You saved me, Ruthless. Thank you. That was brave."

Ruthless licked his jaws. "You're my friend," he said. "You helped kill that zebra for me, didn't you?" He peered up again, puzzled. "But why did you help that cub? He's our enemy."

Fearless hesitated. *Keen isn't the enemy*, he thought. *Your father is.* But he couldn't say that to Ruthless. "I . . . I felt sorry for him," he said instead. "I know what it's like to see your father die."

Ruthless looked at his paws. "Oh," he said. "I forgot."

"Ruthless," Artful called sharply. "Stop talking to Gallant's brat. Come and walk with me." Obediently Ruthless scampered forward as Artful glared at Fearless. "Stay away from my son."

A vulture wheeled in the sky high overhead. With a shudder, Fearless realized it must be heading for the corpses of the Dauntlesspride rebels. Titan was watching the bird too, his shaggy head proudly tilted.

"Now all the lions of Bravelands will know their true leader." Titan tossed his mane. "Nothing's sweeter than the blood of a weak lion."

"No one will dare cross you now, Titan," said Resolute.

"Gallant's dead, and his pride is mine. Dauntless is dead, and his pride is mine. They were fools to think they had any chance of resisting me. It was a pleasure to kill them."

Titanpride's camp came into view, the grass scorched yellow by the heat. Fearless peered, searching for his mother and sister, but they still weren't back. Worry gnawed at him.

Ahead, the young lions were laughing. "So, Titan," called Forceful, "whose blood tasted better—Dauntless's or Gallant's?" Titan guffawed in response.

Fearless couldn't bear to listen anymore. He was terrified of doing something he'd fatally regret, and all he wanted was his mother and sister. He slowed his paws and hung back. Titan was too busy basking in the flattery of his fighters; Artful's attention was all on Ruthless, who gamboled at her side. None of the others had a reason to spy on him.

Fearless sidestepped and darted into a clump of tall grass. Keeping perfectly still, breathing hard and quietly, he watched the other lions pad out of sight.

The sun was lower in the sky now, and though the air remained clammy and hot, shadows stretched out across the grass. Monkeys shrieked in a nearby acacia grove, and from far overhead came the harsh cry of an eagle. Despite the stifling heat, Fearless shivered. With a pang of renewed grief, it occurred to him that even more than Swift and Valor, he wanted his father.

He slunk across the parched grassland, his spine sagging with weariness, his muzzle brushing the grass. It didn't even surprise him that his paws carried him once more to the kopje near Loyal's den.

As he clambered with difficulty up the rocky slope, he caught sight of a herd of antelopes across the savannah. One was on guard, ears swiveling, but even from here its head seemed heavy on its slender neck. A haze of heat shimmered across the herd, but he could still make out that their flanks were bony, their hides coarse. Some of them pawed at the dry slash of a ditch, bending their heads hopelessly in search of water, then lurched on in a slow, despairing line. Fearless hadn't eaten anything since he'd found a rotten lizard for breakfast, but he felt sick at the idea of killing anything right now, especially those pathetically weak grass-eaters.

In the long grass beyond the antelopes, something rippled.

Narrowing his eyes, Fearless recognized Loyal's black-streaked mane and tawny shoulders. The big lion slunk forward, one cautious paw after another. Abruptly his ears twitched and he halted, straightening to stare across the herd at Fearless. With a flash of its white tail the lookout antelope bleated a warning cry, and the herd sprang away, energized by fear. Loyal bounded straight through the stragglers, ignoring them as he ran toward Fearless.

Loyal's forepaws jutted into the earth as he skidded to a halt, sending up clouds of parched red dust. He stared at Fearless, studying him from nose to tail-tip.

"Are you all right?"

Fearless realized he must look as bad as he felt. "I'm fine," he said. "I just . . ." His voice caught. "I just can't stand being with the pride right now. Titan . . ."

"You're exhausted," Loyal said, his gruff voice surprisingly gentle. "Come with me."

He led Fearless up the rocky slope toward his den. By the time they reached the entrance, Fearless was swaying on his paws.

"Just rest," Loyal said, nudging him toward the cave entrance. "We'll figure it out tomorrow."

Fearless ducked under the low-hanging crag and padded into Loyal's cave. In its darkness, the air was blissfully cool after the beating glare of the open grassland, and it was filled with a comforting combination of Loyal's sharp, earthy scent and the faint aroma of zebra and antelope meat.

A few gnawed bones lay in the corner. Sagging, Fearless

stumbled toward them and flopped onto his belly. His eyelids were heavy, his muscles weak and his paws sore, but he needed badly to talk to Loyal—

Darkness swamped him, and he slept.

He woke in the dark, disoriented. *What is this place*—

Then scents flooded his nose: *Loyal*, he recognized, then *gazelle*. His stomach growled.

"Hungry?" Loyal sounded amused. His dark shape was just visible on the other side of the cave. "Here." Something scuffed across the cave floor, and the scent of fresh meat was right under Fearless's nose.

"Thanks." Fearless seized the torn flesh, and the rich taste of gazelle flooded his mouth. His hunger overcoming all his anxiety, he tore into it, gnawing and gulping, relaxing as his belly filled. It felt so good to eat his fill undisturbed, and to feel cool rock beneath him instead of sun-scorched grass.

This was the only den he'd ever slept in; both Gallantpride and Titanpride rested on the grasslands under the stars, and when he'd lived with Brightforest Troop he'd curled up under a bush or stretched himself out between tree roots. *This is better*, he thought. The weight of rock that surrounded him felt blissfully safe, protecting him from both the relentless heat of the savannah and the claws and sharp stares of his enemies.

"Tell me what happened," Loyal said, when Fearless had licked the last shreds of meat from the bone.

With a deep sigh, Fearless rested his head on his paws. It had been good to forget for a while.

"Titan," he said grimly. "It's always Titan." He told Loyal how Titan had invited the young lions to join Titanpride, and how Titan had planned to use them to kill the young elephants and rhinoceroses. It was easier to talk in the dark—he didn't have to look Loyal in the eye as he told him how he'd failed in his mission to protect the young elephants. At last he came to the takeover of Dauntlesspride and the escape of Keen.

"Titan had me pinned down," he growled, his throat aching again with the memory of the big lion's crushing paw. "He would have killed me if Ruthless hadn't stopped him." He hesitated. "But I know he'll do it one day, when he's angry enough. You were right, Loyal. Titan's not going to keep his oath."

Loyal gave a low growl. "It doesn't give me any pleasure to be right. What will you do now?"

"What I should have done before," Fearless said. "Leave Titanpride." Speaking the words out loud made him feel better immediately, and he raised his head. "Can I still live here with you?"

The dim outline of Loyal shifted. "Of course you can."

"And Mother and Valor?" Fearless asked. "They've wandered off somewhere, but I need to find them. Titan will blame them for my absence, and that won't go well for either of them. Is there room for them, too?"

There was a long silence, and Fearless felt his heart skip. *Perhaps I've asked too much of him.*

"They can stay," Loyal rumbled at last. "I would hardly turn away your mother and sister. Would I?"

* * *

It took effort for Fearless to leave the cool shadows of the den for the dazzling glare of the savannah, but it had to be done. Besides, a night in the cave had revived him more than he'd have thought possible when he'd crawled into it like a wounded lizard the previous night. It was early morning when he and Loyal squirmed out of the slit in the rocks and bounded down the kopje. With the most intense heat of the day still to come, they slunk into the thickest clump of bushes they could find and settled down to watch Titanpride from a safe distance.

The savannah already shimmered with heat, warping the pride into a blur of tawny bodies, but still Fearless could make out individuals. The lionesses lounged in the shade as usual, while Titan sprawled on his belly before the pile of prey, holding forth to the youngsters. A knot of lions from the former Dauntlesspride sat a little apart from the group, looking anxious and still out of place. Yet however hard he peered, there was still no sign of Swift or Valor.

"Where could they be, Loyal?" he rumbled. "Mother can't even hunt anymore. And she's too weak to go far." His eyes felt hot. "It doesn't make any sense."

Loyal nudged Fearless with his gold-streaked head. "Your sister's got her wits about her. And your mother might not have eyes, but her instincts are as sharp as ever. They'll be all right."

Fearless nodded, unconvinced. In the rippling grasses he caught sight of something a hundred or so paces away, creeping cautiously toward Titanpride.

"That's strange," Loyal said, following his gaze. "You don't often see lone baboons."

As the baboon came closer, Fearless recognized the small, scrawny limbs and large eyes. "He's looking for me," Fearless said, dismayed. Rising to his paws, he squirmed out of the bushes and bounded low toward his old friend. *"Mud!"* he called, as loudly as he dared. "What are you doing here on your own? It's not safe!"

Mud turned, his face furrowed with misery. "Oh, Fearless," he gasped, flinging his arms around the lion's neck. "I know I shouldn't have come, but I didn't know who else to talk to."

Fearless had never seen him so upset, not even when he'd been wounded by a crocodile. Around his neck he felt Mud's arms tense, and he turned to see Loyal padding toward them, his scarred face creased into a scowl.

"What's this?" Loyal grumbled. "More idiotic advice from Stinger Crownleaf?"

"You remember Mud, don't you?" said Fearless. "He helped us get Ruthless back."

"Hmph. That one?" Loyal studied Mud's scrawny form. "Yes."

"I need to talk to him," Fearless said. "I'll come and find you at the den later, all right?"

Loyal tossed his mane, but he stalked away, his crooked tail twitching with irritation.

Fearless turned his attention back to Mud. "What's wrong?" he pressed him. "Did something happen to Thorn? Is he okay?"

Mud half laughed, half sobbed. "Thorn? No, he's not okay at all. I don't know if he'll ever be okay again."

Fearless frowned, perplexed. "What are you talking about?"

"Mother's missing," Mud whimpered, wringing his paws. "She vanished in the middle of the night, and she *never* would have left by herself. Not without telling me. And then the next morning, Thorn came back into camp—he'd sneaked out. He said he hadn't seen her, but the more I think about it, the more I'm sure he was lying."

"But why would he do that?" Fearless frowned. "You two have been best friends forever. He loves Starleaf almost as much as you do."

Mud shook his head. "He's been acting so strangely, Fearless. Something's changed him. Stinger started this group, this cadre of fighters to protect the troop—the Strongbranches. Thorn's one of them, and they're all the worst baboons. Baboons like Worm and Fang—remember what they're like? He spends all his time with them."

Fearless's heart sank. "I saw Thorn with Nut," he remembered suddenly. "A few days ago."

"See?" Mud's voice rose into a wail. "Nut's the worst of them all!" He clasped his face with his paws. "Has Thorn been visiting Nut the whole time he's been in exile?"

"I don't know," Fearless muttered. "I wonder what's made him like this?"

Mud swallowed. "Maybe it's because he can't be with Berry. And that's because of me."

Fearless paused, unsure what to say. How could he reassure

the little baboon? After all, he knew it was true: Thorn had
forever lost his chance to be a Highleaf when Mud beat him in
a wrestling match for the Third Feat. Thorn had always loved
Berry, that was obvious to anyone, and staying at Middleleaf
status meant he could never be with her. But could even that
awful disappointment change him so terribly?

Fearless had no idea. He'd never been in love.

"It's not your fault." Fearless licked Mud's cheek. "Stinger
will do everything he can to keep the troop safe, won't he?
You should talk to him. Tell him you think Thorn knows
something about Starleaf."

"I don't know," Mud said, his gaze dropping. "If I'm wrong
and I go to the Crownleaf . . ."

"If you're wrong, Stinger will figure it out," Fearless said.
"He's wise. And he'll find your mother, I know it."

Fearless walked with Mud to the edge of the tree line,
then watched until the little baboon had safely vanished into
the undergrowth. But on his way back to Loyal's den—his
den now, too, he supposed—he couldn't shake the memory
of their conversation. It was achingly sad that Thorn could
have changed so much in just a few moons. *And poor Mud*, he
thought. *No Thorn to turn to, no friend to reassure him. But if anyone
can find Starleaf, it's Stinger.*

He had almost reached the den when his nostrils caught
the familiar sharp scent of his sister. Relief flooded him, and
he broke into an eager run. *She's all right!*

She was sitting outside the den entrance, her tail tapping
the rocky earth, her ears stiffly erect. Every inch of her looked

taut with anger. Loyal sat a couple of tail-lengths away.

"Valor?" Fearless bounded to her, but halted when he saw the look in her eyes. "Where have you been?"

"Where have *I* been?" she hissed. "Where have *you* been, Fearless? I've been scouring Bravelands for you. You go off to talk to elephants and you don't come back. You're not at the watering hole, you're not on Titanpride territory. And I finally find you hiding *here*."

Fearless flinched. "I *did* come back," he said. "But I had to leave again. Titan—"

"Why don't you ever think about anyone else?" Her voice was high and tight with fury.

"That's not fair," Loyal cut in gruffly. "You need to let him explain."

Valor whipped around. "Keep out of it, Loyal Prideless. This is about our family!"

Something was very wrong, Fearless realized with a lurch of dread. His sister looked exhausted, and there was tension in her jaw. "Valor. What's going on?"

Valor sagged, as if her whole body had suddenly crumpled. "Fearless. Mother is dying."

A jolt of pain ran through Fearless, worse than Titan's paw on his throat. "Are you sure?" he said stupidly.

"Dying?" Loyal's head whipped around and he stared at Valor as if stunned. "What does she need? Valor, how can we save her?"

"It's too late for that," whispered Valor. "You have to come with me, Fearless. She needs you."

Loyal's scarred face was twisted with shock as Fearless stumbled past him, but Fearless didn't pause. The big lion spoke, but to Fearless it was a meaningless mumble. All the sounds of Bravelands—the birds, the lowing of the wildebeests on the plain—had become an incoherent buzz. In a daze he followed Valor down the kopje, stumbling on loose stones, and across the grasslands. Valor picked up speed, loping fast across the dry earth, and Fearless sprinted after her. For once he didn't even feel the scorching sun. He could only run, bounding pace after pace, as the sun dipped lower in the sky and long bronze shadows striped the yellow grass. He ran despite the pain in his chest, the pain that felt as if he'd been gutted by Titan's claw.

Valor slowed at last to a trot, leading him to a hollow at the edge of the grasslands. There, shielded by a thornbush, lay Swift, her head on her paws and her blind eyes closed.

She was so still that for a moment Fearless forgot to breathe. But as her two Swiftcubs scrambled into the hollow, she stirred, her nostrils pulsing.

Swift managed to tip up her head, by perhaps a claw-length. "Valor?" She snuffed the air, her voice husky. *"Fearless?"*

Fearless sank onto the ground to lie beside her, nuzzling her cheek and neck. "We're both here, Mother." Valor lay down on her other side, burying her face in Swift's fur.

"My cubs," Swift murmured, letting her head sag onto her paws once more. Her breathing was slow and labored. Feeling her jutting bones beneath her fur, Fearless leaned closer, trying desperately to share his warmth. A clenching pain squeezed his chest, and he heard himself whimper like an infant cub.

"Don't be sad," murmured Swift. "I don't want to burden you any longer. You've had so much to bear."

"Mother," Valor wailed. She choked, rubbing her mother's shoulder with her head.

Her distress struck Fearless to the bone. This was his sister, Valor: levelheaded, efficient, bossy Valor, the fierce hunter who could hold her own with the head of the pride, let alone the other lionesses. Now she looked like a tiny helpless cub again, nestling into her mother's flank.

She's been with Mother all her life, he realized. *This is hurting her even more than it hurts me.*

"You've never been a burden, Mother," Fearless croaked. "You taught us everything. You're the best mother in Bravelands."

Swift struggled to take another breath. Her sightless eyes were open only a slit. "You're so young to be alone," she said. "I wish I didn't have to leave. Look after each other, won't you?"

"We will," Fearless promised, and Valor brushed her mother's cheek with her own. "And we won't be on our own," he blurted, frantic to reassure her. "Father's old friend Loyal has been helping me. He says Valor and I can leave Titanpride and stay with him."

Swift jerked, her hind paws pushing at the ground. Fearless realized with shock that she was trying to get up. *"Loyal?"* she gasped. "Loyal's back? What does he want?"

Valor placed a gentle paw on Swift's back. "Mother, please. You must rest."

"Loyal found me after I left the baboons," whispered Fearless. "Don't worry, he just wants to help us."

"You mustn't go near him, Fearless." Swift took a long, shuddering breath and slumped back down. Her voice was faint but urgent. "You can't trust him. Please, stay away from him. He's trouble. He's an oath-breaker."

Fearless flinched. *An oath-breaker?*

Swift was panting with effort, her eyelids drooping heavily. "Promise me," she said again, her voice strained. Valor shot Fearless a terrified look.

"I promise," Fearless blurted desperately. "I'll stay away from Loyal. And Valor and I will take care of each other."

"We will," Valor murmured. She licked the top of her mother's head. Slowly, Swift's breathing steadied.

"Remember the scorpion that day, Fearless?" she said softly. "And the meerkats you both chased? That was a good day, until Titan came."

It was darker now, the sun's last rays staining the lilac horizon with burnt orange and gold.

"Watch out, Gallant," Swift murmured. "There's something in the grass."

"I remember, Mother," Fearless whispered. "I remember everything about that day. You were teaching us to hunt."

Swift didn't reply. Her breathing slowed, jerked, and began again, fainter than ever. As her cubs cuddled close, her ribs expanded, and she gave one more long, rattling sigh.

Fearless blinked. He nestled his cheek against hers and nudged her gently, but there was no twitch of response, no murmur.

No breath.

Something inside Fearless's rib cage cracked and broke. Valor threw back her head and roared in grief, her cry scattering the roosting birds.

Stretching across their mother's body, Fearless nuzzled his sister's cheek. "We'll be all right," he promised her hoarsely. "We'll stick together, Valor. I swear I'll never leave you again."

Valor laid her head on Swift's shoulder, squeezing her eyes shut. Once again, that great invisible claw tore jaggedly along Fearless's belly.

But gradually, through the grief, came hot anger. Without Titan, Fearless knew, his mother would still be the finest hunter in the pride, running across the grasslands in her long, elegant strides.

Yet here she lay, blind and bony. Titan had killed Swift, as surely as he'd murdered her beloved Gallant.

A growl of helpless rage rose in Fearless's throat. "I swear to you, sister," he gritted. Lashing out his tongue, he licked them both fiercely, the grief-stricken Valor and his dead mother.

"I'll make this right. I'll avenge them both. *I swear it.*"

CHAPTER 23

The vulture screeched as she rose with heavy flaps of her wings, then perched on a spindly, windswept ironwood on the side of the mountain. Her talons were still wrapped tightly around the fragment of Great Mother's tusk.

"Up there?" Silverhorn said doubtfully. The ground beneath their feet had sloped steeply as it turned from dusty earth to stone, but the climb ahead was the sharpest yet, straight up the mountainside. "When did we last find water? I don't see any up there."

The sky above remained hard and clear; the mist they had seen from below had turned out to be nothing more than disturbed stone dust from the scorched mountainside, stirred by the feeblest of breezes. It worked into the folds of their skin, worsening the discomfort.

"We can do it," Rock said. He was staring at the mountain

as if it were a rival bull elephant, his ears spread wide and his trunk lifted.

Silverhorn shook her head. "It's too dangerous. I want to go home. With the lion attack and everything . . ." Her voice trailed off, and she shot a sympathetic glance at Sky.

Sky was barely listening. She was thinking of Moon's small wounded body, thinly covered now with the few sticks and branches she had been able to find. It had been so hard to leave him there alone.

Rock's green eyes were soft and kind. "You'll be safe now that I'm with you," he murmured. "The lions ran away, didn't they? If we stick together we're too much for any animal to attack."

Sky scuffed the pale dust with her trunk. *I wish I had called for Rock earlier*, she thought. *I wish . . .*

The vulture screeched again, as if trying to hurry them along.

"Sky needs to find out about the Great Spirit, doesn't she?" Rock said. "The only way to do that, Silverhorn, is to keep going."

Something burned in Sky's eyes, though she was too dehydrated for any tears to fall. *Give me your strength, Great Mother*, she thought. *Please don't let this journey be for nothing. We've lost too much.*

She blinked her scratchy eyelids and set a foot on the mountainside. With a deep, shuddering breath she said, "We keep going."

Up the slope she trudged, following a broad path that swept up toward the blue summit, the others following. It was hard going. Loose rocks shifted and slid beneath their feet as they struggled for purchase on the incline. A stone skittered beneath Sky's foot and she lurched forward, staggering, snatching at the bare rocks. *I'm going to fall straight off the mountain.*

Yet her discomfort was nothing, compared to what had happened to Moon. *I have to keep going. For him.*

Something warm and strong folded across Sky's back. "Careful," Rock said. "Are you all right?"

"Thank you," she gasped. She still felt jittery, but his trunk steadied her and she swallowed. *One more step. One after another. Just like I told Silverhorn.*

Always the vulture was ahead, sometimes circling for height, then plunging again, sometimes perching on a high rock or a scraggy tree to wait for them. The broad path veered ever more sharply upward to become a sheer wall of stone, with a narrow channel slicing through its veined rock. For a moment Sky thought—hoped—they must have reached the end of their journey; but the vulture tilted her black wings and led the way through the cut. The elephants and the rhino squeezed through after her, Rock scraping his shoulders against the sides.

Beyond the slash in the rock face, the track opened to form a narrow pass that wound up the mountain's flank like a snake. On either side rose sloping precipices that blotted out most of the sunlight. Not a single other living thing disturbed the bleak landscape—not so much as a lizard or a beetle. The companions pressed on in semidarkness, the vulture soaring high overhead. Sky gazed up at her forlornly. *How much farther can we go?*

"It's good, traveling with you and Silverhorn." Behind her, Rock's rumbling voice echoed from the stone walls. "Almost like having a herd again."

Like all male elephants, Sky knew, Rock would have left his herd when he was fourteen or so. Only females stayed with their family forever. Her own older brother, Boulder, had left so long ago that Sky barely remembered his face. *And now Moon will never have the chance*, she thought, with a fresh stab of sorrow. *He'll never travel with his brothers or search for a mate.*

She had to stop thinking about the loss of him; it made her want to lie down in misery. She cleared her parched throat. "Will you tell me about your herd?" she asked Rock.

"I was born to the Marcher family," he told her. "They live on the edge of Bravelands, farthest from these mountains. It's flat there, and even drier than the plains." He sounded wistful. "I miss them, but I found new brothers, all around my age. There are five of us, and sometimes we travel together. Thunder—he's the patriarch in our area—he likes to make our lives difficult. But we have fun."

"That sounds nice," Sky said. They rounded a sharp bend in the path. "Do you—" She broke off in astonishment.

On every rock and crag, on the barren stalks of every skeletal tree, vultures hunched. The path opened out to form a circle, but barely any of it was visible beneath the ranks of birds. All were still and silent, their beady eyes on Sky. Perched on the highest rock was the vulture who had led them here, Great Mother's tusk fragment still clutched in one talon.

Silverhorn, rounding the corner behind them, gave a snort

of alarm. She lowered her horn and pawed the rough ground. "Oh, I knew we shouldn't have come!"

Rock spread his ears wide and strode up to the vultures, swinging his long cream tusks. The vultures didn't budge. Their shining black eyes were fixed on Sky. *They were Great Mother's messengers*, she thought. *Do they have a message for me?*

"It's all right," she said, nudging Silverhorn gently with her trunk. "They won't hurt us."

The rhino whimpered, but she let her horn rise a little. Rock stood as still as the mountain.

The lead vulture gave a commanding cry, and the others replied in deafening unison. They launched themselves into the air on vast black wings, swooping toward Sky and her companions; Sky flinched, squeezing her eyes shut. Nothing touched her but the wind of the birds' wings as they soared around her head. When she opened her eyes, the air was a dark chaos of beating feathers.

"Let's get out of here," Rock trumpeted. Silverhorn shrank against Sky.

"Wait." Sky felt oddly calm. Great Mother had trusted these great, sinister birds, and so would she.

The vultures parted, and Sky stepped forward out of the swirling flock. But when Rock made to follow her, the vultures dived in front of him, blocking the way.

The familiar vulture laid Great Mother's broken tusk on the stony path. She rested her talon on it for a moment more, looking at Sky. Then she lurched into flight and soared on up the mountain.

"I understand," Sky said softly. She turned back to where the others stood, half concealed by the black wings that beat around them. "I have to go on alone."

"No!" Silverhorn bellowed, her eyes wide. "It's a trick!"

With a rumble of frustration, Rock tried to pound toward her, but the vultures slashed the air, driving him back.

"Wait here," Sky cried. "They'll leave you alone when they see you're not following."

"But where are they taking you?" blared Rock.

"There's something they have to show me." Sky didn't know why, but she was certain it was true. Something was carrying her to the mountaintop, like a leaf borne on the wind. Turning back was impossible.

"Sky!" She could still hear the frantic calls of Rock and Silverhorn, but she walked on, pausing to pick up Great Mother's tusk. It felt so smooth and cool and familiar, she was reassured.

Up the narrow path she climbed, panting with thirst. She was alone, but she felt a strange sense of a warm, strong body beside her, one she could almost glimpse from the corner of her eye. *Oh, Great Mother*, she thought. *Stay with me.*

The path was steeper than ever, but there were fewer loose stones here. Sky found her energy returning, and she climbed a little faster, her steps more certain, until with a gasp, she crested the mountain.

A breeze whipped around her, fluttering her ears, blissfully cool after the white-hot glare of the pass. Sky caught her breath. Below her, Bravelands swept out in every direction—the dark green of the forests, the pale gold of the grasslands, the misty purple of more distant mountains. She could see the dark blue smear of the watering hole, the lush emerald green around it. Down there, animals hunted and grazed, played and slept and loved, each in their little piece of land. They couldn't see all of it.

But Sky could. And it was *beautiful.*

Sky gazed for a long while, her heart in her throat, letting the wind whip across her face. She searched the great expanse, trying to pick out where her family must be, and where Great Mother and Moon must lie. It was with reluctance that she turned away at last and stared at the mountain's jagged ridge.

A curved wall of jutting gray stones towered above her. Perched on the highest was the vulture she knew. When she caught Sky's eye, she flung herself into the air and flapped between two of the stones. Gathering all her courage, Sky stepped after her.

The space within the stones was almost circular: far smaller than the Plain of Our Ancestors, and bare of any grass or leaf or flower. Its flat surface gleamed with gray and white pebbles, almost blinding in the sunlight. Right in its center lay a perfectly round, small hollow; the vulture glided down to land on its edge. Hunching her shoulders, she gave an eerie screech.

An answering screech echoed behind Sky. She spun, startled.

Another vulture hobbled toward her, his talons clicking against the stones. He looked so ancient, Sky almost flinched.

His eyes were milky white, sightless, and his face was even more shriveled and wrinkled than the other vultures'. His wings were thin and ragged, with great gaps where feathers had fallen out to reveal uneven patches of pale skin.

The old vulture stopped almost under Sky's trunk and craned his neck up toward the tusk fragment she clutched. Sharply, he tapped his beak against it. Then he shuffled past her to the hollow in the rock and tapped the stones in its center.

"You want me to put it there?" Sky asked nervously.

The vulture tapped the stones again.

Sky stepped carefully over the stones and laid down the piece of tusk. As soon as it clicked onto the pebbles, water bubbled up around it, gurgling and swirling.

The sound of it was beautiful, and somehow just the sparkle of sun on the water seemed to slake Sky's thirst. She gazed, mesmerized. The water was flowing ever faster, fountaining up through the stones, soaking them to a dark gray. As the hollow filled, the bubbling surface calmed, glittering with colors Sky hardly recognized: blues and greens and everything in between, and a sparkle of gold. A thrill fluttered within her.

The blind vulture nodded to the pool. It was a clear command she was happy to obey. Sky lowered her trunk, drew up water, and drank.

If the sight of it had eased her burning throat, the taste of it made her think she would never feel thirsty again. The water was clear and cold and sweet, with a scent of mountain air. Sky drew up trunkful after trunkful. It was as if the water was soaking into every part of her, her toes, her tail, her trunk, her ears. And the level of the pool never sank; it lapped at the brim, stirred by the bubbling of the spring at its center.

When Sky lifted her trunk from the water, she felt as if hours had passed, though the sun hung in the same place in the sky.

"You've been brought here for a reason," the old vulture said.

Shock jolted through Sky. Words were woven through the vulture's rasping cackle, as clear as if they'd been spoken by Rock or Silverhorn.

"I can understand you," she whispered, stunned.

The vulture's wingtips twitched. "Here and now, the Great Spirit will let us speak," he said. "You have a vital task, Sky Strider."

"Me?" asked Sky faintly.

The blind bird nodded his wrinkled head. "Great Mother died without the chance to pass on the Great Spirit. It was a great tragedy, unprecedented and unforeseen. But you, Sky, were the first to reach Great Mother's body. You were the one she loved and trusted most. And so the Great Spirit passed into you."

Sky recoiled, her eyes widening. "What? But I *can't* be the Great Mother—I know I'm not!"

"No," said the vulture calmly. "You are not." He shuffled closer, his blind eyes fixed upon her face. "But you carry the Great Spirit, until the new Great Parent is ready. Great

Mother died too soon. You must find that new Great Parent, and, when the time is right, you will pass on the Great Spirit to them."

Something seemed to shift within Sky, as if clouds had scattered to reveal the clear hills beyond. It all made sense now. The Great Spirit had needed her, and this was why.

"How will I find them?" she asked quietly. "Will I know them? Will it be an elephant?"

"I do not know. No creature does. But you *will* find the true Great Parent." He hobbled around the edge of the pool. "You already have the gift of seeing the future, and the water has given you another gift. Come," he called to the other vulture.

She flapped down and hopped in front of Sky, then bent her bald head. Sky understood at once. Gingerly, she laid her trunk-tip on the soft skin of the vulture's head. The world before her blurred and shifted.

She flies, her wings catching the warm wind currents and lifting her high in the infinity of blue. Her flock cry out to her, showing her animals below, and they are calling her name: Windrider. Below her stretches the vast yellow-grass sea, and she eyes every part of it; herds far below travel their own ancient paths across Bravelands.

To her left lies a cluster of flat-topped acacias and beneath them, half in sun and half in shadow, golden lions bask in the sun. Tipping her wings, she spirals lower.

Two cubs, one larger than the other, play-wrestle in the grass, their tails lashing in fierce mimicry of a real fight. As she soars closer, they break apart.

The smaller cub runs a few steps forward and stares up, defiant. His golden eyes meet hers.

The cub opens his jaws and all around her rises a great roar, blotting out all other sound, buffeting the air. Startled, she rocks backward, her wings trembling.

The world shifted, and Sky was on the mountain once more, her feet planted firmly on rock. She snatched her trunk from the vulture's head. *I was in her memory,* she realized. *I was Windrider.*

She looked toward the pool, but the strange water had gone—and with it, Great Mother's tusk. *But how . . . ?*

"She must have had great faith in you, to give you such a gift," the old vulture said. "Use it wisely." He shifted his ragged wings and bowed his head. "The future of Bravelands depends on you." He began to shuffle back into the shadows.

"Wait," Sky cried. "How will I know this new Great Parent? Where should I search? How will I *know*?"

The vulture craned back over his scrawny shoulder and gave a single hoarse cry. No words formed; whatever power had let them speak, it had dissipated with the miraculous pool. Sky stared, dismayed, as he disappeared behind the great stones of the circle. With a rush of wind from her great black wings, Windrider too left her, circling higher until she was no more than a black point in the sky.

Her legs trembling with the weight of her responsibility, Sky shambled out through the circle of stone. She paused to gaze again in wonder at Bravelands, spread out to the horizon in every direction, just as it had been in Windrider's memory.

Sky knew now what she must do; she just could not imagine how.

Somewhere in that vast land is the new Great Parent.

And I alone can find them.

CHAPTER 24

"The plan went perfectly, Stinger," Grass bragged. "The monkeys came home a few at a time, and we chased them into the trees. Off they went, swinging through the branches."

"And then *splat*." Fly gave his jagged grin.

In the sun's glare outside the hyena den, the Strongbranches were reporting with breathless eagerness to Stinger. Other baboons listened as they squatted on rocks or groomed each other. Thorn shuddered inwardly at Fly's words—his fatuous glee didn't come close to the reality of the monkeys screeching as they fell, or the sudden horrific silence as they hit the ground. Catching Mud's bewildered gaze, Thorn felt a wrench of shame.

"I don't think they'll be bothering us for a while," said Worm, grinning cheerfully.

The Strongbranches weren't keeping their boastful voices

down, and one or two baboons exchanged uneasy glances. Hesitantly, Mango Highleaf slipped down from her rock and padded closer.

"This attack . . ." She bit her lip. "Stinger, are you sure this attack fit with the Code?"

Stinger turned to stare coldly at her. "Of course it did. We struck those treacherous brutes before they could attack us again."

"All the same." Mango took a deep breath, visibly summoning her courage. "The plan really should have been discussed in the Council."

"Should it?" murmured Stinger.

"Yes," Mango told him levelly. "That's what Bark would have done."

"Bark Crownleaf?" Stinger mused. "Her days are long over, Mango. But there is certainly something we should discuss. Not with the Council—with the whole troop."

He loped up onto his new makeshift Crown Stone, a heap of small boulders that had been gathered by the Deeproots. Baboons padded forward nervously as the Strongbranches called out Stinger's summons; more emerged from the darkness of the den. The heat of the sun was intense now, and the whole troop looked beaten down by it, exhausted and submissive before Stinger even opened his mouth.

Stinger was the only baboon who looked unaffected by the heat. He gazed around the assembled troop, nodding in satisfaction, as the Council and their retinues shuffled into place behind him. An apprehensive silence fell.

"The Council is now in session," declared Stinger in a ringing voice. "And the Council is herewith disbanded."

The troop erupted. Gasps and hoots rang out; the Council members surged toward Stinger, crying out in disbelieving protest.

"You can't do this!" shouted Mango.

"It's not acceptable. The Council denies your right!" cried Branch angrily.

"Stand aside. *Stand aside.*" Stinger rose up onto his hind paws, looking out across the Council's heads. "Strongbranches, to me. Stand in the Council's place."

The Council looked too shocked to resist as the Strongbranches bounded forward, shoving them aside and ranging themselves in a semicircle behind Stinger. Padding miserably after them, Thorn joined the line; his fellow Strongbranches were grinning at the troop with triumphant malice. He stared at the ground, swamped by shame.

"In these last few days," announced Stinger as the hubbub faded to stunned silence, "there have been challenges to my leadership. This comes at a time when unity is crucial to the survival of our troop, and it is unacceptable. First old Beetle, and now Mango chooses to question me. That's why I have decided that Brightforest Troop will be safer without the mischief-making of its Council. From this moment, Councilors are ordinary Highleaves and have no extra authority over any of you."

In the eyes of more than a few baboons, Thorn recognized glee.

"Do you all understand?" finished Stinger. "Do you *clearly* understand?"

It wasn't just the ones who had looked delighted at the Councilors' demotion; every baboon in the troop nodded, keen to be first to answer. Their eyes bright with fear, even some Council members shouted in agreement.

"Yes, Stinger."

"Yes, we do."

"Long live Stinger!"

Stinger surveyed the troop for a moment longer, then nodded. "Then get back to your duties. My Strongbranches will assist and oversee you." He turned to them. "Make sure everyone plays their part."

"With pleasure." Grass grinned, shifting his grass stalk to the corner of his mouth. "Come on, Fly." The pair bounded toward a cluster of Deeproots, barking orders to forage for food.

Worm made straight for the shocked Mango. "Come on, you. Find fresh bedding for the Strongbranches."

"That's not my job!" blurted Mango, her eyes wide.

"It is now," said Worm, with menacing sweetness. "Or would you like to make your own way in the world, like Beetle?"

Mango stared at her for only a moment longer. Then she turned, shoulders sagging, and padded off to do as she was told.

"Thorn?" Stinger turned to him. "What's the delay?"

He must not show any sign of the revulsion that surged

through him, Thorn knew. He padded dejectedly toward Mud, who stood with a group of Lowleaves.

"Hunting," he managed to croak. "You need to go hunting. There are lizards on top of the escarpment."

Mud said nothing; he didn't even meet Thorn's eyes. In unified silence, the small group began to climb the slope. Thorn stared after them, his heart clenching.

I've got to do something, I've got to force him to reveal what he really is. . . .

Swallowing, he glanced around the sunbaked earth. No one was watching. Quietly, he loped to the den and crept into the darkness of Stinger's sleeping cavern.

His paws crunched on scorpion remains, and he shivered. There were plenty of those up on the plateau, too; no wonder Stinger looked cheerful and well fed. Crouching, Thorn picked through them, then turned to the pile of bedding and searched that too. Wriggling his arm deep into the soft solanum leaves, his fingers closed at last on something cone-shaped, hard, and ridged.

He drew the rhino horn carefully out.

For some reason, Stinger doesn't want Bravelands to know what the rhinos did.

It seemed a very good reason to make sure that Bravelands found out. Clutching the horn tightly, Thorn crept back through the tunnel and edged out of the hyena den.

His heart flipped as he caught Grass's eye. The big baboon was watching him, and his grass stalk had gone still in his lips.

Thorn hesitated, then nodded cheerfully to Grass and loped on. He hated that Grass had seen him, but what could the big brute say? As far as Grass knew, Thorn was going about his Strongbranch business.

Still, his stomach squirmed with fear as he bounded across the plain, and he was seized by an even greater urgency. In the burning distance he could make out the shimmering shapes of a zebra herd, and he ran toward them, gasping with the heat.

The herd looked aimless and hungry, ripping desperately at the parched grass; *Sleekfriend's diminished herd*, he guessed. They didn't look as if they'd fared well without their leader. An edgy-eyed young stallion was making some attempt to coax them to move on to new grass, so Thorn raced up to him.

"Baboon?" The zebra blinked his long lashes. "What do you want?"

"I've got terrible news," Thorn panted. There was no time for polite conversation, and he held out the broken rhino horn. "This was taken from Great Mother's body after she was killed. The rhinos were responsible."

The zebra craned his striped neck forward and sniffed in astonishment. "What?" He flared his nostrils. "Yes, it smells of Great Mother. Is this a trick?"

"No trick," said Thorn grimly as the other zebras gathered, muttering and braying in shock. "Tell as many as you can. Bravelands has to know the truth!"

Without waiting for their response, Thorn spun and ran; wildebeests were grazing by a thin tree line. He trotted to a halt, just out of reach of their twisted horns. Once again he stretched out the horn toward their stunned faces and told his story.

There was no time to waste. Leaving them neighing and bellowing in horror, he cast around and spotted the next group of animals: a sounder of warthogs, snuffling and digging in the drying mud by the watering hole. With grim determination he ran to them and began his tale again.

"And the rhinos can't get away with it," he concluded. "Tell—"

"Thorn. Thorn Strongbranch!"

The familiar voice made his heart lurch. He watched aghast as Stinger strode across the grassland toward him, the Strongbranches at his side. Grass spat out a stalk and smirked at him; so he had told Stinger what he'd seen. Every muscle in Thorn's body tensed to fight for his life.

But Stinger's face was calm; he was even smiling slightly as he padded up to Thorn and the warthogs.

"Thorn Strongbranch," he intoned gravely, with a respectful nod to the warthogs. "Thank you for your service."

What?

Stinger paused to let Thorn speak, tilted his head, then gave a tiny shrug and went on. "Thorn is right," he told the warthogs. "All of Bravelands must know the terrible truth about our so-called Great Father."

"Is it true, Stinger?" grunted a male warthog.

"I'm afraid it is." Stinger closed his eyes in pain. "We have been betrayed. All of us. It is time for Bravelands to confront the deceivers."

Thorn could hardly breathe, let alone speak. How did Stinger do it? He had turned the situation to his advantage yet again, and yet again he'd effectively pinned his own sins on another creature. Had Stinger meant for this to happen? Had he known Thorn would find the horn and do his dirty work for him?

It was impossible to tell anymore, but a tiny voice in Thorn's head told him not. Stinger hadn't wanted this, but now that it was done, the cunning baboon could twist the truth as easily as peeling a scorpion.

That didn't mean Thorn wasn't in trouble. A *lot* of trouble. He swallowed.

Stinger studied him, his expression still mild and almost friendly. "Did you hear me, Thorn? I said you should go back to the den with the other Strongbranches. I'll carry on the good work here."

Thorn knew he had no choice. All he could do was fall in between the Strongbranches and trudge with them back toward the hyena den. His four escorts remained silent the whole way; none of them met his eye.

I'll slip away later, he thought. *I'll go back to the watering hole, find out what lies Stinger has told those herds. I'll get away from the Strong-branches somehow.*

His plan was a doomed one. As the sun sank toward the western horizon, Thorn's hopes faded with it. If he thought he was unwatched and tried to edge away from the den, Fly or Grass would miraculously appear. When he wandered toward the pile of food, Worm walked with him, preventing him from slipping away. Even when he plodded to his sleeping area, thinking he could escape later, Fang followed. The big baboon smiled broadly and sat down next to him, picking his sharp teeth.

When he tried to imagine what Stinger was up to, out on the savannah, panic almost engulfed him. How could he thwart Stinger when he was never allowed to be alone? When the Strongbranches dogged his every step?

There's nothing I can do. Nothing.

CHAPTER 25

Sky had thought it would be easier descending the mountain, but as she picked her way gingerly down the sun-scorched track, her legs jolted and ached. Behind her, Sky could hear Rock's slow, careful footfalls, and ahead, Silverhorn's stocky legs slithered on the loose shale. Above them blazed a dazzling white sun, its baking heat relentless.

No one spoke. Rock and Silverhorn were focused on the path; Sky was turning the old vulture's words over and over in her mind, struggling to accept them. How could any of it be possible? *And how did I understand his words at all?* Her steps felt no lighter, and the loose stony path was no safer beneath her feet. *How can the Great Spirit be in me?*

"So, what happened up there, Sky?" asked Rock at last. "You were gone a long time."

Sky opened her mouth and closed it again. She wasn't ready

to share this with anyone, not until she believed it herself.

"Are you okay, Sky?" Silverhorn peeked back over her shoulder.

"It's hard to explain," Sky said slowly, "or even understand. There was an old vulture on the mountaintop. And a pool."

"*Another* vulture." Silverhorn snorted. "I'm sorry, but they're just creepy. I envy you the pool, though." She gazed ruefully at the heat-cracked mountainside.

"Me too." Rock blew at the arid dust. "Was the Great Spirit there?"

"Not exactly. But . . . I do know the Great Spirit is with us." As she said the words, somehow the pain of Moon's death felt a little less raw. "That one thing is true."

As they reached the lower slopes, Sky paused to tug at tufts of rough grass between the stones; they'd stripped most of the trees on their way up, and she was glad of something to eat. Rock pulled up a tussock by the roots. "It's tough and dry," he said, narrowing his green eyes as he chewed, "but it's food."

"Look, there are shrubs down there with nicer leaves," said Silverhorn. Half turning, she jerked her horn. "Right th—" She broke off with a panicked snort as her feet skidded.

Sky lashed out to grab her, and as her trunk curled around Silverhorn's tail, the world upended. Suddenly she, too, was falling—but it was her head that spun and tumbled, straight into Silverhorn's memory.

Stronghide stood before her in the blue shadows of night. She could see only his haunches and his stiff, twitching tail, but he was talking to someone

*in the undergrowth. Sky craned to make out the shape in the bushes, but it
was no good.*

*She could hear their voices, though. She knew what they were discussing.
She should try to stop them. He was her leader, but she could try—*

Sky gasped for air. She hadn't fallen down the slope at
all; she was on her knees on the sharp ground, her trunk
filled with hot dust. The shapes that loomed above her were
dark and featureless, silhouetted against a blinding sun. She
blinked hard; Rock was kneeling by her side, his trunk on her
forehead. Silverhorn stood beside him, her small eyes wide.

"Sky, what happened?" Rock pleaded. Sky flinched, shuffling away from his touch, and stared at Silverhorn.

"I know what you did," she whispered. Her voice felt hoarse
and strange in her throat.

Silverhorn's ears flattened. "W-what do you mean?"

Sky scrambled to her feet, her forelegs scraping against the
rough stones of the path. Her chest felt hot and tight with
anger.

"You knew!" she cried. "You knew what was going to happen and you didn't stop it!"

Silverhorn tensed in horror.

"What?" Rock lurched to his feet. "Sky, what are you talking about?"

"I saw it when I touched you!" Sky's voice cracked. "Silverhorn, you didn't stop Stronghide. You went along with the
murder! *How could you?*"

"I—I—" Silverhorn stammered, blinking rapidly. "I'm so
sorry, I—"

Sky shouldered Silverhorn aside, making her stumble off the track, and lurched into a run.

"Sky!" she heard Rock trumpet to her, then, harshly to Silverhorn: "Stay back!"

Heavy steps pounded behind her; she heard stones roll and clatter. "Sky! Sky! Wait!"

She couldn't stop, and she had no breath to answer him. Her own weight bore her on down the steep slope, her feet moving faster and faster to save herself.

"Sky, tell me what happened so I can help!" bellowed Rock.

Sky thundered on; she didn't care that she couldn't stop. She only wished she could outrun what she'd seen in Silverhorn's memory.

Suddenly her forefeet sounded hollow and strange as they thudded on the earth. She didn't even have time to understand before she heard an earsplitting crack that echoed from the rock walls of the valley.

At last, Sky dug in and stiffened her legs, and though her body swayed wildly, she jolted to a halt. Panting, she stared up at the mountainside. The cracks in the ground were shivering up into the mountain itself; she could see them widening and splitting. Rocks came loose and tumbled. Then, impossibly, a great chunk of the mountain shuddered and detached itself.

Sky backed a pace, gaping at the mountain. As if a vast invisible claw had hooked it and pulled, part of the slope peeled away and began to slip downward. Huge boulders thundered toward her, and she knew that in moments, much of the mountain would follow them. Pebbles rattled around her feet, but she barely felt the sting as they hit her legs. A billowing cloud of white dust rose, turning the sun to a blot of clouded light.

Frozen with fear, Sky could do nothing but watch the rocks plummet toward her, bouncing wildly. She couldn't breathe, let alone move.

Something huge slammed into Sky, and the falling hillside snapped back in her vision. At first she was sure it was the landslide, that she was dead already; then she felt Rock's warm body against hers. She could hardly breathe. One of the boulders tumbled by with a great crash, so close she felt the wind of its speed. More pale dust billowed around them.

"Go!" Rock shouted over the deafening racket.

Coughing and panting, they ran. Rock shoved her, forcing her to swerve with him, first to one side and then the other. Another boulder careered past, gouging a long scar in the raw mountainside.

A chunk of rock hit Sky's haunch, making her stagger. The noise was deafening, worse than the loudest thunderstorm. She and Rock were half running, half sliding, the mountain seeming to carry them along. Then, abruptly, the ground vanished.

I'm falling! A gash in the earth yawned beneath her, and she felt herself toppling in. Lashing out her trunk, she sought a grip, her helpless feet flailing at the sides of the crevasse.

She thudded onto her flank on a sloping ridge and began to slide, hitting the bottom with a bone-jarring crash. Rock rolled to a stop beside her, his feet churning. His dark gray skin had turned almost white with dust.

Dazed, Sky gasped for breath, her ears still ringing from the roar of the mountain. Rocks were still falling; one struck her trunk, and her eyes watered with the pain, but it brought her to her senses. She staggered to her feet. They were in a sheer valley of stone, but up ahead, carved by the weather, was a shallow recess.

"Over there!" Sky trumpeted over the noise of the landslide, gesturing with her injured trunk. She didn't know if Rock heard her—he replied with a bellow she couldn't understand—but he must have gotten the idea. He pounded with her toward the recess, scree stinging their hides.

Together they huddled beneath the overhanging earth, rumps pressed against the back of the shallow cave, as a new shower of stones pattered down, throwing up clouds of dust. Sky coughed, her eyes stinging and watering.

At last the skittering clatter of the rocks was silenced, and the clouds of dust began to settle. It was still impossible to see far, but the mountain had stopped falling. Craning forward, Rock peered out from their shelter, up toward the slopes.

"Why would the mountain break?" He was breathing hard. "Do you think the Great Spirit's angry at Silverhorn?"

Sky sneezed; the air was heavy with dust, and her mouth and trunk felt scratchy. "The Great Spirit wouldn't bring down a mountain to punish one animal," she said. "I think it happened because the earth was dried out." *And my mad stampede can't have helped.*

"Well, I wish it hadn't." Rock picked his way to the center

of the crevasse. "I don't know how we're going to get out."

In a few heartbeats, the gorge had entirely changed. The two elephants had fallen into a bare, narrow valley; now it was cluttered with boulders and rock shards and broken trees. Sky's heart sank; the slope they had slithered down was blocked by a colossal pile of boulders.

"Maybe we can shift some of these." Rock wrapped his trunk around one of the lower boulders and tugged, his legs and shoulders straining. The boulder moved slightly, but the stack above it shifted, too, and a few small rocks rattled down to the ground.

"Stop." Sky touched his shoulder with her trunk. "The rest are going to come down on our heads."

Rock stepped back, and they eyed the rock pile. The stones had fallen in a jumble, the heaviest barely balanced on the lightest. Near the top, the biggest boulder of all rocked slightly, looking as if a gust of wind might bring it down on them. High above Sky could see the broken side of the mountain, the raw gaping hole as strange as the socket of a lost tusk.

"We have to try to get up there," said Rock. Tentatively, he placed a foot on one of the boulders. But it turned under his weight, and the higher rocks wobbled ominously.

"I'm lighter than you," Sky said. "Let me."

She set one foot onto the lowest boulder, then another. It supported her, but the boulder above it was huge. She stretched her forefeet, but the stones shifted again, showering grit and small stones.

"Get down!" Rock called sharply.

Wobbling, Sky dangled a leg backward as rock grated horribly above her. The pad of her foot grazed the ground, and she lurched backward with a jolt. Rock pulled her away, and they stood panting in fear.

"Stand back," shouted a familiar voice, muffled and distorted.

Sky tilted her ears. Grunts of effort came from behind the rock pile, and she saw them tremble and shift. A fine stream of dust trickled down.

The topmost boulder was shunted violently to one side; it teetered, then toppled to lodge at a wild angle against the cliff. In the new gap Sky glimpsed a horned head. Another stone rolled, then another; finally Silverhorn was fully visible, peering down from the top of the slope. She was filthy, her folds of skin streaked with white dust and grit.

"Are you all right?" Silverhorn sounded fearful, full of concern for her friends. It didn't seem possible this was the same rhino who had done nothing to stop Stronghide's plot.

Lowering her head, Silverhorn got back to work, shunting rocks to the side and gradually forcing her way downward. When she pushed away the teetering boulders at the top, Rock and Sky were at last able to help, rolling and lugging the lower rocks.

When the path was wide and shallow enough, they scrambled up, panting. Stone scraped Sky's belly as she hauled herself up over the edge and onto the firm ground of the track.

"Thank the Great Spirit," she gasped. Rock clambered up next to her, his flanks heaving. A line of dried blood marked his side, but Sky knew they were lucky to be alive at all. Silver-horn hung her head, peeking up at Sky like a frightened calf.

Sky swallowed. "You saved us."

"Of course," Silverhorn pleaded. "I understand you're angry. But please, let me explain?"

Sky nodded stiffly. "All right. But this doesn't mean I've forgiven you."

"Let's find grass and water first," Rock said to Sky. "My throat feels like wildfire. And you'll need your strength."

"On our way up, there was a stream," mumbled Silverhorn. "Remember? I think it's not much farther down the pass."

Raising her dusty trunk, Sky sniffed the air. Through the heat and grit and the pungent odor of her companions' bodies, she caught it: the sweet scent of water. Yearning coursed through her, and she turned urgently toward it, Rock and Silverhorn trotting after her.

The stream was not deep, but it was fresh and clear. The elephants sank their trunks into it, snorting with relief; Silverhorn plunged right in, stirring up mud, then flopping and rolling. The water, it seemed to Sky, tasted almost as sweet as the pool on the mountain's summit. When she and Rock had also rolled, churning the stream to mud and coating their hides, they clambered up and tore ravenously at the straggly thorn trees on the banks.

Silverhorn didn't seem hungry. Her upper lip toyed with the grass, but she looked tired and tense. When Sky and Rock finally turned from the trees, the rhino cleared her throat, her short tail twitching nervously.

Sky tried to harden her heart. "You wanted to tell us what happened," she reminded the rhino.

Silverhorn took a deep breath. "I hated what Stronghide was planning," she moaned. "I didn't know what to do. He said we all had to help—we had to take revenge on Great Mother for all the years of humiliation we rhinos had suffered. That's what he called it," she added hurriedly. "I never felt humiliated. And some others in our crash, they said they wouldn't do it either."

Sky's heart ached for what might have been, if the rhinos had only held fast to their refusal. "So what *happened?*"

"Stronghide . . . he said he had a destiny. That anyone who stood against him was his enemy, and the enemy of all rhinos. He threatened to drive us away—if he didn't kill us first." Silverhorn's voice sank to a whisper. "So I just left. Some of the others fell in with his plan, but I slipped away in the night. I didn't want to murder anyone."

Sky swallowed hard. "You didn't warn Great Mother."

"It was the wrong decision," groaned Silverhorn. "I should have. But I didn't want to betray my crash, any more than I wanted to kill the Great Parent."

"This humiliation story is nonsense." Rock frowned. "So what if rhinos have never been the Great Parent? Nor have any of the other animals. Why did Stronghide really want revenge?"

"It was something that happened to him." Silverhorn's head drooped lower. "Seasons ago, Stronghide and his mate had a calf, a little female named Brighteyes. Everybody loved

Brighteyes, she was so funny and sweet, and Stronghide loved her more than anything." She swallowed. "But she got sick. Really sick. Even though he was so proud, even though he couldn't stand the elephants, Stronghide went to Great Mother and begged her to help."

"I'm sure she did," said Sky, her heart clenching. "Didn't she?"

Silverhorn shook her heavy head. "She told him she couldn't. That if the Great Spirit decided Brighteyes's life was over, it would end. And Brighteyes did grow weaker, and she died." Silverhorn stared at her feet, shuffling the dust. "That's why Stronghide hated Great Mother."

Sky remembered Moon's small lifeless body, and her breath caught in grief. She'd have given anything to save him. How would she have felt if she'd begged for help and been refused?

"Great Mother would have saved Brighteyes if she could," she told Silverhorn desperately.

The rhino nodded. "I know," she said. "I'm sure that's true, Sky. And I think Stronghide knew it too, deep down. I don't believe he ever would have thought of killing her. Not on his own."

"I bet he would," said Rock testily. "Haven't you heard? Stronghide is Great Father now."

Sky and Silverhorn turned to him in shock.

"It's true," Rock said. "This isn't about revenge or what happened to his calf. It sounds to me like he wanted Great Mother dead so he could take her place."

Outrage flooded Sky. "Great Mother's been replaced by her *murderer*?"

"She has indeed." Rock shook his head in disgust. "Why would the Great Spirit choose him?"

Sky said grimly, "It didn't."

Rock blinked, taken aback. "How do you know?"

Because I'm carrying the Great Spirit, Sky thought. *But how can I explain that?* "A true Great Parent would never have broken the Code."

Silverhorn pawed at the ground. "But the old Stronghide— the Stronghide I've known all my life—*he* would never have killed Great Mother. He was always bad-tempered, but he had a good heart. He changed, this last season. That other animal he was plotting with? I'm sure that's who convinced him to do it."

Sky remembered her vision, back on the Plain of Our Ancestors—the rhinoceros balanced in the acacia tree as the wind lashed its branches. He had turned his horn to the sun, unaware of his danger, of the branches about to snap and send him crashing to the ground.

Was that rhinoceros Stronghide? *Surely it was.* This other animal could have learned of his loss of Brighteyes and manipulated his grief, twisting it until Stronghide was convinced Great Mother had to die.

And that creature is the tree. Horror clutched Sky's heart.

They used Stronghide—and soon they'll let him fall to his doom.

CHAPTER 26

The rising sun still dallied behind the horizon, a smear of pink and gold at the edge of the purple sky, but already the heat was unrelenting. Fearless's skin prickled with it. *What happened to chilly nights and cool sweet dawns?* he wondered wistfully. *Have the older lions ever known weather like this?*

Mother could have told me. But it's too late now.

The warm smell of gazelle filled his nose before he saw the herd, grazing a long way off, near the edge of the woods. His shoulder bumped occasionally with Valor's as they walked, but the two lions didn't speak. There was nothing more to say.

They had lain curled by their mother's body all night. Fearless had slept badly, spending wakeful stretches staring at the pale half-moon; any sleep he'd snatched was broken by disturbing dreams. *Titan above him, jaws widening for the killing bite. The*

slip and endless fall from a high branch in Tall Trees, with death waiting for
him on the ground. Keen trapped beneath his own paws, terror and grief in
his young eyes . . .

He knew from Valor's drawn face that she'd fared little
better. By first light Swift's body had been stiff and cold. Fearless had nuzzled her face one last time, breathing in the scent
he knew as well as his own. He would never smell it again.

And a promise was a promise, especially one given on the
point of death: he and Valor had no choice now but to return
to Titanpride. Fearless had thought they'd found a new and
better home, but overnight it had been lost to them forever.
Loyal Oath-breaker.

What had Loyal done? And why had he hidden it from
Fearless? *Because,* a small voice told him, *breaking an oath is the
worst thing a lion can do . . .*

Fearless cleared his throat, his mouth dry. "What do you
think Mother meant about Loyal?"

Valor seemed dazed, as if her thoughts were far from
Bravelands. "What?"

"What do you think Loyal did that made Mother hate
him?"

Valor sighed. She looked exhausted, her whiskers drooping.
"I don't know. And honestly, I don't care. If Mother thought
we should keep our distance, that's good enough for me. Forget him, Fearless."

As they crossed a ridge and came in sight of Titanpride,
Fearless felt as if something heavy clung to his haunches, its
claws digging in and dragging him back. At least, he noticed,

Titan, Resolute, and the young lions were absent. No doubt they were up to something awful, but Fearless wouldn't have to face Titan just yet.

The lionesses were awake, grooming, stretching their muscles, preparing for their early morning hunt. Agile and Sly were gulping down scraps from a kudu; Daring sprawled nearby, yawning, her eyes still half closed. Honor was on her hind legs, sharpening her claws on an acacia. Ruthless was trailing after Regal, pouncing at her tail while she flicked it to amuse him. Artful, seated on the highest point of the rise, watched them closely, her eyes narrowed.

Valor headed toward Honor and sank down beside her friend, closing her eyes.

Honor sheathed her claws and thumped down onto all fours. "What's going on, Valor?"

Fearless lay by his sister, resting his muzzle on his paws. "She's tired," he said. "Our mother . . ." The words caught in his throat.

"Oh, Fearless. I'm sorry." Honor licked Valor's head gently.

Artful approached, her tail switching with irritation. "What are you three up to? Get hunting!" She glared at Fearless and Valor. "I noticed you both disappearing yesterday. When I tell Titan, he'll find out what you've been up to. Where's that wretched mother of yours?"

Honor and Fearless scrambled to their feet, but Valor stayed where she was, eyes tightly closed. "What's the matter with her?" Artful said impatiently, raising a paw to cuff her.

"She's not hunting today," Fearless snapped, his rage

flaring. "Our mother is dead, and Valor needs to rest. So leave her in peace!"

Valor opened her eyes in alarm, but Artful only flicked her ears dismissively. "So, we're rid of Swift at last?" she drawled. "At least the pride's free of *that* burden."

Fearless felt his hackles spring up. His claws protracted. "A *burden*?" he snarled. "*You* blinded her! Can't you leave her alone now? You were jealous of Swift, because you're not half the hunter she was. And you're not half the mother to Ruthless that she was to us!"

Honor and the other lionesses gaped at him. Valor sat upright, her tail-tip flicking nervously. "Fearless, be quiet," she growled.

Artful tensed, her shoulder muscles bunching. "Be careful, Fearless," she hissed. "Your life hangs upon the word of my son."

Valor crouched submissively. "He doesn't mean it, Artful. He's upset." She glared a warning at Fearless. "I can't hunt today. But Fearless—you'll hunt for me, right? Artful, he'll bring back twice as much prey. To make up for my weakness."

Fearless's blood buzzed with the longing to spring at Artful, to tear her eyes with his claws. No matter what happened afterward, it would be so satisfying to take that smirk from her.

But Valor's stare was pleading.

"Of course," he muttered, sheathing his claws. "I'll hunt now."

"You'd better," Artful sneered. "And Titan will hear about this too, Gallantbrat. Don't think you'll get away with *anything*."

As the plump lioness stalked away, Valor gave a murmuring growl. "Idiot brother. Just for once, can you *try* not to annoy her?" She laid her head back down on her paws. "I couldn't bear to lose you too."

"I'm sorry." Fearless licked the top of her head.

He *was* sorry, if only for making trouble for her. But his blood still coursed with rage, and he couldn't stay here. With a lash of his tail he strode out of the camp, feeling the stares of the lionesses burning into his hide.

I don't take orders from Artful.

And I need to talk to Loyal.

His fury distracted him from the broiling heat as the sun rose higher and the kopje came into sight, quivering in the haze. Loyal was near the rocks, crouched over the body of a gazelle.

"Fearless!" the big lion called with delight. Abandoning the carcass, Loyal padded toward him. But as he met Fearless's eyes he hesitated, one paw raised. Then he dipped his great gold-streaked head.

"She's gone, hasn't she?" Closing his eyes, he butted Fearless's nose with his own. "I'm so sorry. I know how much you loved your mother."

Fearless flinched, yanking his head back. "Get off!"

"What? I don't—"

"I told Mother about you."

Loyal froze. A wary look crept across his scarred face. "And what did she say?"

"That you were an *oath-breaker*. One of the *last things* she said was to stay away from you."

Loyal said nothing. He turned to gaze off toward the southern horizon, his face hidden from Fearless.

"You knew she would, didn't you?" Fearless pressed him. "That's why you didn't want me to mention you."

Loyal didn't turn. "Fearless, you don't understand," he muttered.

"I need to know *what you did*. What oath did you break?"

Loyal's crooked tail twitched. "You're not ready to hear about it," he growled more aggressively. "Not yet."

"You wanted us to come and live with you. How could we do that if we can't trust you?"

Loyal turned at last and padded closer. "Listen to me," he said in a tight voice. "You need to eat something. You're exhausted. Eat, rest, and you'll feel better."

Fearless's pelt prickled. "Stop telling me what to do," he spat. "I don't take orders from an oath-breaker!"

Loyal's mane bristled huge, and his pupils narrowed to slits. Fearless took a pace back, suddenly aware of how colossal Loyal was. His shoulders were as broad as Titan's, and each paw was as large as all four of Fearless's put together. The ragged scar beneath his left eye gave him a look of wild, unpredictable ferocity.

"Your mother was right," snarled Loyal. "Yes! I am an oath-breaker. I went against my word, and I caused a lot of pain. But I will never regret it, not as long as I live. No matter what any lion thinks of me—even you."

Fearless stood his ground. "It was *you* who told me oaths are sacred!"

A low, grunting growl came from Loyal's throat. "One day, I'll tell you what happened, and you'll understand. But not yet." He nodded toward the gazelle carcass. "Now, enough of this. Go and eat."

Fearless stared at him, breathing hard. "I will not share food with an oath-breaker."

Loyal blinked, dismayed. "Fearless—"

But Fearless sprang into a bounding run, leaving Loyal standing alone by the kopje. He ran until his chest ached with the burning heat, until he could no longer feel the sting of pain in his heart.

"I can't go on like this," he told Stinger.

He had found the Crownleaf resting on a shelf of ocher rock, looking out to the grassland; it wasn't far from the escarpment where the hyenas had lived until Titan ravaged them. Just the sight of his old friend and mentor had broken the tight constriction of Fearless's throat. His story had come spilling out of him, like water overflowing the banks of a river. Stinger had always understood him best.

Thoughtfully the baboon stroked the scar on his snout as

Fearless paced back and forth. "Do you remember what I told you about Titan?" he asked.

Fearless nodded. "That when the time comes, I can strike like a scorpion. That I should watch and wait. But I don't think I can stand it anymore!" He raked the cracked earth with his claws, sending clouds of dust flying. "My father told me that one day I'd be able to fight anyone in Bravelands. But I won't be full-grown for another year. I don't even have a mane yet. Is Titan going to let me live another year? And if he does, what will things be like by then?"

Stinger stretched out a paw to stroke the lion's muzzle. "Poor Fearless," he said softly. "Brightforest Troop and I will always be here for you. Baboon or not, you are one of us."

Fearless pressed his muzzle into Stinger's paw. "I want to do something about Titan *now*," he growled. "But I don't know what."

Stinger sat up abruptly on his hind legs. His amber eyes gleamed. "But there is something you can do!" he said. "You can prepare for the right time. You'll need to be powerful."

"I know," Fearless broke in, but Stinger raised a finger to silence him.

"Power doesn't just come from strong muscles and sharp claws," he said. "It comes from your allies, too. Titan knows this. It's why he's invited those young lions into the pride. What you need, Fearless, is a pride of your own."

"That's easy to say," rumbled Fearless. "Titan stole my pride."

"He stole your father's pride," Stinger corrected him. "What about those lions who escaped from Dauntlesspride? What if you asked them to join you?" He smiled, his yellow fangs flashing. "Fearlesspride sounds rather good, doesn't it?"

Fearless blinked in surprise. "No cub has ever led a pride."

Stinger shrugged. "Maybe not. But has any cub ever been found in an eagle's nest and raised by baboons? Anything is possible, Cub of the Stars."

Fearless felt his heart lighten, as if Stinger had shouldered a great part of the burden he'd been carrying alone. *Stinger always has a plan!*

And Fearlesspride did sound good. . . .

"I'll do it," he blurted, stiffening his shoulders. "I saved Keen Dauntlesspride, didn't I? I'll find him, ask him to join me!"

Stinger grinned. "Good," he said briskly. He plucked a beetle from a crack in the rock and popped it into his mouth. "Now, my Cub of the Stars, I need to ask for *your* help."

"Anything," Fearless said eagerly.

Stinger's expression grew serious. He leaned a paw on Fearless's neck, as if weariness had overcome him. "I don't need to ask this favor yet," he murmured. "But the time may come soon."

"All you have to do is ask," said Fearless firmly.

"It will be difficult," sighed Stinger. "And perhaps painful. I will be asking a lot of you, my Cub of the Stars. Can I count on your absolute loyalty?"

Fearless pressed his head to his mentor's, wishing he could

rub the tired sadness from the baboon's face. "You have *always* been there for me, Stinger. You've done more for me than I could ever have dreamed."

Bright hope overcame Stinger's expression of misery. Fearless licked his jaw, so happy to have cheered his old friend.

"I'll do anything to help you, Stinger Crownleaf. Anything at all."

CHAPTER 27

The yellow earth was dry and cracked from the relentless heat, and it was easy enough for Thorn to scrape it away, but his breath came in rapid pants and he glanced frequently over his shoulder. He must not be seen.

As his paw-tips touched something thin and fragile, he paused. Digging away the loose earth around it, he drew out a parcel of wrapped leaves, then another. The stuff inside the leaves was still soft and squashy; Grass and Fly had protected their sweetpulp well.

With one more nervous glance around, he peeled aside the leaves and scraped out a pawful of pulp. Beside him was a heap of crushed roots and nuts that he'd brought from the food pile; he mixed the sweetpulp into it, agonizing about the quantity. *Not so much that they'll notice. But enough to have an effect.*

Something rustled behind him, and his heart skipped. It

was time to go. Brushing earth back over the hoard and gathering up the sweetpulp-laden food, he hurried back to the den. He made an effort to look nonchalant as he added the roots and nuts to the Strongbranches' rations.

"Thieving from the supplies, are we?" Worm was right behind him, and Thorn almost jumped out of his pelt.

He took a steadying breath, then rose and turned to Worm with a grin. "I don't see why not. We're Strongbranches, right?" He turned to the Deeproots' rations, grabbed up a wizened spiky melon, and bit into it.

Worm looked taken aback, but then she gave a hoot of amusement. "That's the spirit, Thorn." She crouched and stole a handful of marula nuts for herself. "The Deeproots are so scrawny and lazy, they don't need all this anyway."

"That's right." Thorn stretched his features into a grin. "It's not exactly the tastiest stuff, though." He threw back the half-eaten melon and sat down by the Strongbranch pile, just as the others trooped into the cave. "Let them eat that rubbish. There's a fat lizard on our pile."

As the Strongbranches settled down to eat, Thorn eyed them nervously. He made a slow meal of the lizard he'd snatched, avoiding all the roots and nuts; he didn't want to choose the tainted ones.

"Phew, these roots taste strong," remarked Fang, wrinkling his muzzle.

Thorn's heart skipped. "Probably the heat."

Fly grunted. "I wish the weather would break. Though it was really funny when one of the Deeproots fainted yesterday."

He chomped on a jawful of nuts. "And actually, they taste good like this."

"I was just thinking that." Fang grinned and grabbed another root. "Hey, I ever tell you 'bout the time I killed a python?"

"Yeah, yeah," slurred Grass.

"'S true! It was the biggest one I ever saw. . . ."

The conversation was already growing ridiculous, and before long the Strongbranches were rambling complete nonsense. Fly kept giggling, his lips peeled back from his broken teeth. After a while, Grass slumped against the wall and began to snore, letting nuts tumble from his paw.

Thorn waited, heart in his throat, until he was sure all four of them were dazed with sweetpulp and at least half asleep. When he rose and backed away, Worm mumbled an unintelligible question, Fly giggled again, and the others didn't move at all.

Hardly daring to breathe, Thorn crept from the den.

Bounding over the ridge that led to the watering hole, Thorn halted in surprise. The hillside and the banks were thronged with animals, as densely packed as they had been on the day Stronghide was declared Great Father. But the mood seemed very different. Zebras, gazelles, wildebeests, and kudus tossed their heads and snorted. Close to the water, hippos pawed the ground, jaws wide. At the front of the crowd, a huddle of elephants blocked Thorn's view, their ears spread in aggression.

Everyone's angry, he thought. Unease tugged at him.

A cheetah passed Thorn—the same one he'd seen at the Great Gathering, old, with just one eye. Thorn tailed him as he padded through the mass of hot, sweating bodies down toward the water. A wildebeest shunted her haunches into Thorn, sending him sprawling, but she didn't even notice what she'd done. "I can't believe it," she cried to her herd-mate. "No wonder the Great Spirit has been punishing us."

Thorn's heartbeat quickened. *Do they know already?*

The cheetah's black-tipped tail still twitched ahead of him; he trailed it down the hill, brushing past a group of gazelles and giving the hippos a wide berth. Furious brays and growls rang out all around him. He stumbled out between two grumbling warthogs and saw the water sparkling in front of him.

The elephants had Stronghide surrounded. Their tusks were lowered menacingly at the rhino, their trunks curled for butting. Stronghide faced them bullishly, his horn low.

"Murderer!" the matriarch Rain trumpeted. She reared back, then slammed her forefeet down, making the earth tremble. The nearest animals flinched, but the rest of the crowd took up her cry.

"Murderer! Murderer! Murderer!" The chant was bellowed and snarled along the length and breadth of the shore.

Stronghide was panting now, tossing his horn from side to side, as if he were looking for an escape route. He reminded Thorn of the scorpions trapped by Stinger.

Rain strode forward, vast and menacing. "*You* killed Great Mother!" She lunged at the rhino, but he twisted away with an agility born of desperation.

"Listen to me!" he bellowed. "Please! There are things you don't know!"

"Can you explain the rhino horn found in Great Mother's wounds?" It was the cheetah, prowling along the shore. His hackles were raised, his spotted tail switching. "Stinger Crownleaf told us all about it. He advised us to have mercy, but I don't think so."

"There's nothing you can say, Stronghide." Rain advanced on him. "You're a murderer, and you're no Great Father. If it weren't against the Code, I'd kill you myself."

The crowd surged toward Stronghide, growling and whinnying in agreement. The big rhino lurched backward, an expression of horrified fright on his face.

Thorn stared, his stomach clenching. This was what he had wanted, wasn't it?

So why doesn't it feel right?

"Please," Stronghide begged, "you have to listen—"

"Exile is better than he deserves," a hippo bellowed.

"Get out of Bravelands and don't come back!" came the hoarse cry of a wildebeest.

The elephants thundered forward, and the crowd charged behind them. The ground trembled with the impact of hundreds of hooves, feet, and paws. Stronghide bolted along the shore, wheezing and gasping; Thorn had to splash into the shallows to avoid being trampled, but he saw the rhino's rolling eyes, his contorted snout. The herds pursued him the long length of the watering hole, harrying and snapping and kicking, until at last Stronghide struggled, exhausted, over the crest of a low hill and vanished. The mob of animals trotted and slowed, screeching and roaring in triumph.

Thorn waded back to the empty shore. Despite the heat, he felt bitterly cold. *Listen,* Stronghide had begged the animals. *There are things you don't know. . . .*

Had those things been about Stinger? Thorn could suddenly imagine Bravelands covered in a gigantic spiderweb, with Stinger crouched at the center, drawing in his victims with a twitch of a silky thread. But there was only one way for Thorn to find out what the rhino knew about that web.

I have to go after Stronghide.

Thorn could just make out Stronghide's big, three-toed footprints in the parched dust, but where the rhino had fled across rockier ground, he had to rely on broken twigs and smashed leaves. There were plenty of those to guide him. Stronghide had trampled shrubs and even saplings in his panicked escape.

Ahead, Thorn made out a patch of crushed grass on a low rocky incline. He scrambled up, digging in his front claws to scale the rock. How terrified must the rhino have been to stampede up this slope on his stumpy legs?

Thorn made a final leap to the top—and his forepaw slipped over the edge into nothing. He pulled back, his heart pounding. Edging forward once more, he peered down through disturbed dust. The rocks sloped a little farther, then broke into a sheer drop.

Thorn swallowed. He didn't want to look, but he had to. He squeezed his eyes shut for a moment, then, bracing himself, edged down the slope and peered at the foot of the cliff.

A gray mass huddled there, broken.

The rock face was impossibly steep, but Thorn could make out little outcroppings and ridges of stone. Finding them mostly by touch, he backed down the cliff, clinging to the feeble handholds with uncertain paws. Halfway down he caught hold of a jutting stone that snapped away; Thorn swung wildly, snatching at any hold he could. Finding purchase at last, he hugged the cliff tightly. When he could bear to move again, he lowered himself more slowly, one paw at a time.

Was the rhino even alive? The dark shape down there was terribly still. Failure tasted sour in Thorn's mouth. His only chance of bringing down Stinger might have died with Stronghide.

When his trembling paws hit flat solid ground, he rubbed dust from his eyes, then crept toward the motionless rhino. He was almost close enough to touch him when Stronghide's tail jerked.

He stifled a yelp. The rhino was alive, then. Thorn scratched at his chest nervously. He'd seen plenty of wounded animals, and he knew pain could make any creature dangerous—let alone a rhino.

But Stronghide's eyes were slits of dull black, and his breathing was ragged. There was a bloody gash on the thick hide of his belly, and one of his legs was twisted unnaturally beneath him. Thorn felt a strong pang of pity. Stronghide had lied, he had murdered Great Mother, but no animal deserved this awful fate.

As Thorn moved forward, a dislodged pebble rolled, and Stronghide's eyes opened. Thorn froze. Those small eyes widened, and the rhino staggered up and lurched away, tossing his horn and dragging one foreleg. He swayed, then fell heavily to his knees with a grunt of pain.

He's afraid of me, Thorn realized, shocked.

"Get on with it," Stronghide panted, half rising again. His legs shook violently, and he collapsed into the mud. "Finish me off."

"What?" Thorn exclaimed. "Why would I do that?"

Stronghide glared. "That's why your master sent you, isn't it? To make sure I'm dead?"

"No one sent me," Thorn growled. "I don't have any master. I came to talk to you."

The rhino grunted, eyeing him with mistrust.

"I was there when the other animals drove you away," Thorn said, squatting by his huge head. "Right before you ran, you said there were things no one else knew. What did you mean?"

The big rhinoceros was silent for so long, Thorn was afraid he was already dead. But as he tensed and leaned closer, Stronghide shifted and groaned.

"He could talk an animal into anything," he mumbled. "You should know . . . what he's capable of."

Above them, a guttural screech split the burning sky. With a fearful snort, Stronghide jerked his horn at the sky. Three vultures were circling, their flight path bringing them ever lower and closer, their keen eyes fixed on Stronghide.

"Go away," Thorn cried, waving his paws. "You're not wanted!"

The birds' bald heads dipped to stare at Thorn. After a moment, their wingtips twitched, and they soared out of sight beyond the ridge of the gully. Thorn watched them go, surprised beyond words that they'd obeyed him.

Maybe Stronghide isn't dying after all?

Thorn turned urgently back to him. "Do you mean Stinger? Did he talk you into all this?"

"Who else?" Stronghide rasped.

Thorn slumped down in the dust, his head reeling. It was what he'd suspected from the moment he saw Stronghide cornered by the watering hole—perhaps, deep down, he'd known it all along—but certainty was a horrible thing. *Stinger was behind Great Mother's death.*

Stronghide dragged a pale tongue across his upper lip. "I was so angry with the elephants," he whispered. "And Stinger talked and talked. I don't know how, but I sort of saw it. His words, they made sense in my head. Killing Great Mother, becoming Great Father, it was the only thing to do. The right thing. A noble thing." He gave a rattling cough. "And now I don't know why. It doesn't make sense anymore. I should never have listened to Stinger." His eyelids drifted lower. "If he came to me now, I'd run my horn through him."

Thorn clutched his head to stop it spinning. Stinger's plan had been fully formed, laid out in his mind as neatly as fruit at a Council feast. He must have planned for so long: waiting for a chance to turn a powerful animal against Great Mother, taking the time to coax and convince Stronghide.

What had been happening in Tall Trees, back when Stinger had first visited Stronghide? Nothing that Thorn could remember—everything had seemed normal, yet all along Stinger had been planning Great Mother's death.

Well, he hasn't planned on me.

"I'm going to get rid of him." Tentatively he stroked the rhino's horn; Stronghide's eyes looked distant. "I don't know how, but I'll do it."

Stronghide coughed. "You? Get rid of Stinger? You can't."

"I have to."

Stronghide's tongue lolled. "Good luck, young baboon. Now leave me in peace." His voice was barely audible. "I failed as Great Father, but there's one thing I have learned." He gazed up at three black shapes that once again wheeled overhead. "The vultures always know when death is coming."

Why why why? Why would he do it?

The trudge back to the hyena den was long and slow beneath the glare of the sun; its heat turned the whole savannah into a wobbling blur of pallid brown and yellow. Thorn barely cared that his throat ached from thirst; the agony of not knowing was worse. *Why kill Great Mother, only to set up his own stooge of a Great Father for failure and death?*

Thorn stared unseeing at the horizon as he padded wearily along. *Think like Stinger. What would he do?*

And suddenly, like lightning striking, he remembered what Stinger had said only days ago. *A baboon could do a better job. . . .*

Thorn's heart hammered against his ribs. *Stinger knew Strong-hide was useless.* He told everyone so; he didn't try to hide it. He knew Bravelands would want a Great Father who was strong, and decisive, and clever. He'd always known it. He'd known that when Stronghide failed, the herds would turn to a crea-ture who could lead them through the crisis.

Stinger.

Thorn broke into a panicked sprint. He could not let this happen. It would be a catastrophe; Bravelands might never recover. Words thrummed in his head, over and over again.

Only kill to survive. Only kill to survive. The Code told him what to do. The Code would guide him.

If Bravelands was to survive, he must kill Stinger.

CHAPTER 28

Fang Strongbranch was obsessively focused on a termite mound, breaking away chunks of red earth to dig into the secret tunnels beneath. As Thorn approached, the big baboon plucked out a termite and popped it into his mouth.

"Fang," Thorn greeted him. He could hardly keep his breathing steady.

Fang spun around. "You!" He curled his muzzle. "Very funny trick, lacing the food with sweetpulp. Ha-ha."

"Has Stinger been asking for me?"

"Yes, he has," sneered Fang. "And you're in trouble. He's been wondering where you got to."

"Good," said Thorn, nodding humbly. "I'll explain myself. Will you ask him to meet me here?"

"Why?" asked Fang sharply.

"Because I want to meet him alone. I want to talk to him.

If he doesn't come by himself," said Thorn, raising challenging eyes to Fang, "I'll vanish again."

Fang glared, his jaws working on a termite. "I don't take orders from you. But fine, I'll tell him. I'm sure he'll let us know what you say, anyway."

As soon as Fang slouched out of sight, Thorn peered around frantically. A slab of rock jutted from a small escarpment; it would have to do. Thorn loped behind it, his heart thundering.

If I don't win this fight, Stinger will kill me. He knew it with certainty. *But what if I do succeed?*

The troop will probably kill me instead.

Berry would never forgive him, he knew. That cut him to the heart, but it couldn't be helped. It had to be done. Bravelands needed him to act; every creature's life depended on it. He had no choice.

The wait seemed endless, and the heat only grew worse, glaring off the pale rocks around him. He felt faint with it, but he couldn't let himself pass out. He did not even dare shift position; he could only endure the scorching blaze on his fur and flesh.

Footsteps.

Thorn recognized them at once as Stinger's. Half surprised, half fiercely glad, Thorn felt for one of the chunks of loose rock that lay scattered around him.

Stinger stopped, scratching his muzzle. He looked entirely unconcerned that he'd been summoned to a one-on-one meeting. *He doesn't fear me*, thought Thorn grimly. *He should.*

For a moment Thorn shut his eyes tight, bringing to mind Bark Crownleaf's murdered body. He remembered her smashed skull; her face forever twisted in shock at the betrayal. It seemed a kind of justice that Stinger would die the same way.

Stinger looked puzzled for the first time. Frowning, he turned impatiently to gaze around, and in that moment his back was to Thorn.

Now or never. Thorn sprang from his hiding place, raised the stone, and lunged.

And at precisely the same moment, Stinger spun back, and his amber eyes glowed on Thorn's.

Thorn stumbled, hesitated, froze.

His hand trembled, the rock suddenly far too heavy. As Stinger's golden stare held his, all the air was sucked from Thorn's chest. In a horrible instant he was sharply aware of how much bigger Stinger was, how much stronger and faster.

Stinger glanced from Thorn's face to the rock in his paw and, quite unexpectedly, smiled.

"Put it down, Thorn," he said pleasantly.

Thorn's paw dropped to his side.

"I've been waiting for this," Stinger said. "I knew you would try to kill me."

Thorn stumbled backward a step. His ribs felt as if they were crushing his heart. "No."

"Yes, I *did.*"

"It's not . . . you can't have . . ." Thorn could hardly draw a breath. "You . . ."

"Your view of the world is far too simplistic, Thorn." Stinger gave a sigh. "You think I deserve to die because I did something wrong?"

Thorn's tongue felt dry and thick in his mouth. "You're a murderer," he whispered.

Stinger gazed, his eyes bright and almost amused. "It's in the nature of achieving power to do bad things," he said softly. "You see, Thorn, it's like this. . . ."

He moved so fast, Thorn never saw him coming. Stinger was on him before Thorn knew he'd sprung, and Thorn was slammed backward onto the ground. His skull rang with the impact. Stinger was on top of him, his long fingers wrapped around his throat, and he gasped in pain as claws dug into his skin. Stinger scrabbled at Thorn's paw with his own, and Thorn felt his rock wrenched from his grasp.

Through watering eyes, Thorn saw Stinger raise the rock high. His skull would be cracked like an egg, just like Bark's. . . .

Stinger's eyes gleamed with vicious joy, and for an instant his grip on Thorn's throat loosened. Lunging, Thorn sank his teeth into the Crownleaf's arm.

With a yelp of pain, Stinger released him. Panting, wriggling, Thorn dragged himself paw by paw from beneath him, but at the last moment he felt Stinger's claws sink into his hind leg.

Snarling, Thorn twisted to grapple with him. The two baboons rolled on the hard earth, biting, scratching, tearing.

For a triumphant moment, Stinger was pinned beneath

him. Thorn reared back to strike, all his misgivings forgotten. *I have to kill him!*

Then powerful paws seized his shoulders, dragging him away. Through blurred, bloody vision, he saw Stinger stagger to his feet, and he couldn't bear it. "No!" he howled. *"No!"*

"Shut up." A paw clouted the side of his head, sending him spinning into the dust; then he was dragged up again. Fang's ugly face leered at him.

"I lied," the Strongbranch snarled. "You think I'd let Stinger come alone?"

Grass shoved past Fang, gripping a stone. Thorn had enough time to recognize his own weapon—the one that should have killed Stinger and saved Bravelands—before it was slammed into the side of his skull.

Then there was only darkness.

"Trickery and treason." The voice swam into Thorn's consciousness, solemn and calm and strong. "It was my fault. Forgive me, creatures of Bravelands. I should have known."

The voice was one he knew, one he hated with all his heart. It was enough to give Thorn the strength to shove himself half upright. Groggily, he tried to focus.

"You all believed in Stronghide, but so did I." The voice rang out in clear, sunlit air. "That belief, that faith, blinded me to his deceit. To the fact that he *could not possibly be* the Great Parent."

Thorn blinked hard as the scene came into focus. Great herds were ranged before him: zebras, wildebeests, and gazelles. He could make out leopards and cheetahs, meerkats and hippos; monkeys loitered in branches that rippled with reflected water light. *I'm at the watering hole. At a Great Gathering. And I'm the center of it.*

Fear shot through him, and he tried to lurch to his feet, but Grass and Fly grabbed his shoulders, shoving him back to the ground.

Every creature watched Stinger intently. Animals nearby were repeating his words, relaying them back through the crowd: *"Trickery and treason . . ."*

"The Great Parent is the heart of Bravelands," Stinger went on. "They must be able to solve problems, must understand the news brought from every corner. They must advise, they must judge, and most importantly, they must let the Great Spirit speak through them."

"They must advise, they must judge. . ."

"Let the Great Spirit speak . . ."

Stinger sighed and spread his paws. "Stronghide fooled us all," he declared mournfully. "But we must pick ourselves up and go on. We need a new Great Parent."

Horror clutched at Thorn's belly. This was it—the endpoint of all Stinger's plans. He was making his move right now, and only Thorn knew it.

He struggled in Grass's grip. "Don't listen to Stinger!" he howled. "He's a murderer!"

Stinger shook his head and slanted his eyes.

"Thorn, you fool," he whispered, so softly that only Thorn could hear.

Thorn strained against the powerful arms that pinned him. Gasping, he twisted his head to stare imploringly at the herds. "He tricked Stronghide into killing Great Mother," he screamed at the top of his lungs. "Stinger knew Stronghide would fail, that you'd drive him away. He knew you'd need a strong replacement. *He planned it* because *he wants to be the Great Father!*"

For the first time, he met Stinger's gaze. Thorn expected him to be angry. *Furious.* Perhaps frightened, too.

But Stinger looked, if anything, chillingly triumphant. His eyes were cold, but the corners of his lips twisted in a small, secretive smile. And the nearest animals weren't passing Thorn's words to their herds; they were staring at him in disgust. The anger that had carried Thorn this far collapsed, and he faltered.

"May I speak now, Thorn Strongbranch?" Stinger asked, his voice clear and carrying.

"Please," Thorn begged the animals close to him. "You must believe—"

"Every word from Thorn's mouth is a lie," Stinger said crisply. "He's been working against the Great Spirit for many moons now."

"A lie," the animals at the front repeated.

"No!" Thorn yelped. "It's not true!"

Stinger grabbed Thorn's arm. His fingers dug in, the claws biting painfully. Thorn fought to pull away, but the Strongbranches held him in place.

"Thorn was like a son to me," Stinger told the crowd; his

tone was achingly sad. "It was hard to believe the truth. I did not recognize his pride, his lethal ambition." He shook his head, as if he hated what he must say. "I waited too long, I hoped too long. And Thorn murdered two Crownleaves."

A gang of meerkats gasped in unison as they turned to Thorn. An elderly gazelle glared at him with loathing.

"Murder . . . murder . . . murder . . ."

The words were spreading from creature to creature, across the banks and up the hillside, like a storm cloud rolling over the sky. As it reached each family or herd, they turned toward Thorn. He could feel hundreds of eyes piercing him, filled with horror and disgust.

"I didn't!" Thorn screamed. His heart thrashed against his ribs.

"He used my daughter. Made Berry think he loved her." Stinger's clear voice cracked, and almost broke. "Just to get close to me. You tried to kill me too, didn't you?" His eyes glittered on Thorn. "If I hadn't acted quickly, you'd have smashed my skull with a rock."

Thorn gaped at him, every breath stinging his lungs.

"You can't deny it, can you?" Stinger cocked his head, those amber eyes still brimming with sadness.

"I had to . . . I . . ." Nausea stirred in his gut. All this time, Stinger had been plain-lengths ahead of him.

"How could you?"

Through all the brays and roars and bellows of disgust, he heard a voice he loved. Thorn lifted his head, feeling true despair swamp him. *Berry.*

She stood there before him, half supported between Blossom and Petal Goodleaf, the whole troop ranged protectively around her. For a moment, all Thorn felt was utter relief. Berry was thin and drawn, her tail a ragged stump, but she was alive.

"Berry," he croaked, "I—"

"I trusted you," she whispered. Her beautiful eyes were dark with disgust.

"It's not true, none of it! Berry, all I wanted was to keep you safe!" Thorn struggled, but Stinger's grip on his arm was merciless. Berry turned away, pressing her face to Blossom's shoulder.

"See how he has hurt my daughter?" Stinger flung out a paw toward Berry, and this time his voice held wounded rage. "And his latest crime? *That is the worst of all.*"

For a moment, time seemed to freeze. There was movement in the crowd; someone or something was approaching. Animals backed away, clearing a path as ripples of unease spread. Thorn creased his eyes, trying to focus through a haze of heat and pain.

Worm and Fang paced toward him; between them they carried a limp burden. It was another baboon, Thorn realized.

He strained forward. Crazy, but he thought he saw a white streak of fur on the baboon's forehead. *Starleaf?* he wondered, dazed. It couldn't be. Starleaf was safe, hiding with Nut. Why would she reveal herself? Why would she let Worm and Fang carry her here like a dik-dik corpse?

Then Worm stumbled on a wildebeest's hoof, and her

burden slipped. One of Starleaf's long arms dangled loosely, her knuckles scraping the ground, and her head lolled to face Thorn. He stared in speechless horror into her empty eyes.

Stinger held out his paws toward the body. His eyes were bright with tears of grief. "Starleaf was about to reveal the truth about Thorn. So he murdered her."

"No!" Thorn shrieked. "No, no, no!"

He might have screamed his denial forever, but something slammed into him, knocking him out of Stinger's grip and onto the ground. Small claws slashed and tore at his chest and face, and Thorn felt blood trickle from his snout into his eyes, half blinding him.

It was Mud, but a Mud Thorn had never seen. His eyes were brilliant with fury as he yanked Thorn up by the throat, then slammed his head against the ground.

"Mud, I didn't do this, I didn't, I swear it," Thorn tried to rasp, but the words caught in his strangled gullet. Mud was past listening, anyway. He shook with racking sobs as he tore his claws into Thorn's flesh. "Mud, please—" Thorn gave a shriek of pain as he felt Mud's teeth pierce his shoulder.

"Enough, Mud," said Stinger's calm voice. "Justice will be done, but it must be done fairly."

Strong paws pulled them apart, Grass holding Thorn upright while Fly tugged Mud away. Thorn's whole body was a fire of pain, and he could feel blood trickling from his muzzle and brow and his mauled shoulder.

It didn't matter. It was nothing to the pain of knowing he had lost everyone. Mud hated him. Berry hated him. No one believed him. He wanted to curl up on the bank of the watering hole, to be left alone. There he could wait for night to fall, and the crocodiles to take him.

"Thorn's crimes are terrible," Stinger declared, "but they are only a symptom of what happens when Bravelands has no true Great Parent."

Oh no, Thorn realized through his haze of agony. *Here it comes.*

"It was hard for me to believe," Stinger said. "I have always tried to do what was best for Bravelands and best for my troop. What small talents I had—for organizing, for peacemaking—I was happy to use for the benefit of all animals. But I never suspected . . ." There was no need to pass his words back through the crowd, because every animal was utterly silent, straining to hear. "The Great Spirit has come to me," he said. "I did not ask for this honor, but the Great Spirit whispered what I must do to save Bravelands. I, Stinger Crownleaf, am the only one who can guide us through these terrible times. *I* am the true Great Father."

"No!" Drawing on the last of his strength, Thorn wrenched himself from Grass's grip. He crouched and leaped, his fangs bared, straight at Stinger's throat.

He slammed Stinger to the ground. Beneath him, for the first time, he saw the older baboon's eyes widen in shock.

Then a blur of golden fur engulfed him. Huge and heavy, it crashed into Thorn with stunning force. Thorn sprawled on the bank, but for a moment he didn't know which way was up.

A terrible weight was crushing his chest. He couldn't move, could barely breathe. . . .

Fearless.

The big cub's eyes burned with fury as he forced Thorn down into the hard lake shore. Sharp claws punctured Thorn's chest, and he felt more blood flow down the channels of his ribs. *Fearless*, he tried to say, *Fearless, we're friends*, but no sound would come.

"Great Mother had vultures," Stinger cried to the crowd. "Stronghide *said* he had oxpeckers. And I? I have *lions*."

Gasps and shouts of astonishment rippled through the herds. "He must be the most powerful of all," a giraffe breathed.

Stinger bowed his head. Thorn knew he was the only one who saw the glitter of triumph in the Crownleaf's eyes. "If you trust that the Great Spirit has chosen me—and if you will accept me—I will do my best to be worthy of you all."

The watering hole exploded with noise. Shrieks, yowls, screeches: each animal rapturously proclaimed their enthusiasm. Thorn was crushed against the dusty ground beneath Fearless's heavy, hot paws. He was nothing, he knew that now: a scrap of helpless, useless flesh.

"Fearless," he croaked. "Don't believe Stinger. *Think*."

Fearless glared down. "Quiet," he snarled. "I don't know you anymore, Thorn. Maybe I never did."

Thorn let his head flop back into the mud. He felt utterly empty.

Stinger raised his forepaws, urging the herds to silence. "Before you drink and pledge your allegiance, I must announce my first decision as Great Parent." He stared contemptuously at Thorn. "It gives me no pleasure, but I must judge this breaker of our Code. I have tried to be merciful. I've turned my eyes from Thorn's evils, over and over again, because I loved him too much to believe he was lost to the Great Spirit." He hesitated and drew a paw across his face. "Maybe this time, he can change. Maybe I can give him one more chance."

"What?" gasped a giraffe.

"No!" grunted a cheetah in fury. "No mercy!"

"That one's beyond change." A hippo widened its jaws to display its horrific blunt teeth. "Drive him from Bravelands!"

"What good would that do?" a jackal snarled. "He'll come back. Kill him and be done."

Voices rose on every side: "Kill him! No mercy! *Kill him!*" Thorn thought he could hear Pebble's voice in the chorus, and Bird Lowleaf's, but he tried not to listen. He did not want to hear Berry and Mud calling for his death. He rolled his head back on the gritty earth to stare up at Fearless again. Fearless wasn't shouting for his death, but there was certainly no mercy in his blazing eyes.

Stinger sighed, his shoulders drooping. "And so it must be. The Codebreaker will be killed. Fearless, Strongbranches— take Thorn away."

As Fearless removed his paws from his chest, Thorn rolled over, desperately scrambling for freedom. Moments ago he had wished for a swift end in the jaws of crocodiles; now that death was snapping at his heels, he discovered a fierce urge to live.

But there was no escape. Fang and Worm shoved him back toward Fearless. A wave of Fearless's familiar scent swamped him, mixed now with something bloodier. The lion clamped his jaws around Thorn's arm and dragged him along the sand.

The crowd seemed to swing around him, like treetops in a storm, as Fearless hauled him through it. Fly, Grass, Worm, and Fang strutted at the lion's flanks. Fearless wasn't biting—*Not yet*, a terrified voice murmured inside Thorn's head—but his jaws were tight, and Thorn could sense the suppressed power that would soon crush him between deadly fangs.

"Please, Fearless," he gasped. "*Listen.* I'm not the killer."

A growl sounded in the lion's throat. Fly smacked Thorn on the side of his head. "Shut up, traitor."

As he was dragged through the hollering, baying crowd, Thorn glimpsed Berry, her face hidden behind her paws, and Mud, tightly hugging the body of his mother. Distantly Stinger was wading into the watering hole, his head high. The animals had begun to follow him, eager to declare their allegiance to their new Great Father.

Stinger's victory was absolute.

Helpless, Thorn sagged in Fearless's jaws, his body jolting across grassland and low hillocks. He was beginning to think he would die of the dragging when he heard Fly's voice, tinged with bloodthirsty eagerness.

"Those trees." Fly jerked his head at a thick stretch of forest. "We'll kill him there."

Fearless picked up his pace, and all too soon the shadows of the forest closed around them. Spangled sunlight flashed into Thorn's eyes through the branches, and he glimpsed the pale flowers of a rosewood tree against the blue, blue sky. If death was coming now, he was glad he could see the sky.

Fearless's jaws loosened abruptly, and Thorn thudded to the ground. His nostrils filled with the familiar scents of earth and wood. Sunlight filtered down through the rosewood's leaves, dappling the green moss and his own blood-soaked fur. If it hadn't been for the root that jabbed into his spine, Thorn would almost have been at peace; it was just like the forest glade where he, Mud, and Berry had played when they were very young. *When my parents were alive, and Tall Trees was the only part of Bravelands that mattered.*

"You've known me all my life," he rasped, staring up into the cold eyes of Fly and Grass. From the ground they looked so huge. "Would I really kill two Crownleaves? I threw the Third Feat, and you know it. I didn't even want to be a Highleaf enough."

"Stop arguing," Fly told him, almost kindly. "It's over."

"You do it, Fearless." Grass touched the lion's shoulder. "It'll be fastest."

Panic swept over Thorn. He panted, trying to catch his breath. His heart beat so hard, it seemed to be escaping his chest. "*Please*, Fearless," he moaned. "This is a terrible mistake."

Fearless loomed over him, blotting out the sun. There was

nothing but determination in his eyes.

Fly's right. It's over.

Staring up steadily at his old friend, Thorn fought to subdue the terror. "I know you don't understand," he managed to say, softly and levelly. "This isn't your fault, Fearless, and don't ever forget that. It's Stinger's."

Fearless's ears flicked back and Thorn thought, just for a moment, that he'd reached him. But then, with a grunt of anger, the young lion opened his powerful jaws. His long white fangs glinted, and a rush of hot, blood-tinged breath filled Thorn's nostrils and lungs.

He couldn't watch. He shut his eyes tight and braced himself for death.

EPILOGUE

Babble puffed out his bedraggled feathers, trying to warm himself. The oppressive heat had finally broken, and with it the sky; torrential storms lashed Bravelands with thunder and rain and wind. He and Chatter were drenched. The sky above them was ominously dark; there was little chance the rain would let up anytime soon.

"Horrible," he chittered. "And now this." He pecked a flea from the rhinoceros's hide, but the body beneath his claws was already growing cold in the rain. "That's the last one," he said regretfully, gulping it down.

Chatter clicked his red beak. "Ah, well," he said resignedly. "Plenty more ground-plodders in Bravelands. The pickings were always good on this one, but it's time to move on. You know the saying: *Don't worry about today, because there will still be insects tomorrow.*"

Babble tilted his head to peer down at the motionless gray mass beneath him. A shiver ran through his feathers that had nothing to do with the cold. There would be no tomorrow for the great rhinoceros who had provided them with ticks and fleas for the whole season. "It's hard not to feel sorry for him," he sighed. "It's a bad way to die."

Chatter flicked his tail dismissively. "What did he expect, angering the Great Spirit like that?" He hopped a little farther down the rhino's gray flank, poking at a wrinkle in search of one more overlooked tick. "The vultures say anyone who provokes the Great Spirit will regret it."

Babble tested his wings against the rain, preparing to take off, and a movement in the sky caught his eye. "Speaking of vultures," he said, "they're coming now."

The huge birds spiraled gracefully on the air currents, dropping to settle one by one around the rhino's body. Babble edged closer to Chatter, their wings brushing. He'd heard of this ritual: the great rot-eaters would taste the flesh and judge the death. He was eager to witness the tradition, but the vultures, so big and so wise, were intimidating.

The biggest was the one called Windrider, with her shabby black-and-white feathers and her wrinkled pink head. Babble was overcome with curiosity as Windrider hopped forward, flapped up onto the rhino's rib cage, then tore a strip of flesh from its belly. She tipped her head back and her throat worked as she swallowed. The other vultures watched her calmly; Babble and Chatter stared in awe.

"A good death," she croaked at last. "Though it tastes of

betrayal and deceit." She spread her wings, then paused, peering down at Babble and Chatter.

Babble forgot to breathe. He could feel Chatter trembling along with him, and his friend's yellow eyes were rounder and wider than ever.

"Don't look so frightened, little oxpeckers," Windrider said gently. "I bring news."

With an anxious glance at Chatter, Babble cleared his throat and gave a shy chirp. "What—what kind of news?"

The clouds shifted, sunlight struck the vulture's black wings, and for a moment her feathers shone. Her dark eyes seemed to see into him—no, right through him. Babble was suddenly certain that they saw past Bravelands, to whatever lay above and beyond. Her whisper seemed to fill his whole small body until he felt as big as an eagle.

"*Good* news, Babble Oxpecker. The Great Spirit has returned."

AN ELEPHANT entrusted with a powerful gift.

A LION treading a dangerous path.

A BABOON trapped by the truth.

A great evil has risen—and
the adventure continues in

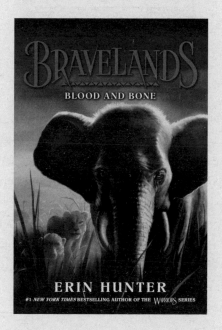

Keep reading for a sneak peek!

CHAPTER 1

Sky Strider's lungs ached, and her hide was soaked to a gray that was almost black. Her legs felt weak, and her feet, usually so powerful and steady, slithered wildly in the mud as she thundered through the forest. She feared that at any moment she might slip and crash to the ground.

Yet she could not stop. Branches whipped her eyes, ears, and trunk, and she almost stumbled on a newly fallen kigelia branch, but she blundered on, driven by a force inside her that she couldn't explain.

I must get there.

Where?

I don't know but I must!

The thick vegetation opened up very suddenly, and Sky stumbled to the edge of a small clearing. Lightning flashed above the canopy, illuminating the whole scene before her, and the young elephant choked on a cry of horror.

A group of baboons stood there, tails stiff, their muzzles peeled back in rage. With them was a young maneless lion, who crouched menacingly over something in the center of the circle. The sight of a lion in the company of baboons no longer shocked Sky—not after all that had happened in the last seasons—but the expression on the lion's face did.

It's Fearless! Cub of the Stars! But I hardly recognize him.

He loomed over another baboon, this one sprawled on the ground, bleeding and terrified. The lion's jaws were open, slaver dripping, his long teeth bared and his amber eyes alight with a killing rage.

"You betrayed us!" Fearless roared at the baboon. With a jolt, Sky saw who it was—Thorn Middleleaf of the Brightforest Troop.

She felt something wrench within her. These two, lion and baboon, had been so close. And now Thorn lay sprawled in the mud beneath Fearless's jaws.

Everything in Bravelands seems broken, Sky thought. She raised her trunk.

"Stop!" Her cry resounded through the clearing.

The baboons turned to her as one, tense with shock, but Fearless didn't even look up. He only glared at his captive with determined fury. "Die, traitor!"

Sky knew she had no choice. She charged.

Before her the baboons scattered in a panic, whooping and hollering the alarm—and clearing her way. Fearless was already lunging for Thorn's throat, but before his lethal fangs could close and kill, Sky smashed into him, her head colliding with his shoulder.

Fearless was flung across the clearing. He slammed into the twisted trunk of a fig tree and collapsed to the ground, limp.

Sky stared at him for a moment, gasping with relief even as the shock of what she had done chilled her blood. At her feet, Thorn Middleleaf gave a whimper and staggered to his paws.

"Sky! *Thank you*," he said hoarsely.

Sky couldn't reply. Drained by her fierce burst of energy, she shambled across the clearing to where Fearless Gallantpride lay unmoving in the rain.

Oh, Great Spirit, let him be alive!

She put her trunk to his tawny flank—and suddenly she was no longer Sky Strider, granddaughter of the last Great Mother: she was a tiny lion cub, prancing across the plains, tail held high as she followed a beautiful lioness. *My name is Swiftcub. My father is Gallant of Gallantpride.*

Startled, Sky yanked her trunk away, her heart pounding painfully in her chest. She stood very still for a moment until the dizziness of the vision passed. She was still getting used to her new gift—the ability to see into the memories of any creature she touched. It was unnerving, but at least it meant Fearless was still alive.

Thorn was beside her. He crouched on his stocky haunches, peering anxiously at the lion who had once been his friend. Blood streaked the young baboon's fur; he looked bedraggled and wretched in the lashing rain. *But his wounds aren't deadly either*, thought Sky with relief: Fearless had not had time to do him mortal damage.

"Oh, Fearless," Thorn murmured, closing his eyes. "It's not his fault, Sky."

"What happened?" she asked. "Why did Fearless attack you?"

"Stinger Crownleaf." Agony contorted Thorn's features. "He's calling himself Great Father now."

A great wave of desolation engulfed Sky. She couldn't move for a moment: the sense of sheer *wrongness* left her breathless and disoriented.

Thorn's expression became bitter. "Stinger turned Fearless against me. And all the others, too. I can't blame Fearless, or my troop. Stinger can be very convincing."

Sky couldn't believe Thorn's words. *Stinger Crownleaf is Great Father? It makes no sense. The Great Spirit is still within me!*

Determination filled her. Damage had been done; it was her job to undo it.

"Thorn, we need to get out of here," she told him grimly. "Fearless will be all right, don't worry. A few cracked ribs, I think, but he'll heal. *We* won't be all right, Thorn—not if we don't leave this place. Those baboons will find their nerve again soon, and they'll be back."

With a shudder, Thorn rose to all fours. Before he could argue, Sky was curling her trunk around his body and lifting him onto her shoulders.

And suddenly there was no rain.

Dappled sunlight filtered through the canopy, warming her fur as she sat on her favorite jackalberry branch. She sank her fangs into a mango, delicious and fragrant. She wished Berry could be with her to share it.

Sky shook herself briskly to chase the vision away. "Hold on tight, Thorn!"

As soon as she felt his paws clutch the edge of her ears, she set off in a trot through the trees. Twigs snapped and leaves pattered down around them. It was impossible to avoid leaving a trail, but the storm was still wild, and with luck the rain would give them enough cover. Filled with urgency, Sky picked up as much speed as she could on the treacherous ground.

But however fast she ran, there was no escaping the memories that passed to her through Thorn's grasp. *A baboon with large, liquid eyes and gold-streaked fur sat close by on the jackalberry branch, smiling shyly when Thorn offered her half the mango.*

"We'll be together," Berry said softly. "I know we'll end up in the same rank, Thorn; I know it in my bones. We're meant to be, you and I."

Thorn's heart felt almost too full of love. "I know it, too, Berry. . . ."

Sky took a sharp gasp of air. *That memory is private!* Clenching her jaws, she plowed on through the teeming rain, trying to think only of the next footfall, and the next.

By the time she felt it was safe to stop, a gray and miserable dawn was paling the sky. Thorn, exhausted, was half dozing against her neck, but she nudged him awake with the tip of her trunk.

The young baboon clambered down to the muddy ground, swiping rain from his eyes, and blinking at the shadowy clearing. "Where are we?"

"We're safe. For now." Sky sank to the ground, flanks heaving. "And we can talk here. Tell me everything, Thorn. I can't believe Fearless tried to kill you."

"And he would have succeeded, if not for you." Thorn shivered. "But I still don't blame him."

"Your own Crownleaf told him to do it?" Sky shook her head, bewildered.

"It's a long, awful story, Sky. But he's got everyone fooled. You know how he got to be Crownleaf? By killing the last two. Bark and Grub."

She stared, stunned. "Surely not—"

"Yes," said Thorn. "I found him out and confronted him; he's been looking for a way to get rid of me ever since. Last night, I was afraid he'd finally found it."

Sky could barely believe it. "And now he's saying he's Great Father? What about Stronghide?"

"Gone," said Thorn. "Stinger didn't need him anymore, so he turned the animals against him. And Sky, that isn't all Stinger's done." He was watching her, his eyes full of sadness and sympathy. "Stronghide killed your grandmother so he could become Great Father—all Bravelands knows it now. But he didn't come up with his plan by himself. It was—"

"Stinger," she said hoarsely.

Thorn was silent for a second. Then he nodded. "He's like a spider, Sky, spinning webs to trap us all."

Sky shook her ears, but not from denial. Aching, helpless anger raced through her blood. *Stinger Crownleaf had Great Mother killed.*

"He did. I'm sorry, Sky. So sorry." Thorn reached for her foreleg. Sky wanted his comfort, but she drew aside to avoid his touch. "Great Mother is a terrible loss to all of us. But especially to you. And to do such a thing before she had the chance to pass on the Great Spirit? It's evil, Sky."

"Oh, it is." Sky felt the hot fury intensify. "He can't get away with this, Thorn. We can't let him. What Stinger did—it didn't just break the Code. I think it's broken all of Bravelands."

"That's why we have to get rid of him," growled Thorn.

"Yes." Her rage turned to fierce determination. "Stinger must be exiled, far away from Bravelands."

Thorn peeled back his lips. He looked straight into Sky's eyes. "I didn't mean we should exile him," he said carefully.

His words cooled her raging blood. Returning his stare, Sky felt a sudden, calm certainty that stilled her trembling limbs.

"No, Thorn. *Only kill to survive*, remember? We'll deal with Stinger according to the Code of Bravelands."

"He doesn't respect the Code!" said Thorn bitterly. "He's broken it already, countless times! How do you think you can just make him leave?"

Sky lowered her trunk and blew at the ground between her feet. "The thing is, Thorn . . . I need to tell you. Something happened to me. I have a mission."

"What kind of mission?"

She took a deep breath and looked up. "The Great Spirit," she told him gravely. "I'm carrying it. It's with me, inside me."

Thorn's eyes were wide, and for a moment he looked stunned. "You mean you're . . . you're the new Great Mother?"

"No!" said Sky hastily. "No, I'm not. My mission is to find the new Great Parent and pass the Spirit to them." She glanced away. "I know it sounds crazy."

Thorn wrinkled his muzzle in deep thought. At last, he nodded slowly.

"I think I understand, Sky. The Great Spirit has to be somewhere, doesn't it? And it certainly isn't with Stinger."

Sky's voice grew grim. "He's got the animals fooled for now, but that will change when the true Great Parent arrives. The animals will drive him into exile as he deserves, and no one will have to break the Code."

The young baboon was watching her with fascination, picking at a wound on his snout. For a few heartbeats, he looked as if he was lost for the right words. At last he asked, "What does it feel like, Sky? The Great Spirit, I mean."

"I can hardly explain it." Sky felt suddenly shy. "It's like a—a force, in my bones and my hide and my blood. But it's separate from me. I think . . ." She recalled the desperate run that had spurred her into the forest, though she hadn't known what she would find. "I think the Great Spirit brought me to you just now. It must have known the Code was about to be broken."

Thorn sat back on his haunches, still staring at her. "Then I'm as grateful to the Great Spirit as I am to you," he said softly. "It really does know everything."

She nodded, silent, and stirred the mud with her trunk.

At last she looked up again.

"But Thorn . . . Bravelands is so vast. Somewhere out there is an animal who'll be our new Great Parent—I must find them, and I don't even know where to start."

"Sky, don't worry. If the Great Spirit brought you to me, it will guide you to the new Great Parent, too. You'll see."

His words made Sky feel lighter. The Great Spirit had trust in her; now she had to return that trust.

From somewhere among the trees, a branch snapped. She started, her ears tilted toward it. "We've been here too long already," she told Thorn. "You should run. Stinger will be looking for you."

"Oh, I know it," he muttered. "He won't give up easily. When Stinger knows what he wants, he just reaches out and takes it." He shook himself, sending rain showering from his fur, then gave her a grin. "But I'll miss your company. Thank you again, Sky Strider. I owe you my life. Good luck."

She watched him turn and lope away into the trees. He moved slowly at first, then abruptly leaped up onto a low branch, scrambled higher, and was gone from sight.

Sky stood still, listening to the fading rustle and crackle of leaves until she was sure he'd finally gone. She shook her ears and blew out a breath through her trunk. At least Thorn was safe for now.

And it's time for me to leave, too—before Stinger strikes again.

ENTER THE
BRAVELANDS

1

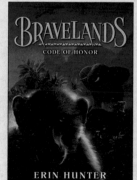

2

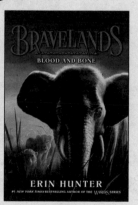

3

Heed the call of the wild in this
action-packed series from **Erin Hunter**.

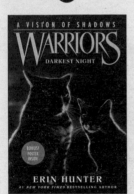

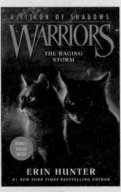

WARRIORS: THE PROPHECIES BEGIN

In the first series, sinister perils threaten the four warrior Clans. Into the midst of this turmoil comes Rusty, an ordinary housecat, who may just be the bravest of them all.

WARRIORS: THE NEW PROPHECY

In the second series, follow the next generation of heroic cats as they set off on a quest to save the Clans from destruction.

WARRIORS: POWER OF THREE

In the third series, Firestar's grandchildren begin their training as warrior cats. Prophecy foretells that they will hold more power than any cats before them.

HARPER
An Imprint of HarperCollinsPublishers

www.warriorcats.com